INSIDE
THE
ECHO

A FLINT K-9 MYSTERY

INSIDE
THE
ECHO

A FLINT K-9 MYSTERY

JEN BLOOD

Adian Press
Maine

INSIDE THE ECHO
Copyright © 2018 Jen Blood
First Edition
ISBN: 978-0-9982296-3-8

Adian Press
Phippsburg, ME 04562
www.adianpress.com

Publisher: Adian Press
Cover Design: damonza.com
Author's Photograph: Amy Wilton Photography

For Ben

Who makes home
my favorite place to be.

1

WildFire Expeditions
Mahoosuc Mountains, Maine
February 4, 1:30 a.m.

MEGAN HUNTER SAT in front of the campfire, a Malamute curled in the snow a couple of feet from her side. Though night had long since fallen, the combination of a full moon, snowy landscape, and the raging fire kept the darkness at bay. Megan had a tin cup of coffee warming her gloved hands, a belly full of franks and beans, and seven other dogs—some Malamute, some husky, some mutts from gods knew where—on a picket line just to the north of their campsite. A birthday card lay in her lap, read so many times in the past week that it was already getting faded.

The others had gone to bed hours ago: nine women including Megan's younger sister, who was running this expedition alongside her. The participants in the group ranged in age from early twenties to late fifties. All strong, reasonably fit, damned determined…and most of them here because they'd dug deep and somehow found the gumption to leave abusive partners within the past six months. Now, they were out to prove to themselves that if they could handle the wilds of Western Maine in the dead of winter, they could handle anything.

Including the spouse or partner they'd recently left behind.

Megan picked up the card and read it again, feeling like a fool.

> *Here's hoping 40 brings the wheel dog of your dreams and all*
> *the ice cream you can handle.*
> *I'll watch the kids till you come home.*
> *Love, H*

She'd been obsessing over the words ever since she'd gotten the card, one week ago today. *Love, H.* He signed it 'love.' It would seem at forty that a woman could stop worrying about what the hell a man meant when he used that word, but here she was again, having the same debate she'd had at fifteen when Rick Cheney signed her valentine that year Love, The Cheenster. It turned out that the Cheenster had signed every girl's valentine with love that year—and had a lot of fun reaping the benefits come spring. Nate Hogan, on the other hand, didn't seem like the kind of man to just toss the L-word around.

Megan was still focused on the card when Recluse, the Malamute by her side, woke with a start, his tufted ears pricked forward. The other dogs followed his lead, on their feet in an instant.

"What is it, Rec?" Megan asked, peering into the darkness. Against her will, she felt a shiver of unease. A byproduct of the horror stories the women had shared around the fire earlier that night. Or so Megan told herself.

The dogs' barking got louder, their attention directed toward that single point in the trees. The long line that held them would keep them all from going far, but Recluse could run if he wanted. Instead, he edged closer to Megan.

A rustling in the trees had the whole team of dogs lunging, while Megan's hand slipped toward the holster strapped to her side. There, she kept her secret weapon: an emergency transponder, which would send a signal for help along with GPS coordinates with the touch of a button.

Before she reached it, the beast from the forest emerged.

"Violet?" Megan said. Fear gave way to embarrassment at her overreaction, but that was quickly replaced by annoyance. She stowed the card from Hogan into her pocket, told Recluse to stay, and stalked across an icy expanse of snow to reach the woman. "You're not supposed to go in the woods alone at night. We've talked about this. If you need to use the bathroom—"

"I know," Violet said, waving her off. Violet was tall, willowy, and blond, with refined features and a delicate way about her. Megan was just as tall and nearly as blond, but willowy or refined would never be used to describe her. Of the women in the group, Violet was the only one who wasn't coming directly from an abusive home, there instead doing research for her dissertation on the long-term impact of fear on women in abusive relationships. Speaking from experience, Megan could have told her exactly what the long-term impact of fear was: it wasn't good.

"I didn't want to go, but I was looking for Gabby and Ava," Violet continued. "Gabby wasn't feeling well, so the two went together to use the bathroom. I fell asleep. When I woke up, it didn't look like either of them ever came back."

Megan thought quickly, immediately concerned. Ava was a Cuban-American woman who'd recently taken her three sons and fled Miami, running from a violent husband who, according to her, had ties to the mob. Gabby was a model originally from Spain who had moved to the U.S. with her husband, a well-known and highly paid quarterback with the NFL. As it turned out, a quarterback with anger issues and little to no impulse control. Neither Ava nor Gabby spoke fluent English, but had arrived on the expedition determined to make it through. Surviving winter in Maine was hardly a skillset in either of their repertoires, however.

"What time did they go?" Megan asked Violet.

"Ten past eleven," Violet said without hesitation. "I looked at my clock, because I was thinking that I hoped I wouldn't have a hard time getting back to sleep. Big day tomorrow and all."

"Right," Megan said hollowly.

Violet was scheduled to drive the dogsled in the morning. The group was led by Megan and her sister Heather, but there was only one sled for the lot of them. That meant Megan and two different students manned the sled each day, while Heather led the other six women on cross country skis. It was Violet's turn at the helm tomorrow, something Megan knew she'd been looking forward to.

On the horizon, the moon hung high over Old Speck, the highest peak in Maine's Mahoosuc Mountains. Megan surveyed the area, aware of Recluse watching her. The rest of the dogs were raucous, sensing that something was up. At the noise, the other women had started to emerge from their tents.

"Go get suited up," Megan told Violet. "I'll get Heather, and we'll start searching."

Violet nodded. She and Megan had been best friends since college, and Megan had always admired her cool head. Violet didn't look like the kind of woman who could handle a crisis, but as a social worker in inner-city D.C., Megan had seen her do exactly that more than once. She looked spooked now, though, like this was somehow bigger than a couple of people in their group simply wandering off. Which it wasn't, Megan told herself firmly. They would find Ava and Gabby. The women weren't idiots; they wouldn't have gone far.

Megan went back to their tent to wake her sister, already formulating a plan. Find Gabby and Ava, get another few hours of sleep, make breakfast, hit the trail. Simple as pie.

Right.

"What do you mean, they're gone?" Heather asked wearily, after Megan had given her the story of the women's disappearance. Heather rubbed her eyes, clearly disoriented.

Three years younger than Megan, Heather had always been the cute one of the sisters. Both had curly blond hair and freckles, but Heather was slender, while Megan had more curves than she knew what to do with. Given a choice between the two, Heather was always the one men gravitated to—there was something innately approachable about her. Being woken from a dead sleep in the middle of the night notwithstanding.

"I mean they're gone," Megan said. "We'll need to gear up to find them."

"Have you called Abe to let him know?"

"Why would I do that?" Megan asked, before she could stop herself. Abe was Heather's husband, a filmmaker who was almost always lost in the hills somewhere, chipping away at a documentary he'd been working on for as long as

Megan had known him. So far, no one but Abe had seen any footage. Megan was beginning to doubt the thing existed.

At the words, Heather frowned. "We need to keep him posted, especially if we're going to get off schedule. He's part of the team."

"We don't know that we'll get off schedule yet," Megan replied. "Just give it half an hour of searching, and then we'll make the call."

"Fine," Heather said, then added, "It might not hurt to give Hogan a call too, you know. See what he says about this."

Megan felt the color rise in her cheeks, and glared at her sister. "Shut up."

"What?" Heather said, all wide-eyed innocence. "He is a warden, right? And a damn fine-looking one, at that. I'm just saying, it wouldn't hurt to have him around."

She swung her legs off her camp cot, wincing at the movement, and her hand went to her stomach automatically. Instantly, Megan felt a twinge of guilt.

"Are you all right?"

"I'm six months' pregnant," Heather said. "I'm host to an alien parasite feeding off me while simultaneously trying to tear me apart from the inside out. Apart from that, I'm fine."

"You're the one who wanted a kid," Megan said, though not without sympathy. "Why don't you stay here while we go out? I can go look with the others, and we'll be back soon."

Heather stood. Her belly still wasn't huge, but there was an unmistakable swell there. Despite her complaints, she seemed to be taking the changes in stride. Those changes were seriously messing with Megan's head, though.

"I'm fine, Meg," she said, with a roll of her eyes. "And

I'm sure you're right. They can't have gone far. We look for half an hour, and then give Abe a call if we don't have any luck."

"Deal," Megan agreed.

Recluse had come into the tent with her, while outside the other dogs on the team were still barking their heads off. Megan made for the entrance, mildly annoyed when Recluse barred her way rather than letting her through.

"I know it's warmer in here," she told the dog. "And God knows it's quieter. But we've got work to do."

She took a step forward. Recluse blocked the exit with his body, growling slightly. Fear pricked its way up her spine —though not of the dog. She looked at Heather, who was watching Recluse's actions with the same confusion.

"What's up with him?" Heather asked.

"No idea," Megan said. She crouched beside the dog and he met her head on, his own head bowed to hers. "What's the problem, buddy? All this weirdness have you spooked, too?"

"Maybe I should give Abe a call now," Heather said. "Just in case."

"Just give it a couple of minutes," Megan said. Her pulse had ticked up a notch, a reaction that annoyed her. What the hell was going on?

Finally, she managed to get Recluse back in hand. She pushed past the Malamute and stepped into the open. The smell of snow was in the air, their insular world of canned light and humming activity in stark contrast to the wilds that lay just beyond. The other dogs were still barking and pacing on the picket line. Megan was pleased to see that Violet had rallied the troops, most of the women already dressed and ready to begin the search.

She took another step forward. Suddenly, there was a sound from the trees just to their right—a ratcheting of steel that was familiar to her, though out of context she had a hard time placing it. Megan turned. If possible it seemed darker out now, the black broken by the ethereal glow of snow and moon and the lanterns their group shared.

Something was in the forest.

The fear that had rankled her earlier returned. Recluse growled again, so low she could barely hear him. Women were talking to her, but she didn't listen. What was out there? Her hand shifted automatically to her holster, going for the transponder. Not for the first time, she wondered if she should start carrying a gun, then dismissed the idea. With two women unaccounted for, the last thing she wanted to do was overreact and inadvertently shoot one of them.

She paused when her fingers brushed the pocket where she kept the transponder; she'd designed the thing herself, specifically for that purpose. For the first time that she could remember, the pocket was empty.

Panicked, she moved to reach for her radio instead.

She was too late.

Suddenly, an explosion shattered the stillness—a sound so real, so hard, that Megan felt as much as heard it. Recluse's growl became a snarl, his focus on the point where the shot originated. Without warning, he slammed his furry body against Megan's so hard that she stumbled. Women screamed. Dogs howled. A second shot came from the same spot in the woods.

Heather started to come out of the tent, but Megan screamed at her. "Stay inside! Call Hogan—get him out here."

"What's happening?" Heather called back.

"Just stay where you are. Tell Hogan there's a shooter."

Recluse was almost on top of Megan, his warm body shielding her, and she fought to order her thoughts. There was blood on his fur. Oh, God. Someone had shot him. The bastard shot Recluse.

The Malamute turned wet brown eyes on her, and started to get up. She reached for his flank, trying to keep him down; trying to find the wound. She couldn't, though. Couldn't figure out where or how badly he was injured. She ran her hands over him once more, but came away with no more blood.

Then, she felt the fire in her own side. She looked down. Ran her hand along a tacky patch at the side of her parka. Only then did she realize, just as another shot tore through the snowy landscape:

The blood was hers.

2

"WE FOUND TESS," I called to Bear, my seventeen-year-old son, as he searched the rocky island shoreline. Casper, Bear's white pit bull, looked up at my words and barked a friendly greeting. Bear caught sight of me at Casper's reaction, and boy and dog ran to me, Bear's head down against the freezing gale.

"Tess," I repeated. "Phantom found her. She's fine." Beside me, my nine-year-old German shepherd raised her head upon hearing her name.

"Good," Bear said. "So that's the last of the cows. That means we've just got the goats to find."

"They're the ones who opened the gate in the first place," I pointed out. "If they wanted to be free so much, maybe we should just let them get a taste of what it's like out here on their own."

"Very funny," Bear said. "It's not their fault they like to cause trouble. They're goats; this is kind of what they do.

We can't punish them for being what they are."

The beasts in question—Randy, Rowdy, and Piper, so-named by Bear—were raggedy-looking pygmy mixes who were way too smart for their own good. Early this morning, for example, we caught the action on our security camera as the trio used each other as a stepladder so they could climb over our six-foot fence. Once Piper was on the other side, she came back and unlocked the gate all on her own. At which point, our donkey, two llamas, three cows, six sheep, and the aforementioned goats, all headed for the hills.

Bear was right, of course. No matter how much I might be tempted, clearly leaving the goats out wasn't a viable option. There wasn't another storm in the forecast for at least the next day, but in the meantime high winds off the Atlantic had driven the temperature down well below freezing. We'd been out for the better part of the past three hours trying to round up the animals, a motley crew of farm rescues Bear had taken in over the course of the past few months.

"All right, fine. They must be on the island somewhere," I said. "Get word to Ren to come in and regroup in the galley."

"We can't leave them out," Bear insisted.

"And we won't," I returned firmly. "But we've already been over this island twice with the dogs. We need a new plan."

Twenty minutes later, Bear and I still waited alone in our newly constructed, 2,000-square-foot galley—an open-concept structure with floors made of salvaged wood, the walls lined with passive solar windows. In addition to a cafeteria for staff and any visitors to the island, the building included a commercial kitchen where we made both the animal and human food on the island.

Bear sat on a bench seat with Casper beside him, his attention on something outside the window. As I often am now that he's getting older, I was struck by his profile, much closer to a man now than to the boy I'd raised. Bear looked more like me when he was little, with my blond hair and a long, lanky build, but as he got older the resemblance to his father grew. Now, with his light-brown hair and dark-brown eyes, his solid shoulders and brooding ways, he was a dead ringer for Brock Campbell. Brock died eight years ago, but I often wondered what he would think of the young man his son had become.

I forced myself out of my reverie to take stock of our current situation. There were seven of us living out on the island year-round, but today three of those seven were working on a search overseas following a recent earthquake. That meant Bear and I were alone on the island with Carl Mensah and his daughter Ren, refugees from Nigeria who had joined Flint K-9 just over five years ago. Ren was Bear's age, and I considered her and her dog Minion nearly as adept at search and rescue as Bear and Casper. At the moment, however, there was no sign of either the girl or her dog.

"Do you have any idea where Ren is?" I asked.

"She was on the western ridge last I knew," Bear said, looking worried himself. "That was an hour ago, though."

Great. Now not only did we have three wayward pygmy goats to find, we were missing a handler and her dog, too.

"Have you tried raising her on the radio?"

"She's not answering," Bear said. "I'm definitely getting worried."

I reached into my back pocket for my radio to try her myself. Before I could do so, however, my cell phone rang. I know all this technology makes things safer and communication easier in the field, but I can't help but wonder sometimes what it would have been like when the only way people could get hold of you were smoke signals. Frankly, it doesn't sound so bad. Juggling my gear, I set the radio aside, hauled the cell out of my pocket, and noted a blocked number on the screen. Definitely not Ren.

"Flint K-9," I answered, more brusque than I'd intended.

"Is this Jamie?" a voice on the other end asked. A familiar voice, though one I hadn't heard in so long that I was sure it couldn't be the man who immediately came to mind.

"This is. Can I help you?"

"Yes," the man replied. "Or, at least I hope you can. I'm actually calling for Sergeant Roger Steiner. There's a group missing in the Mahoosuc Mountains. He's calling in all available K-9s and would like them on ASAP. Is your team available?"

I frowned. "We have three handlers and their dogs overseas right now helping with earthquake recovery, but there are still three teams available. We don't usually send the dogs out in conditions like these, though. In deep snow like this they just get bogged down, so it's not all that efficient." I hesitated. "I'm sorry. Who did you say this was?"

There was a pause on the line. Then: "It's Hogan, Jamie. Nate Hogan. I'm working for the warden service now."

The pause on the line was longer this time, as I tried to sort through a muddled onslaught of emotions inspired by the name. I was all too aware of Bear in the room beside me. The mixed blessing of being a single mom: my son is way too tuned into what—and how—I'm doing at any given moment.

"Jamie?" Hogan prompted, when seconds had passed and I still hadn't said anything.

"Yeah—sorry, Hogan. I just… It was just a little unexpected, that's all."

"I meant to get in touch once I got back to Maine," he said. "I just…"

"I understand," I said quickly. "We can catch up another time. But as I was saying, weather like this—"

"I know," he said, cutting me off. "We've already talked to the handlers in the warden service and in MESARD." MESARD stands for Maine Search and Rescue Dogs, a nonprofit comprised of volunteer handlers and their dogs who help with searches throughout New England and into Canada. "They've all agreed to come. We had rain followed by a hard freeze a couple of days ago—there's a crust of solid ice out there. Your dogs will be able to walk on top of the snow for the duration."

"Another warm front is moving in late tonight, though," I reminded him.

"And we're prepared to send the dogs home at that point, if necessary."

The urgency in his tone finally came through, and curiosity won out over practicality. "Who's missing, exactly?" I asked.

"It's a group called WildFire Expeditions."

"I know them," I said, surprised. "Bear's done a couple of dogsledding courses there. Who's missing?"

"All of them. The leaders of the expedition and all eight students. A snowmobiler came across the camp about an hour ago. Seven dogs still out on the picket line, but not a single member of the group to be found."

I felt a shiver of unease. I knew Megan and Heather, the sisters who ran WildFire Expeditions. Something must have happened for them to leave their dogs unattended. And definitely not something good.

Before I could respond to Hogan's information, the double doors of the galley burst open on a gust of cold air. A second later, three indignant—and very snowy—pygmy goats made their way inside, followed by a little yellow pit bull/lab cross and a very chilled-looking dark-skinned girl. Ren had returned.

Bear cheered her entrance, but I held up my hand for quiet as I ended the conversation with Nate Hogan—a man who had saved my life eight years ago, and then simply walked away.

"We'll be there," I said. "Just text me the details, and we should hit Bethel by noon. How many dogs do you want?"

"As many as you can spare." A second passed before he spoke again. "Thanks, Jamie—I appreciate this. Really. I'll see you soon."

And then he was gone.

I returned my phone to my bag, and Bear was at my side immediately.

"Is there a search?" he asked, always eager to head into the field.

"Up in the Mahoosucs," I said. "WildFire Expeditions." The familiar name triggered a slew of fresh questions, which I answered as quickly as I could before moving on.

"We'll need you both for the search," I said, once I'd gotten them up to speed. "Gear up, and I'll give Jack a call to tell him to be ready. We'll pick him up on the way."

I caught the flash of Bear's frown, and fought a twinge of annoyance of my own at his reaction. Jack Juarez was my newest hire with Flint K-9, brought on board for his investigative skills as a former FBI agent rather than any prowess he might have had with the dogs. Which was good —Jack really had no prowess with dogs. The issue, however, was that since he'd come to work for me four months ago, there was some question as to just what Jack did do for us... and how committed he was to staying.

"Is there a problem?" I asked.

"If he lived out on the island like everyone else on the team, we wouldn't have to go hunting around for him every time we get a call."

"We don't go hunting for him," I answered, keeping my cool. "We go to his apartment in Brunswick, and we pick him up. Or else he just meets us onsite. It's actually pretty simple."

Bear said nothing to that, but his body language suggested he wasn't buying my argument. Not that he was completely off base, I knew. Eventually, I'd need to have a conversation with Jack about just what his intentions were where Flint K-9 was concerned. Based on Bear's reaction, that conversation would need to be sooner rather than later.

"Ren, are you all right joining us?" I asked, switching gears. Ren's cheeks glowed and her snow pants looked like she'd been dragged through a manure pile. Smelled like it, too.

"Yes, definitely," she said, in the thick Nigerian accent I'd become accustomed to over the years. She nodded toward the goats. Piper was the smallest of the three, a little black goat missing her right eye. At the moment, she was trying to chew through the tether attached to Rowdy's collar. "I found these guys up on the ridge." She looked down at herself, wrinkling her nose. "Then I fell into a pile of cow manure at the bottom of the ridge."

"You sure you're okay for a search?" I asked.

"Of course," she said immediately. "Minion was just getting warmed up. I'll get changed, but then we're ready."

Anyone else and I might have doubted them, but I had yet to find a job Ren couldn't handle. "All right, then. I'll talk to your dad about watching the place while we're gone. Get the goats back in the pen—and use the keyed padlocks this time. I don't suppose you'd consider swallowing the key, would you?" I asked her.

"I don't think so," she said, smiling. "They're Bear's goats. Let him do it."

"Fair enough."

I looked at the two of them, and took a breath. The dogs were already settling back in after the search, happy to be somewhere warm again. My handlers, likewise, hardly looked ready to head back out into the field. I knew that wouldn't matter to them any more than it did me, though; in search and rescue, we go where the action is. And, for the most part, we—both handlers and dogs—can't wait to get out there.

"All right, guys," I said. Despite Nate Hogan's sudden return to my life, or the uncertainty of Jack Juarez's role in Flint K-9, or the wayward goats who would no doubt find a way to escape again within the week, I felt a surge of adrenaline at the prospect of what was to come. "It looks like it'll be a long day. Gear up, and let's hit the road."

3

IT WAS JUST PAST NOON when our team finally reached Bethel, a hippie hybrid ski town of about twenty-six hundred people on the Maine/New Hampshire border. We'd driven up in the Flint K-9 cargo van, dogs nestled in welded cages at the back of the rig while I drove the four-hour trek from Littlehope, Maine. During the drive, light flurries that had been predicted early on gave way to a steady snowfall that made for slick roads and tenuous driving conditions. Grateful, I slowed at sight of the roadside sign for Inn of the Rostay, a little yellow inn and motor lodge on Route 2, and pulled into the now-crowded parking lot.

Jack Juarez sat in the passenger seat beside me, Ren and Bear in the bench seat in the far back. Despite Bear's protests, we'd picked Jack up in Brunswick on the way. I noted that, like the rest of us, the former FBI man looked eager for the search.

In the far back, I could hear the dogs pacing in their kennels, sensing that their work was about to begin. We had all three of our dogs with us today: Phantom, Casper, and Minion. Bear and Ren, meanwhile, remained locked in private conversation, seemingly oblivious to the world around them. At least I hoped that was all they were locked in. It was hard to tell when they were way back there.

"There's a space there," Jack said to me, pointing out a parking spot at the far end of the lot.

I managed to stuff the van into the spot with a little maneuvering, and was grateful when I could finally put the vehicle in park and, hopefully, keep it there for a while. Then, I took a second to take in the scene.

Less than six hours into the search, volunteers and law enforcement had flooded the area to help find the missing WildFire expedition. That was hindered only slightly by the weather. From what I'd heard, the combination of high winds and a dusting of snow had effectively wiped out any tracks that might have otherwise been useful. Searchers are used to working in less-than-ideal conditions, though, and based on the way the parking lot was hopping, not many had let conditions keep them off the road.

I took a second to get my bearings by reviewing the laptop mounted on a custom-made adjustable arm between the driver's and passenger's seats at the front of the van. The setup provided me with easy access to a constant stream of information regarding the search: the status of the searchers; whether or not anyone had been found; any weather updates as they became available.

A cursory glance told me nothing had changed in the short time since I'd last checked the stats. Though a good number of searchers had checked themselves in, the missing women still hadn't been found. The temperature outside hovered around the thirty-degree mark—almost too warm for a search like this, as far as I was concerned. Warmer weather made for slushy snow the dogs would sink into with every step, hindering their progress and tiring them out so fast it was usually smartest to just leave them home and work with snowmobiles instead. On the other hand, just as Hogan had promised, the temperature was holding steady following rain and a flash freeze two days ago. If that continued, it would be cold enough to continue to provide a solid crust on top of the snow that we could all walk across, as easy as if it were pavement. Slick pavement, maybe, but pavement all the same.

At the other end of the parking lot, my attention shifted to the 32-foot Maine Warden Service mobile search and rescue unit that dominated the area.

"So I guess we don't have to wonder if this is the right place or not," Jack noted, nodding toward the trailer.

"Guess not," I agreed.

"Can we check out the inside of the SAR mobile unit?" Bear asked, emerging from the back of the van with Ren. "Ren hasn't seen it yet."

"Maybe, once things are settled," I said.

"It's really cool in there," he told Ren. "The tech is insane."

"I would like to see it," she said, addressing me. "I was hoping to speak with someone about a paper I'm doing for school, when we're done."

Both Bear and Ren were technically juniors, home schooled out on the island since our move there a couple of years ago. Bear was never much of a student, however, diagnosed with dyslexia when he was younger and never quite getting the bug for the classroom. Ren, on the other hand, excelled in every line of study she pursued.

"I'll talk to the IC, and make sure you get a tour as soon as they have some down time," I promised.

"Thanks. That would be perfect," she said.

Meanwhile, the dogs were getting wilder in the back,

barks and whimpers and yowls escalating now that we were no longer moving and they could hear the action outside. They were housed in padded steel cages that had been welded into the van, the rest of our gear placed in compartments I'd had specially designed. No more jerry-rigged crates or plastic tubs held in place with bungee cords. The changes had been funded by a grant Flint K-9 was awarded a couple of months before, thanks to Jack's research and surprisingly adept grant-writing skills.

Before getting out of the van, I consulted my favorite technological upgrade: a gauge that monitored the temperature inside the vehicle, setting off an alarm when the interior hit a certain point. Once that happened, the engine would restart and either the heat or the A/C would kick in accordingly. Since we often need to leave the dogs in our vehicles for extended periods of time during a search, regardless of the time of year, this gauge could literally be a lifesaver. Right now, the cab was sixty degrees Fahrenheit—not too cool, not too hot. I didn't anticipate any issues with the temperature one way or the other today, but it was still nice to know there was a failsafe if something did come up.

"Let's let the dogs stretch their legs first, then we can check in with the IC," I told the others.

The IC—or incident commander—would have our assignments ready to go, giving us the coordinates for where we should start searching. I may have been putting off the inevitable moment when I faced Hogan again after our years apart, but I figured in this case it was justified. It had been a long ride, after all.

I got out of the van with my head ducked against the snow. Behind me, van doors opened. Van doors closed. Chatter floated back to me as Bear and Ren rounded up the dogs' gear and opened up the back.

"Thanks for giving me a call," Jack said, startling me as he sidled up alongside.

I turned to look at him. He'd put on a few pounds since leaving the FBI—good pounds, since he'd been downright gaunt during the search in Glastenbury that had ultimately ended his career. Now, he stood in front of me in a blue parka and jeans that seemed to accentuate his height and athletic build. At five foot ten, I'm not exactly a little person, but Jack stands a couple of inches over six feet, with broad shoulders and an easy grace to his movement. He studied me a moment, dark eyes taking me in in a way that always made me feel almost uncomfortably seen.

"Of course," I said. "You're part of the team. With the others overseas right now, we need everyone we can get on this one."

I thought of Bear's words back on the island. Jack looked uncomfortable when I said the word "team," as though sensing my earlier conversation. No doubt about it, we would need to have a chat about this soon.

"Just let me know how I can help," he said. "Without a dog, I'm still not quite sure how I fit into this business."

"There are plenty of members of search and rescue who don't work with K-9s," I reminded him. "You've got your Wilderness First Responder, you're certified in First Aid and wilderness rescue... But if you want me to, I can get you a dog whenever you want. Just say the word."

He looked a little stricken at the thought. "Thanks, but I don't think I'm ready for that yet."

Not ready for a dog. Not ready to move out to the island. Despite myself, I couldn't help but wonder just what he was doing with us. I didn't say the words aloud, but I suspected the same thought had occurred to Jack more than once over the past few months.

"Come on," I said, rather than pushing. "Let's walk. We can figure out assignments once we get briefed."

He agreed with a silent nod. He still seemed out of place, and I wondered suddenly if Jack had ever felt like he was part of a team before. Or had he always been the one sitting on the sidelines, locked in a world where he never quite belonged?

At the back of the van, all three dogs were harnessed and ready to go, so we headed toward an area at the back of the motel where Hogan had said we'd be able to let the dogs run. Only about ten feet behind the building was a thick stand of trees, a path cleared out among them. The dogs were all squirrelly by now, anxious to move, so we released the hounds as soon as it was safe. While the younger dogs immediately dove for one another, Minion and Casper practically colliding in midair, Phantom was more sedate. She left me and headed for the trees, tail waving slowly.

Phantom is more a fan of people than other dogs as a general rule. Casper in particular has always rubbed her the wrong way, so she tends to either ignore him outright or lean toward overt hostility with the dog. His enthusiasm just isn't her style. Of course, as soon as he saw a window Casper raced to the older dog, trying in vain to get her to join in on the play.

He bounded toward the shepherd, play bowed, and raced away. He got no response, so tried again a second later. And again. Finally, Phantom rushed him, grabbed him by the scruff of the neck, and wrestled him to the ground. Casper either didn't realize or chose to ignore the fact that she wasn't playing. As soon as she let him go, he was at it again—though with more care the second time around. He'd still rush the shepherd and bow, but he was a little more serious about running away if she showed any interest.

"Looks like that dog's playing with fire," a voice behind me said. Bear and Ren were at the other side of the clearing, Jack and I on our own, but I saw Bear look up when he heard the words. Jack and I both turned, startled. At sight of the man who emerged from the darkened woods, I steeled myself for the meeting I'd known was coming.

"Sorry," Nate Hogan said. "I didn't mean to startle you. I saw you pull up, though, and figured I should come say hello."

The dogs had of course taken notice of the stranger, and raced toward him. He was a solid, good-looking man in his forties, his dark hair now tinged with silver. It had been jet black when I'd seen him last.

"Hello, Hogan," I said. We stood there awkwardly for a second, trying to decide whether or not a hug was appropriate. He moved in at the same time that I extended my hand, unfortunately jabbing him in the gut when I'd only meant to shake his hand. He winced. "Sorry. This is a little…"

"Unexpected?" he said helpfully. Not the word I was thinking of, but I didn't correct him. "I know. I thought I'd had enough of Maine when I left the PD. I got a call when the job in the forest service opened up last year, though. It turns out I missed it here more than I thought I would."

The others on the team converged at that point, calling their dogs to heel before Hogan was completely overwhelmed. I introduced him to Jack and Ren, then paused when I came to Bear. That sick sense I'd felt from the second I got Hogan's call returned. The last time we'd seen Hogan had been shortly after Bear's father died, under what the police had deemed suspicious circumstances. Despite the fact that Hogan and I were friends, and I was a chief suspect in Brock's death, Hogan had insisted on remaining part of the investigation at the time. It was shortly after that investigation closed that Hogan told me he was leaving the force, and the area. Though he hadn't been a huge part of Bear's life before that time, his absence after Brock's death had not gone unnoticed.

"I guess you know who this is," I said.

Hogan nodded. "I can't quite believe it, but yes." He extended a hand, which Bear shook reluctantly. He looked as nervous as I felt. "Hard to believe how much can change in a few years. You look good. All grown up."

Bear shrugged. "It's been eight years. It'd be a little sad if I hadn't changed since then."

"True," Hogan conceded. "Still. Nothing makes you feel quite so old as meeting a man when you remember a boy." He shifted gears, sensing the tension radiating from Bear. "What about the rest of your crew? The four-leggeds, I mean."

I relaxed. When in doubt, talk about the dogs. "The white dervish over there is Casper—Bear's dog. The shepherd is Phantom. And Minion is Ren's dog." The little lab/pit bull was glued to Ren's side, clearly uneasy at the stranger's presence.

Silence fell over the group, and I looked at Hogan expectantly. "Do you have our room info, or do I need to check in with the IC first?"

"No, I've got it." He produced a yellow envelope from his pocket. "There are actually a couple of ski lodges next door. Your team will stay in one of those with some of the wardens, and MESARD's in the other one. We figured it would be easiest if we could keep the K-9s together."

"Nice," Bear said, with genuine enthusiasm. "It's about time we start getting the royal treatment."

"I wouldn't get too excited before you see the place," Hogan said.

With the stranger in our midst no longer quite so strange, Phantom loped back into the woods to stretch her legs and take a much-needed break from Casper, who was still pushing his luck. I wished I could follow her. Casper, on the other hand, happily rolled onto his back and let Hogan rub his pink belly while we continued with our conversation.

"A pit bull search dog?" Hogan asked. Casper bicycled his legs and wriggled his body in the snow, making puppy snow angels. "I know this isn't my field, but that isn't usual, is it?"

"We train all different types of dogs," Bear said. If he was bothered by the question, he didn't show it. "That's part of the Flint K-9 mission: save dogs from high-kill shelters, move them to our place, and train them for service. We do a lot with search and rescue, but we also train for therapy, visually or hearing impaired owners, wounded veterans or those suffering from PTSD."

Hogan looked at me. "Wow. Quite a difference from the days when Brock was running the show, huh?"

I could feel Jack watching the interaction, studying my reactions to Hogan's words. I struggled to seem unaffected at mention of Brock's name, more concerned with how Bear might react. Brock Campbell had been my mentor in the world of dog handling when I first got started as a teenager; ours was hardly a romance for the ages. The fact that Brock was Bear's father had been a poorly kept secret for years— one I still hadn't shared with Jack. The relationship between Brock and me was, at its very best, complicated. Apart from Bear, no one knew that better than Hogan.

"How do things stand with the search?" I asked, deliberately changing the subject. "Any luck yet?"

A shadow darkened Hogan's blue eyes. He shook his head. "Not yet. I don't know what the hell happened out there. We've got planes in the air and snowmobiles on the ground, but after the wind and snow we had overnight we can't tell a damned thing about what happened in that camp. And forget trying to find a trail up there."

"What about the people in charge of the dogsledding operation at WildFire?" Bear asked. "They're usually on top of things out here. Haven't they been able to give you any information?"

"Your mom said you had some background with WildFire," Hogan said. "That could come in handy. So far, we haven't gotten much from them."

"I've done some courses there. They run the dogsledding stuff for teens, but they also teach K-9 wilderness first aid. It's good stuff to know if you're out in the field with dogs."

"As far as we knew," I added, "they worked primarily with high school students. These are adults though, right?"

"That's right," Hogan said. He looked uncomfortable. "It's a little complicated."

"What do you mean?" Jack asked. "Adults should be easier to deal with—at the very least, they're more likely to be able to take care of themselves until they're found."

"That much is true," Hogan agreed. "But not everything is so cut and dried. This is a women's course." He looked at me, his gaze strangely calculating. "Battered women, actually. Which means we have to be careful what information the press gets hold of."

The way he said 'battered' pierced me. I felt a flush of embarrassment, shame, that Hogan might consider me part of those ranks, even in the distant past.

"You're trying to make sure their partners don't figure

out where they are," Jack guessed. "Things could get ugly if a bunch of abusive husbands show up here." If he sensed anything in the exchange between Hogan and me, he didn't mention it. Bear, however, had gone conspicuously quiet.

"Very ugly," Hogan agreed. "And as if that weren't enough to deal with, Senator Price's daughter is also on the course—"

"Robert Price?" I interrupted. Robert Price had been elected to the U.S. Senate six years ago, after a distinguished career in law enforcement with the Portland Police Department. I knew nothing of his daughter, but I couldn't imagine him taking it lightly if someone had abused her.

"She's working on her dissertation," Hogan said, reading my mind. "She and Megan Hunter were undergrads together at Georgetown. She's apparently a social worker in D.C. right now, working with one of the women going on the course. They arranged this whole thing together."

"The press must be going nuts," I said.

"They haven't caught wind of any of it yet. We're trying to keep them in the dark as long as possible."

"Any chance one of the husbands or boyfriends of the other women on the expedition could be involved in this?" I asked.

"There's always a chance," Hogan said. I noted the darkness in his eyes again, and for the first time it occurred to me that he didn't look nearly as good as I'd imagined he would when I'd pictured this reunion. Obviously I didn't have all the information about the women missing, but I wondered if there was something Hogan wasn't telling me.

"Right now, the IC's not running things like there's a third party we need to worry about," Hogan continued, his tone brusque now. "We'll change course if we need to, but for now we're just working on the assumption that something went wrong on the trail and they got separated from their dogs."

"No way," Bear said definitively. "Have you met Megan and Heather? They wouldn't just leave their dogs without a fight. Not unless something went seriously wrong."

Hogan frowned, but I spoke up before he could argue the point. "How's Heather's husband taking this? He must be going nuts."

"He is," Hogan agreed. "He spoke to them at check-in last night at nineteen hundred, and at that point he says everything was fine. Then he gets word that the whole camp is missing."

"Where was the camp set up?" I asked. "They usually stick pretty close to Grafton Park, don't they?"

"That's right," Hogan said. "This trip was no exception. They were camped out at the Step Falls Preserve for the night, then were supposed to make their way to Old Speck—that mountain over there." Hogan pointed into the distance, at a high peak barely visible between the clouds and snow. "Abe—Heather's husband—has been going crazy from the moment he heard about this. Seems bent on taking all of us with him."

I didn't blame him. The more I learned about this search, the less I liked it. Generally when you lose a large group, there's a rational explanation and everyone shows up just fine a few hours later. Alarm bells were ringing in my head. Not only had the dogs been found half-buried in the snow with no humans in sight, but those humans were still MIA hours later. I was getting the feeling more and more that this wouldn't be the simple search and rescue I'd hoped for.

"So I assume you've set the camp as the PLS, then?" I

said. In search and rescue, PLS stands for Place Last Seen, and it serves as the center point for most searches.

"That's right," Hogan agreed. "We're gridding out from there. We've got an air team covering waterways and roadways, since we figure Megan and Heather will know enough to head for open land so we can find them. There are a couple of snowmobile clubs that are helping out, too. They're out combing the trails now, and checking any hunting lodges or shacks in case people got separated or needed to find shelter."

Casper had tired of belly rubs by this time and was back on his feet in search of Phantom. I could see my shepherd off about fifty yards to our right, and kept one eye trained on her while we continued our impromptu briefing.

"This shouldn't be that tough, then," I said. "Especially if you have a lot of scent dogs on the job. If everyone was traveling on foot, they couldn't have gotten that far from the camp in the time between their check-in and the snowmobiler finding the camp."

"We've set a radius of ten miles," Hogan said, with a nod. "We thought they might have gone out on skis, but we found their equipment still stowed in one of the tents." That shadow returned to his face, his expression darkening. He shook his head. "To be honest, I don't know what in hell could have happened up there. I'm trying not to think the worst, but it's not easy with this one."

He said the words quietly, almost reluctantly, and I knew this at least was the truth. Before I could reply, Phantom chose that moment to explain to Casper in no uncertain terms that she was not interested in his games, filling the silence with snarls and Casper's answering yelp.

"Phantom!" I called. "Leave him be."

Casper was on the ground with Phantom on top of him, her jaws at his throat. She looked up at my voice, gave the pit bull one final snarl, and trotted off. It took Casper all of thirty seconds to gather his courage and trail after her. This time, he kept a respectful distance between himself and the female. Maybe there was hope for the boy after all.

"If your dogs are set, we should probably head in so you can report to the sergeant and get your assignment," Hogan said. "You can stop at the lodge and dump your gear, get the dogs settled. I'll meet you at the trailer."

He turned back toward the path. Just as he did, I heard something on the air—a voice, distant but distinct, that grabbed hold like a human hand at the back of my neck.

I told you not to run, baby girl.

My head jerked up. Jack was saying something, Hogan already on his way down the trail, but I could do nothing but listen to that voice.

Running won't get you anywhere. Don't you know that by now?

I knew that voice all too well.

Brock Campbell.

I'm what's known as 'sensitive' to things others can't see or hear, but for all my interactions with ghosts of my past and others', I had never seen Brock, never heard him, never sensed him, after he took his last breath. A blessing I've thanked God for every day.

So why would I suddenly hear him now?

"Did you hear something?" I asked Jack. Bear trailed behind with Ren and their dogs, but I wondered immediately if my son—himself an even stronger empath than me—had heard the same thing.

Jack looked at me. "No. What's the matter?"

"Nothing. I just…" I shook my head. "I don't know."

I fell silent, waiting for the voice again. It didn't come.

"Jamie?" Jack pressed. "What's going on? Did you see something, like in Glastenbury?"

"No, it's nothing," I tried to reassure him. I've been able to pick up on subtleties that others can't from the time I was a kid, occasionally able to catch glimpses into the future that I've never been able to explain; sometimes hearing the voices of the dead. Bear's gifts go far beyond that. He sees the dead, speaks with them, experiences things the rest of us can't even imagine. I only came close to that once, during the search in Glastenbury.

While there, I saw the spirit of a young girl who had been murdered in 1945; she became something like a guide for me during that search. She appeared to Bear, too. Nothing like that had happened in the five months since that search, though, and I'd never experienced anything like it before that time.

This wasn't a spirit, though. At least I hoped to God it wasn't.

"What's up?" Bear asked, catching up to us. "Is something wrong?"

I forced myself to return to the present. Whatever—or whoever—I'd heard, it was gone now. "I'm fine. We should get going, though."

We called the dogs to us. Phantom and Minion came willingly, while Casper continued racing around us in a game of tag in which only one of us was a willing participant. Eventually, though, he settled down.

The snow had stopped for the moment, and the parking lot continued to fill with searchers, both volunteer and paid, along with the inevitable influx of news vans. Meanwhile, we headed in to get the dogs settled.

The ski lodge Hogan had arranged was definitely not the kind of accommodations we were used to. I knocked at the front door since Hogan had said we'd be staying with others, and was met with a deep-throated bark that set our own dogs off beside us.

"Can it, Whippet," I heard on the other side of the door before a woman opened up. She was petite and curly-haired, dressed in a warden's uniform sans the boots. Corporal Michelle Wassel, a K-9 trainer and handler I'd worked with before, and had always liked.

"Hey!" she said at sight of us. "Hogan said we'd have roomies—you never know how that's gonna go. Glad to see it's you guys. Welcome to the Copa."

She stepped aside, giving us our first look inside the lodge. Bear whistled softly.

"Wow," he said. "Definitely a step up from the crap hotels they usually put us up in."

"Right?" Michelle said. "We lucked out this time."

Michelle's dog, Whippet, was a Dutch shepherd—an athletic breed whose high energy and drive to work make it ideal for search and rescue. Now, the little brindle shepherd decided that she'd had enough of the niceties, and bolted toward the door to get in on the action. The dogs had all met before, so I wasn't as concerned as I might have been otherwise. Still, it gave us an excuse to skip the greetings and just get through the door already. As soon as we'd crossed the threshold, we let our own dogs loose. Michelle already knew Bear and Ren, but I made a quick requisite introduction to Jack since the two had never met.

She gave me a sideways, approving glance when Jack wasn't looking, and I felt the color rise in my cheeks. "Nice. Way to class up the joint," she whispered to me. I gave her what I hoped was a stern enough scowl for her to be quiet, and hoped to high heaven that Jack hadn't heard. He continued further into the lodge, seemingly oblivious of our exchange.

The lodge opened into an expansive great room with a wood stove at the center, a fire already roaring within.

"Whoa," Bear said as he stepped inside. "Now I could definitely get used to this."

"Well, don't," I said evenly. "How many bedrooms are there?"

"Five," Michelle said. "There's another warden who'll be staying with us: Charlie Babcock. He doesn't have a dog, but he's always happy to be around them. He's a good guy, you'll like him. We already claimed our rooms, which means two in your team will need to double up. Hope that's all right."

"I'll do it," Bear volunteered immediately. I caught the look he exchanged with Ren, but was more concerned with the blush climbing his cheeks. "Ren and I could—"

I held up my hand. "Not on your life."

"Bear and I can bunk together," Jack volunteered. Bear started to argue, but I just raised an eyebrow.

"You're seriously gonna fight me on that?"

He opened his mouth, then closed it. Frowned. "No, ma'am."

"Thank you." I looked at Jack. "Are you sure you're all right with that?"

He shrugged, with a slight grin in Bear's direction. "I think we'll manage."

After introductions were through and room assignments had been settled, I went to my room to set my things down. As soon as I made it through the door, I took a deep breath at sight of the queen-sized bed and down comforter, not to mention the large flat-screen TV mounted on the wall. I even had a bathroom to myself. Out on the island, we'd just finished building dormitory-style housing for the group. I had a twin-sized bed that I usually shared with Phantom, and a bathroom that was anything but private.

I turned the water on in the shower and slipped my hand under the spray. *Oh, God.* Water pressure. Actual water pressure.

"Jamie?" There was a knock on the bedroom door. I opened up to find Jack in the hallway, now without his parka and ski hat.

"Yeah?" I said. "Is there a problem with the room? I know it's not ideal sharing with a teenage boy—"

"No, it's no problem," he said quickly, waving me off. Surprisingly, I got the sense he genuinely didn't mind. "I was just wondering if you'd mind me coming along when you get briefed by the IC? I'd be interested to hear some more details on the case. And I haven't actually been inside the SAR mobile unit yet…"

"And you'd like to see what kind of toys they get to play with in there?" I guessed.

He grinned, a little sheepish. "Yeah. Kind of."

"Of course," I agreed. "Let me grab my coat, and I'll meet you in the great room in five."

"Perfect."

He left, and I closed the door after him. I allowed myself two minutes to lie on the giant bed, Phantom stretched out beside me.

"Don't get used to it," I said to the dog. She sighed, and lay her head on my arm. My sentiments exactly.

I managed to pry myself off the bed and was at the front door right on time when Jack met me. He was bundled up again, a spark in his eye that I was beginning to enjoy. I hadn't seen that when he was with the FBI, but it always seemed to turn up when I called him in for a search.

As we were headed out the door, his hand settled at the small of my back as he ushered me through. Warmth spread where his fingers connected with my body, despite my multiple layers of clothing.

And then, that voice returned.

Just hold tight, baby girl. I'm on my way.

I shrank from Jack's touch, hoping he didn't notice, and focused on the words. The voice. And then, I steeled myself. There had to be a reason I was hearing Brock again. I thought of the women lost in the snow at this very moment. *Battered women.* It was a term I had no love for. I'd always refused to label myself that way, despite what I went through with Brock. I wasn't so delusional that I didn't recognize that was mostly vanity on my part, though.

"Are you coming, Jamie?" Jack asked. He was watching me again, clearly aware something was going on. I was relieved when he didn't press me on it.

"Yeah. Sorry—I'm coming."

I stepped into the cold air. Jack closed the door behind us. I waited for that clear, distant voice I loathed to return. This time, it didn't.

I knew the reprieve was only temporary. One thing you could always count on with Brock Campbell: once he got his claws in, he didn't let go. He would be back.

4

HOGAN CAUGHT UP TO US again in the parking lot outside the mobile search and rescue unit, looking more harassed than he had before. Barely twenty minutes had passed, but clearly tension was mounting around this search.

"Any news?"

"Vultures are circling," he said, nodding toward the news vans. "I thought maybe the weather would keep them away, but no such luck. Other than that, not much."

Before we made it inside the trailer, a handsome older man accompanied by an equally attractive woman in her mid- to late sixties made a beeline for us from across the parking lot. I recognized the man as Senator Robert Price immediately, and cringed at sight of the reporters and camera crews trailing him. At the same time that the senator and his wife were headed our way, I noticed a ruggedly good-looking man in a navy blue ski jacket and knit cap as he stepped out of a black SUV across the lot. He made no move to join us, but I was acutely aware of his attention.

"Thank you for meeting us here," Hogan said to the senator, extending his hand. "Senator Price, this is Jamie Flint and her colleague, Jack Juarez. Jamie will be coordinating with the warden service's K-9 unit for the operation."

Jack and I shook the senator's hand, and he introduced us to the woman beside him—his wife, Sally. As we exchanged pleasantries, the press took a steady stream of photos, shouting questions that were mostly ignored.

"I'm happy to help in any way I can, Lieutenant Hogan," the senator said.

"Can you tell us why you've been asked to assist in this search, Senator?" a female reporter called out from the crowd. For a second, I saw a weariness, a glimpse of pain cross Sally Price's face before it vanished. The senator, however, remained unwavering.

"Law enforcement background," he said vaguely. "I've helped with a lot of searches in my years on the force, and I still know this area. Times have changed, but I'm happy to lend a hand when I can."

"Does it have anything to do with the individuals on this expedition?" another reporter, this one a man, asked. "Why hasn't the warden service issued a statement on the participants, or any other details about the trip? What's with all the secrecy?"

"As the lead agency on this search, it's up to the warden service what information they do or do not release," the senator said. This prompted another flurry of questions.

"Excuse us," Hogan said smoothly, interrupting the assault. "We need to get to work. IC Roger Steiner will have a statement prepared as soon as we have any new information."

He opened the trailer door and stood aside as Sally Price entered first, her husband's hand at her elbow, his own head bowed. Jack and I followed behind, silent.

The Maine Warden Service's mobile unit was a thirty-two-foot, state-of-the-art trailer decked out with the latest in law enforcement technology and communications. A digital whiteboard was the centerpiece of the room, with several computer stations on either side. All of them were occupied at the moment, the place buzzing with activity.

"My son-in-law should be here shortly to help with the search," the senator said the moment the door was closed behind him. "He's a registered Maine Guide, so I expect his expertise will come in handy."

"I'll have him coordinate with the IC, sir," Hogan said. "We'll take any help we can get."

The mobile unit door opened once more, letting in a flurry of shouted reporters' questions as the good-looking man I'd seen in the parking lot entered, another warden beside him.

"Chase! Thank God you could make it," the senator said. He turned to Hogan. "This is my son-in-law, Chase Carter."

"Good to meet you, Mr. Carter, though I'm sorry about the circumstances," Hogan said. He extended his hand and the men shook, though I could tell from the tension on his face that Hogan wasn't happy about this new addition. "It looks like you made quite a stir out there with the reporters. We're trying to keep a low profile on this as much as possible."

"Chase is running for U.S. Senate next term," the senator explained. "He's a crowd favorite. Low profile isn't even in his vocabulary right now."

He didn't look the least bit familiar to me, but I got the sense simply in the way Chase Carter carried himself that he expected others to know who he was. At the words, I caught a glimpse of a frown on Sally Price's face, accompanied by a fleeting glance in her son-in-law's direction that got my own antennae up. However much the senator might like Chase, I wasn't sure that Sally held him in the same esteem.

"I tried to tell him he could meet with IC Steiner later, inside the motel," the warden who had accompanied Chase said. He was wiry and blond, not more than twenty-five years old, and clearly feeling a little out of his depth right now.

"It's in your best interest to listen to the corporal from here on out," Hogan said to Chase, then shifted focus back to the corporal. "You can join the briefing now, Charlie. I've got it from here."

The corporal moved to find a seat in the briefing area, where it appeared things were about to get started. Hogan took me aside briefly. "I'm going to talk to the senator and his family out back, get them briefed and find out whatever I can. Make yourselves comfortable. IC Steiner should be here shortly."

Sure enough, Hogan had barely shepherded the others away before Sergeant Roger Steiner entered the unit, another volley of questions following him before reporters were shut out behind the closing door. He was a tall, angular man who always reminded me a little of Abe Lincoln, minus the mutton-chop sideburns. Corporal Charlie, the warden who had accompanied Chase Carter, stepped to the front of the room.

"We'll begin the briefing now," the corporal said. "Assignments will be given out at the end, and if you'll sign up with your phone number on the sheet I'm sending around, I'll text updates to the group as we get them."

There was a flurry of conversation as others found seats or chose to stand, as Jack and I had. Corporal Charlie went to the whiteboard, and a digital topographic map of the area appeared. The map was covered with lines—solid, dashed, and dotted—of varying colors, a coded spider web that would have been hard to decipher if I hadn't been in search and rescue for the better part of a decade and a half. Today, the yellow dashed lines represented snowmobiles; solid red was the overhead crew; solid green were the "ground pounders"—volunteers searching the area on foot. K-9 units were represented by a series of blue lines concentrated in the area around Grafton Notch State Park, a 3,000+ acre park in the Mahoosuc Mountains first established in 1963.

The map was tangled enough right now, but I knew that by the end of the search we'd barely be able to identify the major landmarks for all the markups covering it.

Up front and off to one side stood Sergeant Roger Steiner, a man I'd worked with before and had always respected. Roger had been in the warden service for decades. He loved the outdoors, had forgotten more than most people would ever know about the job, and knew the Maine woods better than just about anyone out there. If there was anyone suited to head the search, it was him.

Beside Roger stood a man I barely recognized, though I had met him a few times in the years that Bear had been active with WildFire Expeditions. Abe Wright, Heather's husband, had always been good looking, gregarious, and creative—an artist trapped in the body of a mountain man, and someone Bear always looked up to. Now, the man looked wrecked. Unwashed, eyes shadowed, clothes rumpled. He stood beside Roger with his hands deep in his pockets and his head down, forehead furrowed as though he were in pain.

"Jamie," Roger said, when the wardens at the map were quiet. "Good to see you, though I wish it were under different circumstances."

I nodded my agreement. "Of course."

Abe acknowledged me with a curt nod. If he recognized me, he gave no indication. Of course, the way he looked I'm not sure he would have recognized his own shadow.

"I've asked Abe here to provide some background for searchers," Steiner said, nodding toward the younger man. Abe nodded, appearing more focused now that he had something to do.

"This map indicates where Heather's expedition was supposed to be yesterday, last night, and today. They were traveling on skis and by dogsled, so it's not likely they'd be too far beyond this."

I studied the map. The Mahoosuc Mountain Range is a northern extension of the White Mountains, straddling the Maine/New Hampshire border. Some of the toughest miles in the Appalachian Trail are part of the range, including Mahoosuc Notch—generally agreed to be the slowest mile on the trail, with its steep climbs, massive boulders, and notable lack of any actual walking trail.

"This is a pretty standard route for them, isn't it?" I asked Abe. "My son did a couple of courses with you. I think the trails at that point were in and around Grafton Park—the same area I'm seeing here."

"That's right," Abe said. "I wanted them to stay more central. I tried to talk them into sticking near Sunday River, but Megan overruled me. Said it would be better to stay on familiar ground." He paused. Studied me. "You're Bear's mom, aren't you?"

I nodded, and he smiled almost absently. "He's a good kid. I'm sorry I didn't recognize you. I'm a little..." He trailed off, looking suddenly lost.

"Don't worry about that, I understand. You were saying,

about the trail choices?" I prompted, getting him back on topic.

"Right," he said. "They wanted to be more accessible, in case there was a problem. With some of the women, there was a concern about spouses getting involved."

"You're aware of the type of expedition this was?" Steiner interrupted, directing the question at me. I nodded wordlessly.

"Between that and Heather's condition…" Abe trailed off just as Hogan returned, the senator and his wife nowhere in sight. I waited for someone to elaborate on Abe's words; when no one did, Hogan volunteered the information.

"Heather is six months' pregnant," he explained.

"I wanted to make sure they could get help if they needed it," Abe said. "Megan said it wouldn't be a problem staying out toward Grafton Notch, though." His voice failed, and he shifted his gaze to the ground abruptly, trying to get himself back under control.

"We still have no idea what happened out there," Steiner said to him gently. "But you don't find women tougher than Megan and Heather. We'll find them, Abe. They'll be all right."

Abe nodded, but said nothing more.

"Anyway," Steiner said, his focus on me and the other wardens in the room now. "The way we figure it, the group traveled at most ten miles from where the camp was found. That's where we're focusing our efforts, so we'll start the dogs out there."

He nodded toward the map on the whiteboard. "This is accessible to everyone on the search, of course. You'll need to sync with everyone else, and Charlie—" he nodded to the corporal, who was fast becoming a familiar face—"will get you the passwords you need so you can download and share your GPS coordinates as you finish your assignments."

Michelle Wassel, our roommate back at the lodge, cleared her throat. As leader of the warden service's K-9 unit, I would report directly to her over the course of the search. Meanwhile, the IC oversaw the operations for multiple agencies until the missing were either found or the search was called off.

"I still have my doubts about taking the dogs out in this weather," she said. "It'll be fine while things are frozen over tonight, but it's supposed to warm up by morning. I don't want my dogs plowing through a foot of slush tomorrow."

"How many teams do you have out there?" I asked.

"Six warden service teams, and eight MESARD handlers. Add your three to that, and we've got an army of dogs and handlers. Hopefully that'll be enough to bring everybody home before the weather turns again. Tonight should be fun, though. We just slip on our ice skates and let the dogs have at it." Jack looked mildly concerned. "Not literally," she assured him, and there was a ripple of laughter in the room. "But it'll be damned slick. Not that the dogs mind that kind of thing. Should be a good night for a search."

"Hopefully so," I agreed. "Especially if we bring everybody home fast."

That earned nods all around. The rest of the briefing took only a few minutes before Charlie took me aside and supplied me with the passwords I'd need to get on the shared online search page for this operation. As soon as Jack and I were done, Hogan found us again.

"You ready? Once we get to the park entrance, we'll have a sled bring you and the dogs up to the camp."

"A sled?" Jack asked. "As in…"

"Not a bobsled," I assured him. "It's what all the guys in the know call snowmobiles."

"Ah. One of these days I'm going to write down all the lingo I run into with these searches. Half the time I feel like I need Google Translate just to keep up."

"Let me know if you do," IC Steiner said, approaching Jack, Hogan, and me. "I'm sure our volunteers could use it."

"We'll do that," I said. "Do you need us for further briefing, or should I just meet up with the others and move out?"

"Yeah, go ahead and get started," he said. Someone else was trying to get his attention, while a third officer held a phone, waiting for the sergeant's first available second. Ah, the life of an incident commander; definitely not something I ever aspired to. Before Steiner took the phone, he shifted focus back to me. "Report back at fourteen hundred, and make sure you're checking in with your people every hour."

Two p.m., military time. It was twelve-thirty now. "Yes, sir," I agreed.

At this point, I was eager to get started with the dogs myself. I glanced back toward the cordoned-off area where the senator, his wife, and son-in-law were all still sequestered. I could hear voices—tense voices, based on the tone and volume—but could make out no words. None of which really mattered to me, as long as they all stayed put. My job was to find the missing, not navigate the politics and emotions of those close to them.

We started toward the door with Hogan beside me, Jack just behind, maneuvering past several officers crowded in the narrow space.

"I'm glad you brought Bear along," Hogan said just as we reached the door, surprising me. "I'll be interested to see how he does out there. He was always good at thinking on his feet."

His tone made me uneasy, and a dozen memories of the year Hogan came into my life flashed through my mind. It had been the worst year of my life, in any number of ways. I still wasn't sure how I would have survived if he hadn't been there—something I had never really told him. I wondered if he had any idea what his presence had meant back then. Or just how much it was spinning me to see him now.

I pushed those thoughts away. Our energy needed to be focused in one direction and one direction only: on finding the WildFire group that had vanished, seemingly without a trace. Everything else would wait.

5

I DROVE THE TEAM up to the Grafton Notch State Park entrance, where half a dozen other SUVs were already parked—the first wave of K-9s to go out searching, I assumed. We parked and Bear and Ren got their dogs while Jack and I took Phantom and made our way to the head of the trail. Michelle Wassel waited there with Whippet, the rest of her team close behind and clearly eager to get to work.

The sun was bright by now and the snow subsided for the moment, the day cold and clear with a wind biting enough to cut to the bone. Both Phantom and Whippet wore weatherproof jackets, Phantom with the Flint K-9 logo on the side, Whippet with MAINE WARDEN SERVICE.

A snowmobile pulling a covered trailer idled nearby, a helmeted figure in the driver's seat. Michelle nodded toward him.

"That's our ride up, and we've got a squad of others on the way. Two dogs to a trailer; two riders and a driver to each sled. It'll be a little crowded, but it shouldn't take long. Is your team ready? I want to head out."

"We're more than ready," Bear said, from behind me. "Casper's gonna set out on his own if somebody doesn't give us something to find soon."

"Well, then, let's get moving," Michelle said. She barely got the words out before three more snowmobiles showed up with engines revved.

Phantom and Whippet hopped into the trailer at the front of the fleet willingly, and Michelle climbed behind the driver. I crowded on behind and held on tight.

"Ready?" the driver called back in a muffled voice. Casper and Minion were loaded into trailers behind us, while Jack, Bear, and Ren climbed onto the other snowmobiles.

Before I could answer, the machine jerked to a start and we bounded up the mountain.

With a crust of ice topping the pure white snow, the snowmobile made easy work of the path, taking us up about a mile along a narrow trail until, suddenly, the trees opened up and we were in a clearing with a perfect view of Old Speck and the valley below. We came to a stop about a hundred feet from three brightly colored tents that stuck out of the snow. The WildFire Expeditions camp, now abandoned. Michelle and I got off the snowmobile, and the driver removed his helmet. An older man with a scraggly beard peered at us, eyes squinted and head ducked against the wind.

"Here you go," he said. "Creepy as all get out, but this is it. Whatever happened to them, it happened right here. I can't imagine they would've left their dogs otherwise."

I considered that before nodding. He was right, just as Bear had said earlier: Heather and Megan wouldn't have left their dogs without a fight. Looking around, though, I saw no sign of that fight. Of course, the high winds and light snow they'd had on the mountain overnight could easily have wiped away any surface traces we might have seen.

"Agreed," Michelle said. "So, we start here. We've done

flybys and we've had snowmobiles canvassing out here since we got started. There's no sign of anyone, which doesn't make a lot of sense. There wasn't enough snow last night to bury a body—if they're out here, we should have gotten a visual pretty quickly."

"Which is where the dogs come in," I said. "They might not be readily visible, but they didn't just disappear."

"Exactly."

After Michelle had gotten Whippet from the trailer, I retrieved Phantom and tightened the straps of her vest at her chest and belly. Within five minutes, the other snowmobiles came in with the rest of the team, and Bear and Ren got their own dogs and prepped them for work while Jack retrieved our gear. Meanwhile, I took stock of the scene that had been found.

The snowmobile driver had been right: it *was* eerie being in the abandoned camp—there was really no other word for it. The WildFire dogsled and three tents, blown down and half buried in snow, marked the space. Phantom looked at me, whined, and sat. Even she seemed overwhelmed at what we had found.

"I want your crew covering the northeast quadrant," Michelle said to me. "MESARD's got dogs covering the south. We only have a couple of K-9s from the warden service on right now, but they're covering the northwest."

"Got it," I agreed. The wind was worse here, though I was grateful that no more snow fell.

"Remember, check-in's at fourteen hundred," Michelle continued, consulting her watch. "And let me know if the going is too rough for your dogs. I'll definitely be watching Whippet."

"Will do." I looked around once more. Jack, Bear, and

Ren waited at the edge of camp, trying not to disturb what we knew could prove to be a crime scene. On the horizon, I could see MESARD handlers already out with their dogs, working the grid.

"So, what's the plan?" Bear asked at my approach. Casper was already pacing at the end of his long lead, while Minion sat calmly beside Ren.

"We've got the northeast quadrant," I said. "Wind's been blowing too much to tell when the camp was abandoned, but it had to be sometime between their check-in at nineteen hundred last night and when the camp was discovered this morning. We're working with a radius of ten miles, assuming they were on foot."

The others nodded, silent. Digesting. There was something so sinister about this place. Vaguely haunting. I looked at Bear, trying to figure out whether he'd sensed any kind of presence. If he had, he gave no sign of it.

"Okay," I said. "We have our orders. We should head out, but keep your radios on. If your dog alerts, follow up with them to see if the find is good, then call it in. Everyone reports back at fourteen hundred."

There was agreement all around, and we set out—Jack with me, while Ren and Bear took their dogs in the opposite direction. With the others on their way, I shifted my focus to Phantom. I got down on one ski-pant-clad knee and looked her in the eye.

I rescued Phantom literally minutes before she was scheduled to be euthanized at a shelter down in Georgia, seeing something in the skeletal frame and sunken eyes that spoke to me even then. Seven years later, she's become the best dog of my career. Every decision that I make in the work we do is, of necessity, with her best interests in mind.

"What do you say, girl?" I asked. "You ready for the game?" Her tail waved, her focus absolute. No sign of hesitation to be found. I gave her the scent article we were working with: an old scarf of Heather's that her husband had given the team. She snuffled it thoroughly, getting more worked up with every second, kinetic energy buzzing now.

"Good girl, Phantom," I said, infusing my words with as much enthusiasm as possible. "That's my girl! Let's go. Find her!"

The moment she had the command, Phantom let go with an energized *woof* and set out.

I sent her off without the leash, a GPS affixed to her collar while I used a handheld device to track her progress in case I lost sight of her. A bell on her collar, meanwhile, gave me an immediate auditory cue to follow if I lost a visual.

We'd been hiking for nearly an hour, uphill much of that time, when I caught sight of Phantom up ahead again. She was moving more slowly now, her head up as she continued sniffing the air. When a dog is actively searching for a scent on the air—called air scenting—their head will be up, nose going nonstop, while they try to find those all-important scent particles. Once they're locked on, the head usually goes down and they start following the active trail from there.

Today, however, we had the deck stacked against us. There are four factors that impact how well a scent dog does her job: airflow, temperature, moisture, and density. Moisture traps scent particles in the air, making tracking considerably easier. In subzero temperatures, that moisture freezes and it's harder to follow any kind of scent trail. Combine that with the high winds we were experiencing, and I sincerely doubted the dogs would be able to come up with anything at all today.

Regardless, we kept going, Phantom gamely searching for that elusive scent trail. The world darkened as we moved deeper into the woods. The path beneath our feet was solid but slick, more of a challenge for we humans than the canines on our team. Or so I thought.

Phantom had gone on ahead but I kept a close eye on her, trying to figure out if there was actually a point in us continuing. The women in the camp hadn't just levitated out of here; there had to be a trail somewhere. The fact that none of the dogs had been able to pick it up spoke to the difficulty of the conditions. It might be better to pull them now and have the IC get some infrared cameras that could track body heat, and rely on those instead. Of course, if the women's core body temperatures had lowered, they were buried deep, or the unthinkable had happened and they were actually dead, an infrared camera would do no good. All scenarios my dogs could work with.

Up ahead, I caught a glimpse of Phantom once more. Her head was down this time, her body tight, and she moved with a purpose that had been missing before. The shepherd's tail was stiff and held high, and I felt my own tension build as I watched her move.

"She's got something," I said to Jack, now a couple of steps behind me. He picked up his own pace, and soon the two of us were moving all-out to keep up with her.

Then, when Phantom was still about twenty yards from me, I watched as she hit a slick of ice on the surface of the snow. The dog skidded, stumbled, and then went down hard on her front legs, faltering a second later as she righted herself. I felt the pain of the jolt in my own bones, even though the dog hadn't made a sound. In the wild, it's in an animal's best interest to hide their physical discomfort to discourage anyone who might challenge them. Dogs still have that instinct, and Phantom had always been stoic to the core.

"Phantom!" I called after her as she set back out, though I couldn't detect a limp. "Stop."

She glanced back over her shoulder at the command, took another two steps, and finally came to a halt. No question based on the look on her face, however, that she wasn't happy about the interruption.

"Is she okay?" Jack asked.

"Hang on," I said. "I'll just check. She's probably fine." I said the words as much to reassure myself as him. I made my way across the snow on my own, leaving Jack behind.

"You all right there, girl?" I asked the dog as I approached. There was no tension in the way she held herself, and I saw no pain in her brown eyes when she met my gaze.

I knelt beside her in the snow, then carefully felt along her legs and feet for any sign of injury. She didn't flinch when I extended her front legs, and seemed to resign herself to my ministrations as I ran through a basic exam. Definitely no break. Based on the way she was acting, no sprain or strain either.

"All right, girl," I said. "Looks like you're good." Another bullet dodged. I was silently grateful that this wasn't the dreaded injury that finally sidelined her for good— something I worried about more and more as she got older.

"She'd caught a scent before," Jack said.

"It definitely seemed that way," I agreed. I looked around, but if whatever it was she'd smelled was nearby, I saw no sign of it.

"Maybe we should stop and give her time to rest," Jack said. "Or switch her out for one of the other dogs. I know your friend thinks it's fine for the dogs, but she's obviously having a hard time."

I looked at him, surprised. It was clear from the time Jack started working with me that he wasn't a dog person, but it seemed he'd developed a soft spot for Phantom.

"It's actually not as bad as you think," I said. "The temperature's ideal for something like this, especially for dogs. No bugs. No ticks. And while it's slick underfoot, the fact that she's not falling through the snow is a huge point in our favor. To be honest, these are kind of ideal conditions."

All that said, I was equally uneasy continuing—though not necessarily just because I was worried about Phantom. Truth be told, I was more worried about that creeping feeling that had been dogging me all morning. Regardless, I shoved that aside. Ten women were missing, counting on us to come find them.

"Okay, Phantom," I said to the dog. She looked up at me eagerly, tension coiling her body tight as she waited for the word. "Go ahead, girl. Find them."

The moment she got the command, she was off again. There was no question based on her reaction that Phantom had the scent now. She rushed forward, paying no attention to me after that, her nose back down in the snow. I focused on following her, Jack silent beside me as we walked on once more. And continued walking. The wind grew teeth but the sky was clear overhead, cloudless and blue. The ice cleats I'd strapped to my boots helped me stay on my feet on the ice-slicked snow, and I was glad I'd insisted on a shopping trip for Jack early in the season so he was equally prepared for the elements.

About half an hour later, with Phantom a good twenty-five feet ahead of us now, I saw her put on a sudden burst of speed as we approached denser forest. Though we were off trail now, the time of year meant we were able to move through the thick of the trees easier than we ever would have managed in summer, when everything was in full bloom. We trekked through the forest, going alternately over, under, and around felled trees. I knew searchers would keep looking overnight if the women weren't found by then, but having the daylight right now was a huge advantage.

"What would they have been doing out here?" Jack asked me, his breath coming faster as we raced to keep up with the dog.

"No idea," I said over my shoulder. He was right: what could have brought Megan and the others out this far, more than three miles from the dogs and their campsite?

Suddenly, Phantom's clear alert—two sharp barks in close succession—sounded. I consulted the GPS I held. She'd veered to the west and out of sight, but the blinking orange beacon on my screen made it easy to follow her. Wordlessly, Jack and I sped to a run, my adrenaline pumping now.

Come out, come out, wherever you are, a familiar voice said in my ear, the tone as wheedling as it was menacing. *Come on, baby girl. Show me that pretty face.*

My vision blurred, my stomach cramping. With my focus split, I lost track of where I was going or what was in front of me. Running full on, breath coming hard in the darkened forest, I completely missed the felled spruce across my path until Jack shouted a warning. He was too late.

I was going full tilt when I collided with the tree, hitting me square in the gut. My momentum propelled me over the obstacle and straight to the other side. I extended my arms to break my fall, but still caught myself pretty good on the chin, snapping my head back. Somewhere in the distance, both too close and far, far out of reach, I heard Brock's laughter.

"Are you all right?" Jack asked, at my side immediately. My cheeks flamed with embarrassment as I scrambled to my feet, ignoring the pain in my chin, back, arms, and gut.

"I'm fine," I said briskly. "I just…" I sucked in a painful breath. "Damn. Who put a tree in the middle of the forest like that?"

He flashed a smile at the weak joke, but clearly was still worried. There was no time for that, though; Phantom's impatient bark reminded us both of our mission. I stooped to pick up the GPS where it had landed when I fell, and paused. My pulse ticked up another notch.

A dark patch of crimson marked a snow-covered boulder just a couple of feet from me.

"Jamie?" Jack said, when he realized I wasn't following him. The wind had been knocked out of me with the fall, but the feeling in my gut right now had nothing to do with that. I nodded to the pool of blood—it could be nothing else, I knew. Jack frowned.

"We can come back to it," I said, and clicked a marker into the GPS so we wouldn't lose the spot.

Then, we set out once more.

Fifty yards on, Phantom sat waiting for me. Wind buffeted her, and I was surprised she hadn't come back to get me rather than just waiting.

Until I saw her find.

"Oh, God," I said, half under my breath, still ten yards away. "Call Hogan," I instructed Jack.

Phantom sat beside a wind-worn fir tree, her head down. Beside her, a woman lay with one hand wrapped tight around my dog's leg, as though reaching for a lifeline.

She lay on her back, eyes closed, a pool of crimson bleeding to pink in the snow beside her. Her face was deathly pale.

"Who is it?" Jack called to me, radio already up to his mouth.

The woman opened her eyes at my approach, plainly terrified. I knelt beside her. "It's all right," I said. "We're getting help."

"He shot Megan—" she began.

"Jamie?" Jack called, closer now.

"Tell Hogan we found Heather," I instructed him, then returned my focus to the woman before me. "Who shot her, Heather?" I asked. "What happened? Where are the others?"

She shook her head, tears coursing down her cheeks. "I don't know. It happened so fast. It came from the woods. I never saw anybody. And then we were running away, and I…" She stopped, forcing herself to slow down. "Then, he shot me. Everything just happened so damned fast."

I took a few seconds to assess her condition and realized that the bleeding seemed to be minimal, confined to what looked like a graze in her right leg.

I turned back to Jack, already on the horn with Hogan. "Give him our coordinates and get somebody out here. We need a Medevac. Fast."

Phantom lay down beside the woman, and Heather tipped her head to the side so she could touch the soft fur. I remained beside her, trying to keep her calm, as the minutes passed.

Buckle up, baby girl, Brock whispered in my ear. *I'm just getting started.* My stomach turned. With the radio call made, Jack stood beside us, silent, as we waited for help to come.

6

WITHIN TEN MINUTES, Hogan reached the site where we'd found Heather. He was accompanied by two other wardens and Heather's husband, Abe. As soon as we were in sight, Abe broke into a run. He half-slid to a spot beside his wife, eyes frantic.

"Heather. Oh my God, baby." When he got no response, he looked at me. "Why isn't she saying anything? Has she woken up since you found her?"

"She was conscious when we got here," I said, directing the words to both Abe and Hogan. "But she passed out a few minutes later, and I haven't been able to get her back."

"Is she hurt? What the hell happened to her?"

"We're not sure," I said. "We'll need to wait and have the paramedics check her out."

Abe had another dozen questions for us that we couldn't answer, while Hogan alternately sent updates to the IC and stared at the sky, waiting for help to come. Mercifully, that help arrived twenty minutes later, noise like a firestorm sounding over the horizon. Seconds later, the Medevac helicopter came into view. It landed in a clearing fifty yards away, blowing snow and debris in every direction. I snapped Phantom's leash onto her collar and kept her out of the way as paramedics rushed toward us, crouched low to avoid the chopper's rotors.

"Vitals?" a short, stout woman demanded as she knelt beside Heather. I rattled them off and the woman nodded. Meanwhile, Hogan and Jack worked together to strong-arm Abe out of the way.

Satisfied that we had done what we could, Hogan, Jack, and I stood by as they lifted Heather onto a stretcher and carried her back to the chopper. Once she was loaded in, the medics made room for Abe, since there was no way in hell he would have been left behind. We remained silent as they lifted off. I reached down and scratched Phantom behind her ears as the helicopter flew away, and tried not to think about what would have happened if she hadn't caught that scent and pushed on.

"The IC is pulling us in to regroup," Hogan said, once the chopper was up and away. "The fact that there's a gunman changes everything. State police are on their way out to analyze the scene, and the sergeant needs to figure out how he wants to play things if we have an active shooter out there somewhere. My hunch is that he'll pull the ground pounders out of the field now."

The fact that I worked with the trained K-9 units meant I was slightly more valuable than the civilian searchers Hogan was referring to, but I still technically qualified as a civilian volunteer.

"He doesn't need to do that," I said. I thought of the search in Glastenbury and the deadly standoff that resulted because I hadn't pulled my searchers off, and reconsidered. "At least, not with me. I'll keep Bear and Ren out of it from here on out. Issue Kevlar if you need to, but I'm not stopping as long as those women are still out there. Especially not now."

Jack frowned. I glanced at him, noting the worry in his dark eyes. "You don't have to come," I said. "I'll understand. There's no shame in playing it safe."

"I'm not worried about myself," he said quietly.

"We'll need to report back to the IC regardless," Hogan said. "He was clear on that. We've got a new PLS to work from, and with the hasty search of the area already done, we're moving into a type 2 search. That means I'll need more teams on the ground, including K-9s. Whatever way you slice it, this is gonna be a shit show."

In search and rescue, there are several categories of searches, the most basic being the 'hasty search,' which is exactly what it sounds like: searchers divide segments of a large search area into a grid and do a quick scan of the area, often using planes or helicopters to cover open spaces like roads and waterways. In this case, the hasty search had employed both air teams and snowmobiles, but had yielded nothing.

Type 2 searches are more organized than hasty searches, but are still considered a rapid, basic search. In type 2, an area is divided into grids and searchers are sent out to cover each section in a focused, consistent pattern. In the vast majority of search operations, the missing person is found during either the hasty search or the subsequent type 2 phase. I was hoping that would be the case this time, but the discovery of Heather and the story she told made me doubt we'd be so lucky.

"Based on what we saw here," Hogan continued, "Heather couldn't have been in the snow more than a few hours. Did she say when she got separated from the others?"

"She was fuzzy on the details. She was with another group, but she broke away so she could go back to the camp for Megan, who was the first one hit. Heather spent some time looking, and that was when she was shot."

Hogan looked at me sharply. "Megan was hit, too? So where the hell is she? We've searched the camp. There's no way she's there."

"We don't have any more answers than you do," Jack said. "But according to Heather, they were at the campsite when the first shot was fired."

"So our radius has to be right," Hogan said, half to himself. "This is three and a half miles from the campsite. They must have run like hell once the shooter came on the scene."

The image ran through my mind: the group, panicked, running for their lives, Heather aware that her sister was hurt, that the dogs had been left behind, desperate to get back to them. I could imagine her begging the others to let her go, and then insisting. Only to find herself a target, just like Megan.

"The fact is, we don't know what happened," Hogan continued, his frustration clear. "We can finish speculating at base. We need to head in." I frowned, catching Jack's eye. He looked equally unhappy. Hogan caught the exchange, and paused. "What?"

"What if the others aren't that far from here?" I asked. "They could be close, in which case us leaving the scene to go talk about what we should do rather than just doing it, especially if we already know what that something is… It's a waste of time. And it could be time that Megan and the others don't have."

To my surprise, he nodded rather than arguing. "I know. But my orders are to bring you back in. We'll get someone out here as soon as we can."

"But you already have someone out here," I insisted. "I could swap Phantom out for Casper so Phantom can rest up—Casper has more energy than he knows what to do with. That dog can do a ten-hour shift and still be ready to play when we get home. I want us to keep looking as long as we can."

Hogan ran a hand through his hair. I'm not usually one to argue with my superiors on a search, but I will if I know they're making the wrong call. In this case, everything in me was saying we were wasting valuable time. We were looking at an active shooter and nine women still missing; time was the enemy right now. We couldn't afford to waste a minute.

"Let me give the sergeant a call, see what he says," Hogan finally said. "I want to check in with Michelle, though. See how long she thinks the K-9s on her team can handle the terrain out here."

"Whatever you need to do," I said, then added, "Thank you."

He shrugged. "I just want to get everybody home safe. And if Megan's still out there, and she's hurt..." He fell silent for a moment, seemingly at war with himself. When he spoke again, there was an intimacy there that he hadn't allowed in before. I saw Jack shift, and knew he must be wondering about our past. "I need you to be smart about this, Jamie. Because to be honest, I'm not sure I can be."

The truth was clear in his eyes, whether or not he chose to acknowledge it: he knew Megan. Maybe they were just friends, but that wasn't what I was seeing. Right now, I saw a man being torn up by a ticking clock and the knowledge that everything he was doing, everything he could do, might not be enough.

"Just let me get Casper out here," I said to him. "Send

us back out. In the end, I'll do what's best for my dog. If I think he's in danger, I'll pull out."

"Good." He paused, looking out toward the horizon. His jaw was hard, pain clear in his eyes. "Thank you, Jamie. I'm glad you're here."

"Don't thank me yet," I said. "Wait till we see how this thing ends."

•

My next call was to Bear. I expected a fight about making him sit the search out while I took his dog with me. Instead, I was more than slightly uneasy about the underlying note of joy I detected in my son's voice when he learned that he and Ren would be alone and unsupervised in a romantic lodge on a cold winter's night, instead of trekking through the wilderness until the wee hours.

"You have separate rooms for a reason," I reminded him, a tinny echo over the radio repeating the words back to me. It felt like I was being mocked by the danged thing, though I knew that wasn't true. My son might not be taking me seriously, but the radio probably didn't care one way or the other.

"I know that, Mom," Bear said. "Relax. Geez. We'll hang out, watch something on TV, and get some sleep. Hopefully once everything gets figured out, we'll be able to get back out on the trail tomorrow to look for Megan and the others."

I didn't tell him that I doubted that, since that was my one and only bargaining chip at the moment. "Good. There's a little bit of food in the fridge, but if you can't find anything you like you can always order in."

"We're seventeen, Mom—I hope at this point we can figure out how to feed ourselves."

"Funny how I never hear you say that back home when you're wandering around complaining that there's nothing to eat." He didn't dignify that with a response, which I could understand. I hesitated a second, that voice from our shared past echoing in my mind once more. Had he heard anything? Seen Brock?

"We'll be fine, Mom," he said, when a second of silence had passed between us.

"I know you will," I said. Unless he said something to me about Brock, I decided, I would keep the echo of Bear's father to myself. "Look after Phantom, and I'll check in later. Love you, bud."

We'd already gone through the phase where those three little words inspired embarrassment or overt horror. Particularly since the events in Glastenbury, that seemed to be a thing of the past.

"Love you too," he said. "Now go on out there and find Megan, would you?"

I smiled. "You got it."

I ended the call, and got my head back in the game.

Three hours later, we were still going strong. Any precipitation had long since ended by this time and the moon was out, the night unnaturally bright thanks to the light given off by the world of white around us. Casper kept going without complaint, his body insulated with his thermal jacket and his paws protected in specially designed thermal booties. We'd been joined by Michelle and Whippet and another half-dozen dog teams, each of them focused on an area within the grid we'd established based on the discovery of Heather Wright.

Jack remained by my side, while Hogan returned

periodically to check on us but, clearly, had too many other things going on to hold my hand. Which was just fine, as far as I was concerned.

I hadn't heard Brock's voice again for hours, but I couldn't shake the memory. More than once, I felt the cold, hard eyes of some malevolent force following me, but when I turned around there was no one. I kept going back over the words I'd heard, both back at the hotel and then later in the woods. There was no question that it was Brock's voice. He may have been dead for eight years, but I would never forget what he sounded like whispering his threats in my ear.

There was one key difference here, though: *Baby girl*. In our entire troubled history, Brock had never once called me 'baby girl.' 'Sweetheart' was his preferred term of endearment, said typically with an underlying bite that made it feel as pointed as a knife's edge by the time we were through. So was it actually Brock I was hearing, or could it be someone else? And could that someone actually be Heather's shooter?

My thoughts were interrupted by the rustle of branches and the sound of footsteps behind us. It was just past ten p.m. Hogan pushed through the undergrowth, his breath a cloud of white preceding him.

"All right," he said. "Time's up. I want you back at base."

"But—" I began. He held up a hand to stop me.

"No buts—I'm serious. You've been over the same area three times now, and so has everyone else out tonight. We've got a fresh group coming on. They'll work through the night, expanding the grid another five miles. But you're dead on your feet, and I know that dog could stand a break."

Reluctantly, I nodded. I hadn't worked Casper any harder than I should have; the dog's eyes were still bright and his tail up, but extending the day any longer would definitely push the line. Jack looked ready to drop, and I was anxious to get back to the lodge to check on Phantom, who had gone back with Bear and Ren.

"All right, fine," I said. Hogan looked pleasantly surprised that invoking the needs of the dog had worked on me.

"Really? We're going back now? I was just getting warmed up," Jack said, up ahead on the trail. Jack usually wasn't one for sarcasm, but there was no missing it in his tone this time.

"You could have gone back sooner, you know," I said.

"And leave you alone out here? Not a chance," he said. At my look in his direction, he added quickly, "Not that I was here because I thought you needed protection. It's just..." He faded out, his eyes still caught on mine.

"We're partners," I said. "I wouldn't have left you, either. That's how this thing works."

It felt strangely intimate saying the words aloud. Another beat of silence passed before Hogan cleared his throat. "Well, nobody has to leave anyone out here alone now. Let's get back to town."

I called Casper back to me and snapped his leash on at his return. He looked discouraged at the unsatisfying end. Just like humans, working dogs thrive on knowing they've completed the day with a job well done. But while Phantom had found Heather, Casper had been chasing dead ends for hours. I hesitated, then turned to Jack.

"You up for one last job?"

He narrowed his eyes at me, his fatigue apparent even in the darkness.

"Jamie—" Hogan interrupted.

"It will only take a few minutes," I said, barely glancing

in Hogan's direction before I refocused on Jack. "You mind playing the vic in a quick game?"

He caught my meaning immediately and nodded. "Casper needs a win for the day? Sure, I can do that. Just give me five minutes."

Jack took a handkerchief from his pocket and handed it to me. "Here. Use this as a scent article. It should smell like me, but I swear I haven't actually used it."

I shoved it into a plastic baggie I took from my own pocket, holding it by one corner between thumb and forefinger. "Sure you haven't."

Seconds later, he vanished into the darkness. I turned to Hogan, who stood beside me with weary acceptance.

"The dogs need to feel like they've done something. This has been a frustrating day for everyone."

"Tell me about it," Hogan said darkly. "Do what your dog needs—I'm not about to stand in the way of that."

After five minutes had passed, I knelt and unsnapped Casper's leash one more time, then stuck the baggie with Jack's handkerchief under the dog's nose.

"Smell familiar, boy?" I asked him. He wriggled from head to toe, sensing that things were finally about to get good again. "All right, Casper. Ready? Find him!"

Instantly, Casper was on the move. His head was up for only a second while he searched for the scent. Then, three seconds in, his body snapped to attention. His nose hit the ground. Trotting easily across the frozen ground, he weaved in and out of the trees with Hogan and me close behind. Less than a minute later, I heard his alerting bark, then the pound of his paws on the frozen snow as he returned to me, barked, and ran off again.

"Where is he, Casper?" I called, pouring my last shred

of energy into the words. "Come on, boy! Show me!"

He came back around to get me one more time, and I followed him through the woods until he stopped and sat down, barking pointedly into a den of branches. I shone my flashlight in, and Jack grinned back at me.

"Good boy, Casper!" I said. "That's my boy!" I pulled out his tug toy, continuing to praise him like a nut while Jack and Hogan looked on and Casper latched onto the tug, teeth bared, tail waving. When you're a dog handler, you can't have too much stock in your own dignity—part of the job is acting like a complete idiot to keep your dog motivated and enthusiastic about the job.

After a two-minute celebration, I snapped Casper's leash on again, stuffed his slobbery tug toy into my pocket, and looked to Hogan and Jack.

"Okay. Now we can go."

"Good enough," Hogan said. "God forbid we bring one of your dogs back less than ecstatic."

I snuck a side glance at him, and noted just a trace of a smile. Small as it was, it was a relief to me. I'd worked with Hogan on a couple of searches when he was with the state police, back when I was doing search and rescue on the side while working for Brock. That was nearly ten years ago. What I remembered most about those days, apart from how much he cared about his job, was his sense of humor. Verbal sparring had come with the territory back then, and I couldn't help but wonder whether the change I saw now was a result of the years apart, or something more immediate was affecting him.

As we talked, I shone my flashlight beam around us. We'd strayed farther from the path than I'd intended while searching for Jack. To my left, I spotted a plastic orange marker wrapped around the branch of a spruce tree, its branches heavy with fresh snow. When I shone my flashlight to the right, however, expecting to find another marker, the trees were empty. I paused.

The search team working the grid area adjacent to ours had used blue ties to indicate where they'd searched, while Jack and I had used orange. Right now, though, I didn't see either blue or orange ties. Strange. I made a mental note to mention it once we were back at base, then pushed it out of my head in favor of the thought of a blazing fire, warm food, and a soft bed.

I'd no sooner had the thought than Casper froze where he stood, nose up, then turned toward me with the same intensity he'd shown during our game a few minutes before. He barked at me, his gaze this time fixed to the west—the exact area where I'd noted the absence of plastic ties.

"Where are we?" I asked Hogan. "I'm not seeing any markers around here. I thought Michelle's team was supposed to cover this area."

"There's a ravine not far from here. If Jack had gone another twenty feet looking for a hiding place, he would have found a hundred-foot drop instead."

"And you didn't think to mention that before we started the game?" Jack asked.

Hogan shrugged. "You're a smart guy. I figured you'd notice before you hit the end of the world."

"So no one searched the ravine?" I pressed. At my feet, Casper was growing more and more agitated, his body tense and his focus locked on some invisible point in the distance.

"I don't know," Hogan admitted. "I assumed the IC sent a team out here, but it's not an easy trail to get down. He may have figured that if somebody fell down there…" He faded.

"It wouldn't be an easy drop to survive," he summarized.

Regardless, there was no question that Casper was locked on scent now, and it seemed to be coming from the direction of the ravine.

"What are you saying?" Hogan asked, new energy in his voice. "You think they're down there? We had our team do flybys—they didn't see anyone."

Casper tugged at the leash once more, impatient. If it was as treacherous as Hogan made it sound, there was no way I'd risk letting Casper off leash for this part of the search. I switched out his regular leash for a ten-foot length of rope we used for training, my own pulse rate climbing.

Before we set out, Hogan radioed Michelle to let her know our plan.

"Are you sure about this?" Michelle asked, her voice a tinny echo on the radio. "How solid is Casper, over?"

I looked at my dog. His stubby ears were pointed forward, his body leaning into the harness in a desperate effort to move me along.

"I'm not positive," I replied, leaning in when Hogan shifted the radio to me. "He looks solid, though. Over."

There was what seemed like an endless pause before Michelle replied. "Careful. I'm sending fresh teams to the southern quad. Be there in ten to lend a hand. Over and out."

I looked at Hogan once she was gone. "Looks like we have the go-ahead," I said. "Okay?"

"If Hunter might be down there, you've got my blessing," he said. I glanced at him, and watched his face change when he realized what he'd said. "Megan, I mean. I call her Hunter—because it's her last name. And the others. All the women who are missing," he amended awkwardly.

"Sure," I said. I shifted my focus to Jack. "If you'd

rather head back to the lodge, I understand. You don't have to come."

He smiled. He looked tired, but I could tell he was excited at the possible break. "You'd really drag me all over this mountainside and then send me home just when it's getting good?"

"You sure?"

"Positive. Let's do this."

Buoyed by his enthusiasm and the prospective find, I knelt in front of Casper and cupped the dog's block head in my hands.

"You need to be careful this time, okay, boy?" I said. "Bear would never forgive me if I let something happen to you."

I got a big, enthusiastic lick on the cheek for my concern, followed by an impatient bark. *Come on already*, I could practically hear him say.

"Okay, Casper. Okay." I straightened, gripped the lead tighter, and prepared myself to get hauled through the woods and, potentially, down a mountain. "All right—find them!"

I let him go. And boy oh boy, did that dog go.

7

THE MOUNTAINSIDE WAS LIT like a New York City block in December within just a few minutes of alerting the higher-ups of our potential find. Helicopters hovered above as best they could in rising winds, spotlights shining into the trees. Other search teams set up spotlights on the ground, spaced evenly around the rim of the ravine. Casper ignored all the action, having no need for all that hubbub so long as he had his nose and a dog's keen night vision. For my part, I was grateful for both the lights and the company.

At the edge of the ravine, I pulled Casper up short. All around us, searchers called the names of the missing.

"Megan! Violet! Ava! Shonda!" On and on it went, interrupted by the occasional bark of another search dog on the scent.

Over the course of the night, the state police had arrived, and Hogan told Jack and me that they were hard at work trying to piece together the details of everything that had happened at the camp. Meanwhile, they were waiting for the go-ahead from medical staff before interviewing Heather at the hospital.

Since the police were now working under the assumption that there was an active shooter loose in the woods, they were restricting the search to law enforcement, including those in the warden service and state and local police. Jack, me, and a few members of the snowmobile club were the only exceptions.

The temperature dropped the higher we climbed, until it was so cold that my nose and fingertips stung, and I eventually lost all feeling in my toes. I stopped periodically to wiggle them, afraid that I'd have nothing but blackened stubs left by the time we got back to base. My back ached; my legs ached; my lungs ached. Hell, even my skin hurt. Regardless, Casper had my full attention when I pulled him up short at the edge of a cliff that looked down into a hundred-foot void below.

He pawed at the snow with a whine, gently at first, then with more urgency.

"He's got something," I called back to Hogan and Jack, who were trailing me by a good thirty yards. I called Casper back to me, winding his long lead around my arm, and waited for the men to reach us. Hogan arrived first, Jack just behind him, both men out of breath.

"There," I said, pointing to the area where Casper had alerted. Hogan went to the spot and, to my amazement, dropped to his knees and began to dig, using the baton in his belt to crack through the frozen snow.

It took only a few seconds before he stopped. I heard him swear under his breath before he got his phone.

"What is it?" I asked. Not far from us, I heard other teams approaching. Before long, they would all wind up here.

Hogan straightened and trained his flashlight beam on a single, orange rappelling anchor driven into the ground. I stepped closer. The WildFire logo was stamped at the head of the anchor.

"They climbed down?" I said, incredulous. Hogan stepped a little to his right and started digging again. Sure enough, he found a second anchor.

"But that's suicide," Jack said.

Come out, come out, wherever you are, a familiar voice whispered to me. I'll be right here waiting till you do, baby girl.

I shivered, the knot clenching in my belly once more.

"Unless they had no choice," I said.

•

The wind had picked up and the sky had started spitting icy snow while we were trekking through the woods. Now, standing as we were at the edge of the world, we found ourselves facing a landscape of black and white: driving snow and ice-coated trees, while below was an abyss blanketed in pure white.

"What now?" I asked Hogan.

He responded by leaning out over the ravine, hands cupped around his mouth. "Hunter! The Maine Warden Service is here—if you or your students are down there, please respond!"

The words echoed in the stillness until they rang, empty, through the air one last time. No reply came.

How was it even possible for Megan, who had been shot according to Heather, to make this kind of descent? Could the shooter have forced them down into the ravine at gunpoint?

Probably not, I finally decided. It was logistically unlikely, if not downright impossible. If they did climb down there, they did it as a means of escape, not because someone had coerced them. I cleared my throat, and followed Hogan's lead by cupping my hands around my mouth to amplify the sound.

"Megan, this is Jamie Flint. Bear Flint's mom." I wet my chapped lips with my tongue, and tried to imagine what might reassure me if I were in Megan's place. I thought back to my days with Brock, pushing aside the shiver that always seemed to accompany that memory.

"Your dogs are all right," was eventually what I came up with. The dogs had always been a point of contention between Brock and me, despite the fact that they were technically what brought us together in the first place. "Someone found them this morning, and they're waiting for you. If you're down there, you need to tell us where so we can come for you."

Another long, laden silence followed. And then, like it was rising from the bottom of the ocean, I heard a woman's voice.

"We need help," the woman called. "Two of us are hurt down here. You gotta get down here." She faltered, then continued. "I don't know how much longer we're gonna last."

"We'll be right down," Hogan called. No response. I thought again of Brock's voice. Where I'd been, emotionally, when things finally hit rock bottom. Despite Hogan's presence, there was no way in hell I had wanted a man riding in to save me back then. Hogan must have figured the same thing, because he looked to me with a nod.

"That's the warden you heard," I called down. "His name is Nate Hogan. Can you tell me your name?"

The pause that followed this time was shorter. "Shonda," the voice called up. "Shonda Waylon."

I recalled the name from the roster. We'd found them!

And, at least for now, they were safe.

"You have no idea how good it is to hear your voice, Shonda. Just hang tight. We'll get you out of there."

"I've got climbing gear on the sled," Michelle volunteered, coming up behind me. She was alone now, Whippet apparently retired for the night. "The guys are on their way with it."

"How's your team with this kind of rescue?" Hogan asked her.

"I've got a couple of guys who just got their WFR recerts. They're not the best with heights, but they can handle it in a pinch." She hesitated, but only for a second before she looked my way. "What about you? Megan knows you..."

"I re-certified this fall," I said with a nod. I expected Hogan to argue, but instead I watched with some amazement as he stripped his coat off and started gearing up himself.

"What are you doing?" I asked.

"I'm going too," he said. "If you get in trouble—"

"I won't," I said. "And you heard how quiet they got when they heard a man's voice. Michelle and I can go down there, calm them down..."

"She's right," Michelle said. "And God knows I'd put Jamie up against half the guys on our team when it comes to this kind of thing. She's got mountain goat blood running in her veins."

"Are you sure you don't need a third?" Jack asked. Hogan shook his head before I could do the same.

"No way in hell you're going down there if I'm not. We send two down to assess: Jamie and Michelle. Figure out what it looks like, and then we can decide what happens next. I need all other hands up here assisting, at least until we know what we're dealing with."

Jack didn't argue, but I could tell from the look on his face that he wasn't happy with the decision.

Within a few minutes, Michelle's team was on the scene with a snowmobile packed with climbing gear: harnesses, ropes, carabiners, hardware, helmets. With Casper at a reluctant heel at his side, Jack fastened the helmet strap at my chin, then checked the safety lines on my harness.

"You don't have to do this, you know," he said. "I could go. Or Hogan—isn't that supposed to be his job?"

"Michelle's right: these women may not respond well to a man being there. We have no idea what happened to them out here, much less what they've gone through that landed them on this course in the first place. We need to make the rescue as easy as possible on them. I'll be fine."

He held my eye as he checked the last line.

"Promise?" he said. Though I had so many layers on I could barely feel the brush of his gloved hand on my arm, the gesture still somehow warmed me.

"Promise."

He stepped back with a grim nod, still uneasy. "Then do what you have to."

I stepped to the edge of the ravine beside Michelle, both our backs to the abyss. Rather than using the rappelling anchors left behind by the WildFire crew, we'd decided to tie off to the snowmobiles. Not only was it more secure, but it had the added bonus of providing a handy tow if we needed it. Given the circumstances, that seemed more than likely.

"Ready to fly?" Michelle asked, eyes on mine. The lightness in her tone was infectious, and I couldn't deny the bubble of excitement rising in my chest.

"Let's do it."

We both eased ourselves backward, behinds hanging over the edge. Michelle had floated the idea of getting one of the helicopters down here, but the winds were too strong. I felt those winds buffeting my backside now, and wondered just how I thought I was in a better position to fight them than a two-ton, state-of-the-art bucket of steel.

I was about to find out.

"Make sure you hang on to him," I called back to Jack, who held tightly to Casper's leash now.

"Let me worry about that," he said, his own face tense as he watched me prepare for my descent. "You just focus on staying in one piece."

"Got it."

Since we didn't have an exact location of where Megan and the others might be, our approach was admittedly low tech: as we lowered ourselves down the side of the icy cliff, occasionally slammed into the granite by the raging wind, we shouted. Stopped. Listened for a response.

Hoped to God we were gauging right based on the distant voices we heard call back.

Twenty minutes later, we'd descended maybe fifteen feet. My legs and arms were shaking with the strain of trying to hang on, and I was beginning to think it would be easier to wrestle a greased pig in a tornado than it was to hang on to an ice-coated granite cliff face in this kind of wind.

Michelle seemed to feel the same, since she doubled her rate of descent before long. I fought to keep up, battling fatigue and fear, focused on keeping my body balanced and my legs tight and bent at the knees as we continued to rappel.

"We can see you!" I heard a voice say suddenly, blessedly close by.

The same woman's voice that had been guiding us along

this entire nightmarish descent was so welcome this time that I felt myself tear up, though that could have been from the cold air whipping past my face. "Just a few more feet down, maybe ten. Heather had her climbing gear—she helped us find this cave thing."

Heather, I repeated to myself silently. Not Megan.

"You hear that?" I shouted to Michelle, who nodded. She looked more solid than I felt, her certification as a rock climbing instructor serving her well right now.

Suddenly, a fresh gust of wind blew through the canyon. It was so intense that it picked me up and moved me like I was on a rope swing, a solid ten feet to my right. I slammed into the cliff face. My head bashed into the rock so hard that I was sure my skull would have cracked if I hadn't had the helmet on. Stomach churning, I fought to hang on.

I heard Michelle swear beside me, but couldn't check on her until I had a grip on the rope again myself and was safely back clinging to the rock. I was shaking violently by now, the adrenaline too much for my overloaded system.

Not much farther, I told myself. *You've done tougher than this.* Though right now I wasn't sure that was true.

"You okay?" Michelle shouted over.

"Just got my marbles rattled a little," I shouted back. "But yeah. I'm okay."

I looked to my left and saw her looking at me, concern apparent on her face. "Really," I assured her. "Let's do this thing already."

"It won't be much longer now," she assured me. I hoped not, but I said nothing. Whatever happened, there was no turning back now.

Thirty-five minutes after beginning our descent, we landed on the ledge where Megan and her students had been waiting for rescue.

Once on solid ground, legs still shaking, I blinked my eyes as I tried to adjust to the darkness. The cavern was maybe five feet high, and extended no more than seven or eight feet into the mountainside. A small space for a group any size to hide for any period of time, especially when some were injured.

"Holy crap," a slightly overweight, dark-skinned woman sighed at sight of us. "I didn't think you'd ever get here."

I recognized her voice immediately as the one who had guided us here: Shonda. She crouched close to an unnaturally still figure lying on the ground, the others in the group crowded in behind them.

"Sorry you had to wait so long," I said. Michelle called in our position and our status while I moved in for an assessment of the group. "You said two people were injured?"

Shonda turned large dark eyes on me, fear shining through now. "Becky…" she started, nodding to the figure on the floor. I knelt beside the woman, whose eyes fluttered open when I touched her hand. Her left arm was wrapped tightly in what looked like strips from someone's T-shirt, the homemade bandage soaked with blood.

"She's been shot?" I said.

"Yeah," Shonda said. "Some crazy son of a bitch opened fire from the woods, and we all took off. Becky got hit in the arm. We were headed out to look for Gabby, and all hell broke loose."

"Hang on," Michelle said, holding up her hand. "Slow down a second. Who's Gabby?"

"Gabriella Garcia. One of the ladies on the course with us—a big-time fashion model, married to that football player, right? You know the guy? He just got out of jail for beating the crap out of her."

"And she was missing," I said, trying to follow along. At the same time, I checked Becky's vitals and was relieved to find her stable. Though she'd clearly lost some blood, it wasn't nearly as much as she would have if Shonda hadn't been thinking on her feet.

"Yeah," Shonda said. She sounded a little put out that we weren't better informed. When she continued, she spoke more slowly, giving the sequence of events in bullet points. "We were getting ready for bed, and Violet tells us Gabby and Ava took off because Gabby wasn't feeling good, but she never came back. So Violet goes into the woods, just thinking they were off using the bathroom and got hung up or something. But then she didn't find them, so she came back to get the rest of us. Then we're just gearing up to go out and find Gabby and Ava, and some fool shoots at us from the woods. Hits Megan." She paused, and took a long, shuddering breath.

"I was on my way to help her, and then Megan says no, don't stop for her, just get the hell out of there. We start going like the devil's on our asses, and Becky gets clipped. Then Heather gets us out to the cliff here and down the ropes, which, I'm sorry, is not what I signed up for. Next thing we know, Heather says she's gotta go back for her sister, and we never hear a thing more."

"Is she okay? What about Megan?" Becky asked. She was likely in her thirties, with blond hair going dark at the roots and a complexion pitted with old acne scars.

"We found Heather," I said. "A Medevac unit came in a few hours ago and transported her to Maine Med. We thought Megan was with you, though."

"No. We haven't seen her since the shooting." Becky's eyes filled with tears, but she swallowed past them. "What about Heather's baby?"

"We don't know yet," I said. I was still trying to process the realization that Megan wasn't here, and figure out how I was going to break the news to Hogan. "But Heather's alive, and it didn't appear her injuries were life threatening. Did any of you see who did this?"

"Some asshole too much of a coward to show his face," Shonda said. "Never even got up the balls to leave the cover of the trees."

Another woman in the back began to cry, and I forced myself to breathe. We had to get everyone out of here.

"What have we got?" Michelle asked me.

"Gunshot wound to the upper shoulder," Shonda said. Becky tried to sit up, pain flashing across her face. Shonda pushed her back, none too gently. "How many times do I have to tell you?" she asked her patient. "You might think you know everything about being out in the woods just because you been out here for five days without a shower, and maybe that's true. But if you get shot, I'm in charge. Just lay back and wait for somebody to haul us out of here."

"Shonda is a nurse," Becky explained darkly.

"And you're damn lucky I am, too," Shonda returned.

"No kidding," I agreed. "But you said two people down here were injured. Where's the other one?"

She shifted a bit, moving into the light of our lanterns enough for me to see her more clearly. Her right arm was cradled in a sling I hadn't even seen in the semi-darkness.

"Dislocated," she explained. "It happened while we were climbing, or falling, or whatever it was we did that landed us here. Edie over there gave me a hand, though." She nodded toward the crying woman in the back. "Got it popped right back in."

"You've done a fine job," I told her honestly. "And now if everybody can hang on a little bit longer, we'll have you all up top, safe and dry and fed in no time."

A murmur of relief ran through the group as Michelle and I set to work getting the logistics in place to get everyone home again.

I did a head count once Michelle and I had assessed Becky and done a quick exam of Shonda's arm. My stomach took a nose dive yet again when I only came up with five people in total: Shonda, and four other women.

"What happened to the rest of the group? I know you said you got separated from Megan and Heather..." I said, fighting for calm.

"Violet stayed back with Megan," Shonda said. "We never found Gabby and Ava—the ones I told you about before."

"Crap," I heard Michelle say under her breath before she turned to me. "I'll get on the radio with Hogan, let him know who's still missing. We'll need to have teams keep looking for the others. You start getting people lined up to get out of here."

For the next hour, the focus was on the painstaking process of getting the injured and the rest of the group safely up the cliff face. The winds were starting to die down, the temperature holding steady at around ten above zero with the wind chill. I'd made rescues in worse conditions; then again, I'd also made them in better. Michelle and I debated keeping everyone who wasn't injured in the cave until the wind died down completely, but we had the manpower to make it happen then and there and neither of us was keen on any more delays—particularly knowing a shooter was out there somewhere gunning for these women.

Thankfully, the evac process went smoothly. I was sweaty and shaking with exhaustion by the time we sent the last women up. I allowed myself a minute of rest, leaning against the cold granite of the cave wall as Michelle and I watched the slow ascent of the rescue baskets containing Edie and Mary, the last two WildFire women.

Once they were at the edge of the cliff, we began our own painstaking ascent. I climbed the rope occasionally, but more often was content to let the others haul me up.

That is, until we reached the halfway mark, wind battering us, fingers frozen with cold.

Suddenly, a woman's scream rose above the sound of the wind. I looked at Michelle climbing parallel to me, and I'm sure my expression mirrored hers.

What now?

Spurred by a fresh burst of adrenaline, we climbed faster.

By the time we reached the top, my imagination had painted a dozen grim scenarios for what could possibly have happened.

At the lip of the cliff, I scrambled for a hold until I felt strong hands close around my wrists. Jack's eyes met mine as he pulled me back to solid ground, holding me steady when I stumbled.

"You okay?" he asked.

"Sort of. What happened? We heard a scream."

I scanned the scene. Becky had already been whisked off for emergency care, but Shonda and the others were still there, wrapped in thermal blankets. A medic attended to Shonda's arm while Casper sat attentively beside her, happily accepting whatever spare scraps the women sent his way from the food the rescue team provided.

"Sorry," Edie—historically, the crier in the group—said sheepishly. She was small and pale, and looked considerably younger than the other women. She nodded toward Casper. "Where I come from, a dog like that comes for you and you just pray to God he finds somebody bigger to eat before he gets to you. I maybe overreacted."

"Imagine that," Shonda said dryly, as she gave Casper a scrap of bologna.

"Hogan already has teams out looking for the others," Jack told me as we stepped away from the chaos.

"Good," I said. "I have a bad feeling finding them won't be quite so easy."

"Right. Because this was a walk in the park."

I smiled faintly, then froze as a shiver swept up my spine and the dark, low voice I'd heard earlier filled my head once more.

I'm here for you, baby girl. Just show me that pretty face, and I'll show you what happens to traitors.

"Jamie?" Jack said.

I shook my head. "Yeah," I said. "Sorry. I'm here. And honestly? Compared to what the women still missing are going through, I think what we just did was definitely the easy part."

8

"MEG? HEY—COME ON, Megan. Wake up. Please."

Hogan's hand rested on her cheek, his blue eyes gone dark with concern. God, he had good eyes. And hands: long and lean, surprisingly gentle. He never called her Megan, though—always Hunter. *Give me a break, Hunter.* She focused on his eyes, his hands, and pushed aside those niggling doubts. Tried to ignore the pounding of her head; the flames of pain that licked at her side.

"You have to get up," Hogan said to her. "Please, Megan."

"Yeah, right. You first," she said—or tried to say. Her lips were so chapped, her mouth so dry, that nothing came out but a groan.

"Damn it, Megan." His face wavered in front of her. Blurred. God, she was so damned cold.

"Megan!" This time, it wasn't Hogan's voice. No doubt about it, this voice belonged to a woman. An angry woman, based on the tone. Hogan vanished, receding into darkness.

Megan tried to blink him back, but he stayed gone. Typical man.

She opened her eyes.

"Please, Meg," Violet whispered. Her eyes were wide, utterly terrified. "You were talking in your sleep. You have to be quiet. He could hear otherwise. We can't risk him finding us again."

Megan looked around, painfully awake now. At the movement, a furry head appeared beside her, tongue slopping kisses on her cheek. Recluse. She felt a lightening at the knowledge that at least the dog was okay.

They were inside, in a little hunting shack with an unlit woodstove at the center of the room. Megan lay on a lumpy double bed. Apart from a cupboard of rusty canned goods that the women had already made a dent in, that was the extent of the amenities.

"Sorry. You should have woken me sooner—I didn't mean to fall asleep," she said.

Another face appeared in front of her, this one darker than Violet's, with big brown eyes and full lips. Ava.

"We thought you were in a coma or something," she said, in heavily accented English. "Don't do that again, okay?"

"I'll do my best."

She sat up, reorienting herself to everything that had happened. *Someone tried to kill us.* Just thinking the words made it hard to breathe. Once she'd realized she was shot, she and Recluse had hunkered down there in the open while the other women ran like hell. Then came a pause in the gunfire. Megan had known she was bleeding, but she had no idea how bad her wound might be; for all she knew, she would die right there. And then Violet had swooped in like some kind of skinny blond superhero, got her on her feet, and dragged her to safety.

"Do you think Heather's all right?" she asked, thinking of her sister. The last she'd known, Heather had been holed up in the tent. She imagined the shooter coming out of the woods after everyone else had gone. Opening the tent flap. Megan closed her eyes, trying to shut out the rest of that scene.

"We don't know," Violet said. "Everybody just ran. She was in the tent when I grabbed you, though, and the shots were still coming at us. I don't think he was after her."

"I still want to know what happened to Gabriella," she said, thinking of the first woman to go missing.

"I lose her," Ava said, though she'd told the story before. "We are in the woods. She had to use the bathroom, so I give her privacy for that. I am looking for her when I hear the gunshots, and then I couldn't find her no more. Then Violet finds me, and we get you."

"They must have started the search by now," Megan said. "We should send up a distress call."

"Pretty hard to do without a radio," Violet reminded her. "Or a transponder. You must have dropped it when we were running away."

"I didn't drop it," Megan said. Again, a conversation they'd had before. She had reached for the transponder just before the shooting started, but it wasn't there. "I never had it. Someone must have taken it."

"It seems more likely maybe you just forget," Ava said, doubt clear in her voice.

"Of course I didn't forget it. And I didn't drop it. The shooter must have come into the camp and taken it from me."

"The dogs wouldn't have let anybody do that," Ava pointed out. "They would have barked their heads off. That man came for a visit yesterday, and they try to eat him."

"They didn't try to eat Chase," Violet said. "They were just…surprised."

"Weren't we all," Megan said dryly. The unexpected appearance of Violet's husband yesterday during the expedition remained a sore spot between them, though she knew it hadn't been Violet's idea.

"My point is," Ava continued, "if they want to eat a good looking guy like that who doesn't mean anybody no harm, what you think they do if a bad guy starts sneaking around?"

Megan started to argue her point, but Violet interrupted smoothly. "It doesn't matter. The point is, we don't have the transponder now. I don't know how we're supposed to reach the searchers without something, though. We're miles from nowhere at this point."

For much of the day, they'd been running. Whoever was chasing them, he hadn't simply gone back into the woods after the first shots were fired. He hadn't shown himself, had never spoken, but nonetheless he'd been herding them as effectively as cattle since one-thirty the previous morning. His goal couldn't have been clearer, as far as Megan was concerned: get them as far as possible from the track searchers would be following to find them.

"We'll figure something out," Megan said. She didn't know what in hell that something might be, but she knew she had to do something.

Recluse whined beside her, jockeying for a better position to reach Megan. She lay her hand on the dog's head, drawing strength and some measure of calm from him.

"We have to do something to get someone's attention," Violet said.

"How do we do that without the shooter seeing us?" Ava asked.

An excellent question—one Megan had no answer for, at least not yet. She shifted on the bed, swinging her feet to the floor, and winced at a twinge of pain.

"How bad is it?" Violet asked her.

"You're the one who cleaned it, you tell me."

"Not as bad as it could be," Violet returned. "It's just a graze. As long as it doesn't get infected, you'll be fine."

"Good thing you have those love handles," Ava said. "It could have been a lot worse."

"I don't have love handles," Megan said irritably.

"You have less now," Ava noted.

"If Recluse hadn't pushed you out of the way, who knows where you would have been hit," Violet said. Megan scratched behind the dog's ears, and Recluse lay his muzzle on her leg with a sigh.

"Thanks, buddy. Good boy," she said to the dog.

"If we don't get word out to someone soon, it won't matter that he saved you," Violet said.

"And how do you suggest we do that? Smoke signals?"

"Maybe he's taken off by now," Violet said. "He did what he came to do—scare the bejeezus out of us—and now he's gone back into whatever hole he crawled out of."

"He is not gone," Ava said. Her eyes were serious, wide with fear. "He won't leave. Not until he's done."

Violet looked away at Ava's words, but Megan caught the frown before she did.

"Done with what?" Megan asked. "What are we talking about here?"

"Ava believes her husband may be the shooter," Violet said.

"What do you mean?" Megan said. "What makes you think it's him?" Even as she was saying the words, though, she felt a bizarre surge of relief. If it was Ava's husband, it couldn't be the man she'd feared might be out there from the moment that first shot was fired.

"I'm so sorry—I never think he'll find me here," Ava said soberly. "He was in the Marines, then he works for himself. He hurts people. Kills them—this is what he does for a living. And I take his children from him. I should have known that he would find me."

"I was the one who encouraged you to come on this trip," Violet insisted. "There's no way you would have even dreamed of something like this if I hadn't pushed you into it."

"That's true," Ava said, deadpan. "I never would come if you didn't say it would be so good for me. 'Just think of the dogs, Ava. Imagine all that snow, Ava.' Now look at us. You are not the best social worker ever."

Violet laughed. "Well, at least you're not pulling any punches."

"We can't blame each other for this," Megan said, relieved that the tension seemed diffused for the moment. "If this is really your husband, Ava, the fault lies at his feet. Not ours."

Despite the brave words, Megan battled through the pain in her side and a growing sense of panic herself. They were trapped. Inevitably, she flashed on her own history with Justin, her ex-husband—the man she'd initially thought could be behind this nightmare. In prison for the past five years, Justin was the reason Megan was so committed to working with abused women now. She pushed the thought away, struggling to retain reason. It didn't change what she knew to be true, though:

Justin would do this.

Justin would love a game like this.

However, Justin wouldn't be up for parole for another five years.

This couldn't be him.

"Regardless of whether it's your husband or not," she said to Ava, "we have to do something. We'll freeze or starve if we don't. We can't just sit here waiting for that to happen."

Ava stood abruptly. She walked away, moving to a small window on the other side of the room. Careful to stay to the side of the glass, Megan noted. They had two small oil lanterns going, the only sources of light in an otherwise dark space. Of course, that would be all it took to alert someone if there was, in fact, a man out there looking for them.

"I've been talking to her about this," Violet said, voice lower now. "Someone needs to go get help, and I think it should be me. I know these woods better than Ava, and I'm more used to the cold. If we've found shelter, we can't possibly be that far off the beaten path."

Megan hated to argue, but she was afraid the opposite could be true: a shelter this primitive was built by someone with no need for creature comforts. Who knew how long someone might stay in a place like this, as far from others as humanly possible?

Before she could respond, Recluse's head came up abruptly, a low growl in his throat. At the same time, Ava gasped at the window.

"Douse the lanterns," she hissed to Violet. Recluse got up and padded over to the window, hackles raised. Fear ran through Megan in a wave, pain close on its heels.

"What is it?" Megan hissed back, even as Violet turned the dials on each of the lanterns in turn and the flames flickered out. The room went black around them.

"He's out there," Ava whispered. It sounded like she was talking to herself as much as anyone else. A flurry of Spanish followed, whispered under her breath—a prayer, Megan thought.

"We don't know it's him," Megan insisted. "It could be a search party."

No one replied. In the sudden stillness, Megan heard the crunch of footsteps on the snow. Recluse's growl deepened, until Violet knelt beside the dog and wrapped her arms around him, trying to quiet him. A branch snapped, not far from the window.

The silence that followed was so loaded that Megan thought she'd explode from the tension alone. Then, as though someone had whispered it in her ear, she knew:

It wasn't the searchers out there.

Something was about to happen.

"Get down!" she shouted, an instant before the nightmare started all over again.

Violet and Ava both dove to the ground, Violet pulling Recluse with her. Megan was trapped on the bed with nowhere to hide, no way to move, when the bullet pierced the glass and the window shattered.

He'd found them.

•

Megan lay flat on the bed, paralyzed, waiting for the next shot to come. For some masked man to appear in the open window. For something to happen that would put an end to this nightmare.

There was nothing.

Wind and snow gusted in, chilling them all. Recluse continued to growl, but Violet kept a tight hold on him.

"What's happening out there?" Megan whispered to the others.

Recluse escaped from Violet's grasp at Megan's voice, but thankfully made no move for the open window. Instead, he went straight to Megan. A step into the journey, he paused with ears up. Megan listened as well, hearing the sound an instant before Recluse started barking.

Dogs.

They were far off, but unmistakable.

"Can you see any lights out there?" she asked Violet.

She crawled carefully over the broken glass and peered into the night, keeping her head low. "All I see are trees," she said. "And snow. No sign of anyone else out there now, though."

"He must have gotten spooked," Megan said. "The searchers are out there right now, I just know it. It sounds like maybe they found someone." She thought briefly of Heather, and sent up a quick prayer that her sister was safe. That she and the baby got out of this alive, whatever might happen to Megan.

"Can you send up a flare or something?" Violet asked. "Some way of letting people know we're here?"

"We could if we had one to send up. You don't happen to have one in your back pocket, do you?"

Violet shook her head regretfully, and they turned their attention to Ava. She'd been silent through most of this. Now that Megan tuned in to the other woman, she realized something was definitely wrong. Something beyond being pinned down by a psychopath in the dead of winter in the Maine woods, that is.

"He's playing games," Ava said. The words came in a low whisper, terror palpable in her voice. Her dark eyes were luminous, almost ethereal in the moonlight.

"Who's playing games?" Violet asked.

"Frank. My husband. This is what he does—he likes to play. He shoots Megan but doesn't kill her; tracks us through the night; shoots again, forcing us into the open so he can track us again."

"Or else he's just really shitty at his job," Megan said. She knew she should be more patient, more sympathetic to Ava's fear, but right now she didn't have it in her.

"No," Ava insisted. "I know him. This is his way of making me pay."

Megan thought of the games Justin had played with her over the years: subtle little comments, barely discernible moves, and then the sudden explosions—all designed to terrify and control.

"Maybe so," Megan conceded. "But we're not going to let him win. We're not even going to play the game."

"How?" Ava hissed. "You should let me go out there. Let me give up. Maybe if I just go with him, he won't hurt you." She shook her head. "I never should have tried to leave him."

Recluse stood again, eyes back on the open window. Megan felt a fresh surge of adrenaline. "We can't stay in here unarmed," she said. "Right now, our only hope is to get out there and find help before the shooter finds us again."

"What if he's out there waiting for us, though?" Violet insisted.

Megan hesitated. She had no answers, no ideas. Right

now she only knew what her gut was telling her: if they stayed in this cabin a minute longer, they would die here.

"You trust me, right?" she asked the two women. She thought suddenly of Hogan. He'd asked her that once, not so long ago. *Do you trust me?* He'd been frustrated with her non-answer, her inability to just believe in him.

Here and now, though, the two women nodded without hesitation. She would not betray that trust, no matter what it took. Not as long as she was still breathing.

"Then trust me on this," she said, ignoring the pain as she hauled herself out of bed. "We need to get out of here. Now."

Violet and Ava exchanged a look, some silent exchange that Megan couldn't read, before both women nodded.

"Whatever you say," Violet said. "We're with you."

"Good." It was all Megan could manage as she levered herself up off the bed, one hand on Recluse's sturdy shoulder to steady herself. "Then let's go."

9

Flint K-9 Search and Rescue
February 4, 11:30 p.m.

"WE NEVER SAW ANYTHING," Shonda said an hour later, when the women were being debriefed in the Maine Warden Service mobile unit. Hogan had asked me to stay behind to download my notes and coordinates for the day. Now, I sat a curtain away from Shonda as the detective in charge from the state police walked her through the events of the past twenty-four hours. I'd sent Jack back to the lodge with Casper and the promise that I would finish up as soon as I could.

"You're sure it was a he, then?" the detective asked. "How do you know?"

There was a pause before she replied. "Well... I don't, I guess. I mean, somebody starts shooting at you all of a sudden in the middle of the woods, you just kind of assume it's some asshole man, don't you?"

"So the shooter never said anything."

"Nope. Didn't say a thing."

"And the first shot he fired was at the instructor: Megan

Hunter. Was there any possibility that he could have been firing at someone else?"

"Far as I could tell he was shooting at anything that moved—didn't matter whether it was Megan or Heather or someone else."

"But you're sure he hit Ms. Hunter."

"I'm not sure of much of anything that happened after that, you want the truth. Shots came out of the woods, Recluse knocked Megan down, there was a whole lot of screaming, and then everybody just started running."

"And the four women who haven't been found yet: Megan, Violet Carter, Gabriella Garcia, and Ava..." He paused, and I heard a shuffling of paperwork as he confirmed the last name, "Jones. Where were they when this happened?"

"We were all heading out to try and find Gabby and Ava—that's the only reason everybody was dressed. Violet was sharing a tent with them, and I guess Gabby was sick. So Ava went to find her, but she never came back. So Violet went to look for them, couldn't find 'em, and came back to get the rest of us. So I don't know where Gabby and Ava were. Violet was right there, though—I saw her go back for Megan before I took off with the others."

There was a pause, the detective still shuffling through paperwork, before Shonda cleared her throat. "When we were holed up in the cave, we started thinking about who it could be. I mean, it's not like any of us are married to angels, but you've gotta be a special kind of psycho to go in for something like this."

I came to attention. The detective's voice, likewise, took on a new energy. "Did you come up with any suspects in particular?"

"You want a list?" Shonda asked. "Everybody on that course is married to a nut job who'll do violence rather than lose them. You got Gabriella and her famous football husband—you know him, right? Maybe he wouldn't get his hands dirty himself, but he could sure hire somebody to come out here. My ex is too lazy for something like this, but he wouldn't waste any tears knowing it happened." She paused, and I sensed something more coming before she spoke again.

"You might want to check out Ava, though," she said.

"Ava Jones?" the detective prompted. "That Ava?"

"That's the name she gave. I don't think it's her real name, though—a couple of us were talking about it. She's from Mexico, then moved to Miami with her ex. English isn't her first language. Not exactly the 'Jones' type, you know what I'm saying? And she told us some stories…"

"What kind of stories?" the detective asked.

"Not great ones," Shonda said. "At first, we thought she was full of it. I mean, everybody out there had some pretty crappy memories, but Ava's were different."

"In what way?" the detective asked, with impressive patience.

The pause this time was longer, and I wished I could see Shonda's face as she thought through the question.

"He's a bad guy," she finally said. "I mean—like, professionally. Ava told us the second night in that he hurt people for a living. It was a big risk her taking the boys—she's got three sons, you know—from him, but she'd finally had enough. So she took the kids, and she disappeared."

The story stopped me. Why would Ava go to the trouble of taking her kids and escaping only to risk that by enrolling in an expedition like this?

Before I could hear the detective's response, Hogan returned. "You ready to get out of here?" he asked. He looked exhausted, and I wondered when he'd gotten a full night's sleep last. Before Megan went missing, I suspected.

I couldn't exactly shush him so I could keep eavesdropping, so I nodded and got to my aching feet once more. "Definitely. You look like you could use a break yourself."

"I'm fine," he said shortly. "The IC wants me to hit my bunk for a couple of hours, but then I'm headed right back out."

That didn't sound like the best idea to me, but I chose not to push him on it. As we were leaving, Hogan checked in with the detective questioning Shonda. While the two men were talking, I smiled at the woman, still seated in front of the desk.

"Thanks again for everything you did for the others," I said. "You did a great job out there. Your patients are lucky to have you."

"I'll be glad to get back to them," she said, then managed a weary laugh. "You know things are bad if I'm saying something like that. The job's been driving me crazy, the last few months. Now, I can't wait to get back."

"I'm sure they'll be glad to have you again." I glanced at the detective, now busy with Hogan. "The questions shouldn't take much longer. Then make sure you get some rest tonight."

She shivered. "I don't know if I'll ever sleep again. I just keep hearing that sound—that gunshot. Seeing Megan go down. Last thing I want to do about now is close my eyes."

"I know," I said. "And I know it's hard to believe, but sleep will help. And time." I thought about that for a second, remembering my own experiences after Brock died. "Mostly time. Be patient with yourself."

"I'll do what I do," she said, with a shrug. "I got patients at work, kids at home. Lot of reasons to keep myself together and keep going."

Hogan returned before I could respond. "You ready?" he asked me.

"Definitely," I said. I wished Shonda a final goodbye and made for the exit, then was so tired I nearly face planted on my way down the steps. Hogan caught me by the arm before I hit the ground.

"You should take your own advice and get some sleep," he said. "You're every bit as exhausted as I am."

"I need to get back to the house, see how everything's going there. I left Bear alone in a ski lodge with his very pretty seventeen-year-old BFF for the better part of the past six hours. I'm thinking it's about time I make an appearance."

"Probably smart," he agreed, then hesitated. "Listen, they're serving late dinners over at this local place in town— the Funky Red Barn. Kind of a dive, but I hear they serve a great veggie burger there. Meals are free for searchers, and they're staying open till midnight. If you get home and find there's nothing in the pantry…"

"I'll keep it in mind."

There were so many things I wanted to say to him. He'd left the police department shortly after Brock's death, but I often wondered if things would have been different if I had asked him to stay. There had never been anything overtly romantic between Hogan and me, despite what Brock may have thought, but there had undeniably been feelings there—on both our parts, I thought. With the insanity of Brock's death and the investigation that followed, though, my focus had been on getting Bear through the worst of it all. I had never regretted that decision, but I had wondered about Hogan over the years. Had he thought about me? Been tempted to call? What had he been doing in the eight years since we'd seen each other last?

And what, really, was his relationship with Megan Hunter?

"All right, then," he said, when I said nothing more. "I'll see you tomorrow. Good work today."

"You too," I said.

And, with so much more to say and no idea how to say any of it, I headed back toward the lodge.

It was a short walk, the dark sky too cloudy for stars overhead. Just before I reached my destination, I realized something was off. First of all, every light in the house appeared to be on. So much for Bear and Ren getting to bed early.

As I turned onto the walk leading to the front door, the dogs went berserk inside. I heard Michelle shout a couple of choice expletives that didn't slow anyone down in the least, and picked up the pace. I managed a painful jog up the front steps, and Michelle opened the door before my hand was even on the knob.

"Hey," she said. She looked surprised. She had her boots and jacket on, gloves in her hand. "Sorry, didn't realize you were there. The dogs have been going ballistic at everything that moves ever since we got home. I didn't expect they actually heard something real this time."

"It's pretty busy out here," I said. "Lots to hear, with everyone coming and going in the search. Where are you going?"

The corporal I'd met earlier stepped up. Charlie, I

recalled. Apparently, he was the sixth in the house. "They're serving free food at a local place, so we figured we'd take advantage while we could. Michelle and I are going back out in a couple of hours. We want to fuel up while we can." He glanced farther into the house, toward something just out of my line of sight, and lowered his voice. "And to be honest, it's not exactly a party in this place."

I stepped past the threshold and looked around. Whippet and Casper were up and intent on mauling me, while Phantom lay sedately by the woodstove. She waved her tail slightly and raised her head to acknowledge me, then lay it back down again.

Meanwhile, now that I was inside I could see that the big-screen TV in the great room was on, the volume up. Bear sat alone watching what looked like an old Austin Powers movie. The fact that he was still up, the volume was high, and he was sitting with his arms folded over his chest and his jaw set all clued me into one thing:

Things hadn't gone well tonight.

And, my kid was mad as a teenage hornet.

"Do you mind waiting a minute?" I asked Michelle. "We might join you."

"Of course," she assured me, then kept her voice low when she added, "Ren's in her room. Bear's not talking, but things definitely didn't go according to plan here."

I didn't even want to think about what that plan might have been, though I could guess what Michelle and Charlie probably thought it was. "Give me two minutes," I said. "I promise, if I haven't gotten things figured out by then you can go without me."

"No problem." Michelle gave me a sympathetic tip of the head. "Sorry—I know you're tired."

"It's what I signed up for when I had the kid. I'll be right back."

I paused to greet the dogs, realizing that Minion must be up in the room with Ren. Jack stood at the bar in the kitchen, beer in hand, watching the proceedings with weary bemusement.

"You didn't want to go into town for food?" I asked.

"I thought it might be a good idea for someone to stick around," he said, looking in Bear's direction.

"Thanks."

The dogs quieted and returned to their separate corners when they realized my presence didn't mean something exciting was about to happen. Casper went back to Bear, climbed up on the couch, and settled with his head on the teenager's lap. Bear's hand went absently to the dog's head, but his focus remained on the TV. I sat down on a far corner of the sofa—the only space available.

"Hey," I said.

"Hey," Bear returned, gaze never leaving the TV. Frown never leaving his lips.

"We found some of the others in the group. Not everyone, but five others."

"I heard." Monotone. Still not so much as a glance in my direction. A commercial came on the TV; Bear remained fixed on the screen.

"So, how did things go here?"

"Fine."

Oh, boy. One of the remarkable things about teenage boys: just how much contempt they can load into one-word answers. I continued gamely.

"What did you eat?"

"Nothing."

That stopped me. "Nothing at all? What do you mean?"

"There's nothing to eat here."

"There's a fridge full of food. What happened to the whole, 'I'm seventeen, Mom—it'd be pretty sad if I couldn't feed myself.'?"

No answer.

I took the remote from him, and turned off the TV. That got his attention.

"Hey! I was watching that."

"You've seen that movie a hundred times, and we have it on DVD back home. Talk to me, please. Why didn't you eat something? And where is Ren?"

"She went to bed. I stayed up. We didn't eat anything because there was nothing to eat." He reached for the remote. I shifted it to my other hand and held it away from him, and Bear groaned. "Mom, just give me the damn thing. Leave me alone, all right?"

It wasn't all right, actually, but I knew my son well enough to know nothing would be resolved until he had something in that bottomless teenage belly of his. I stood.

"Get your boots and coat. There's a place in town that apparently makes great veggie burgers, and they're serving them free to searchers."

I expected him to argue, but he actually lightened at the mention of free food. He got up and stalked over to the closet, and I left him to dress while I dragged myself up the stairs to the second bedroom on the right—the one Ren had claimed. A sliver of light glowed beneath the door, which I took to mean Ren was still up.

I knocked lightly on the door, and heard Minion's answering, soft *woof* immediately. Ren's response was a few seconds delayed, and even softer than the dog's.

"Yes?" she said.

"We're going to get some food in town," I said through the door. "Would you like to come?"

"No thanks," she said. There was a nasal quality to her voice, and my Mom radar was immediately on alert. Had she been crying? "I'm tired, I'm just going to go to sleep."

I hesitated. If Ren were my kid, I would be pushier. I would go into the room, and find out just what was going on. She wasn't my kid, though. She was a mature, intelligent, strong young woman who just happened to *have* no mother of her own.

"All right," I said. "I'll bring you something back if you want. And we'll have a good breakfast tomorrow. Just try and get a good night's sleep."

"I will." She sniffled. Oh, crap. "Goodnight, Jamie."

"Goodnight, sweetie. I'll see you in the morning."

10

AT TEN TILL MIDNIGHT on a Tuesday night, my bedraggled team, my sullen teen, and my weary, weary self all dragged ourselves out for dinner. Bethel's trendy main stretch was shut down at that time of night, though twinkling white lights still lit the way along snow-covered streets. The whole scene had a Norman Rockwell feel to it that didn't mesh with my aching bones, the memory of Brock's voice, or the blood that still stained my clothes from Heather Wright.

We took a left on Mechanic Street and then another left onto Summer, where we found a narrow space in the crowded lot outside the Funky Red Barn.

"Are you sure they're still serving food?" I asked Michelle, seated beside me in the passenger's seat.

"Till midnight," she said. "If you had any doubt whether people really liked Megan and Heather, this should put it to rest. Restaurants don't keep their doors open past closing and supply food for the masses for free for just anyone."

No doubt about that. With just minutes to spare before the kitchen closed, Jack, Bear, and I staggered over the threshold. A weathered Christmas tree still stood in one corner, an American flag on the opposite wall, while a Bud Light poster featuring two large-breasted blonds in white bikinis dominated the space above the pool tables. A generously proportioned platinum blond met us at the door.

"You with the search?" she asked.

"K-9 unit," I said.

"And you didn't bring the dogs?"

"They're home, resting up for tomorrow."

She harrumphed at that. "Next time, bring them too. They deserve a home-cooked meal as much as anybody. We've got a couple of 'em already here, had more earlier."

I looked around and saw that, indeed, another handler was at a table in the corner with his dog asleep on the floor at his feet, another couple of searchers from the team seated next to him. I recognized almost everyone in the place, including wardens at the pool tables in the next room and members of the snowmobile club with pints at the bar. The state police who had been brought in this evening after Heather's discovery were conspicuously absent, however.

"Go on over and sit down wherever you can find space," the waitress said, nodding toward a couple of tables in the back. "I'll bring you over some menus. You want beer?" She directed the question at the group. I declined, but Michelle, Charlie, and Jack all ordered. Bear looked at me with a raised eyebrow, but didn't push it beyond that.

Hogan was already at a table in the corner with an untouched burger in front of him, flanked by the senator and his wife. Despite having managed to find six of the ten women missing today, the fact that the senator's daughter wasn't among them was not lost on me. Any feeling of celebration I may have been feeling disappeared the moment I saw their faces.

"You mind if we join you?" I asked him as we approached.

"No," he said. "Have a seat. You remember Senator and Mrs. Price?"

"Of course," I said. I introduced them to the others in our party, and we all sat. I ended up next to Sally Price, who looked utterly exhausted.

"You were there when they found the others, weren't you?" she asked, as conversation buzzed around us.

"That's right," I said. "It looks like everyone we found will be just fine."

"Violet wasn't with them." She faltered, looking embarrassed. "Of course, you know that—you were there. When we got word they'd found everyone, I could scarcely breathe. And then to find out Violet…"

"It's still early in the search," I said. "The fact that we found the women we did is a good thing. Don't give up hope yet. People are still out there looking. I'll be going out again first thing myself."

She nodded. "Of course. I didn't mean to imply everyone isn't doing their best. I just…" Her eyes welled, and she looked away quickly. "She's such a good girl—always doing things for others. To know she's out there with someone pursuing her…"

The senator patted her arm, and for the first time I caught a glimpse of the fear he was hiding so adeptly. "We'll find her, Sally. I'll see to it. I promise you that."

Unable to cement that promise myself, I fell silent.

"Any word on how Heather's doing?" Bear asked.

"It looks like she'll be fine," Hogan said. "They're keeping her at the hospital overnight for observation, but she got lucky."

"And the baby?" Jack asked.

"Okay so far," Hogan said. "They're both strong—the doctors are optimistic at this point."

Jack nodded, looking more relieved than seemed natural given he'd never met any of these people before. I knew a lot of this story was probably hitting close to home for Jack, though. Seven years ago, his wife was murdered when she was six months pregnant. The event had changed the trajectory of his life, and I was sure the memories had been replaying themselves when we found Heather in the condition we had.

"Has she been able to shed any light on what happened?" I asked. "I know the others don't seem to know who it was, but does she have any theories?"

"She's been pretty out of it from what I've heard," Hogan said. He stared disconsolately at his beer. "She knows Meg got hit, though—no question of that. Shot in the side, she thinks."

"If we haven't found her yet, she must not have been hit too bad," I said. "Otherwise, she wouldn't have been able to travel so far."

"Unless he took her," Hogan said. "Whoever the hell 'he' is."

I noted again how weary he looked; how broken.

"How well do you know Heather and Megan?" Jack asked him. Hogan shrugged, eyes downcast.

"They're friends of mine," he said. "Good friends. Megan and I worked together on a commission investigating the oil pipeline not far from here. She cares a lot about this area. We got to know each other then."

"From everything I've heard, they sound like amazing women," Jack said. "I can understand being worried."

"They're pretty great," Bear agreed. "I don't get how something like this could've happened on their watch. They're always so careful out in the field, all these protocols in place."

I looked up as a cold wind swept through the bar when the front door opened. Chase Carter stepped inside, accompanied by three reporters I recognized from earlier in the day. Beside me, Sally Price frowned.

The hostess at the front of the bar swept in before anyone else had to and booted the reporters before they'd gotten more than a few feet inside. She gave Chase a dressing down for inviting them in in the first place, and I saw a small, vindictive smile from Sally before her son-in-law approached the table.

"Lieutenant Hogan," he said to Hogan, surprisingly at ease given the circumstances. "Do you mind if I join you all? It's been a long day."

"Of course," Hogan said. "Take a seat wherever you can find one. I'm not sure they're still serving anything in the kitchen, though."

"That's fine," Chase said. He sighed. "I don't think I could eat anyway. I just wanted the company."

"You've been doing a wonderful job managing the press," the senator told him. "You've earned a break. You should eat, though. I'll see if I can't convince the kitchen to stay on a few minutes more."

"We don't want to bother them any more than we need to," Sally said. "They've been up working hard—"

"It won't kill them to take a few more minutes to make a burger for our son," the senator interrupted, his tone biting. "It's not as though they have somewhere important they need to be. He needs his strength."

"Thank you, Robert," Chase said to the senator. "I suppose I should force something down."

Sally stared down at the table without arguing the point any further, but I could feel the anger bubbling beneath the surface. I didn't blame her, personally. Chase may have won over the masses, but so far I was less than impressed.

Chase extended his hand toward me and introduced himself then, his gaze fixed on mine. I had the uncomfortable feeling that he'd somehow read my thoughts.

"I saw you briefly earlier," he said. "But I didn't catch your name."

"Jamie Flint," I said, offering a reluctant handshake before I introduced him to Jack and Bear.

When our hands touched, a shiver of cold ran through me—a reaction that I couldn't shake, particularly when our eyes met. He was even better looking than I'd thought based on our first meeting, with a strong jaw and striking blue eyes. There was a coolness to those blue eyes that chilled me, though the pained smile he offered seemed genuine enough. I withdrew my hand, inexplicably eager to get away from him.

The waitress came and took our orders, and there was polite chitchat around the table before Chase refocused on me while the others continued their conversations.

"Did Lieutenant Hogan explain to you the circumstances for Violet being on the expedition?" he asked, directing the question to me.

"About her dissertation?" I said. "He did. It's an important topic. It sounds like your wife is doing good work."

"She is," Chase said. "She really is remarkable. If something happens to her..." He fell off, eyes brimming with tears, and looked away abruptly.

"I'll tell you what I've told Sally," the senator said, his own brow furrowed at his son-in-law's evident pain. "We're going to find her, Chase. We're bringing her home. You've got my word on that."

Chase nodded, but seemed too emotional to say anything further.

Jack sat across the table from me. I caught a glimpse of skepticism as he studied the distraught man, but he looked away from me when our eyes met. I made a mental note to check in with him later for his impressions on Chase Carter's theatrics.

"How did you and Violet meet?" Jack asked Chase.

"Megan introduced us, actually," he said.

"Megan's husband," Sally corrected him, her frown firmly back in place.

Hogan looked up sharply. "You know Justin?"

"Do you?" Chase countered. A trace of something ugly flickered in his eyes, his voice, as he turned the question around on Hogan.

"Only by reputation," Hogan said. "My understanding is that he's still in prison."

Chase nodded, his expression darkening. "That's right."

"But you knew him," Hogan pressed.

"They were best friends," Sally replied for him, when Chase didn't answer the question himself. "And of course Violet and Megan had been friends for years at that point. Justin was the one who suggested Chase would be a perfect fit for Violet."

"We weren't best friends," Chase said quickly. "We went to high school together. Our families traveled together sometimes, and we had similar interests."

Which sounded a lot like best friends, but I wasn't going to get into semantics with the man.

"I had no idea he would turn out to be...what he was," he finished lamely. "He showed no signs of it when we were young."

Bear was listening intently by now. I fought the urge to shield him from the direction the conversation was turning. At seventeen, I had to stop feeling like I had to protect him from the uglier things in the world. Particularly given all that he'd seen firsthand between Brock and me.

"What's he in prison for?" Bear asked.

Both the senator and his wife looked flustered, staring intently down at their half-finished plates.

"He tried to hurt Megan a few years ago," Hogan said quietly. He kept his focus entirely on Bear. I thought of the soothing presence he had been for my son in those last weeks before Brock died, and was grateful that he didn't try to sugarcoat things now. "But he's safely behind bars now. There's no reason to worry."

"You're sure about that?" Jack said, his FBI experience showing. "Have you checked into it?"

"The police are on it," Hogan said. "They're checking into the whereabouts of the partner of everyone on the course."

"Good," Chase said. "I've made a couple of calls myself, just to make sure. Someone would have let Megan know if he was out for any reason, though. Trust me: Justin is still safely doing time at the Maine State Prison. He's not going anywhere."

Silence fell over the table as the waitress delivered food to our party and cleared plates for Hogan, the senator, and Sally. I watched with no small measure of annoyance as the senator plead the case for his son-in-law, and the waitress ultimately agreed that they could reopen the kitchen long enough to make him a burger. Sally said nothing further on the subject, but there was no mistaking the fact that she wasn't on Chase's side.

Shortly after the waitress left and conversation had resumed, I noticed that Sally had effectively faded beside me.

"Why don't you get back to your room and try to get some sleep?" I asked.

"I'm not sure I could," she said. "Not knowing Violet is still out there."

The senator had been deep in conversation, but refocused on his wife the moment she spoke. There were unquestionably things I didn't care for about this man, chief among them the way he just seemed to assume the rest of the world was here to serve him. The way he looked at Sally softened my opinion, however.

"She's right, Sal," he said quietly, and stood. He got his wallet and withdrew a couple of twenties, and tossed them on the table. "That's for the waitress," he said quietly to Hogan. "Tell her we appreciate everything they've done for the search." Then, he pulled Sally's chair back gently and helped her to her feet. "I assume you'll be in touch if there are any developments, Lieutenant?"

"Of course," Hogan assured him, then stood himself. "I'm going to get going myself. I need to get a couple hours' sleep before I head back out. I'll walk with you."

"Thank you, Lieutenant," Sally said.

Hogan tossed a few bills on the table after the senator's twenties, and addressed the crew.

"When are you guys back on?" he asked, directing the question to Michelle and Charlie.

"They want us back out at o-three-hundred," Charlie said. "I wish we didn't have to wait. I'm way too juiced to sleep."

"The true sign of a rookie," Michelle said. "You'll learn

soon enough: when you get a few minutes' rack time, you take it."

"Exactly," Hogan agreed. "Listen to her. Finish up here, then get back to the lodge and sleep as long as you can. That's an order."

"Yes, sir," Charlie said respectfully. "Will do."

Then, Hogan left alongside Sally and Senator Price, Sally leaning heavily against her husband as we watched them go.

"It makes me nuts, you know," Chase said suddenly, just seconds after they were out the door. All heads turned to him as we waited for him to continue. "What these men do to the women in their lives. The terror they instill. The damage they cause—for everyone, not just the wives or girlfriends. The kids, the rest of the family… This is a prime example. Look how much Sally and Robert are suffering here, and this has nothing to do with them."

The anger in his voice seemed genuine enough, but I still couldn't shake the feeling that this was a performance for him. That everything he did and said had a specific audience in mind. I caught the same skepticism on Jack's face, though he remained silent.

"You know what pisses me off more than anything else," Michelle said. "It's these women who stay. I mean, yeah, the women on this course finally got the guts to leave their abusers, but how long did it take? Who knows what the final straw must've been to get them off their asses and out the door."

How many times had I heard that argument before? As soon as the words were out, I felt as though the entire table was looking at me. Most of them had no idea of my history, but it didn't change what had happened—the fact that I was the worst of the worst in the eyes of people like Michelle. Once upon a time, I had been a woman who stayed.

"That's kind of an ignorant thing to say," Bear said. I looked at him in surprise. He continued without looking at me, his focus instead on Michelle. "You don't know what their situations were. Maybe they had kids they were worried about. Maybe they didn't have the money to go off on their own. Maybe the guy wouldn't let them leave. There are plenty of reasons somebody would stay with a guy who hurt them."

"Bear—" I said, trying to get him to back off, but Michelle didn't seem to take offense to the fact that a seventeen-year-old was calling her out.

"No, that's all right," she said, waving me off. She kept her focus on Bear, her tone respectful despite her clear disagreement with his point. "But why stay with them in the first place?" she asked him. "The first time a man laid a hand on me, he'd be flat on his ass and I'd be out the door."

"It's not like it starts out that way," Bear said. He kept his voice level, but there was no mistaking the emotion there. "One in four women experience severe abuse at the hands of a partner at some point in their lives. You really think one in four women are just doormats who get hit on the first date and decide, 'yeah, this is definitely the guy for me'? It happens over time, and a lot of these guys are master manipulators. And making the decision to leave is hardly an easy one. A woman is *seventy times* more likely to be murdered in the first few weeks after she leaves an abusive partner than at any other point in the relationship. They're right to be afraid of making the break."

"It sounds like you've done some studying on the subject," Jack said, his own tone quiet. Everyone else might be getting riled up by the debate, but Jack just seemed more contemplative. Bear reddened at the question, looking down quickly. Once again, it felt like a spotlight was shining down on me.

"I did a report for school," he said. "The whole thing makes me sick. Any guy who would hit a woman is totally pathetic."

"Agreed," Chase said. "Which is why I have such respect for the work Violet does. Bear is right: things aren't nearly as cut and dried in these situations as you might think."

"I don't know," Charlie said, adding his two cents. "My sister goes out with losers all the time who beat the tar out of her. She doesn't seem to be getting any smarter about it. She finally gets rid of one only to wind up doing the same dance with another one."

"It's a tough subject," I intervened before Bear could address that—which I had no doubt he would—by asking something personal about Charlie's family history. "And hardly one we're going to solve tonight."

"True," Jack agreed. He glanced at his phone and yawned widely before anyone could argue his point. "It's twelve-thirty. We should probably head back and try to get some sleep."

That was all it took to break things up for the night, for which I was grateful. We left Chase still waiting for his burger, added another generous tip for the wait staff to the growing stack of bills, and piled into the van.

Bear was quiet on the short drive back to the lodge. That could have been because he was tired, of course, but I worried that the conversation at the restaurant had triggered bad memories for him. Despite my concern, I was proud of how clearly he had stated his case, and how well-armed with facts he seemed to be about an issue I hadn't even realized he'd given much thought to.

When we got back, I caught his arm and stopped him outside while the others were headed in.

"It seems like you've had a pretty tense night all the way around," I said. "You okay?"

"I'm fine," he said wearily. The hostility had returned, but he checked himself on it before I had to. "I just want to get some sleep, okay? I don't want to have some big heart-to-heart right now."

"That's fine," I said. "I was just checking in. I can take Casper out with Phantom if you want, and you can just go straight up."

"That'd be good, actually. Thanks."

"Brush your teeth."

"Mm hmm."

"And give me a hug."

He groaned, but complied with the command. I held on for a second too long, then kissed his cheek as he pulled away. "I'll see you in the morning."

He grunted at me, which I chose to take as affirmation, and went inside.

•

The final out with Casper and Phantom that night was a welcome reprieve from the madness of the rest of the day. I was happy to see that Phantom was moving easily now, with no signs of stiffness from her earlier fall or the other challenges she'd faced. Casper, meanwhile, was uncharacteristically slow going on the trail. Miracle of miracles, it seemed we'd actually worn the dog out today.

Jack asked to join me, and I readily agreed. Not just because I enjoyed his company; I honestly didn't want to be alone right now, giving Brock—or Brock's voice—any opportunity to creep back inside my brain.

For several minutes, we walked in silence along a trail out behind the lodge. Casper and Phantom walked side by side, Casper uncharacteristically uninterested in starting something. I watched as they sniffed at the bushes and pawed at the snow. Phantom's gait was easy, and she seemed happy to be outside in the crisp air, whether she was working or not. Maybe she wouldn't have as hard a time with retirement as I thought. God knew there were enough goings-on to keep her occupied out on the island.

"It was nice of Hogan to arrange the lodge for us," Jack said abruptly, interrupting my thoughts. "Bear was right. It is a pretty sweet place."

"We'll see how sweet you think it is after spending a night in the same room with him. The smells alone…"

"You forget—I was seventeen myself once," Jack said. "I think I can handle it."

"He's actually not that bad," I said, after a moment's thought. "When he was a little younger, I used to dread sharing a room with him during searches. He's worked hard on organizational skills, though. You're less likely to get to the room to find your bed buried under dog gear and empty food wrappers now."

"I guess it could be worse," he said with a laugh, before continuing. "He seems like a cool kid, actually. I look forward to getting to know him better."

"He's pretty special," I agreed.

"You did a good job with him."

"Most times, I feel like he grew up well despite me, but thank you. It's nice to imagine I had some kind of positive influence."

"I have no doubt."

Without warning, we suddenly reached the edge of the tree line, opening onto a cleared area now completely iced over.

"I remember seeing something about this in a brochure in the lodge," I said. "They use it as an ice skating rink during the winter."

At sight of an open play area to explore, Casper took off running. He managed only a few steps before his feet slid out from under him. For a couple of seconds he just lay there looking comically crestfallen, before he managed to get up again.

"You'd think he'd never been on ice before," I said, as he hesitantly took a step. Phantom remained at the edge looking on. I was afraid she might slip and take another fall, but she avoided the issue by sticking to the perimeter. Meanwhile, as Casper gained confidence, his antics on the ice grew more brazen at center stage.

"I bet it's pretty here when everyone comes out," Jack said. He sat at a wooden bench off to the side of the rink, then moved aside so I could join him.

"I'm sure. Do you skate?"

"I never had much reason growing up in Florida. I learned when I was in D.C., but didn't go that often."

"Now that you're in Maine, maybe it's time to dust off the skates and get out there again," I said.

I felt his gaze on me, and he bumped my shoulder lightly with his own. "I will if you will."

I laughed. "I haven't been in years. Not since Bear was little."

"All the more reason."

I turned to look at him, to see if he was serious. In the

darkness, his eyes shone like starlight. Before I could say anything more, Jack's gaze shifted abruptly. He pointed up to the sky, just beyond the Little Dipper.

"Shooting star. Do you make wishes on that kind of thing?"

"Not really. I've never been much for wishes."

"Ah."

That effectively killed the conversation, at least for a couple of minutes. I watched Casper race across the ice. He'd found a hockey puck, and carried that in his mouth for a few feet before he'd fling it away from him and then race after as it slid across the ice. With his big paws and wide grin, he actually reminded me a little of a hockey player. With slightly less grace, of course. Phantom, meanwhile, settled on the ground beside us, lying at my feet. Jack's attention remained split between Casper's antics and the sky above.

"I was in Nicaragua last month during that big meteor shower," he said. "Did you see it?"

I looked at him in surprise. "When did you go to Nicaragua?"

He smiled slightly. "Last month."

"Right—yeah, you said. But I mean... You didn't say anything about going."

"I know. Sorry about that. I was following a lead in Lucia's case."

Lucia had been Jack's wife. She was killed in Nicaragua while volunteering at an orphanage there.

"Did you learn anything new?"

"No. I know who did it, of course—I just can't find them. I heard there might be someone there who could provide information, but it didn't pan out."

"I'm sorry."

The people behind the murder were a mystery to me, as I suspected they might still be to Jack, at least to some extent. I knew there were government conspiracies involved. Kidnappings. An experiment on mind control gone wrong. I'd been on the periphery when Jack had learned all of these things, but I still couldn't quite get my head around it. I wondered if Jack felt the same.

"You know," I said, reluctantly brought back to my responsibilities as team leader at Flint K-9. "If you're going to be unavailable, even if it's just for a couple of days, it would be great if you could give me a heads-up. Just so I know I can't count on you."

He frowned. "You can always count on me—"

"In a search, I mean," I said quickly. "If something had come up, it would have been important to know where you were."

"Of course," he agreed. "It came up suddenly, but that's no excuse. I'll keep you updated next time."

"Thanks."

It got quiet again. Casper trotted over, tired of his solitary game, and tried to rally Phantom. When it was clear she wasn't interested, he lay down with a heavy sigh. I listened to the wind, allowing my eyes to close. My body to relax. I really was beyond tired.

I've been waiting a long time for this, baby girl.

My head snapped up at the words. The sound of that insipid, familiar voice.

"Jamie?"

I held up my hand for Jack to be quiet, and continued listening. Nothing came, though.

"What's going on?" Jack pressed. I hesitated. "This has happened a couple of times since we got here. What are you hearing?"

"A voice," I finally admitted. So far Jack had been surprisingly open to my "abilities," but it still felt strange sharing my secret. "I think it might belong to the gunman."

"What does he sound like? What does he say?"

"He sounds like a man," I said. No way was I going to tell him *which* man he sounded like. "I just get snippets of things, a random sentence or two."

"Nothing to identify who it might be?"

"Not really. He calls the woman—whoever he's talking to—'baby girl.' Other than that, nothing."

He made a face at the term of endearment.

"It's not my favorite, either," I agreed. "So far, that's all I've really heard, though."

He considered that for a few seconds while we continued to listen to the wind. My butt was frozen on the cold bench, and I knew it had to be getting late. As much as I might be enjoying the company—or maybe because I was enjoying it a little too much—I stood.

"We should probably get back. Bear will wonder what we did with his dog."

"Of course."

We got up, my ears still trained on the distance as we walked. Jack was beside me, close enough that I felt his warmth every time he brushed against my shoulder. I caught him sneaking glances at me, and did the same myself more than once. His hand brushed against mine. I wondered, suddenly, what it would be like to hold hands with Jack Juarez. What it would feel like for him to touch me—more than just a casual brush against my jacket, all those layers no longer between us.

Casper yelped suddenly, jolting me out of my reverie before I followed it down a dangerous path. I realized in the midst of my fantasizing, I'd stepped on the poor dog's foot. He looked at me reproachfully, while Phantom fixed me with a knowing gaze. She might not really know what I'd been thinking, but I chose to believe she had an idea. Her judgment seemed undeniable.

And she was right.

Jack Juarez was an employee. An employee with long, strong hands and sculpted features and really, really great eyes.

But an employee, regardless.

"Sorry, buddy," I said to Casper, patting him quickly on the head. "I'll pay more attention."

"Everything okay?" Jack asked, as we continued the rest of the way back. "You seem a little distracted."

"A little," I admitted. "But I'll get over it."

11

THEY WERE DRY. They'd found food. They had all slept, at least a little. No one was badly injured. People were searching for them. Megan kept reciting the points working in their favor in her head, as the three women trekked through the forest. Violet and Ava followed her without complaint or question, Recluse steady by her side.

We can do this, Megan thought, as the sun came up over the mountains. The day was cold but clear, and while the pain in her side from the shot the sniper had taken was painful, it wasn't life threatening.

"Do you have any idea where we are?" Violet asked, breathless, as they crested another ascent.

Megan looked around, but she was already pretty sure she knew. One quick glance confirmed it, and she pointed to a ribbon of water moving through the valley below.

"That's Bear River. If we can get down there and into the open, someone should spot us. They've been flying planes overhead regularly for the past twenty-four hours. It's just a matter of getting somewhere where we can be seen."

"If we go in the open, Frank finds us," Ava pointed out.

"We still don't know it's Frank," Megan countered. "And if we don't go in the open, we die out here. At some point, we have to be willing to take the chance."

"What about up here? Can't we just stay here and wait to be spotted?" Violet asked. She sat down heavily in the snow, then lay back. Megan was struck by the dark circles under the woman's eyes; how thin, frail, she looked. Megan's stomach grumbled, but she ignored it. They'd taken what rations they could carry from the cabin, but it would hardly keep them going for long.

"It's too heavily forested here," Megan said. "Besides, there are too many places where the shooter can sneak up on us. We have to be smart about this."

Ava sat down beside Violet, but Megan resisted the urge to join them. She needed to keep her feet under her. Recluse seemed just as reticent about settling, despite how tired he must be. For Megan, every rustle in the brush, every time Recluse growled or started or even turned his head, she was sure their time was up.

"Five minutes," she told Violet and Ava. "Then we need to start moving again. Eat something from the stash. Take some water. We can do this."

"What about you?" Violet asked. "Don't you need food or water, or are you Wonder Woman now?"

"Wonder Woman needs food and water," Megan said idly.

"Now she's better than Wonder Woman," Violet said, speaking in a loud aside to Ava. The woman chuckled, and even Megan managed a smile. She wasn't hungry, but she accepted her part of the ration—a handful of stale nuts and one-third of a protein bar—regardless. It went down dry despite the scant amount of water she allowed herself, then settled like rocks at the pit of her stomach.

Overhead, a bald eagle soared close enough for Megan to see his white head. He was flying toward the river. *Good fishing and hunting grounds at the river,* she remembered Justin telling her once. *Everybody needs a drink now and then. That's where we want to be. Pick those deer off one by one, baby girl.*

She shivered at the memory of his voice. Would the shooter be moving in that direction, for exactly that reason? What if he were there waiting for them?

Unnerved at the thought, she pushed it aside. They had to do something, and going toward open water was the surest way she knew for searchers to find them.

"Okay," she said, after only four minutes had passed. "Pack your trash. Let's get moving again."

They struck out without following a trail, Megan focused on making the descent as quickly and as safely as they could. She figured it would take about three hours as long as the weather held, and they would reach the river.

Behind them, she imagined the sniper loading his gun. Following their tracks—because right now, she knew they were leaving a trail behind. If he looked in the right place, he would find them.

"Step up the pace," she said to Violet and Ava, the two traveling in front of her. "You can do this. You've done harder things than this in your lives. Just keep moving."

Weary but determined, that was exactly what they did.

12

"I'VE BEEN WAITING FOR YOU, baby girl."

That voice again, sickly sweet and terrifyingly familiar. I was in the woods, though not in Bethel. The snow gone. Instead, the trees were in full bloom, the sky dark overhead. There was a cabin off to my right, another to my left.

I needed to get home. I didn't want to be back here.

"Let me walk you to your room," the voice said, somewhere behind me. I remembered those words from nearly twenty years ago, but felt none of the anticipation I had then. My stomach rolled, fear prickling my skin. *It's just a dream,* I told myself. The fear remained.

"Look at me when I talk to you, sweetheart."

I froze. Slowly, unable to refuse, I turned on the path.

Instead of the man I expected, however, a figure in black stood before me.

"Stay out of this, baby girl," he said to me, in Brock's voice. "This is my business, nobody else's."

"Who are you?" I asked.

He took a step toward me. Phantom was suddenly

beside me, though she hadn't been before. She bared her teeth, hackles raised.

"Easy," I said to the dog. The man stared at her, and I saw fear in blue eyes. "I thought you liked dogs," I said.

"I'm not him," the man said. "Don't make that mistake. I'm my own man."

"Your own kind of demon," I said, recalling distantly that Brock had said that to me, once. He laughed, showing his teeth.

"That's right, baby girl. I'm my own kind of demon. Leave me to my business, and you'll be just fine." Phantom wasn't growling anymore, but she still sat alert by my side. Above us, the clouds darkened. "Tell your people to let this go. I've got business in these woods. This is my world now."

"We're bringing Megan and those other women home," I said. "We're not leaving without them."

"Then you're not leaving here," the man said simply. "You've been burned before—I promise you, he was nothing compared to me. I'm the devil, baby girl. He was just a bad imitation."

He walked back into the woods, the clouds so dark now that I could barely see him as he disappeared into the trees.

I looked down, and realized that I stood on a wooden box shaped like a coffin, but several times larger. Beside it was a pile of dirt. I knelt in the cool earth and reached my hands in. As though compelled by some force, I began dropping handfuls of the dirt onto the box at my feet. With every handful dropped, it seemed the box grew another foot longer.

"You can't keep that thing buried, sweetheart," Brock said. "Dig all you want. There's not enough dirt on the planet to keep that thing underground."

I looked up, my hands still clutching a fistful of dirt. Brock stood there—the real Brock this time, flesh rotting from his skull.

"I need to do this," I said.

He shook his head. "Go ahead, sweetheart. Keep at it. It's your funeral."

I worked harder, putting my back into it, trying to move just a little bit more earth at a time. The box just kept getting bigger, though, while the pile of dirt beside me continued to shrink.

I woke with a stone in my gut, the room still dark. Phantom snored softly at the end of the bed.

I'm the devil, baby girl. He was just a bad imitation.

I pushed past a wave of nausea and delved deeper into the dream. So that first voice—the one I kept hearing in the woods—wasn't Brock. He'd said as much, in my dream. I didn't know why I was hearing Brock's voice, or how I'd somehow locked into this stranger's experiences, but I had. I felt sure of that now.

Whoever the man in my dreams was, this was the shooter.

I rolled over and looked at the clock. 3:35 a.m. Definitely too early to get up. I closed my eyes and took a few deep breaths. Brock's face appeared on the back of my eyelids, as though burned there. My hand drifted to my side, tracing the rough, raised patch of skin that ran just below my breast all the way down to my upper thigh. Brock's gift to me, eight years ago. Something to remember him by.

"It's good to be back, sweetheart," a voice said, just behind my left ear. A breath, a breeze, something tangible crept across my skin. I jumped, as though burned yet again. "I've missed you, James."

I clenched my teeth through the sudden clutch of fear that gripped me. I'd already established that this wasn't Brock, hadn't I? But even as I thought it, I wondered if I were wrong. What if somehow, the presence of this new force in my thoughts had provided an opening for Brock—or his spirit, whatever thread was left of him—to find his way back to me?

"Go back to hell," I whispered into the darkness.

"Not without you," Brock said into my ear.

The night closed in around me. I squeezed my eyes shut tighter, the way I had against the voices as a child. Slowly, I felt the presence weaken, then disappear completely.

Exhausted, terrified, I waited for sleep to come once more.

•

The others were still asleep when I woke again at five o'clock. I got up, dressed, and took Phantom out while it was still dark outside, though there were lights on inside the mobile search and rescue unit and plenty of reporters still milling around the parking lot. I avoided everyone, and directed the dog toward the back of the inn. My mind was still locked on the dream I'd had, and the exchange afterward. Had I been asleep then? Or had I imagined the voice, so real that I could feel his breath on my skin?

The alternative—that Brock truly had somehow found a way back to me—was unthinkable.

It was just below freezing now, and we'd already done a type 2 search of the entire area where we'd found the women the night before. I didn't have a clue where the wardens would want to send searchers today. Despite the cold, I couldn't help but revel in the clear air. Phantom seemed likewise invigorated, mouth open in a toothy grin, tail waving as we headed down an icy path toward the back of the hotel.

I'd received no report that Michelle and her team had found anyone else while they were searching overnight. If they had, I was sure she would have let me know before now.

"All right, Phan," I said to my shepherd. "Get a little energy out, but take it easy. I don't know what kind of day we've got in store."

Phantom started to wander off to do her business, but stopped abruptly. She turned on the path, ears pricked forward, tail still waving. I likewise turned, and smiled at sight of Bear and Casper headed toward us. I was surprised Ren and Minion weren't with them, but then remembered the dark mood in the house when we first got back last night. There was definitely something going on there.

"Morning, Phan," Bear greeted the shepherd, giving her head a quick pat.

Casper held still long enough for me to give him a similar greeting, but then play bowed three times in succession in front of Phantom, hopping from one spot to the next while the shepherd held still glaring at him. To my surprise, however, on the third bow, she reciprocated—going down on her front paws with a low *woof* before she darted away. For a second, Casper was too dumbfounded to move. *Really? You really want to play?*

The paralysis didn't last long, though. Half a second later, the pit bull was on the move, darting after Phantom with such speed and vigor that I was afraid it would be too much for the older dog. I was grateful when he slowed his approach the closer he got, however, and the most he did when they caught up was bump up against Phantom before he backed off.

Bear and I stood in companionable silence for a few minutes, laughing out loud at the dogs' antics. Finally, when Phantom and Casper had both slowed down and were just meandering around the clearing, I shifted focus back to my son.

"Did you sleep all right? Is the room comfortable?"

"Definitely," he said. "Jack's a lot quieter sleeper than Monty. He talks in his sleep, but at least he doesn't snore." Monty was my second-in-command out on the island, someone Bear had bunked with more than his share over the years.

"He talks in his sleep?" I couldn't help but ask. "Could you tell what he was saying?"

He shook his head. "Not really, no. Just mumbling. Sounded like maybe he was having a bad dream. Still, it's a lot better than trying to sleep with Monty in the next bed."

"I'm glad to hear the room assignment worked out," I said. I wondered about the dream. Would Jack tell me if I asked him about it? I suspected the nightmares weren't new, and thought yet again of the wife he'd lost.

"Do you know what the schedule's supposed to be today?" Bear asked, interrupting my thoughts. "I really want to get out and start doing some searching."

"I'm not sure how they'll approach that today. There's potentially still a shooter out there," I reminded him. "Do we really want to put the dogs at risk like that?"

"Then I'll leave the dogs home and go out with the ground pounders," he said with a shrug. "It's stupid just sitting around in the lodge while everyone else is out looking."

"You and Ren didn't seem to mind it so much last night when you got sidelined."

He merely grunted. So much for subtlety. "If you want to talk about whatever's going on between the two of you…" I began.

Another grunt. Then, before I could follow up, he countered with a question of his own. "Does Hogan have a thing for Megan Hunter?"

The question was so unexpected that I had to pause before responding, unsure how to frame my answer. "What makes you say that?"

"I don't know. He just seems weird about her," Bear said. "Plus he looks like crap. I don't think he's been sleeping."

"Hogan says they're just friends."

"Right," Bear said, with a snort. "Just friends. I know how that goes." The bitterness in the words surprised me.

"He may have feelings that she doesn't return," I said carefully. "That's never an easy thing to handle."

Bear looked at me sideways, then returned his focus to the dogs. Phantom had long since tired of playing with Casper, but Casper was still doing everything in his power to re-engage her.

"Has that ever happened to you?" Bear asked, surprising me.

"Has what ever happened to me?"

"You liking someone, and they don't like you back."

Ah. That. I considered the question, surprised when Hogan's face flashed in my mind. "It has," I admitted. "A few times. I think it happens to everyone, at some point or other." I paused. Should I continue with the charade that we were talking about someone else, or did I give up the ghost and just ask outright?

"Bear, I know how much Ren cares about you…"

His jaw tensed. He stared into the distance, unable to meet my gaze. "She's going away, you know," he said, after a second's tortured silence.

"Eventually," I agreed. "But you both have another year of school. A lot can happen in that time."

"No," he said. He shook his head vigorously. "I'm not supposed to say anything, because Carl hasn't talked to you yet. But they're leaving. There's some stupid job in California…and it's not even a stupid job." He sighed, working hard to keep himself together. "God, this sucks."

Though this was the first I'd officially heard of Ren's father leaving, I wasn't completely surprised—particularly at mention of California. There was a program Carl had spoken of before, working with Nigerian refugees suffering from PTSD. Though Carl had been trained as a dog handler, he didn't have the passion for it that the rest of us did; I wasn't surprised to think he might leave it behind to work with people instead.

I thought of all the things I could say. *Maybe it won't happen—maybe they'll stay; you can keep in touch online; she can still visit in the summer.* All of it pointless for my son right now. Instead, I rubbed his back the way I used to when he was a little boy.

"I'm sorry," I said. "That does suck."

"Yeah," he agreed. "It totally does."

We stood that way for a while, Bear leaning toward me just slightly, my hand resting on his broad back. Against my will, Brock's voice returned to me—the mocking laugh that I had heard yesterday out in the woods. Despite everything, Brock truly had loved Bear. I never would have agreed to come back to Maine if he hadn't, and certainly wouldn't have stayed. Unfortunately, the way Brock treated me killed any chance he might have had for a good relationship with his only heir. I wondered, though, if Brock had ever tried to make contact with Bear after that fateful night in his home eight years ago.

As though sensing the turn my thoughts had taken, Bear turned to glance at me. "Yesterday when we were in the woods, you heard something, didn't you?"

"I'm not sure. Maybe. I've been wondering about something, actually."

Casper had gotten bored with being ignored by Phantom, and returned to Bear with expectation in his eyes. Time to play. Bear pulled a tennis ball from his pocket and tossed it across the clearing. Then, he turned to me, waiting for me to continue.

"What exactly were you wondering about?" he asked. "I've got some cool tricks up my sleeve, but I'm not a mind reader."

I smiled, grateful for at least a little show of humor. "I was wondering if you ever hear voices. I know you see things, connect with spirits visually, but do you ever just hear a voice?"

"Not really," he said. "There's usually a visual that goes with it. Who are you hearing?" Was I imagining the tension in his voice, that sense that he already knew?

"I'm not sure," I admitted. "I think it had something to do with this search, but the voice..." I paused, not sure how to continue. I almost regretted bringing it up in the first place.

"What about the voice?" he prompted.

I wet my lips, watching as Bear tossed the ball for Casper one more time before I spoke. "Since he died, have you seen

Brock again?"

The tension returned to his jawline, extending to his entire body this time. "What did he say to you?" His voice was tight, and I caught an edge of fear there that did little for my own state of mind.

"He's saying things that don't make sense based on our history. Things like, 'I told you I'd find you, baby girl.' Brock never once called me baby girl—whoever this is says it all the time."

"But you're sure it's his voice."

"Positive." Casper returned. Bear threw the ball once more as Phantom came trotting over.

"What else does he say?" Bear asked.

"Creepy things that horrible people say, mostly," I said, unwilling to be more specific than that. "Whoever it is I'm hearing has some issues. So you haven't heard anything?"

He frowned. "I haven't seen or heard Brock since the night he died. I've been a little surprised, to be honest. Grateful, but surprised. If the person you're hearing is coming through with his voice, though..." He hesitated. "Have you heard anything that makes you think maybe Brock is there, too?"

I've missed you, sweetheart. The words sounded in my head yet again, the memory of his breath on my neck.

"Mom?" Bear pressed. I couldn't find words to say it out loud. "Crap," he said. "You're giving him an opening. Maybe he just hasn't had the chance to cross back all these years—but now, for whatever reason, you're locked in this...echo, or whatever, that's coming off the mountain. And that echo is manifesting as Brock, or his voice at least. But if that's opening a door for him, you have to be careful."

"I know," I agreed. "I will. Please don't worry about this—I'm sure there's an explanation. Brock is dead and buried, and he has been for years now. He's not coming back."

Even as I said it, though, I heard that voice again. Bear was right: I was giving him an opening. And Brock had always been a man who took advantage of an opening when he saw one. Bear grimaced at my words, but he didn't argue any further. Instead, he took a deep breath and looked back toward the lodge.

"I think I'll go back and see if I can convince Ren to come out with Minion," he said.

"Sounds like a good plan."

"I was thinking maybe they could use some help out at the WildFire base," he continued, eying me. "If we're not allowed to work on the search with everyone, do you think it'd be cool for Ren and me to go over there? They have like twenty dogs. It's crazy for Abe to try and handle the whole place himself."

"That's a great idea," I agreed. "Depending on when they want the searchers to head out, we can probably give you a lift out there if you'd like."

It was good to see him lightening up a little. A minute later, he called Casper back and the two headed back to the lodge. I resisted calling Phantom yet, enjoying the stillness of the morning. The shepherd kept close by now that we were on our own, her attention split between me and the sounds and smells of the wilderness around. I welcomed the peace, grateful that no familiar voices whispered to me in the darkness this time.

Regardless, I kept looking for some threat.

You know I'll always find you, baby girl. The words sounded again in my head, the low rasp grating along the base of my spine.

Was the shooter someone Megan knew? She had been the first victim, after all. According to Chase, her ex-husband was still in prison. Ava and Gabriella, however, both had husbands with pretty dire reputations. It could have been one of them, and Megan was simply in the way.

If the words I was hearing hadn't actually been spoken by Brock, and I was in fact hearing the shooter, did that mean I had information I should be giving the police? By saying nothing rather than coming forward, was I putting Megan and the others in even more danger?

Phantom meandered back over to me as I pondered, clearly bored now. The relatively warm air meant I had yet to get chilled, but my stomach was rumbling and time was marching on. Definitely time to get inside.

"You're right," I said. "We'll go in and get some breakfast, get on with our day."

She sat and tipped her head to the right, eyes intent on mine. The difference between her and the other dogs really was amazing. As much as I loved every dog on our team, there was a bond with Phantom that I had never experienced with another animal. A sense of understanding, of trust, that I worried I would never find with another K-9 partner.

"She's a beautiful dog," a woman said behind me. I turned, startled. Phantom stood, eying the newcomer with suspicion, but she didn't bark.

Sally Price, the senator's wife, halted her advance, tensing slightly at the dog's posture.

"Thank you," I said. "She's a great partner."

Sally took a hesitant step forward. "May I pet her?"

"Of course," I said, then shifted focus to Phantom. "Say hi, girl."

With the requisite permission to advance, the shepherd's

posture relaxed. Tail wagging, she trotted over and allowed Sally to lay a hesitant hand on her head.

"Is she purebred?"

"I'm not sure," I said. "I found her at a shelter in Georgia. She didn't exactly come with papers."

"I see," Sally murmured, gently stroking Phantom's silky fur. I was relieved when she offered a pained smile. The deep circles under her eyes belied a long night, and her red, swollen eyes suggested she'd been crying recently. A little comfort from a friendly four-legged couldn't hurt.

After a few seconds of silence, she returned her focus to me. "I was just getting some fresh air. The suite feels too stuffy with the three of us crammed in there together."

"You're staying with Chase, then."

"Of course. He's part of the family." Was I imagining the bitterness in those words?

"I'm sure he must be beside himself about Violet," I said.

She turned to look at me at that, a furrow in her brow, her eyes shadowed. She wore a white fur hat and a white parka with fur at the cuffs and hood, with matching, tailored white ski pants. The ensemble probably cost more than my entire wardrobe.

"He must be," she agreed, without conviction. She seemed scattered, detached, and I wondered if she'd taken something. She'd stopped petting Phantom, appearing to forget the dog was even there.

"Do they have any theories about the shooter?" she asked me after a few seconds. I looked at her, surprised, as the image of the man in black from my dream flashed through my mind.

"I'm sorry," I said. "I can't really talk about the investigation—not that they've shared any of it with me anyway. But the police take this kind of thing very seriously. You need to speak with them if you're looking for information."

"They won't tell me anything," she said. Her voice broke. I thought of the agony I'd gone through when Bear was in danger in Glastenbury last fall. Would I be doing anything differently than this woman, in her place? "I'm just trying to find out what's going on with my daughter. What Chase said…"

"What did Chase say?" I prompted.

"It's not…" She sighed, then lowered her voice when she spoke again, as though sharing some shameful secret. "Violet had some problems when she was younger. We don't talk about them—she's worked hard to overcome that period, but her work in Washington makes it clear that period had an impact on her life."

I didn't press her despite my interest, instead letting her tell the story in her own time.

"Violet was hospitalized when she was younger, her first year of college. She'd always been a high achiever, and I think the pressure of an Ivy League school was more than she had anticipated. We learned that she was…hurting herself. Cutting?" Her eyes welled at the memory, and I felt a tug of sympathy. "We got her the very best care, of course, and she was released after a week. After that, she began seeing a therapist."

"It's not uncommon for girls to have issues like that, especially if they put a lot of pressure on themselves," I said. "I don't mean to be insensitive, but I'm not sure I see the connection to what's happening now."

"I'm sorry. I know I'm not doing this very well—I'm not used to talking about any of this." She took a deep breath, working herself up to whatever it was she wanted to say. "While Violet was in therapy, some issues came up. Regarding her father." She fell silent.

"What kind of issues?" I prompted, when she didn't continue.

"He could be strict—hard at times, with both of us. He was just trying to be a good father, a good husband, but he had no idea the impact it had on Violet. As soon as she came to him, the three of us began seeing a family counselor. It could have ruined his career, but he didn't care; he did everything he could to make sure she knew how much he loved her. It made a huge difference, for all of us."

"And what happened from there?"

"Violet went back to school, and she excelled even more than before. She met Megan—the two were fast friends by sophomore year, and have remained close since then. There was a peace to her that I'd never seen. The whole thing set a fire in her, though, and she became passionate about helping women and girls in abusive situations."

"When did she and Chase get together?" I asked.

Sally frowned, an expression so fleeting that I second guessed myself the moment it was gone. "She met Chase shortly after graduating—his friend introduced them. He was an actor, you know. And a Maine Guide. An entrepreneur. Horse breeder. Inventor. Now, he wants to be a politician. The curse of being born with money—that's what Violet always says. Though from what I gather, he's gone through most of that now."

She hesitated. I waited for her to complete her thought, sensing that something was coming. "He was orphaned when he was a teenager; his parents died in a fire. And his first wife was killed, too. Did you know that?"

The revelation stopped me. I fought to remain steady, unable to forget the feeling I'd gotten the first time I'd set eyes on the man. "I didn't know," I said, working to keep a level tone. "That must have been hard for him."

"Yes," she said distractedly. "It must have. He'll tell you that it was, if you ask. He'll even cry, sometimes."

The pause went on for nearly thirty seconds this time, until I finally spoke up. "Sally, what exactly are you trying to tell me?"

She shook her head. "I don't know. I don't know what I'm trying to say. Robert was always a good father to Violet— he adores her. You have no idea how sorry he was when he realized how badly he'd frightened her when she was a child. He's spent years trying to make that up to her. And Chase is a good husband. He says all the right things."

It struck me as a strange thing to say. "But..." I prompted, when she fell silent.

"No buts," she insisted. "He is. They're the perfect couple. He's the perfect man." She stopped.

"If he's the perfect man, why are you talking to me right now? Clearly something is bothering you."

"There you are!" a voice called from the woods. At the sound of Chase's voice, Sally flinched. He jogged toward us, but slowed to a walk when Phantom came to attention at his approach.

"Steady, girl," I said, not willing to completely call her off just yet.

"We've been looking everywhere for you," Chase said, once he'd reached us. "I was worried, seeing you leave the room so early this morning."

"I just needed some fresh air, Chase. I'm fine."

"I'm sorry to interrupt." He studied me a moment, with

a strangely calculating gaze. "What are you ladies talking about? It looked pretty serious."

"My daughter is missing," Sally said witheringly. "You expected us to be trading sewing tips?" Chase said nothing for as much as a second, awkwardness building between us. "I'm sorry," Sally said. "We're all so worried right now—I didn't mean to be rude."

The apology was delivered to me as much as Chase, and I was struck by the way she was looking at her son-in-law. Or not looking at him, actually. Even when speaking directly to him, she wouldn't meet his eye. It reminded me of some scene from the wild: the more submissive animals in most species will avoid direct eye contact with a dominant member of the pack. I couldn't shake the feeling that Sally was doing everything possible to avoid the impression that she was challenging her son-in-law.

"We were just talking about the search," I said. "I'll be headed out again soon, and I was telling Sally a little about what my team does."

"Ah. Well, I appreciate you taking the time to talk about that. I know you must be very busy."

Chase put his arm around Sally's shoulders. She stiffened. Phantom stood, hackles raised, her focus on the man who now stood between Sally and me.

"I think we'd better go, Sally," Chase said. We need to let Jamie get to work. I'll take you over to the dining hall. Breakfast is on."

"She's fine," I said. I glared at his arm until he removed it from around his mother-in-law's thin shoulders, though he put no distance between himself and the woman. "I was headed over there myself anyway. We'll just go there together."

"That's all right," Sally said quickly. She didn't even look at me, casting a sideways glance in Chase's direction. "He's right, I should let you go. I'm sure my husband is worried about me."

"If there's anything more you'd like to talk about," I said, "please, don't hesitate to come to me. We're staying right next door, at the ski lodge. If I'm not there, someone else will be."

"Thank you," she murmured. "It will be fine once Violet's home. Just find her. Please."

"I'll do everything I can," I promised.

Chase began walking away, his hand at Sally's back—not quite touching her, but I got the sense that was only because I was watching.

"Thanks again for your hard work, Jamie," Chase said over his shoulder as he departed. "We appreciate everything you're doing. We won't bother you again."

Before I could insist that it had been no bother, they were moving back up the trail.

Once they had gone, Phantom and I headed back to the lodge ourselves. After the strange encounter, I was eager to get back on the search as soon as possible. I had no idea how the higher-ups may have scheduled the day, but I hoped plenty of field time would be included. Right now, all I wanted to do was get out there with my dog and do our job.

13

OVER THE COURSE OF THE MORNING, Megan, Violet, and Ava struggled on some of the most rugged terrain in the Mahoosucs. By the time they finally reached relatively even ground, they were exhausted, with mouths parched and stomachs rumbling. Even here, they had to watch out for tree roots just beneath the snow or low-hanging branches that seemed to reach for them with deadly intent.

"If we ever get out of here," Violet announced at one point, "I'm going for the biggest, juiciest burger you've ever seen in your life. And lobster. And cake." She groaned. "Oh, God. Cake."

Personally, the thought of food wasn't what spurred Megan on—in fact, the mere mention turned her stomach. The idea of home, on the other hand, pushed her forward. She'd been dreaming for months of the day when her nephew came into the world. If she had anything to say about it, she would be there for that. And her nephew wasn't the only guy on her mind. Two days before leaving on the expedition, Hogan had asked her to go to Boston with him. She'd been so flustered she'd almost laughed out loud.

"Why would we go to Boston?"

He'd shrugged, looking a little flustered himself. "There's an exhibit at the Science Museum— the evolution of man's best friend through the ages. I thought maybe we could get some dinner, make a night of it."

She'd actually been wanting to make it to that exhibit. And it wasn't that she wasn't interested in going with Hogan; they were friends. Good friends, as a matter of fact, when they weren't driving each other crazy. But going to Boston with him? Dinner, the museum, the long ride home afterward. Maybe things would run late, and he'd want to spend the night there. In a hotel. With her.

A few days ago, the thought of dealing with that had almost blown her mind. Now, she wished she could go back there and kick her own cowardly ass. She was lost in the woods with a psycho hunting her down. What she wouldn't give if the biggest thing she had to face was her first date with Hogan— something that, if she were being honest, had been featured in daydreams a lot lately.

Despite the sun climbing higher in the sky, Megan wasn't getting any warmer. Her head ached and her side burned from the gunshot graze, which she was afraid might be getting infected. Recluse walked alongside her, his fur matted now, his gait no longer as easy as it had been when they'd first started this ill-fated WildFire expedition. How many days ago had that been? Five? Six? More? It felt like a lifetime.

Megan scanned the forest, taking full advantage of daylight. They weren't far from the river now, she knew.

Occasional, earth-shaking booms vibrated the ground beneath their feet— the ice shifting as it melted. They were close. She just wished they could find some of those many searchers who should be looking for them.

She spotted something on a ragged, somewhat lopsided spruce tree, and paused.

"What is it?" Ava asked her.

She reached up and plucked the object from the branch, her forehead furrowed. A closer examination of the area revealed others, at a rate of one tie every twenty trees or so.

"Are we on private property?" Violet asked. "Or are these just to mark the trails in the area?"

"Trails are marked with paint blazes on the rocks and trees," Megan said. "They wouldn't use plastic ties. And no one would mark private property this way."

Which meant one thing: the searchers had been out here. They'd marked the area off to indicate where they'd looked. Would they come back if they had already been here? How far away could they possibly be by now, even if they had moved on?

Old Speck was just ahead of them. There was no way in hell any of them could handle climbing the mountain at this point, too weak from cold, fear, and lack of food, water, and rest. In the best of circumstances, she considered it the perfect way to spend a weekend. Now, though, she seriously doubted she had the strength.

"We can't be far from searchers by now," she said to the others. "Let's continue up this trail a little farther and see if we can find anyone."

Ava and Violet agreed, though neither seemed to have strength for more than a grunt. Recluse glanced up at her, tail waving briefly, and waited for Megan to lead the way.

Suddenly, the dog went stiff. His ears came up, head tilted to the left. Megan watched the fur stand up along the ridge of his back, the dog growling all the while.

"Stop," she whispered to the others.

The three of them froze. Megan wrapped her hand around Recluse's collar, and held on tight.

Somewhere close by, she could hear someone moving through the brush. It wasn't an animal— the footsteps and the rustling of branches were too lumbering for that. Ava started to speak, but Megan put her finger up to her mouth. They stood like that for at least three minutes as they listened to the sounds move farther and farther away, never sure whether they were in fact hearing the shooter.

Another five minutes ticked by. Then ten. Recluse had relaxed. The forest sounds Megan heard now, she was sure, were native to these woods. The monster had gone.

Maybe their luck was turning. They'd been able to rest in the cabin; not much, but enough to get them through another day. People would still be looking. Recluse was still with them. And the wind and occasional flurries meant that any tracks they left on top of the solid-crusted snow were obliterated almost as soon as they left them, making tracking them that much harder.

"Should we keep going?" Violet finally asked, breaking the silence.

Megan nodded. They'd been still for so long that her limbs ached once she got them moving again. They walked on regardless, Megan's hand resting at the top of Recluse's head.

●

An hour later, they were headed down a darkened path slick with snow and ice when Megan heard the sound of an engine in the distance. Recluse tensed beside her, while a rush of excitement sent a surge of much-needed adrenaline through her veins. Violet grabbed her arm, the woman's blue eyes wide.

"Do you hear that?"

Megan nodded, unable to hide her own excitement. "It's a snowmobile," she whispered, then gestured toward a patch of trees just off the trail. "Go in there—hide until they get here. I don't want anyone getting run over." She didn't say what she knew they were all thinking: if it wasn't searchers, if it was in fact the shooter, she wanted to make sure they had a chance to get away.

Recluse, meanwhile, had done a full 180-degree turn on the path, searching for the source of the noise. Judging by the roar of the engine, whoever was driving was going like hell.

Obediently, Ava and Violet went into the woods. Violet tried to drag Recluse along with her, but the dog would have none of it. After a minute's struggle, Megan took hold of the dog's collar herself and shooed the other women away.

The sound of the engine got louder. It was definitely headed in their direction. Recluse pranced where he stood, nervous himself. Megan held tight to his collar to keep him from running away, or getting hit. This could be their salvation... Or, she reminded herself, it could be the shooter, coming for them with a mode of transportation that all but guaranteed he would catch up to them. Megan sent up a silent prayer that their nightmare was about to end, and help truly was just a few meters away.

A few seconds before the snowmobile rounded the bend

and came into view, Megan made her decision. Through the trees, she saw the blaze of yellow on the machine itself, and tried desperately to see the driver. When she failed, she grabbed Recluse and yanked him into the trees with her. She crouched there, waiting, until the snowmobile rounded the bend.

She almost wept at sight of the MAINE WARDEN SERVICE insignia on the side of the sled when it finally came into view. She stood abruptly, one hand still wrapped tight around Recluse's collar, and shouted as she waved her other arm over her head.

"Hey! Stop! I'm with WildFire Expeditions—"

She'd barely completed the sentence when the driver slowed the machine, though the fact that she was still well off the trail and partially hidden in the brush meant she couldn't be positive whoever it was had seen her. At the same time, she felt a change in Recluse beside her. A low growl escaped the dog's throat, something she felt more than heard above the roar of the engine.

"It's all right, Rec," she told the dog. "This is a good guy."

The snowmobile slid to a stop. The driver turned to look in her direction, his helmet making it impossible for her to see his face. The weight of his stare and Recluse's ratcheting anxiety raised her own enough that she paused where she stood. She didn't step farther out into the open, painfully aware of her own vulnerability. Of the danger she may have brought to all of them.

The driver continued to stare in her direction, trying to see through the patchy brush. He wore a heavy-duty Carhartt snowmobile suit over his clothes, so she couldn't tell whether there was a Maine Warden Service uniform on under that or not. She wondered for a split second whether it might be Hogan, but dismissed the thought. She would know if it were him, whether she could see his face or not. Before she could decide whether to stay or run, she caught another glimpse of movement in the distance—this one slower. Someone on foot.

"Hey!" Megan shouted again, louder this time, as a fresh surge of fear spurred her forward.

At last, the driver spotted her through the trees. He killed the engine and started to get off the machine. As he did, Recluse started barking so violently that Megan thought he would tear the collar right out of her hands. The man on the snowmobile held his hands up in a gesture clearly meant to indicate that he meant no harm, but Recluse didn't ease up. He continued barking, straining so much that Megan had to fight to hold him at bay.

"Recluse, settle!" she shouted, but the dog ignored her.

The driver moved to remove his helmet, not trying to get any closer. Megan, likewise, remained where she was. She was eager for rescue, but preferred to do it without more bloodshed—something that seemed inevitable the way Recluse was going at it.

"You're with the WildFire group?" the man asked, once his helmet was off. He was younger than she had expected, most likely mid-twenties, with blond hair and a pale complexion. She'd never seen him before.

"I was," she said. "Damn, are we glad to see you." She had to shout to be heard over Recluse, who still wasn't giving an inch.

"It's okay, buddy," the man said, his voice low, extending a hand. Thankfully, he didn't take a step closer.

"I'm sorry about this," she apologized. "He's been

through a lot the last few days. We all have."

"I bet," the warden said. He took a step closer, and Recluse responded with even more ferocity than before, forcing Megan to yank him back with all her strength.

"Maybe you should take a step back," she suggested. "I'm not sure what his problem is, but he seems serious. Have the others been found yet? My sister—Heather?"

"We've got them," the man assured her. "They're okay. Your sister's in the hospital, but she's all right." Though he looked a little hurt at Recluse's reaction, the warden didn't hesitate to retreat a couple of steps.

Even with the additional space and Megan's renewed hope, however, Recluse continued to bark. The warden put the radio to his ear, plugging his other ear to shut out the mad dog Megan struggled to keep under control.

And then, suddenly, something changed. In that instant, it felt as though the wind shifted. The world slowed. Megan heard the sound of thunder, familiar enough now that she knew even before the bullet struck…

The warden fell to his knees, the radio falling from his hand. The shot had come from behind him; the exit wound sprayed blood across the snow, far enough that Megan felt it wet her face, stain her clothes. Someone—Ava, Megan thought—screamed. Megan stood for a second, frozen, until there was a rustling in the trees where the shot originated.

A man dressed in black from head to foot stepped out, his face the only thing uncovered.

"Hey, baby girl," Justin drawled. His smile was thin, his face drawn. Prison hadn't been good to her ex-husband. "I'm home."

Recluse had stopped barking, leaving behind an absence of sound more deafening even than the gunshot. Now, though, he began to growl once more. Megan yanked his collar hard as she turned back toward the woods.

"Come, Recluse," she shouted. Panic rode high within her, shutting out any intelligent thought she might have had.

Summoning what she was sure was the last of her strength, she dragged the dog along until he kept pace, then bolted ahead. She could hear footsteps behind her. The monster, in pursuit. If she lost this race, she knew without a doubt what her end—their end—would be.

"Keep going," she urged the dog, shouting the words loud enough that she hoped Ava and Violet heard her. "Don't stop."

They ran.

14

Flint K-9 Search and Rescue
February 4, 7:00 a.m.

I RECEIVED A TEXT from Hogan just before getting back to the lodge:

Report for duty 0800 Grafton Park Entrance. OK?

I texted back confirmation, then waited for any subsequent information. Not surprisingly, none came. He provided no information about the status of the search, but I assumed he would have told me if anyone else had been found overnight.

My mind was going a hundred miles an hour as Phantom and I skipped up the steps to the lodge. Did they have any more information about what had happened? Was Heather Wright awake yet? Had she been able to tell them anything about the shooter? And what was the deal with Sally Price—and, specifically, her bizarre reaction to her even more bizarre son-in-law?

My thoughts were interrupted once I reached the top step and the front door burst open, nearly knocking me off my feet.

"It's about time," Bear said. "I just got off the phone with Abe Wright—he said he can definitely use the help. We're ready to go. I want to show Ren around the place." He and Ren were both bundled up and in good spirits, their earlier argument apparently forgotten. Casper and Minion, meanwhile, were underfoot and unmistakably unhappy about being left behind.

"Just give me a minute to get my gear. Have you seen Jack yet?"

"Right here," Jack said from the kitchen, and appeared with a mug of coffee in hand. He looked freshly showered, and was already shaved and dressed. "Do we know how the day's supposed to play out?"

"Just heard from Hogan," I confirmed. "He wants us at the park entrance in an hour. That gives us enough time to drop Bear and Ren over at WildFire before we go to the park."

"Sounds good. I've already replenished my pack—I'm ready whenever you are."

That, in a nutshell, was what I'd been expecting when I first decided to bring Jack on board at Flint K-9. Punctual, professional, ready to go at a moment's notice. I told the others to give me five minutes, ran upstairs and got my own gear, and was back down with two minutes to spare.

It was ten past seven by the time we loaded the van and set out, with me at the wheel and Jack once more in the co-pilot's seat. Phantom was the only dog traveling with us today, Bear and Ren in the bench seat in the back. I glanced in the rearview and smiled at sight of the two of them sharing earbuds, one in Bear's ear, the other in Ren's, as they sat locked in their own little world.

A light snow had started and winds were picking up, but

overall it looked like the weather was going to cooperate today. A storm system coming through that night, however, could mean trouble, with high winds and mixed precipitation predicted. I pointed our van north, up the mountain toward the WildFire base. My windshield wipers beat a steady rhythm as the snow continued. Jack and I chatted about the search, what I knew about the area, where else I thought we might be looking today... Everything and nothing, my encounter with Sally Price effectively forgotten.

Half an hour later, we passed a sign indicating WildFire Expeditions in one mile. We were traveling up a steep, narrow grade with just a guardrail to protect us from a sheer drop to our right. With the increased elevation, the wind and snow had picked up and I was starting to second-guess my earlier thoughts about the weather.

Meanwhile, Jack remained silent, tense, beside me.

"It's not much farther," I said, as we rounded a bend in the road.

"Not that I don't trust your driving, but that's good to hear," Jack said.

"Definitely," Bear said, inserting himself into the conversation for the first time since we'd set out.

I glanced in the rearview mirror. The road was empty, no sign of a vehicle for at least that small stretch of highway visible. When I returned my gaze to the road ahead, I saw a car come out of the turnoff to the WildFire place, about a half mile up ahead.

The vehicle got up to speed fast once it hit the road. It quickly surpassed that speed, barreling toward us at a pace that would have unnerved me in the best driving conditions.

"What the hell are they doing?" Jack asked, gripping his armrest tight. I kept my eyes on the road, my hands locked on the wheel.

It was a dark SUV coming toward us—an expensive one, by the look of it. When the vehicle was just up ahead, nearly upon us, a crawl of dread worked through me as the license plate registered.

SENATOR

I shifted my gaze to the driver as the car sped past, Sally Price's terrified eyes locked on the road.

"What's she thinking?" Bear asked, his own voice panicked at sight of the rogue SUV. "She's going to get herself killed."

"Or someone else," I said.

I slowed down and pulled a U-turn, focused on keeping all four wheels on the road, everyone in the car stone silent. In the back, Phantom had picked up the strange vibe, and I could sense as much as hear her pacing and pants.

I got the van turned around and had time for a single deep breath, my eyes on Sally's SUV up ahead, when I saw her front tires hit a patch of ice. She fishtailed, drifting into the opposite lane on the steep grade headed back down the mountain—directly into the path of a plow truck that hadn't been there earlier. Her brake lights locked on as she ground the brakes, but found no purchase on the snowy road.

The sound of the oncoming plow's horn sounded, surreal and almost mournful on the isolated road. But it was the scream of tires and the clash of metal as the two vehicles collided that, I knew, would follow me into my dreams.

I watched in horror as the SUV hit the plow head-on at speed, pushing it back until both vehicles were barreling backward down the mountain, the drivers powerless to slow the descent.

I cursed under my breath as I drove on slowly, inexorably, toward the crash. Meanwhile, Jack fumbled with his phone, then swore himself when he realized we had no signal.

Phantom was barking in the back of the vehicle, and I glanced in the rearview just long enough to see Bear and Ren paralyzed, terrified, in the rear seat. I reminded myself of their safety, of our safety, and slowed our van to a crawl as we approached the scene of the accident.

Sally's SUV came to a halt only when it hit a steel guardrail, nearly taking the rail out before the vehicle finally stopped. The plow rested on its side a few feet beyond, in the middle of the road. With snow flying and wind blowing, I could tell nothing beyond that.

I found a spot as far over on the shoulder as possible and pulled our van to the side, already calling orders over my shoulder.

"Bear, if we can't get cell reception get the radio. Let them know we need an ambulance and somebody to help get these vehicles off the road before somebody else comes along and makes this even worse."

"Got it," Bear said, already pulling out the radio. "Where do you want us?"

I hesitated, but only for an instant. We were off the road as far as I could safely get with the van, but that didn't mean we were completely out of harm's way if another vehicle came around that corner.

"Get Phantom and take her out toward the tree line— not beyond, but far enough that you're away from the road."

I expected an argument, but was relieved when I didn't get one.

"Jack," I began, before he cut me off.

"I'm with you," he said.

I got out of the van with my heart racing, sick to my stomach. We went first to Sally's SUV since it was closest, and I froze there. The windshield of the senator's vehicle was cracked, with blood and white hair at the center of the spider webbed glass. The passenger's door was open; Sally wasn't in the vehicle. I looked around, perplexed.

"Come check the plow with me first. Then we'll go look for her, once we've got backup."

I nodded. Head down, I ran beside Jack to the up-ended snowplow.

The engine was still going, music—Led Zeppelin, I thought—blaring inside the cab. Jack got down on his hands and knees in the snow to peer inside, and I followed suit. A young man, no more than twenty-two, was in the driver's seat, eyes open but bleary.

"We need to get him out fast," I said to Jack. "If another car comes around that turn before help arrives, they won't have time to slow before they hit the truck."

He nodded his agreement, then leaned down and knocked on the window to get the driver's attention. "We're going to get you out," he shouted, over the competing sounds of the engine, the music, and the storm.

The driver snapped to attention, his eyes widening. He said something that I couldn't hear, then began to cry—the sobs of someone deep in shock. I looked at Jack.

"We've got to get him out of there," he said. I agreed, though at the moment I didn't have a lot of ideas as to how to do that.

I moved in as close to the windshield as possible, hands cupping my mouth to magnify the sound, and shouted. "Can you reach the button for the window?"

It took him a minute, but the directive seemed to pull the man slightly out of the grip of hysteria. He looked around, orienting himself—not easy, I was sure, in his current state. Then slowly, painfully, he reached to the door beside him and pressed the button. For a second, nothing happened. I was already deciding whether I would go back to the van to get a crowbar myself or just send Jack when, finally, the passenger's side window moved. Jack forced it down the rest of the way. I winced as the music got that much louder, and called in one more time.

"Turn off the truck," I said. "Can you do that?"

The man nodded. He took a deep breath, apparently focusing, and his hand moved to the ignition. Two endless seconds of fumbling later, and the world went blissfully still.

"Good," I said, quieter now. "You're doing great. Can you tell me your name?"

"What the heck was she doing?" the young man asked, rather than responding. His eyes were haunted, pupils enlarged from shock or concussion. "What was she thinking? She came straight at me."

"I know," Jack said, his voice low, soothing. "It's not your fault. But right now I need you to focus. I want you to stay as still as you can, and we're coming in to get you. Can you do that?"

"I think so," he said.

"Will you get the kit from the van?" Jack asked me. I nodded and stepped away from the plow, grateful to get away from the diesel fumes.

I slid twice on my way back, going down hard once before I recovered as I raced for the emergency kit we kept in the van at all times. Bear and Ren had Phantom over by the tree line, but came closer at my approach.

"What can we do?" Ren asked.

"Come on over to the plow," I said, after a moment's hesitation. "Both of you. Bring Phantom. We may need her. Did you reach someone on the radio?"

"Yeah," Bear said. "They're on their way—they said it shouldn't be too long."

"Good."

We returned to the plow with Phantom at a heel by my side. Ren and Bear trailed behind me, and I wondered as I have a hundred times before in raising Bear, whether I had exposed him to too much by allowing him to be this much a part of search and rescue from the time he was small.

To my surprise, the plow driver was already out of the vehicle when we returned, and was seated beside Jack in the snow, well clear of the road.

"He climbed out before I could stop him," Jack said.

"I told you, I'm not hurt," the man said. His speech was slurred, ragged, and blood still oozed from a gash in his head. Definitely a concussion, at the very least. "I need to get back. My boss is going to kill me." He looked at me, awareness slowly sinking in. "What about that lady? Is she okay?"

"We don't know how she is," I said. "I'm going to find her now."

Phantom left my side and approached the injured man with her head down, tail waving slowly.

"What's your name?" I asked the man, for the second time that morning.

"Corey," he said. Phantom sat down beside him and licked his face, not a move she was known for with strangers. Corey pet her head, eyes sinking shut. I watched the calm I knew so well descend on the man as he focused on the dog, his ragged breath gradually evening out. "Corey Haskell." He opened his eyes and met my gaze, tears welling once more. "I didn't even see her coming."

"There was nothing you could do," I told him honestly.

"This isn't your fault."

He lay his head against Phantom's neck, blood and snow and tears mixing in the dog's fur. Phantom sat, tail still waving slowly, and I wondered at the empathy of dogs, as I have countless times in my life.

"I'm going to look for Sally," I said to Jack, speaking low to keep from disturbing the unfolding scene.

"I'll come too," Jack said.

"That's all right. Just stay here, keep everyone together."

"What if you need help with the rescue?"

"I'll bring the radio, and keep in contact. Come after me as soon as emergency vehicles arrive."

"Stay safe."

I nodded grimly, my mind stuck on that patch of blood and hair we'd found on Sally's windshield. What the hell had she been doing out here. "I'll do my best."

•

I took Phantom with me as far as the SUV, the grinding in my stomach growing with every step. Once we reached the vehicle, I wrangled the door open and found a pair of women's gloves on the floor of the passenger's seat. Sally's, I presumed.

I took them out and let Phantom take a good, long whiff, then bagged them in one of the Ziploc baggies I carry with me. I looked at my dog as she stood in the snow, head up, tail at half mast, ears perked. She was ready.

"Okay, girl," I said. "Find her!" My voice shook with the words, in time with my body. I forced myself to pull it together. Focused on my dog as she raised her head, nostrils flared, oblivious to the snow that continued to fall.

She trotted toward the guardrail. I followed along behind, managing to stay on my feet through sheer stubbornness as I skated along behind her on the slick pavement.

It took just under five minutes before Phantom locked on scent. She continued along the embankment, head up, and then paused suddenly. I watched as she held her nose high, nostrils quivering, ears tipped forward. Then, she maneuvered past the guardrail and began making her way down the steep embankment.

Phantom glanced back at me, a question in her eyes before her gaze returned to the ravine.

"Stop," I said. She froze. Sat. Waited until I reached her. "She's down there, girl?"

She turned intelligent eyes on me and barked, twice. I had no doubt: Sally Price was there.

Phantom and I half walked, half slid down the embankment beside the guardrail. The woods were thick here. I didn't understand how Sally ended up out this far, but I knew enough to trust my dog. Despite the fresh powder, the underlying blanket of snow was still solid. Phantom was able to trot along on top without a problem, something I was grateful for. Regardless, I knew this wouldn't take long.

Sure enough, it was only another three minutes before Phantom paused. She glanced back at me, then at the snow in front of her. My stomach turned. There was a blood trail on the ground, the snow compacted as though someone had dragged herself—or been dragged—deeper into the woods.

"Keep going, Phan," I said. "Find her." My mouth was dry. I followed more slowly than I usually would, dreading what we were about to find.

Ten feet later, Phantom led me to Sally Price.

The senator's wife lay on her back at the end of the blood

trail in the snow, eyes closed. Why had she left the vehicle? What had she been running from? Or to? I knelt in the snow beside the woman, giving Phantom only perfunctory praise for her find before I focused on our victim.

Blood ran down her face from a deep gash in her scalp, where her head had hit the windshield. I was dimly aware of sirens approaching, the realization that help had arrived, but my attention returned quickly to the woman before me.

"Sally?" I said. I wasn't surprised when she didn't respond to my voice, but I continued searching for vital signs until I found a faint pulse at her throat. "Sally!" I said again. I shook her lightly, trying to get her to come to, and then radioed Jack to let him know where I was before beginning CPR.

I ran through the training in my head, starting with thirty chest compressions. I'd finished the first cycle when I became aware of voices in the distance—Jack and the paramedics, as he briefed them on the situation. They would be here soon.

And then, bubbling up from the earth like some insipid black tar, I heard laughter.

Low and familiar.

Are we having fun yet, sweetheart? Brock asked me.

This wasn't someone with his voice anymore, I was sure of it. This was him.

I ignored him and continued working on Sally Price's inert body, though his voice echoed in my head. What did he want?

The instant I thought it, his answer came.

I want you to tell them the truth, he said. *I want you to stop lying. I want you to pay for what you did to me. What you took.*

I put my ear down to Sally's chest, listening for any

sign of a heartbeat. Would Brock appear to me now? Take physical form? Punish me, in ways I knew he'd dreamed about when he was alive?

"Sally!" a voice called, before I could reply to the ghost now haunting me. This voice was fully grounded in the real world, though. Young. Masculine. Phantom stood beside me, and I noted with surprise that her hackles were raised. In response to Brock, or this new presence?

Someone rustled in the underbrush, shouting Sally's name again, and Phantom tensed further. So this wasn't a reaction to Brock, then. The voice was sickeningly familiar, and I knew exactly who it was well before the brush parted and Chase Carter stepped into view.

I caught a glimpse of his face as I continued working on his mother-in-law's body, and I watched something cross his face at the sight.

Delight.

Pure, unadulterated delight.

The look vanished, but only just, when he realized I'd seen him.

"She just took off," he said, out of breath. "I'd tracked her down with you and I was going to have breakfast with her in the dining hall. But the next thing I knew, she was gone again. Then I heard about the accident." He stopped. "Is she alive? What can I do?"

The paramedics arrived before I could answer, taking over for me as I gave them a rundown of what I'd found and what I'd done thus far. Jack joined me, his hand at my back, and I was honestly prepared to stand there and watch Sally Price die.

Instead, the paramedics worked for less than a minute before a stocky man monitoring her vitals ordered them to stop.

"We've got a heartbeat," he said to the others. "Get her to the bus."

Sally still wasn't moving, certainly wasn't conscious, but my own pulse sped at the implication. She might actually survive this. I suddenly, desperately wanted Sally Price to survive.

Chase remained beside us after the paramedics had gone, rather than insisting on going with them to be with his mother-in-law. Jack and I walked with him back topside, my adrenaline still pumping after the rescue.

"I can't believe this," Chase said eventually, when we were back at the road. Jack had returned to Bear and Ren, leaving Phantom and I alone with Chase for the moment.

"Do you have any idea why she would have gone to the WildFire camp?" I asked.

"Is that where she was? I don't have a clue. She just... left. We were talking about Violet and Megan, and she said something about wanting to talk to the other women on the expedition. I told her she shouldn't be driving in her state."

His gaze returned to me, complete innocence in the words. But I hadn't imagined the look I had seen on his face when he'd first set eyes on Sally's body, I was sure of it. He might be a good actor, but there was no question in my mind that what I was seeing now was anything but authentic emotion.

"Did she say what she wanted to talk to them about?" I asked. "What was so important that she couldn't use the phone? Or wait until they came to the lodge—I'm sure someone would have been onsite at search headquarters at some point today."

"She didn't mention anything. Frankly, she probably said more to you today than she did to me. What did you talk about?"

"I already told you," I said. I didn't care for the way he was looking at me, the pressure I felt in his words. "We talked about the search. And she gave me some information she thought might be helpful in looking for Violet."

"What information?"

"A little about Violet's background." I paused. "A little about your background."

If I hadn't been watching for the reaction, I wouldn't have noticed a fleeting moment of tension before it vanished. "What did she say about my background?" he asked, trying to laugh it off. "I don't see how that could help you find my wife."

"She said you've lost some people in your life. I'm sorry about that," I added. "It must make what's happening with Violet that much harder."

He held my eye, though I saw what appeared to be genuine pain on his face now. "You have no idea what it's been like, from the moment I heard she was missing. I don't know what Sally might have implied about my past, but I love my wife. I would do anything to get her back."

The last was said with actual tears standing in his eyes. Phantom remained vigilant by my side, though, and I couldn't shake the memory of the look I'd seen on his face when he saw me working on Sally. The feeling I got when we first shook hands.

"Do you have a name you call your wife?" I asked. "Like a term of endearment? Honey? Sweetheart?"

His forehead furrowed. For the first time I got the sense I was seeing a genuine, unfiltered reaction from him. "Of course—doesn't everyone? It's something a little more intimate than I care to share—"

"Baby girl," I guessed.

He cringed. "God, no. Vivvy—I call Violet Vivvy. The only person I've ever heard use something as crass as 'baby girl' is Justin."

It felt like an actual electric current ran through me. I imagined it as the same feeling the dogs got when they finally caught odor on a trail.

"Justin, as in Megan's ex-husband?"

"That's right."

"And you said he's still in prison?"

"The last I knew." He hedged, watching me closely now. "I can't be sure, though. We haven't stayed in touch."

I didn't believe that for a second. Hogan and a group of wardens arrived on scene then, and I fought between relief at no longer being alone with Chase and annoyance that I could ask no more questions. One thing was certain, though: the first thing I planned to do was double check to make sure Megan's ex-husband really was still safely locked away in prison.

"We're going to need you to clear out of this area," I heard Hogan say behind me as he reached Chase and me. "Both you and Mr. Carter. We're getting the vehicles out of here now."

"Of course," Chase said. He cast a glance toward me that was as icy as the world around us. Then, as if by magic, his eyes welled. "I don't know how I'm going to tell the senator about this."

"She's still alive," I reminded him. "Tell him that. I think she's tougher than she looks."

Chase shook his head. "Maybe. I just don't know..." His voice faded as he walked away, hands in his pockets, shoulders hunched. It reminded me of the way someone might play grief on screen. Nothing about it rang true in life, however.

"Do you have any clue what she was doing out here?" Hogan asked me, as soon as Chase was out of sight.

"I don't," I said. "She was just coming out of the WildFire road as we approached, driving like a bat out of hell. I turned around because she was obviously in trouble, and she hit the plow."

His gaze shifted to the body, and I saw the emotion that had been missing from Chase. "Jesus. What was she doing? The kid in the plow said she drove straight into him. Why?"

"I think she lost control of the SUV," I said. "But it's no wonder considering how fast she was going." I shook my head. I heard that toxic laughter well up from below again, and forced myself to ignore it. "Something's going on, Hogan. I don't have a clue what it is, but I think it might have something to do with Chase Carter. Sally may know something—I saw her this morning, and she was definitely spooked as soon as her son-in-law came around."

I hesitated, not sure how to frame my next words. Unlike Jack Juarez, Hogan was a skeptic when it came to my sensitivity to the world around me.

"Have you double checked yet on whether Megan's ex-husband is still in prison?" I asked. "Confirmed what Chase said last night?"

"The police were supposed to be on that, but I haven't heard back."

Something in the way he phrased it and the tension in his voice told me that wasn't the end of the story. "So you made the call yourself," I guessed.

"I'm not sure what's going on, but I'm having a hard time getting any answers," he said. "I think there may have been a mistake somewhere along the line and they're covering their tracks. But I'm not getting a clear answer one way or the other."

"I think you need to find him," I said. He met my eye, and read the intensity there. I expected dismissal. Instead, fear flickered in his eyes.

"You think he's the one behind this."

"I don't know. I just… I have a feeling—which I know you don't believe in. But I think you should follow up. And figure out what you're dealing with, if he is the one out there right now."

"Okay," he agreed gravely. "I'll do that."

He studied me for a moment, emotion sliding easily across his face. Had he always been this easy to read?

"Please don't get caught up in this, Jamie. I'll dig deeper to try and get some answers about Megan's ex, but don't get tangled up with Chase Carter. This is a powerful family, and the senator is already going through hell with his daughter missing. That hell is about to get a hundred times worse. Let us handle this."

I thought of the pleasure on Chase's face when he'd seen his mother-in-law's body. Recalled Sally's all-too-obvious fear when she'd spoken with me. I nodded, but this time I knew there was no way I could just let it go. Somehow or other, Chase had something to do with the WildFire shooter. If that shooter did indeed turn out to be Megan's ex-husband, we already knew the connection: the two were long-time best friends. Whatever it took, I planned to find out what Chase's role in this had been. And then, I would make sure he paid for the pain he'd inflicted.

15

MEGAN KNELT IN THE SNOW on all fours until her stomach was empty, retching like a dog. Almost nothing came up, regardless—all she'd eaten in the past twelve hours were nuts and protein bars, and those sparingly.

Recluse whined beside her, pawing at her shoulder with one massive foot.

"Just give me a second, buddy," she said wearily. Empty, exhausted, and still shaking, she crawled away from the scant pile of yellow vomit in the snow and collapsed.

Where were Ava and Violet? For that matter, where was *she?* She longed for her pack, with its compass and cell phone, first aid kit and emergency stash of Clif Bars and water.

"Where the hell are you, Hogan?" she muttered to the sky.

Unsurprisingly, there was no answer. Still, she knew he would be out here looking. Heather would be, too—the warden had said she was okay. Megan just hoped her sister left the searching to everyone else. It might prove to be too much for the baby.

"Take care of that kid, Heath," she said, still talking to the sky. "That's all that really matters."

Would Heather's husband be looking too, she wondered? Hell, he probably had his camera going this whole time, recording every damned minute of the search.

"God, this is getting bad," she said to Recluse. "I even miss my idiot brother-in-law."

She had her breath back, and her stomach was beginning to settle. What was the next step? Find Violet and Ava. So far she'd managed to avoid thinking about the fact that, against everything she thought was good and stable in the world, her ex-husband was out of prison. She wasn't thinking about the look in his eye when she'd finally been in his sights again. She definitely wasn't reliving that last night the two of them spent together, six years ago in a cabin in the Rockies. The night he imagined she'd looked twice at a busboy at the restaurant where they'd had dinner.

The night he broke her nose. Bruised two ribs. Held a knife to her throat, and raped her before she finally got away.

She swallowed hard. She was sweating. She closed her eyes, then opened them quickly when she thought she heard movement in the bushes.

She had to stay focused.

Where were Ava and Violet? It seemed in that moment when Justin killed the warden that everyone had scattered in different directions, but maybe the two women had stayed together.

Megan struggled to her feet, wincing at the pain in her side. She stood there a second, swaying slightly at a wave of lightheadedness, but it passed soon enough. She kept thinking, trying to figure out that mystical next move.

And then, she had it.

She would go back the way she'd come. Justin would never even imagine she'd have the guts to go back there. The warden had been on a snowmobile. It should still be there, abandoned. Waiting for her. All she had to do was get there.

She rallied herself once more, searching for a sign of her tracks in the snow. God, she was parched. She let a snowball melt in her hand, then drank what remained; actually eating the snow risked lowering her core body temperature when she definitely couldn't afford it.

The trail back was easy to find. Panicked as she'd been at that first sight of Justin's face, she'd hardly been in stealth mode. She lay her hand on Recluse's head for a boost of strength, and began retracing their steps.

16

AFTER WE HAD ANSWERED the police's questions and the plow truck driver—shaken, but rallying—had been taken to the hospital, Hogan gave me permission to report for duty a late given the circumstances. I returned to my original mission: dropping Bear and Ren at the WildFire base camp before Jack and I headed out on the search once more. I knew that it was only a matter of time before the police descended on Abe Wright to find out why Sally had paid him a visit moments before her accident. I had to admit, I was burning with curiosity about that myself.

All conversation inside the van had quieted as I navigated along a deeply rutted gravel drive to the WildFire camp. A six-foot fence ran along the driveway to my left, enclosing at least three acres. Dogs—hearty, thick-coated, but otherwise sharing very few obvious similarities with the stereotypical sled dog—barked a warning at our arrival, running along the fence line. They kept pace easily with the truck, their bodies lean, their coats wet with snow.

"It's like a wildlife park," Jack said. "Do you think any of them ever get inside?" I heard the note of disapproval, and squelched a smile. Jack was new to the dog world, but he'd become protective fast.

"These breeds are different from your average household pet," I said. "If you tried to keep them inside, especially in winter, they'd be miserable. Megan and Heather have a good setup for them, or at least they used to. I've never heard any complaints."

"It's actually pretty great here," Bear said, calling up from the back. "I came back to Flint K-9 last time with a lot of ideas on how to improve conditions for our own dogs, thanks to everything Megan and Heather do here."

Jack looked skeptical, but seemed to accept our view. To our right as we approached the house was a small parking lot with a pickup truck and a little Toyota covered in about an inch of ice and snow. I drove past and pulled up in front of a rough two-story structure with a tar-paper roof and solar panels. The dogs' barking reached a crescendo.

A rope course was strung above the house and part of the dog yard, while giant tire swings, wooden platforms, and dog houses were scattered throughout the fenced area. The whole place looked to be in slightly worse repair than I remembered it, but I wasn't sure whether that was reality, a trick of the season, or influenced by my own state of mind.

I parked the van, turned off the engine, and left Phantom while Jack and I got out with Bear and Ren, Bear keeping up a running dialogue on everything he remembered about the place.

"The first couple of trips I did here, we were camped out most of the time. When I did the canine wilderness first aid, though," he told her, "we stayed right here. They've got like barracks or something out back. Wait till you meet their dogs."

"You did tell Abe you were coming, right?" I said to Bear, though we'd been over this before.

"Of course," he said. "I'm not an idiot. I called and told him I'd help out in whatever way he needed with the dogs. He seemed kind of out of it, but he said he was grateful for the help."

The walkway leading up to the house was covered with a dusting of fresh snow, a sheen of ice beneath that. We skated our way to the door and I braced myself for whatever may come next. After the morning we'd had, I had no idea what to expect anymore.

Predictably, barking ensued as soon as I knocked. A lot of barking.

"They must not keep all of the dogs outside then," Ren said.

"Last time I was here, there were six who lived inside," Bear said. I had no doubt he knew all six of those dogs' names; he probably also knew the names of every dog in that enclosure.

"Just a second!" a woman's voice bellowed from within. She opened the door, nearly taking me out, and a Malamute the size of a pony barreled past.

"It's you," Shonda said, staring at me.

"I brought my son—he talked to Abe, and said he'd volunteer to help with the dogs." The explanation felt inadequate now that I was actually here, at the heart of the chaos.

Shonda gestured broadly out the door, toward the dog now running wild and the dozen or more others going berserk inside the fenced area.

"Sure. You like a lost cause, have at it. I'm going before it gets any colder and the whole world freezes over."

"Where are the others?" I asked.

"They left first thing this morning, the second they got the go-ahead. I stuck around a little longer, just in case the police needed me to say something more."

"What about Abe?" Jack said. "Where is he now?"

"At the hospital with Heather. Some lady showed up asking for him a couple of hours ago. I'll tell you what I told her: I don't know when he left, don't know when he'll be back, and don't know how Heather's doing. At this point, I'm in the dark."

"So he didn't talk to the woman?" I paused, just registering that the Malamute was headed for the fences, where several other dogs didn't look at all happy to see him coming.

"Is that Denmark?" Bear interrupted, following my line of thought. "He's not supposed to be out there, is he?"

"No," Shonda said grudgingly. "But he goes out all the time to torture the dogs in the yard. Damn it, Denmark. Come!" she bellowed toward the dog. Unsurprisingly, Denmark didn't look at all interested in obeying the command.

"Hang on," Bear said. He pulled half a dozen pieces of chicken liver and a slip lead from his jacket pocket. Truly his mother's son. "I'll get him."

Denmark was gorgeous and fluffy, a healthy burnished grey color dusted with snow. He was getting dangerously close to the fence, though he stayed just far enough out of reach to avoid trouble. That didn't matter, though—I've been around dogs enough to know that if they get amped up and can't reach the object of their frustration, they often turn on each other. A fight between a dozen dogs in a pit of snow and ice seemed fitting given the events of the rest of the day, but if we could avoid it, that would be my preference.

"Denmark," Bear called, keeping his voice light. "Come on over here, buddy."

The dog turned toward Bear, intrigued at his voice, and Bear held out a piece of the chicken liver. Though he was still at least twenty feet away, Denmark was clearly interested.

"You need a hand?" I asked, though I kept back.

"Just hang there," Bear said. "Give us a minute."

The other dogs were still barking, though the vitriol had lessened as Denmark moved farther away. "Good boy," Bear praised the dog, then crouched low and turned his body to the side, avoiding eye contact.

"Come on, buddy," he said once more. "Come, Denmark."

At last, Denmark made up his mind. He turned his back on the other dogs, head and tail held high, and trotted toward Bear.

For all his show of bravado with the other dogs, he was a perfect gentleman as he delicately the slip lead went over his head. Bear stood, roughing the top of the dog's head as he turned back toward the house.

By this time, another half dozen dogs of varying sizes and breeds—none of them under sixty pounds—had gathered at the threshold. They were all well behaved, though, offering only a perfunctory sniff before they went back to lie down once more. Shonda, meanwhile, stood with her suitcase in hand, clearly preparing to make a run for it. She set it down when Bear brought Denmark inside again, and closed the door behind him.

"I know you're trying to get out of here," I said to the

woman, "but I'm afraid the police will probably be out with some more questions soon. I'm surprised they're not here yet."

"And why is that, exactly?" Shonda asked.

Before I launched into that dire story, I held up my index finger to indicate I needed a minute and shifted focus to Bear and Ren. "Unless you wanted to hang out in here for this, you two can go out and start working with the dogs if you want." I looked at Shonda again. "Have they been fed?"

"Not that I know of," she said, with a shake of her head. "Abe was gone when we got up this morning, and it doesn't look like he did anything out there. Megan was always telling me to stay out of that pen—too much dog for me to handle, she says."

"Are you sure you're up for it in that case?" I asked Bear.

"Definitely," he said, without a second thought. "I was in there all the time at the last workshop. You just have to know how to approach them."

"Whatever you say," Shonda said doubtfully. "No way I'd risk it, though."

"Ren, maybe it would be best if you stayed out of the enclosure." I expected Bear to protest, but he and Ren both nodded their agreement.

"I'm sure I can find ways to help outside the pen," she said. "Maybe when Heather and Megan return, I'll have a chance to take one of the workshops myself."

"That would be awesome," Bear said. "They're running one this summer. We could do it together."

She smiled, with none of the regret I would have expected if she were really leaving with her father soon, as Bear had said.

Hmm.

The two teens headed back out into the snow. I was caught for a moment when Bear slipped his hand into Ren's, and the two continued on hand in hand.

"They're cute," Shonda said. "I don't even remember what it was like to be that young. Definitely not that in love."

I resisted the urge to protest. Bear and Ren in love? They were friends—good friends. And, yes, it had been clear for a while that there might be a little bit more to it than that. But not *love*. Right?

"Okay, spill," Shonda said, interrupting my reverie as I closed the front door once more. "Why the hell can't I leave? It's not like the roads are gonna get any better as the day goes on. There's a flight with my name on it going out of Logan this afternoon, before things get bad out. I plan to be on it."

I could understand being anxious to get out of here, but I planned to take full advantage of Shonda's presence before she left.

"You said a woman came here looking for Abe," Jack said, rather than answering her question. "Did you get a chance to talk to her?"

"She just asked if we were okay," Shonda said. "And then she said she wanted to talk to Abe. Seemed pretty anxious to have a word with him, but I couldn't tell her much except that he was at the hospital. I got the feeling she wanted to say something to us, maybe had some questions, but she took off in a hurry."

Jack and I exchanged a glance. "Any idea why?" I asked.

"She got a text," Shonda said. "Whatever it said, it shook her up. She took off out of the parking lot like she was trying out for NASCAR—not the smartest way to go on a road like this."

Shonda studied me, keen eyes taking in my reaction to her words.

"Did something happen to her? Is that why the cops want to talk to me again?"

"There was an accident," Jack said. "Down the road from here. She was going too fast for the conditions."

"Is she all right?" Shonda asked.

"We're not sure yet," I said. "They were still working on her when they took her to the hospital."

Shonda swore under her breath, shaking her head. "I knew she was going too fast."

"You don't have any idea what was in that text message?" I asked.

She didn't. I made a mental note to contact Hogan as soon as we were finished here to make sure the police knew to access Sally's phone and text messages. That alone could go a long way toward solving this puzzle.

"Listen, if the cops aren't here yet, I don't know when they're coming," Shonda said abruptly. "I haven't heard anybody saying I have to stay, and I want to get home to my kids before I get stuck here a minute longer."

"I understand," I agreed. Where the hell were the police? "They have your contact information. I'm sure I'd be doing the same thing in your place. Just please drive carefully—it was just flurries this morning, but even that can mean trouble if you're not paying attention."

She agreed with a grim nod. At the door just before she left, Shonda stood for a second, looking back at Jack and me. Her face was drawn, her eyes weary, but there was a determined set there that I appreciated.

"They've got a good thing going out here, you know," she said. "It all went to hell this time, no doubt, but Heather and Megan do good work. Once they find Megan, you tell her that for me, okay? Tell her I learned some things. I'm not going home empty handed."

"I'll let her know," I said quietly.

And with that, Shonda shifted gears one more time, waving off Jack's offer to help with her bags. She told us to lock up when we left, and I watched as she made her way carefully to the car. The temperature was stuck in the mid-twenties by now, and the snow had stopped. Even if she crawled down the mountain, Shonda should hit the airport well before her flight. Silently, I wished her safe travels.

●

The WildFire base camp was just two miles down the road from the Grafton Notch park entrance. By ten-thirty that morning, Bear and Ren were happily mucking out the enclosure while a dozen husky mixes danced around them. Shonda had gone and Abe was still nowhere in sight, but I had faith that the teens could handle themselves. Clearly, Jack and I weren't needed here.

When we arrived at Grafton Notch, SUVs and snowmobiles were already parked, searchers bundled up and the dogs raring to go. Michelle and Hogan met us outside the van as I unloaded Phantom, while Jack double checked our kit to make sure it was ready for the trail.

"Looks like you've got a full house," I observed.

"We could use a few more actually," Hogan said. "There are a couple of theories going around about the shooter, and Steiner isn't approving anyone else until we have some clue what we're dealing with."

"Which makes sense," Michelle said. "We all want to

find Megan and the others, but it doesn't help anyone if other people end up getting hurt out here. It just winds up taking resources away from the search."

"I know," Hogan agreed grudgingly. "Doesn't mean I have to be happy about it."

"We were just down at the WildFire base," I said. "Shonda, that woman who was interviewed last night, had to get going to make a flight in Boston. I was surprised the police didn't show up while we were there to talk to her."

"As far as I know, they're done with her for now. I guess they may have some follow-ups about the shooter, but it didn't seem like she was able to offer much in the way of information," Hogan said.

"Not about the shooter," I said. "About the accident with Sally Price."

Hogan frowned. "Why would they need to talk to her about the accident?" he asked. "I don't think Shonda or any of the WildFire crew would have much to say about that. Other than don't drive like a bat out of hell on a slick road when you're medicated."

"You know for sure she was on something?" I asked. I recalled my own impressions of her that morning, and found I wasn't surprised at the news.

"The son-in-law said he gave her something this morning. She was worked up, and he had a prescription he thought might do her some good. Not a great idea, but I've got bigger fish to fry than worrying about rich folks swapping prescription meds."

"But why would she have gotten behind the wheel?" I persisted. "She didn't seem like the type to take a risk like that. And why did she go to the WildFire base to begin with? Shonda said she got a text, freaked out, and left right afterward. Aren't you at least curious what was in that text?"

"I wrote that text," a voice said from behind me. I turned, and had to work to keep from frowning at sight of Chase Carter bearing down on us. "I don't know why she reacted the way she did, unless she just decided she needed to get out of there."

"What did you say?" I asked.

"Here, see for yourself," he said. The smug look on his face was enough to make me want to kick him. He handed me his phone, the text already pulled up. *Don't go far. I'm coming for you.* I stared at him.

"You wrote this?" Jack asked, stepping to my side to read the message as well.

"I did. I was just letting her know I'd come get her if she needed any help." He looked morose for a second, sighing dramatically. "I just wish she had stayed to wait for me."

"Have you heard anything from the hospital about her status?" I asked.

"She's made it so far, but she's unconscious," Chase said. "We just have to wait and see."

I looked at Hogan to see if he was buying what seemed to me a completely transparent act, but he was deep in discussion with Michelle. Jack, however, looked unimpressed.

"What are you doing here, anyway?" I asked, unable to keep the annoyance from my voice. "Shouldn't you be with your father-in-law right now?"

"He's been sedated," Chase said. "I'm not sure how much more of this he can take. I can't stand sitting still waiting for the phone to ring, so I figured I would volunteer."

This time, I didn't wait for Hogan to shift focus back to us, interrupting his conversation with Michelle. "I thought you weren't taking any more civilian volunteers," I said.

"He's a civilian, isn't he?"

"'He' is standing right here," Chase said coolly. "And I'm a certified Maine Guide with extensive knowledge of this area. I've already signed a waiver, I don't care if I'm putting myself at risk. I need to find my wife."

"We need all the qualified hands we can get," Hogan said. "Chase has worked with the warden service on a lot of searches in the past. We're lucky to have him out here."

Sure we were. Beside me, Phantom was starting to get restless, and personally I was starting to feel the same way.

"So, where do you want us?" I asked, rather than pursuing the conversation while Chase was still around.

"We're going further out today," Michelle said. "We were working with a radius of ten miles yesterday, but they could have gone farther by now. We've got sleds that'll take you out to the edge of the perimeter we finished last night, so you'll be working fresh ground today."

"Sounds good," I said.

"How are you pairing us up today?" Jack asked.

"We're doing teams of three this time out," Hogan said. "One dog-and-handler team, plus two from law enforcement."

"You really think that's necessary?"

"We're not taking any chances," Michelle said.

"Okay, so… How are we doing this?" I asked.

"I'll go with Jamie," Chase said, much to my surprise.

"He's not law enforcement," Jack pointed out.

"I might as well be, though," Chase argued, focused on Hogan. Hogan waved off the argument.

"No, he's right. Jack and I will go with Jamie. Chase, you're with Michelle."

I thought for a minute that Chase might actually argue, but after a second's thought he nodded.

"Sure," he said. "Wherever you need me."

When he and Michelle left, we were finally clear to get started. Snowmobiles were already lined up like cabs outside an airport, waiting for the next paying customer. I loaded Phantom into one of the trailers, hopped on behind an unidentifiable man in a snowsuit and helmet, and felt my adrenaline kick in once more. Jack climbed on behind me, his body warm and reassuringly solid cradling mine as we headed out.

And then stopped.

We were no more than fifty yards along before the snowmobile up ahead came to an abrupt halt. Hogan got off, radio at his ear. Our snowmobile slowed to a stop and idled while we waited to find out what was happening. Hogan was pacing, definitely unhappy, and I watched as he put the radio away and stalked toward us with his jaw set.

"We've got a warden who's MIA," he said. "Charlie Babcock was due for check-in at o-seven-hundred, but we never heard from him. We haven't been able to raise him since."

"Can you track his phone?" Jack asked.

"Not out here. We're doing what we can, but I don't like this. Charlie can be a pain in the ass, but he never misses check-in."

He'd barely gotten the words out before his radio crackled to life once more.

"Excuse me," he said to me, and walked away with shoulders tensed.

"What do you think's going on?" Jack asked behind me, his mouth at my ear to be heard over the roar of the snowmobile engine.

"No idea. It doesn't feel like a good thing, though."

"No."

At sight of Hogan's face when he returned a few minutes later, it was clear that we were right: this was definitely not a good thing. Before he could tell us anything, however, another snowmobile came rocketing back from up the trail. I recognized Chase and Michelle on the back. The snowmobile stopped close to ours and Michelle got off, stumbling in her scramble to reach us. Chase got off more slowly, but my focus was definitely on the K-9 handler.

"Something's wrong with Whippet," she called as she approached. "I need to get her to the vet. Her pulse is going crazy."

My own heart thundered at the words, knowing the implication.

"Go!" Hogan commanded. "We'll figure things out on my end, don't worry about it. Just take care of your dog."

She nodded numbly and ran back to the snowmobile as Chase ambled toward us. The look on his face made my skin crawl—a smugness that I couldn't imagine the others could possibly miss.

"Looks like I'm missing a partner," he said casually.

"There's a team farther up the trail who could use a third," Hogan said, clearly distracted. "I'll radio ahead and let them know."

Chase's face fell. "I thought I would just work with your group."

"We don't need a fourth, especially not when other teams are short. It's either that or head back and wait at the hotel with the senator."

"No," Chase said shortly. "That's fine. I'll go with them." He was clearly unhappy; Chase Carter was a man used to getting his own way.

"Great. Just wait here, and someone will be by to pick you up."

Before Chase could argue, Hogan gave our driver the signal and we were headed up the mountain once more. I looked behind us, but could see little beyond Jack's form behind me. I imagined Chase still there, sulking and seething, and was grateful that Hogan had stuck to his guns.

It took half an hour of steady riding before we reached our section of the grid. The day was clear and cold, the sky cloudless after the morning flurries. Once the sled came to a halt, we dismounted and I retrieved Phantom. I thought of Whippet, and wasted no time running Phantom through a quick check-up while we waited for Hogan to join us.

"What do you think is wrong with Michelle's dog?" Jack asked me.

"No idea. I hate thinking about it—it's every handler's nightmare." I had Phantom sit, and crouched beside her, then held out my right hand. Phantom dutifully offered her left paw. She sat back on her haunches, but her focus was keen on the world around us. I gave her leg a gentle stretch, supporting her elbow and monitoring for any foreign pops or creaks in the joints.

"It's a strange coincidence, the dog being fine up until the moment Chase joined the group," Jack said, too casually. I dropped Phantom's left foreleg and moved on to the right, weighing my words.

"Remember what I told you about the voice I've been hearing?" I asked. I glanced up to find Jack's attention on me. He nodded.

"'Baby girl'? It's too creepy to forget."

"I was talking to Chase this morning. He says Justin used to call Megan that."

Jack frowned. Phantom whined, and I realized I'd been holding her paw without doing anything for the past minute.

"Sorry, girl," I said. I stretched the foreleg gently, then set it down.

"Did you tell Hogan?" Jack asked.

"Not what I've been hearing, but I did tell him to follow up and figure out where Megan's ex-husband is."

"And?"

I shrugged, then straightened and gave a hand signal for Phantom to stand. "He's looking into it. Last I knew, he hadn't heard anything."

"I wonder if that's what that second radio call was about."

Hogan arrived as I was finishing up with Phantom, and strode across the frozen ground from his snowmobile with clear purpose.

"Megan?" I guessed, simply by the look on his face.

"You were right about her ex," Hogan confirmed. "There was apparently some kind of error at the prison. That's why I had such a hard time getting my information. They were too busy covering their own asses to contact Megan about the release."

"The release?" Jack echoed. "So he's out?"

"He was on some kind of work program. Just walked out of the damned facility three days ago. He had paperwork or something, I don't know. All I know is, heads will roll once this gets out. And if this is really the guy out there doing the shooting…"

"If?" I said. "Doesn't this kind of confirm that he's the one out there?"

"There's another guy: Frank Mooney. Husband of Ava Jones, the woman Violet had been working with in D.C.

We've been trying to get additional information from the FBI about him. It turns out he's a contract killer with a lot of connections. It could just as easily be him."

"Frank Mooney?" Jack said. "That's not good. I don't know anything about Megan's ex, but Frank Mooney is notorious in the Bureau. Given the choice, I'd take just about anyone else going up against those women right now."

"Either way," I said, as Phantom tugged impatiently at her lead and the sun climbed higher in the sky, "our job remains the same. We have to find them."

"Agreed," Hogan said. He looked at me, then out at the wide expanse around us. "Lead on."

17

RECLUSE BY HER SIDE, Megan made her way back through the forest as fast as her legs would carry her, intent on finding the dead warden's snowmobile. When she finally stopped, it was because she was so completely disoriented that she was afraid she'd circled back and would wind up right back where she'd started. She took a few minutes to catch her breath and settle her nerves, the events of the past twenty-four hours running through her head on a continuous loop. Where were Ava and Violet? Who was the warden Justin had shot? Hogan must know him; all those warden types knew each other, whether they worked in Maine, Alaska, or anywhere in between.

She continued moving through the woods with Recluse beside her through the morning and into early afternoon, mindful of every sound they made. If she could just get back to that damned snowmobile, they would be fine. She could save the others. The police would catch Justin, and put him away for life this time.

It was beautiful out, something she was grateful for. Sun high in a blue sky, the temperature hovering just around the freezing mark. A perfect day to be out on the sled with the dogs. She thought longingly of her workshop. Of being there with the smell of sawdust in her nose, heat from the woodstove taking off the chill while she worked.

She would get back there.

She kept going with her head up, eyes and ears alert for anything foreign. Recluse was just as on edge. Twice, he chased, caught, and killed squirrels that crossed their paths. Megan didn't like watching, but she didn't begrudge him the meal.

She looked up at the sky. It had to be at least noon. She should be back there by now. The trail she'd left when running away had gotten muddled by a thin layer of snow that fell after the fact. That and wind and melting meant a trail that should have been simple to follow had gotten garbled somehow.

Suddenly, she heard something in the distance. A dog barking. She stood still, straining to hear even as Recluse came to attention beside her. She couldn't be that far from the site of the killing. She froze at the sound of someone shouting.

"Megan! If you're within the sound of my voice, call out!"

A searcher.

How far were they?

If she could hear them, they could absolutely hear her.

She opened her mouth, heart pounding, an instant before Recluse whirled. Something in the air, a sudden weight in her chest, told her before he'd even spoken, exactly who was there.

"You left before we got a chance to talk," Justin said.

She could have cried.

Megan turned to find a rifle pointed at her, Justin smiling behind it. He had hazel eyes and dusty brown hair; a good-looking guy, according to most who met him. Witty. He and Chase had lived a charmed life, getting everything they wanted from the time they were kids. The ugliness Megan had experienced had wiped away any physical beauty she might have seen in the man, though. She fought bowel-clenching fear; a profound desire to melt into the earth.

"What happened?" She tried to steady herself, managing to sound almost normal. "You're not up for parole for another five years."

"Computer glitch," he said cheerfully, then shrugged. "Technology. What can you do?"

"What do you want?"

"That isn't obvious by now?" he asked. He kept the gun level with her breast. "I want you. Well... I want you to pay, specifically. You ruined my life. You really thought I would just forget about that?"

Throughout the exchange, Recluse had been standing stock still, held back by Megan's hand around his collar. If she let him go, she knew he would lunge.

And Justin would shoot.

"You have a leash for that thing?" he asked, nodding toward Recluse.

"Left it home. We don't really worry about leash laws out here."

"Funny."

Justin looked around, for the first time appearing to lose some of that eerie calm she'd first seen at the site of the warden's killing.

"What's wrong?" she asked. "Didn't quite think this all the way through?"

"Shut up."

She was right, though. He hadn't thought through the logistics. She could see his dilemma now. If he fired the gun, it would attract the attention of searchers so close now that Megan could hear them. If he made a move toward her, Recluse would take him down in a second. Justin had never been great with details, and it was about to bite him in the ass. If Recluse didn't get there first.

"Get on the ground," he said.

She straightened to her full five foot six inches. "No."

He took a step toward her. The fur stood tall at the back of Recluse's neck all the way to his tail, his growl reverberating in the stillness.

And then, Justin shifted the gun. He pointed it directly at Recluse, and took a step back.

"You think you have me, right, baby girl? You always thought you were so much smarter than me. Well, think about this:

"I get off one shot, and it hits that dog. Maybe I'm not the best shot, but chances are pretty good I'll make this one. I promise you this: that dog won't survive a point-blank bullet from this gun. Then, I go for you. And we run like hell, before the searchers ever figure out where we are."

He looked Megan in the eye, giving her a glimpse into the darkness she'd learned to loathe during their marriage.

"Tell me I won't do it," he challenged. "Baby girl, I got nothing to lose. You saw to that."

Megan knelt. He ordered her to put one hand on her head, holding Recluse back with the other. Trembling now, and hating herself for it, she complied.

She watched as Justin took his pack off his back and removed a length of rope from inside. He saw her eying his gear, and smiled.

"Nice, huh? Good old Chase. Never lets a brother down."

Megan was stopped by the information, for just a second. Why would Chase give him money for camping gear? Had he told Violet what he was doing?

Justin zipped the pack again and put it back on. He was shaking even more than she was, and Megan wondered if he was on something or this was just nerves.

He tossed her the rope. "Loop it around the dog's collar, and tie him to that tree." He indicated a sturdy maple not far from them. "Make sure it'll hold."

"I'm not just leaving him here."

"We either do that or we leave him dead. Your choice."

Silent, fuming, she did as he instructed. When she was through, Justin ordered her away from the dog. Her stomach felt like it was lined with razorblades. Furious, she choked back tears.

"Please don't hurt him." God, how she hated the weakness in her voice. It was a drug for Justin, though. He stood a moment, taking it in, as he watched Recluse lunge at him, trying to break free of the rope. Justin hefted his gun. He looked at Megan, then at the dog.

If he hurt her dog, she would kill him, she silently pledged. Any moral dilemma she may have had—and that was already questionable—would be gone.

He grinned at her suddenly. "It's good to see you again, Meg. I forgot how much fun we used to have."

He took a threatening step toward Recluse, the gun raised as a club now. Recluse held his ground, teeth bared.

Justin started to whip the gun down toward the furious animal, stopped abruptly, and laughed. He aimed the rifle once more at Megan.

"Just kidding. I'm not going to hurt the damn dog. What kind of monster do you think I am?"

A chill filled the air, settling deep in her bones. All humor gone, he looked at her once more. "Now, get away from him. Walk."

Impotent, seething, Megan did as she was told.

18

WE WORKED STEADILY for an hour, trekking through the undergrowth with Phantom constantly on the move up ahead. Jack, Hogan, and I were largely quiet during that time, but I could sense Hogan's growing frustration. Megan and the other women had now been missing for over twenty-four hours. Every hour that passed without us finding them made it less likely our search would be successful.

The one thing we had on our side today was the weather. It was beautiful out, and—apart from the reason why we were here—I couldn't think of a place I would rather be.

Since setting out that morning, I had yet to hear Brock's voice. Did that mean we were moving farther from the shooter? I didn't think so. The first time I'd heard him, we had been just out behind the hotel. Would the shooter have been out there talking to Megan? I sincerely doubted it. Which meant it must be something else that was triggering these bizarre echoes. I just wished I could figure out what it was.

At twelve thirty that afternoon, just as we were finishing up with a good-sized swath of search area, Hogan got another call.

"Keep going," he told Jack and me. "I'll catch up."

Jack and I walked behind Phantom in silence for a couple of minutes. I loved watching Phantom work. She was a natural athlete, every move fluid and graceful. The shepherd continued along the snowy terrain, her focus entirely on the search. Behind us, I could hear Hogan on the radio. He didn't sound happy, though I could make out no words.

When he came back, I braced myself for bad news.

"What's going on?" I asked.

"More stonewalling from the Feds," he said. "We're still not getting a clear answer on whether they know where Frank Mooney is. He's supposed to be under surveillance, but no one will tell me if that's actually true and, if so, where he is now."

"If you don't find anything out soon, I can call some of my contacts there," Jack offered. "I made some enemies before I left, but I still have a few people I can check in with."

"That would be good," Hogan agreed. "Thank you. I'll take whatever we can get at this point."

"So no word about Whippet?" I asked.

"It looks like she'll be fine. They think she ate something, but it'll be a while before toxicology comes back. In the meantime, Michelle was on it fast enough to get her the help she needed. They won't be back in the field today, though."

•

The afternoon wore on. Shortly before one, we reached a narrow trail of snow and ice that skirted along a frozen waterfall, one of many in this park. Hogan had been called away a couple of times as he tried to help marshal the warden service's dwindling forces. Jack had taken a quick break to answer nature's call, which meant I was on my own. Phantom moved closer to the edge of the waterfall, peering down below. I went to her, following her gaze with my own.

Water frozen mid-stream hung like crystals, some of them as much as a foot thick, while down below portions of the fast-moving creek still flowed. It wasn't a huge drop, only about twenty feet, but it was high enough to be deadly if one of us fell. I ordered her back, keeping my distance as well.

"It's pretty stunning, isn't it?" someone asked behind me. I started. When I turned, Chase stood watching me.

"What are you doing here? I thought you were working with another team."

"Got separated," he said with a shrug. "I'm lucky I found you. I could have been wandering out here for hours." The response sounded rehearsed. He didn't even try to inject some realism into his tone, and I realized that right now, for whatever reason, he wanted me to know who he was. Beyond the façade he'd built for years now, he wanted me to see the darkness he hid from the rest of the world.

"What's she looking at?" Chase asked, nodding toward Phantom.

My focus shifted below once more, trying to see whatever it was that Phantom had spotted. The dog seemed to decide that, whatever it was, it wasn't worth her attention. She moved and left me standing there.

"Check out that spot there," Chase said, pointing to a

narrow overhang of rock that looked out over the whole scene. "Come on—I bet we'd get a great view from there."

"That's all right. I can see just fine from here."

"Afraid of heights?"

"No," I said evenly. I held his gaze, willing myself not to look away. "I'm not afraid of much, actually."

"Really? Hmm." He paused, seeming to consider my words. "That sounds like a challenge to me."

I couldn't hide my surprise—shock, even—at his words. Had he really just said that out loud? He studied me, appearing to enjoy the reaction.

"Didn't Sally tell you I like games during your chat?"

I wet my lips. Phantom had moved on ahead, and Jack still wasn't in sight. Suddenly, a shiver of fear inched under my skin. "I told you: Sally didn't tell me much of anything this morning. It was an innocent, unexpected meeting. We parted ways, and I never saw her again."

"Did she tell you that she doesn't like me? That she tried to convince Violet not to marry me?"

"No," I said. His eyes darkened.

"Why are you lying to me?"

He stepped closer. I held my ground. He was tall, over six feet, broad and muscular. A man who took his time at the gym seriously.

"I'm not lying. Step back, please," I said. I kept my tone even, but my anger was rising.

"Or what?" he said quietly.

"Or I'll make you take a step back," I said.

A grin touched his lips, and a spark of something—arousal?—sparked in his eyes. I fought the urge to wipe the look off his face.

"I'd like to see that," he said.

Before I could respond, or push him back, or throw him over the side of the damned waterfall myself, Phantom's barking pulled us back out of the moment.

Rather than her usual double bark to alert me to a find, she let loose with several throaty woofs and low growls that raised the hairs at the back of my neck. This wasn't an alert; it was a confrontation.

"Phantom!" I shouted.

More snarling followed, along with growls that I knew didn't belong to my dog. A fresh rush of adrenaline had me pushing past Chase to get to my dog. On the way, I caught a quick glimpse of his face again, and almost stopped at the cruelty there; the cool cast of his eyes, and the venomous smile.

I felt his hand at my back before I could react—a quick brush, barely making contact at all, but he caught me at just the right angle. My foot hit the patch of ice beneath me, and lost purchase.

19

IF I WERE A FOOT HIGHER UP on solid ground, it would have been fine.

But I wasn't.

I landed hard on my tailbone at the very edge of the falls, slid an inch or two farther, and grabbed for a hold to catch myself before I fell straight down. I caught nothing but empty air. I screamed, as much out of surprise as fear, and managed to catch hold of an icicle that made up part of the falls long enough for it to slow my descent—only to have it break an instant later. Meanwhile, my handheld GPS—my link to Phantom—plummeted to the water below.

"Jamie!" Jack shouted.

An instant later he was there, his hands wrapped around my wrists as he fought to pull me back up.

"Help me, damn it!" he shouted to Chase.

I could feel his gloves starting to slip off. On top of that, I could still hear the snarls and yaps of Phantom and another, as-yet-unidentified animal. Jack shouted at Chase one more time, this time with a violence I'd never heard from him before.

Finally, mercifully, Chase lay down on his stomach beside Jack and grabbed hold of my arms. Together, they pulled me back to solid ground.

I lay on the ground beside Jack, Chase on his feet and safely away from us. Jack stood, and helped pull me to my feet.

"You hurt yourself," he said. He brushed at my cheek, coming away with blood.

"I'm okay," I said. "Phantom…" I didn't bother finishing the sentence before I turned my back on them both and took off, running for my dog. The sounds that had been coming from the brush had stilled, the silence painful.

"Phantom!" I called. Without the GPS now at the bottom of the waterfall, I had no way to find the dog unless she led me to her. "Sound off, girl."

It was a command I'd taught her early on for exactly this reason. If we were ever separated and an electronic tracker failed, I wanted some way for her to reach me.

An endless few seconds passed before I heard the dog's answering bark. My stomach was tied in knots, my body shaking, but I kept going.

Within another five minutes, I found her. Phantom sat holding one paw in the air, her head down. As I got closer, I could see blood on her neck and torso. My attention was momentarily diverted, however, by the dog's find.

A body.

Lying on its back in a snowmobile suit, face unrecognizable after what looked like a gunshot followed by the first stages of animal predation. A Maine State Warden Service snowmobile was stopped on the trail just a few feet away.

I went straight to Phantom, careful to avoid the body she'd found. Pink-tinged snow and scuff marks marred the area, signs of the struggle she had just survived.

"Hey, girl," I said, my voice choked with emotion. "Good find."

She leaned away from me as I touched the wound at her neck. There were puncture marks, but no tearing. Her foot, likewise, didn't look badly damaged. I did a more extensive exam, but saw no evidence of further injuries. That meant the biggest dangers were infection and shock. Whatever else might be happening around us, I needed to get her to a vet stat.

Jack and Chase came down the path after me a minute or two later, and stopped short at the scene they found.

"Oh my God," Chase said, and I hated that trace of theater in his voice at sight of the body. "Who is that?"

"I don't know," I said shortly. I ignored him and my own rage, and focused on Jack. "Phantom must have caught the scent and startled an animal who thought they'd found a free meal—fisher or maybe a mama coyote, based on how hard they fought. Anything else just would have run away."

"Is she okay?" Jack asked.

I shook my head. "I'm not sure. I have to get her looked at."

"She looks fine to me," Chase said. "A little bloody, but not too bad. I guess she's a scrapper, huh?"

The words were all it took for my rage to finally boil over. I stalked over and pushed him full in the chest when I reached him, catching him off balance enough that he had to take a step back to keep from falling.

"What the hell is wrong with you? Huh? You almost killed me back there."

"I'm sorry," he said. "I lost my footing and bumped into you—I didn't do it on purpose. When I saw what was happening, I froze."

"You didn't lose your footing. You pushed me." I stayed in his face, something so patently not my style that I felt like I'd somehow left my body. "Don't lie to me. I know what you did."

Jack pulled me away, but I was grateful that he said nothing to defend Chase's actions. "Take it easy," he said. It was good that he didn't try to touch me just then—I thought for sure I would spontaneously combust if he did.

"Keep him away from me," I spit out.

"I will," Jack promised, an edge of anger seeping into his own words.

After a few seconds, I came back to myself enough to make the call to IC Steiner that we needed assistance. I used the code for officer down rather than saying the words aloud, uncertain whether the press might be monitoring the channel. Of course, chances were good that they knew the code as well as I did, but it was the best I could come up with on the fly.

Hogan and half a dozen other wardens, along with police and paramedics, showed up within twenty endless minutes. Hogan took one look at the body and paled before he turned away.

"Can you tell who it is?" I asked.

"Charlie Babcock," he said, and I thought immediately of the young man who'd been rooming with us at the house. "The kid was just getting started."

He shifted gears, taking in the blood on Phantom's fur and my own disheveled state, then Chase's presence among us. "What else is going on out here? What the hell are you doing here, Chase?"

"I got separated from my team," he said. "Jamie was nice enough to invite me to join you guys."

I ignored him, focused instead on my dog. "Phantom got into it with someone who thought he'd found a free lunch. She chased him off, but not without a fight."

Hogan took in my state with some concern, and I realized I'd never wiped away the blood on my face or pulled myself back together in my concern for the dog.

"And what about you?" he asked, his tone softening. "Did you get in the middle of the fight too?"

"No," I began. My anger returned as I cast a glance toward Chase, who stood just off to the side of us now. "We were over by one of the waterfalls, and he pushed me—"

"I think Jamie's got things a little bit off, thanks to all the drama," Chase said, stepping in. "I've already apologized—I inadvertently bumped into her beside the waterfall, and she slipped and fell—"

"—and if Jack hadn't come when he did, you would have let me drop all the way to the bottom of the falls," I said. "That's not me being hysterical. That's fact."

"Hogan," Chase said smoothly, a shadow falling across his face, "I swear to you, I never meant for any of that to happen. I guess maybe I'm a little more shaken by all that's happened than I realized. I froze."

"You were there," Hogan said to Jack. "Did you see what happened?"

Jack reluctantly shook his head. "I was farther back on the path—I'm sorry. I got there just as Jamie fell."

Hogan shifted back to me only briefly before he looked at Chase once more, forehead furrowed and anger barely contained. "If you're that shook up, you're no help to us out here," he said. "We'll take you back to the hotel, and you can stay with the senator while we continue searching."

"But—" Chase protested, but Hogan cut him off.

"No arguments," he said. "We've got enough problems without having to worry that one of our own will freeze at a critical moment."

I expected more of an argument, but this time Chase merely nodded. "You're probably right, Jamie," he said, tears standing in his eyes. "I really am so sorry for what happened. Please know, I would never purposely hurt you. Or anyone."

I held his gaze, not taken in for a second. My stomach turned when a familiar voice whispered on the wind.

Looks like you've got two devils on you now, sweetheart.

I fought to remain impassive, but I thought I saw something in Chase's eyes—some recognition of, and delight in, my fear. He may not have any idea what I was hearing or experiencing, but there was no doubt in my mind that Chase Carter was a man who fed off the fear of women. God knew, I'd dealt with the type before.

"Why don't you catch a ride back to the hotel with those guys heading out now," Hogan said to him. "They'll drop you there." He nodded toward a trio of wardens walking toward the trail back down the mountain. "You'll need to run to catch up."

Stubbornly, jaw set now, Hogan waited for Chase to argue. This time, he didn't. Once he'd gone, I returned my attention to the most pressing issue right now.

"I need to get Phantom to a vet," I said.

"I'll give you a lift," Hogan said.

"I can carry her back if you need me to," Jack said, to my surprise. He was crouched beside the dog, his eyes dark with concern. I couldn't help but smile.

"You're going to carry my seventy-pound dog back to the truck?"

His cheeks flamed, but he shrugged as he continued petting the dog. "If she needs me to, then yeah."

"I called in a trailer to come with one of the snowmobiles," Hogan said. "I don't think you need to carry anyone." Jack looked at me as if to confirm, and I nodded.

"She'll be fine in the trailer."

He looked relieved, but only marginally. I got the sense that, like me, he wouldn't believe that until we actually got word from the veterinarian.

"Lieutenant Hogan," a police officer called, striding toward our group.

"Just give me one minute," Hogan said. "Go on over and get her set in the trailer. I'll be right there." He nodded toward a snowmobile and trailer just coming up the trail.

"You okay to walk, girl?" I asked Phantom, but evidently Jack wasn't willing to risk it.

Rather than waiting, he gently picked up the dog and stood for a second, Phantom curled in his arms as though she were a puppy. Men of the world, if you want to make an impression on a woman? Forget playing knight in shining armor to her—try doing it for her dog. Panties will drop.

I walked alongside talking to Phantom the whole while, then explained to the driver of the snowmobile what was happening and loaded Phantom inside the trailer. There wasn't a lot of room back there, but I didn't care; without consulting the driver, I climbed into the trailer with my dog and settled in with her head in my lap. I knew it would be a bumpy ride.

It took half an hour to get back to the Grafton Notch park entrance. During that time, Phantom was clearly uncomfortable, and I worried that her injuries were more extensive than they appeared. Once we reached the entrance,

Jack carried her to Hogan's SUV and I climbed into the backseat with her beside me, while Hogan and Jack got in front.

Phantom lifted her head to look out the window as Hogan started the engine. I'd checked her wounds repeatedly, trying to figure out why she was acting so squirrely. She'd been in a couple of fights when I'd first gotten her, but none in years. Was she just traumatized by the incident itself, or was there something more going on that I wasn't seeing?

"I wish you could speak, girl," I said. She thumped her tail against the seat at the sound of my voice, and lay her head back down on my lap. This promised to be one of the longer car rides of my life.

In front, Hogan got the SUV on the road and pointed down the mountain. He kept his gaze fixed on the road as he drove, his speed down as we navigated along the stretch down the mountain where Sally Price had already lost control earlier today. I glanced at Phantom, eyes closed and now apparently resting comfortably. Her breathing was no longer labored, her body completely relaxed.

"How's she doing?" Jack asked, looking back over his shoulder at us.

"Better, I think. She's tough. I think she'll be okay."

I stroked her head, thinking of those early days with the dog, back when she didn't trust a soul—including me. What a gift it was that she'd taken that leap and allowed me into her heart. I knew she was getting older, and retirement would come all too soon. I just prayed I had at least a couple more years with the shepherd at my side, trekking through the woods as a team more unified than any human partnership I'd known.

"Right, girl?" I said quietly. I leaned down and kissed the top of her head. "You'll be okay."

20

WildFire Expeditions
February 5, 1:00 p.m.

AS SOON AS JUSTIN HAD HER away from the dog, he produced a zip tie and wrapped it across her wrists, pulling her hands tight behind her back. He lingered behind her, one hand stroking her arm while she cringed. Try as she might to steel herself, she couldn't help but flinch when she felt a whisper of fabric around her throat. This was how he would kill her. She'd always known this would be the way. He'd always said that, at the end, he wanted to look her in the eye while he squeezed the life from her.

She tensed as the fabric tightened around her neck. His body was pressed to her, his front to her back, and she could feel him breathing in her ear. Excitement mounting. She tried not to struggle, knowing that would only spur him on, but couldn't help it when spots started to float in front of her eyes. Her lungs would burst. She flailed, furious when she heard his low laughter.

And then, mercifully, seconds before she would have blacked out, the fabric slipped away.

"Not so fast, baby girl. Don't worry. I've got bigger plans than that for you."

He slid the fabric up her neck, past her chin. Whispered in her ear. "Open your mouth."

She refused.

He wrenched her arm until the pain was almost unbearable, but she kept her mouth closed. Furious, Justin spun her around so she was facing him. He cupped her jaw with one hand.

"When I tell you to do something, you do it," he bit out. A response would have required opening her mouth, and she wouldn't give him that satisfaction. She kept her own jaw clenched, her body rigid, while he fought to get the gag around her mouth.

She didn't see the punch coming until it was too late—a single blow to the stomach that had her gasping for breath like a land-locked trout. Justin laughed as he fastened the silk scarf around her mouth, while she was still trying to get her breath back.

She might be humiliated, but she refused to let him see her cry. Hands behind her back, gag over her mouth, she moved forward with her shoulders squared and her head up. No matter how much it hurt.

21

WHEN WE ARRIVED at the hotel, Hogan pulled into a space beside an old Jeep 4x4. The driver's side door of the Jeep opened immediately, and a plump older woman in a wool coat, leggings, and snow boots met me at my door.

"I'm Dr. Wallace—Michelle said you were on your way," she said. "Come on into the hotel. They let me set up a space in the main office while the search is ongoing."

"Do you need me to carry her in?" Jack asked me, at my side once more. I couldn't help but smile.

"Thanks, but no—I think she's all right to walk, Jack."

"Are you sure? Maybe she broke something."

"She looks just fine to me," the vet said. "I'll let you know if I change my mind."

Jack looked skeptical, but stepped aside nevertheless.

"I need to get going," Hogan said. "I want to check in with Steiner, figure out what our next move is considering the latest find."

"When do you want to meet up so we can head back

out?" I asked. I knew as soon as I saw the look on his face what his answer would be. "Hogan—you need us out there. Now more than ever, you need as many searchers as you can get."

He shook his head, hand up to stop my argument. "Just let me talk to Steiner first, all right? We'll figure it out from there. I'll give you a call when we're through."

I agreed, anxious to get inside to look after Phantom. When he was gone, Jack and I went in with Phantom and Dr. Wallace, and followed the vet to the office they'd designated as her exam room. Phantom was still walking with a limp by this time, but she was up and alert.

Over the course of the next twenty minutes, Dr. Wallace conducted a more thorough exam than I'd seen some vets do in state-of-the-art facilities, attentive to every detail of my shepherd. Phantom sat patiently, shaking slightly and with downcast eyes, as the veterinarian gently shaved the fur away from the bite wounds at her neck and hock.

"What do you think attacked her?" Jack asked. He hovered at the edge of the room watching the vet's every move.

"Most likely a coyote—it's been a cold winter, and there are a few up in the park who've been getting too close to people's camps for comfort. If they found an easy meal, one of them might not have taken kindly to being interrupted. Though based on how superficial these bite wounds are, I'd say she wasn't much of a fighter."

"Or Phantom's a serious contender," Jack said, pride in his voice.

"Or that," Dr. Wallace agreed, with a bit of a smile as she stroked the dog's head. "We can take her in for ex-rays if you want. I think what you saw after the fact and the shaking she's doing now is a result of the adrenaline that rushed her system. Nothing too serious, based on what I'm seeing. She may have sprained her foot, but there's no break there. She'll need to take a round of antibiotics to fight infection from the bites, but overall everything is superficial."

"I'm assuming she's out of commission for the rest of the search, though," I said.

The vet nodded, adjusting her glasses as she did so. "Absolutely, I'm sorry. I'd do just about anything to help find Megan, but I can't in good conscience approve this dog for the field."

"I understand," I agreed. Hogan wouldn't be happy to hear this, though I knew he'd already suspected as much. "Did you examine Whippet earlier?" I asked, thinking of the sudden illness that had eliminated Michelle's dog from the search.

"I did," Dr. Wallace confirmed. "I think she'll be all right, but it's lucky they got to me as fast as they did. She was in rough shape."

"Any idea what happened to her?"

"Chocolate," the vet said, with a frown. "You'd think with this group people would know better than to allow something like that near a dog, but we think she got hold of a block of it somehow."

I glanced at Jack, who looked equally disturbed. Immediately, Chase Carter's face flashed in my mind. "I'm not the most knowledgeable when it comes to dogs," Jack said, "but you gave me that lecture on day one."

"What's the prognosis?" I asked.

"We caught it before there were any real symptoms, and induced vomiting as soon as he got here. If Michelle hadn't been paying attention to her dog's behavior or spotted that candy bar wrapper, the theobromine could have killed her while she was still out in the field. As it is, though, she'll be fine tomorrow. She's definitely out of commission tonight, though."

There was a knock on the door, and Phantom woofed lightly.

"Come on in," Dr. Wallace said.

Hogan poked his head inside. The storm cloud on his face suggested that, impossibly, things had gotten worse in the time we'd been apart.

"Is she going to be all right?" he asked me, nodding toward Phantom.

"She will, but she's off the search. She's old enough that something like this needs to be taken seriously."

"Of course," Hogan said. "I figured that was probably the case." He hesitated, looking thoroughly defeated. "I guess that means your team can head out whenever you want. If you want to hang out tonight and see if you can help out a little more at the WildFire base, that's fine. I've arranged for us to foot the bill for the lodge for one more night."

I shook my head. "I'll work with Bear's dog again. You saw how good he was in the field yesterday."

"The pit bull?" he asked. He frowned, though I thought I saw a faint spark of hope in his eyes.

"He's a good search dog," I insisted.

Hogan hesitated. "I know he is, but we still have to clear it with Steiner. I'm not sure he'll go for sending you back out."

"I'll talk to him," I said. "At this point, it seems like you guys need everyone you can get."

He nodded grimly. "You're not wrong."

I left Phantom with Jack and Dr. Wallace for the moment, and Hogan and I made the trek across the snowy parking lot to the SAR mobile unit. The unit was filled to the gills when I arrived, between detectives, wardens, and leaders of the civilian teams now being pulled out of the field. Hogan pulled Steiner aside, and the three of us met in the cordoned-off area at the far end of the unit where Shonda had been questioned the night before.

"Our searchers are dropping like flies," Steiner said, staring out a tiny window that looked out on the parking lot. In any search I'd ever worked on with him before, he'd always given the impression of being almost impossibly together: pressed uniform, freshly shaven, rigid posture. Two days into this search, it was clear from his wrinkled uniform and the five o'clock shadow on his weathered face that the pressure was getting to him.

"I'm pulling all civilians out," he continued. "The weather's good right now, but it'll be bad tonight. Ice and freezing rain mean we won't have a chance in hell of raising anyone by radio once everything ices over. Babcock is dead. Michelle's dog is out. Your dog is out. I can't risk civilian lives—"

"I'm not leaving until we've exhausted every possibility," I said stubbornly. That familiar voice was driving me now. Haunting me. No way in hell could I imagine going home now, with four women still missing and a demon tracking them out there. "You know you need me."

He grimaced, still staring out the window. It was after four p.m. by now, the sky darkening rapidly despite the fact that the sun wouldn't officially set for another hour.

"What do you think, Hogan?" he asked, without turning to look at the other warden. Hogan frowned.

"You know I can do this," I said to him, when he didn't answer Steiner's question.

"But *should* you?" he said. "That's the bigger issue. You could run the search backwards, whatever dog you choose—I know that. But how safe is it with this guy out there, and am I throwing you in the crosshairs because I can't see straight ever since I found out Hunter was missing?"

Steiner turned during our exchange, and I was struck by the compassion on his face. Whatever was between Hogan and "Hunter," he was aware of it—and of the toll it was taking on one of his lead wardens. I'd never seen Hogan more torn, and I couldn't help but wonder if he'd acted the same way about me in those final weeks before everything came to a head with Brock. Somehow, I didn't think so. I had no doubt that Hogan was fond of me; maybe he'd even had romantic feelings for me at one time. But it paled in comparison to whatever was going on between him and Megan Hunter.

"Why don't you let me worry about that, okay?" I said, as gently as possible. "When I first got here, you told me you needed me to be smart about this, didn't you? I say this is my call. I want to be out there."

He nodded wearily, scrubbing a hand through his hair. "Yeah—okay." He shifted focus back to Steiner, who looked satisfied with the conclusion, if not exactly enthusiastic.

"Take a couple of hours to get yourself and the dog situated," Steiner said. "I assume Juarez will still be going out with you?"

"That would be my preference," I agreed.

"Good," Steiner said. "I spoke to a couple of friends in the Bureau today—they had good things to say about him. I think it serves us well if we can keep using him out

220 · JEN BLOOD

there." He looked at Hogan. "Hogan, you'll go with them. The three of you pick up where Charlie was found. I already have teams out there. Just check in with Michelle to get your exact coordinates. She and Whippet are out of the field tonight, but she'll still be coordinating the K-9 teams we have left."

Eager to get everything settled so I could get out in the field and searching once more, I agreed.

•

I thanked Dr. Wallace for her help when I returned to the hotel, and Jack and I got Phantom back to the lodge a few minutes later with a handful of painkillers and a round of antibiotics. Michelle was settled by the fire with Whippet on the couch beside her when we arrived, the Dutch shepherd's head resting in her lap. Whippet looked up when we came in, but barely stirred beyond that as I tried to get Casper and Minion back in hand. Jack brought Phantom in afterward, insisting on carrying her up the front steps. When he set her down, Phantom came through the door slowly, bandaged and shaved and shaken.

Casper raced up to her as soon as she crossed the threshold, but thankfully all it took from Phantom was a single growl, lips curled back, before the pit bull slunk off once more.

"I heard what happened," Michelle said. I noticed as I got closer that her eyes were puffy, and the realization struck that Charlie Babcock had been her friend and colleague. The combination of Whippet's trials and the loss of the fellow warden had to be taking a toll. "Is Phantom okay?"

"She's a little stiff, but the vet says she'll be fine. What happened with Whippet? Dr. Wallace said she got hold of some chocolate?"

"Yeah," Michelle said, clearly still angry. "Apparently, one of the cops dropped it. It sure as hell never would have come from anyone on our team."

"Who told you it was one of the police officers?" Jack asked.

"It was actually the detective who dropped it—he 'fessed up as soon as he heard what happened. I don't remember his name. He said he was sure he'd left it in his car, but he guessed he'd put it in his pocket at some point and forgot about it."

Which ruled out Chase Carter for this particular calamity, at least in theory. Unless…

"Do you know who Chase rode up with before we started the search today?" I asked.

Michelle shrugged. "Chase? No idea. He just kind of showed up—I sure as hell never invited him."

"You don't like him, I take it?" Jack asked.

She made a face. "He's too pretty for my taste, and way too smooth. He might as well have 'Made in DC' stamped on his forehead."

I would have pursued the conversation further, but Bear and Ren were still at the WildFire base, and I was eager to get them home again before time ran out and I needed to meet Hogan for the next leg of the search.

"So, are you going out again?" Michelle asked. "Whippet's feeling a little better. I was thinking I'd leave her here and join the ground search. Without Charlie, I'm sure they can use somebody else."

Rather than breaking down, her voice hardened on Charlie's name—a reaction that almost made me smile. Women like Michelle Wassel didn't fall apart in moments like these; they came together. Focused. Fought. And, ultimately, they got the job done.

"Jack and I are going back out at eighteen hundred," I said. "I'll take Casper. It seems like he could use the exercise."

Michelle smiled. "You think?" she asked dryly.

At the moment, the pit bull in question had a tea towel he'd stolen from the kitchen, and was trying to tempt Minion into a game of tug o' war. Unfortunately for him, it looked like Minion wasn't interested. He tried one more play bow, dropping the towel in front of her as he bowed. Minion turned her head, refusing to engage. Gamely, he pushed the object across the floor with his nose. Still no response from Minion. He woofed. She got up and walked away.

It turned out that was too much for the boy. He let out another sharp woof, play bowed, skidded forward on his elbows, grabbed the towel himself, and tossed it into the air. Caught it. Glanced at Minion.

She yawned.

I took a step toward the pit bull. That was all it took for him to decide the chase was on—another of his favorite games. With the tea towel clamped tight in his jaws, he bounded away from me. He raced around the room and up the stairs. I could hear him galloping down the hallway, feet pounding on the hardwood floor.

Both Jack and Michelle laughed out loud. Casper peered around the corner of the stairwell, then took two tentative steps to see why I wasn't playing along. All I had to do was take a single, quick step in his direction and he was off again, grinning like mad, towel still between his teeth.

"How long does it take before he figures out you're not really playing along?" Michelle asked.

"He figures it out eventually," I said. "It makes it easy to wear him out, though."

Casper appeared on the stairs again, tail whipping like mad, set the tea towel down, and play bowed at the top of the stairs. *Come get me! You know you want to!*

This time, Jack was the one who took the step toward him. Someone new was playing along? Casper went completely berserk at the notion. He grabbed the towel, raced halfway down the stairs, went back up, and disappeared down the hallway, groaning and growling the whole way.

Minion, meanwhile, was starting to get the itch to join in herself. On Casper's third time down the stairs, she raced up after him—something I was very happy to see. At five years old, the yellow lab/pit bull mix had been raised by Ren from the time she was four weeks old. As a result of that early relationship, Minion was almost unhealthily bonded to her handler. Being apart from Ren for even a few hours was not a common experience for the sensitive little mutt, so I was glad to see her able to set her anxiety aside for a brief play session.

"I'll take them with me to pick up Bear and Ren," I told Michelle, as we listened to the dogs galloping up and down the upstairs hall. "Minion's been cooped up with this lunatic all day—I'm sure she could use a break."

"Couldn't we all," Michelle said.

"You mind if I hang back?" Jack asked. "I'd like to take a shower, maybe freshen up a little before we head out again tonight. I wanted to follow up for Hogan, too, make a couple of calls to see if I can learn anything new about the Mooney investigation."

I assured him that would be fine, then got Phantom settled in my room and harnessed a panting Casper and Minion before setting out on my own.

It was getting colder as the day transitioned to evening,

but the sky was still clear at this point. Precipitation was predicted to start sometime after seven o'clock, most likely in the form of a mix of rain and snow. It was dinner time by now, the hotel next door swamped with guests and searchers looking for food. I avoided them all, including the bevy of reporters skulking just outside the action, and took the dogs straight to the van.

Happily, the trip to WildFire Expeditions was uneventful this time. When I got there, I noted that the Wright's truck was back in the driveway, while the little Toyota that had been there before was gone. The WildFire dogs greeted us with the customary barks and howls, something Casper and Minion didn't take nearly as well as Phantom had.

I was met with the same chaos I'd experienced earlier when I knocked on the front door. To my surprise, Heather Wright was the one who greeted me. She was pale and drawn, propped up on crutches, but she still looked marginally better than she had when I'd seen her last.

"I assume you're here to pick up your tribe," she said. "Unless you're okay with us adopting them, of course."

"We still have use for them around Flint K-9, unfortunately," I said. "But I'll let you know if that changes."

Denmark—the giant Malamute I'd met earlier—had stationed himself at Heather's side, and didn't look like he would be moving anytime soon.

"How are you doing?" I asked Heather. "I didn't think you'd be out of the hospital so soon."

She shrugged. A pained smile belied the fatigue in her eyes. "I didn't want to stay away knowing Meg's still out there somewhere."

"I understand."

"Have you heard anything more?"

I wasn't sure how much the police were saying about the presence of Megan's ex-husband, so shook my head. "Nothing much," I said. "Have you talked to Hogan about it?"

"He's been so busy. I know he's making himself sick worrying about Meg out there. If I can't be searching myself right now, I'm glad he's the one leading the charge." She frowned. "I just wish we knew who the hell was doing this."

Ah. So that answered the question of whether she'd been told about Justin. Apparently, the police were keeping that detail close to the vest.

"If you have a minute, come on in. We were just finishing up dinner."

I followed her through the house to a large, well-lit dining room painted a pale, soothing green. A long trestle dining table was the centerpiece of the room, which was lit by a chandelier that looked like it had been forged from old bicycle parts.

"Megan's creations," Heather said, noting my interest. "Table, benches, chandelier, and the sideboard."

"I thought she just made the dogsleds," I said.

"She's branching out lately," Heather said. "With Hogan's help. He's got good business sense. Doesn't hurt that he's crazy about her, of course."

"Just don't let him hear you say that," Abe—Heather's husband—warned.

He sat at one side of the table, Ren and Bear at the other. If anything, he looked more worn than Heather. Considering how bad he'd looked yesterday, though, this was a marked improvement. Meanwhile, both my teenagers were filthy after their day's labor, but neither showed any interest in leaving.

"Can you stay?" Abe asked. "These two saved our butts today. The least we can do is feed you for letting them come out."

I was still processing the latest information about Hogan's connection with Megan. It was definitely more than he'd first let on, but considering the way he'd been reacting from the moment we got here, I was hardly surprised.

"We actually need to get back," I said, pulling myself back into the conversation. "I'm headed out again in about an hour, and I'd like to get everyone settled before I go."

The plates in front of Bear and Ren had been scraped clean, while a large bowl of what looked like pasta and roasted cauliflower sat half-eaten at the center of the table. It smelled delicious. I noted the half-dozen dogs who lived inside the house had all taken up residence at the door, looking on with hangdog expressions.

"Bring dessert to go, then," Heather said. She hobbled to the sideboard, where a heaping plate of brownies waited. "I bake when I'm nervous," she explained. "After everything that's been going on, I think we'll have enough brownies to feed the state if Meg doesn't come home soon."

She forced a smile, but it looked tenuous at best. Abe rose as Ren and Bear stood to clear their plates. He went to Heather and put an arm around her shoulders. "They're going to find her, Heath. Everyone in this county loves Megan. They won't rest until she's home, safe and sound."

He looked at me. "Have you talked to Chase lately? I know he must be losing his mind about Sally. That, combined with Violet still out there... I can't imagine what he's going through."

Heather closed her eyes. A tear squeezed from behind her lid, despite her best efforts. "It's just a nightmare. I keep telling myself that. That I'll wake up soon, and everything will be back to normal."

"Did Sally ever talk to either of you about Chase?" I asked. I knew this probably wasn't the time for it, but I couldn't just forget the feeling I got around that man. "About any concerns she might have had? She came to this base just before she died. Do you know what she might have wanted to talk about?"

"No idea," Abe said seriously. "We've been asking ourselves the same question. I mean, she was never a huge fan of Chase's, but he can be a little much sometimes. He has a good heart, though."

The doubt must have shown on my face, because Heather added quickly. "He's financing Abe's movie. The guy can't be that bad." Abe frowned. "Sorry. That was supposed to be a secret. But Abe has been working on this project forever, and we just couldn't get the money together to finish it and deal with the promotion and distribution. And then a week ago, Chase just comes to him…"

"He wants to keep it quiet for now," Abe said, though I could sense his own excitement now. "Violet isn't always crazy about the way he spends his money, but apparently he's working on something right now. He said he'd have everything we needed within a couple of months."

"But he didn't say where he was getting that money?" I asked.

"No, and I figured I wouldn't look a gift horse in the mouth," Abe said. Heather looked a little less comfortable with that approach, but said nothing.

Bear and Ren had cleared the dishes and were standing by waiting for me to finish—Ren quietly, Bear with the tapping and fidgeting I'd come to expect from my son over the years. I didn't know what more to ask Heather anyway, so said goodnight, assuring both that someone would be in touch as soon as we knew anything. All the while, though, I couldn't shake the feeling that what I had just learned had something to do with Sally Price's wild ride that morning. And, possibly, could explain what Chase had to do with the sudden return of his old best friend: Megan's violent ex-husband.

•

"So, did you get a lot done?" I asked Bear and Ren, as the two loaded back into the van. They left the passenger's seat empty so they could sit together, just in case I thought for a minute I was anything but their chauffeur.

"We did—it was disgusting," Ren said. My rearview mirror gave me a perfect view of her hind end as she draped herself over the seat to greet Minion. "I missed you, girl!" I heard her say, and smiled. "None of those dogs are half as nice as you."

"They want us to come back this summer," Bear said. "There's a K-9 first aid course for kids, and they want us to be counselors. It's just a five-day program, so it wouldn't eat up much of our time."

I grimaced inwardly, thinking of what Bear had told me that morning: Ren was leaving soon. Based on what he'd said, she wouldn't even be here by summer. To my surprise, however, Ren gave no sign of trepidation when she joined in.

"He said we can use Casper and Minion in the programs. I think it would be so good for Min's confidence."

"Can we do it?" Bear asked. "I know there's a lot going

on in the summers, but it wouldn't be for that long. And it will be really good experience."

"I'll talk to Abe and Heather about it," I said. "But I don't see why not."

Once we were on the road, I glanced back at Bear and Ren in the back of the van together. Bear's arm was draped across the back of the seat—not exactly around Ren's shoulders, but there was an unmistakable implication. Because I'm only human, I lasted only until about halfway back to the lodge before I finally gave in and had to ask what was eating up most of my mental energy at the moment.

"So... Are you two really thinking you'd be interested in that camp at WildFire this summer?" I asked. In the rearview mirror, I caught a flash of annoyance on Bear's face. Ren, on the other hand, remained completely open.

"We are," she said. "But we needed to talk to you about something first. Or, I needed to talk to you."

"No time like the present," I said.

She unbuckled her seatbelt and made her way to the front, climbing over and settling into the front passenger seat with a grace she'd grown into in the five years since I'd first met her. She put her seatbelt on without being prompted, and turned to face me gravely.

"I know Bear told you my father is planning to take a job in California," she began. I nodded. "It was a difficult decision, but that organization's mission is very important to him." She hesitated. "To both of us, but I don't have the memories of Nigeria that he does. He had a happy childhood there, and many happy years with my mother. But I remember nothing of my time with my family. The first place where I have felt safe is here."

I smiled, moved by her words. "You know you'll always

have a home with us, Ren. Whatever else happens, that won't change."

"I know. Bear said the same—I know that it's true."

She had been such a shy, broken little girl when she came to us at twelve years old. Ren was three years old when soldiers came into her home and killed her mother and brothers, while she hid beneath the bodies and prayed to be spared. Her father was a soldier himself; when he came home, he found his family gone. It took years before he was finally reunited with his daughter, who had been taken in by a neighbor and then sent to a local convent. Years later, when she and her father made it to the United States and eventually found their way to Flint K-9, she knew almost no English. I would wake to her screams every night from nightmares that still haunted her. I had no idea whether our outfit was right for her until Minion came along. The two saved one another…and from that point on, there was never any doubt in my mind that Ren and her father had found us for a reason.

"That's why I wanted to talk to you," she continued. "I spoke with my father on the phone this morning. He is determined that he is meant to take this job, and I'm happy that he has found the opportunity."

"But…" I prompted, when she didn't continue.

"But, I am farther ahead in my studies than Bear. If I work at it, I could get my high school diploma by summer. I would like to finish out the year here, before going to join my father in California."

"And your dad is okay with that?" I asked, glancing at her again. Carl, Ren's dad, was notoriously protective of his only surviving child. Despite the fact that she was seventeen, I was surprised that he'd agreed to the separation.

"I'm almost of age—I will be going to college soon. He knows we won't be together forever. He told me that if you agreed, he would be all right with me staying on the island and continuing with Flint K-9 until the fall."

"And then what happens?" I asked.

She glanced back over her shoulder, in Bear's direction. I followed her gaze in the rearview mirror and saw Bear poised at the edge of his seat, waiting for my verdict. Ren's eyes returned to me. She straightened in her seat.

"I've already been accepted to the undergraduate program in zoology at the University of Maine. Once that's completed, I'll be able to go on to earn a doctorate in veterinary science."

I looked at her in surprise. I'd been talking to Bear for the past year about the need to think about what he would do when he was finished with school. He'd been ambivalent at best; I had no idea Ren had been so focused on her own future while my son had been waffling about his.

"You've given this a lot of thought, then," I said.

"It's what I've wanted since I first began working with animals. I would like to continue living at Flint K-9 until Bear and I have finished our courses, however. And if I could keep working through the summer…"

"Of course you can," I said immediately.

I resisted the urge to ask whether she had talked to Bear about this next part of the plan. Was he also planning on going to college, or did he just plan to move to Orono and hang out while his girlfriend went to school? Or had they even thought that far ahead? That was definitely a conversation better reserved for solo time with my son, so I settled for simply calling to the back of the van,

"She can stay as long as Carl says it's all right."

Bear grinned wider than I'd seen him in months. "He already said it was up to you."

"Then I guess it's settled."

"Thank you," Ren said quietly.

"My pleasure, sweetie," I returned, just as quietly. "Whatever happens, I'm here for you."

I snuck another look at her before I settled my eyes on the road ahead. At seventeen, I'd had an active, sensitive two-year-old son to take care of on my own. I love Bear more than anything on this earth, but my road still isn't the one I would choose for most teenage girls out there. I vowed to do whatever I could to make sure that Ren remained focused on her future, even if my son didn't turn out to be a permanent fixture in it.

22

WITHOUT RECLUSE BESIDE HER, Megan didn't know when she'd last felt so helpless. What if no one found him, and he just wound up tied to that tree indefinitely? She hadn't tied it that tightly, and she knew the dog was more than capable of chewing through rope like that… That didn't mean he would do it, though. He could die of thirst. Die of hunger. He would think she didn't care.

That she had abandoned him.

"Faster," Justin said, behind her.

The sounds of search and rescue were all around them now. They were at the epicenter of the search grid, Megan was sure. With her hands bound and the gag tight around her mouth, though, the searchers might as well have been looking on another planet. They would never find her.

If she could have called for help, Megan vowed that she would have. Even if it meant Justin shot her on the spot, she would have screamed her bloody head off. As it was, though, she could do nothing but move. Breathe. Try to function, despite the fact that she was growing thirstier with every passing step, thanks to the gag. And more weary. God, when had she ever been this tired?

She brushed against every scrap of foliage she could find, intent on leaving a scent trail the search dogs could follow. She was sure they hadn't been that far from the site of the warden's slaying when Justin found her. Surely Hogan and his team would see it. Find Recluse. And from there, track Megan. Ideally, before Justin raped and killed her—which, she had no doubt, he'd been fantasizing about the entire time he'd been in prison.

The sun was already sinking lower in the sky and Megan had completely lost track of where they were when she finally stopped dead on the rough trail they'd been following.

"What are you doing?" Justin growled. He poked her in the base of the spine with his rifle, hard enough to push her forward. She stumbled. Fell.

Unable to catch herself with her hands tied behind her back, she face planted in the snow before rolling herself over. Justin stood above her, always his favorite place to be. When they'd first gotten together, she'd been so stupid. Naïve. She thought it was just a quirk, the way he always had to lead the way. Make the agenda. Decide who she talked to, and when.

Now, she understood exactly what that was called. Violet had warned her about it then. *He's isolating, you, Meg. A good boyfriend doesn't have to know where his girlfriend is every second of the day. I don't even understand why he and Chase are friends.*

"Get up," Justin said, pulling her back to the present.

He looked back over his shoulder nervously. She wondered again if he was on something. He'd been straight as an arrow when they first started dating. Or she'd thought he was, anyway. She learned later that that was only because he couldn't control himself when he drank. He saved that for home. For her, once he had her and had no intention of letting her go.

She shook her head, hating the gag and the snow and the cold and, above all else, Justin.

"What's the matter?" he demanded.

She gave a muffled response through the gag that nearly choked her. Justin set his rifle against a tree and knelt on the ground beside her. He straddled her, still on his knees, weight pressed solidly against her groin, and wrapped his left hand around her throat.

"Scream, and I kill you here," he said. He pulled the gag away from her mouth, but kept the pressure so tight around her neck that she could barely squeak a word out.

"Water," she whispered.

His eyes lit. It was a triumph to him, she realized: she had asked for something. Needed him for something.

"I guess I can arrange that."

He replaced the gag, and got off her. She watched as he removed his pack, eyes on her always, and took a water bottle from the side pocket. Had Chase really supplied all this gear? Justin's parents still loathed Megan and believed every word their precious son said, but they had moved to Hawaii the last she knew. If they weren't available, she couldn't think of anyone other than Chase who could have gotten this stuff for him. But why?

While Justin was juggling gear, eyes fixed on her, a sound in the woods drew her attention. Megan coughed behind her scarf to cover it, her eyes drawn momentarily to the trees.

She fought to remain impassive despite what she saw, returning her gaze to Justin. From the edge of the forest,

Violet's finger moved to her lips, signaling Megan to stay quiet. Recluse was beside her, ready to pounce. Violet must have been holding the beast back with everything she had.

"Here you go, baby girl," Justin said. He resumed his position straddling her, one hand around her neck while with his other he roughly shoved the gag aside. He put the water bottle to her lips. Tipped the bottle up.

Megan drank hungrily, eager for more, but panic soon overtook her when he tipped the bottle farther up. The water kept coming. It spilled over her lips, down her chin, as his other hand tightened around her neck. She fought to stay calm. Breathe through her nose. Not let the bastard drown her here and now.

When she began to cough the water up, he finally removed the bottle from her lips. He didn't bother replacing the lid, instead tossing the bottle aside. It was sacrilege to waste water out here like that, but Megan figured on Justin's list of sins, that ranked pretty low.

"What are you going to do with me?" she asked, when she could finally speak again.

Justin moved closer. She could feel him, excitement growing, pupils dilated to pinpoints. His mouth moved over her ear, his breath hot. Wet.

"I want to take everything from you," he whispered, his hand still around her throat. "I want you to beg me for your life. And then, when I'm done with you, I'll watch you beg me to put a bullet in your skull."

She wished she could think of a comeback. Wished she could be calm, cool, like the heroines in movies. So little oxygen was getting to her brain, though, she considered it a triumph just to stay conscious.

Suddenly, she heard an eruption in the brush. A growl

burst from Recluse's throat, and the dog leapt away from Violet. At the same time, she watched as her friend ran full-out for the rifle Justin had left propped against the tree.

Recluse knocked Justin off Megan with the wild abandon of a defensive tackle. Meanwhile, Megan was worried about her friend's ability to deal with the firearm Justin wielded so easily. She had forgotten, however, that Violet was the daughter of a military man. The rifle was already cocked and ready to fire, something Violet thankfully recognized. The more difficult issue, however, was where to aim. Justin was pinned to the ground with Recluse on top of him, jaws wrapped around the man's right arm.

Violet focused on Megan instead, tearing the gag from her mouth.

"Recluse, off!" Megan shouted, the moment she was able.

The dog, well trained as he might be, was so far gone it took Megan another sharp command before he backed away. Blood flecked his muzzle, while Justin lay pale, inert, on the snowy ground.

For all the show, however, the damage could have been worse. Justin would need stitches, and there would be a scar on his right arm where Recluse had taken him down. Beyond that, the man would be fine. Despite herself, Megan was grateful—not for Justin, but for her dog. Whether the victim is a bad guy or not, a dog known for fatally injuring a human doesn't usually have a bright future ahead.

"Good boy, Rec," Megan said. Her voice was raw, her nerves fried.

"Is he…dead?" Violet asked, nodding toward Justin. For the first time, Megan realized that her friend was shaking badly.

"I think he passed out," she said. "He might be on something. Or he might just be a spineless loser who can't handle it when things don't go his way. Hang on."

She forced herself to her feet, and turned slightly—careful to keep Justin in her sights—so Violet could cut the ties from around her hands. Once she had, she ordered her feet forward. One step at a time, until she was standing above Justin. She kicked him lightly in the side, and he came to with a start. Megan jumped backward, out of the way.

Violet's gun came up.

"Stay where you are," Megan ordered.

His response was a string of curses, blood coursing down his arm. Despite her terror, Megan was proud to note that Violet kept the rifle steady on her target. The senator had trained her well, apparently.

"Get up, Justin," Megan said.

"Fuck you." He was crying. Actually crying. He wiped his nose with the back of his sleeve—or started to, then saw the blood and paled even further. He turned his head away from them, trying to get hold of himself.

"No, thank you. Don't be such a pussy. Get up." It had been one of his favorite insults, whenever she showed any kind of emotional response to his abuse during their brief marriage. If he got the significance of her words here, he showed no sign of it now.

"What do you plan on doing if I just sit here?" Justin said, gradually pulling himself together. He looked at Violet, his chin up. "Little Miss High and Mighty over there. What are you going to do? Call your daddy?"

She aimed the rifle. Megan noted that she had steadied considerably since this whole thing began. Without even giving a warning, she fired. The shot kicked up snow a foot away from Justin's butt, making Recluse yelp and Megan's ears ring.

Justin was on his feet in half a second.

"What the hell, Vi?!" Megan said. "Give some warning next time, would you?"

"Sorry," Violet said. Her eyes never left Justin, rifle still held high. "I'll do better next time. Do you have any other weapons on you?"

"Why don't you come closer and find out?"

Violet nodded her head toward Megan, and Megan steeled herself for the inevitable. Recluse growled the moment she took a step toward the man.

"Stay, Rec," she ordered.

She moved toward him—the devil incarnate. Bleeding and pale, a trail of snot and tears on his face. "Try anything and I won't call my dog off this time," she said.

She ordered him to stand back to her, his good arm raised while his other hung useless by his side. Moving as quickly as she could without running the risk of missing something, she patted him down. All the while, ignoring his ugly comments, his endless dialogue.

She came away with a survival knife she'd found strapped to his leg and a pistol he kept in a holster behind his back. More exciting was the cell phone in the pocket of his backpack. It wasn't inconceivable that he had more weapons hidden on him somewhere, but short of making him strip naked she wasn't sure how to find it.

Instead of prolonging the search any longer, she took a zip tie from the stash in his pack and repeated the procedure he'd done to her a short time before, binding his hands behind his back. It was a cruel thing to do given his injury, something that made her own stomach twist, but she knew how stupid it would be to let that keep her from securing him somehow. The instant he saw an opening, regardless of how much pain he might be in, she knew he wouldn't hesitate to act.

"Now what?" Violet asked. "My arms are getting tired."

"You can put the rifle down for a minute," Megan said. "He's not going anywhere."

She took the phone she'd found in Justin's pack, and turned it on. Megan wasn't surprised to see it password protected. Nor was she surprised when she was able to unlock it on the first try.

030175DIEMEGAN

Justin's birthday, and the mantra that had most likely helped get him through his stint in prison for the past five years. Justin had never been the most creative guy on the block.

"We don't have any bars out here," she said to Violet, looking at the screen. "Big shock there. We'll need to get to higher ground if we're going to reach someone."

"What do we do with him?" Violet asked, nodding toward Justin. He sat on the ground now, hands bound behind him, eyes closed.

"He comes too," Megan said. "There are coyotes. If they find him out here bleeding and bound, they won't hesitate to finish him off." Why should that matter to her, she wondered? Somehow, it made her feel better that there was something left in her that still worried about such things.

Violet nodded, unsurprised. Together, they got Justin on his feet and moving. Without a psychopath on her heels tracking her every move, Megan figured they would be found within the hour. They just had to get to higher ground, and keep moving.

23

WE RETURNED TO THE LODGE half an hour after leaving the WildFire base, where Jack was still waiting for a callback from his contacts in the FBI. An hour later the call still hadn't come, and we agreed that waiting any longer would do little to save Megan or the other women still missing. Casper was eager to get on the trail despite the darkness or the snow that had begun to fall. Personally, I didn't care about my fatigue or the conditions outside; the search had long since lost its luster, and I just wanted our victims home safe and sound.

The search teams were considerably more sober now than they had been earlier, the forest cold and quiet as snow continued to fall. One group had been ordered back to the site of the original camp, on the off chance that something had been missed or someone had returned to the scene after the fact. The rest of us, bundled up tight and with dogs still eager to get the job done, gridded out from the location where Charlie Babcock had been found earlier that day.

An hour passed. The wind picked up. Casper was already in Kevlar and foul weather gear, but the snow beneath our feet was turning to slush and I worried he wouldn't be able to handle the worsening conditions.

"How are your paws holding up in this?" I asked the pit bull at one point, as he trudged across ice and snow with his head up, forever searching for that elusive scent.

His tail waved, far more sedate than usual, and he dutifully lifted one paw at a time as I checked to make sure his booties were still intact and securely attached.

"Does he show any sign of…anything?" Hogan asked me. The exhaustion was beginning to show on him. I wondered how he would handle it if the search went on much longer.

"He can't smell something that isn't here," I said. "Why don't you go check on some of the other teams? Jack and I are fine out here on our own."

I expected him to refuse, but after another few minutes following Casper's wagging tail and seemingly aimless trek, he fell back and got on his radio.

I glanced at Jack, who had insisted on walking alongside me ever since the incident on the trail with Chase and the waterfall.

"Still no word from your guy in the FBI, huh?" I said.

"Who knows," he said. "It's not like we get reception out here. Even if he gets back to me, I won't get the message until we head in again."

"You don't seem too concerned by that," I noted.

He shrugged. "Honestly? I don't think it will be that helpful."

I raised an eyebrow at that, waiting for him to explain, then realized he couldn't see my expression in the dark. "Why not?"

"If it's Frank Mooney, he's already out here doing what he does. How does it help us to know how he found out his wife was here?"

"I don't know—you're the investigator, right? Or the former investigator, at least. Details like that must help, or people wouldn't bother with them."

"They matter when you're prosecuting. They definitely matter if you're trying to figure out who did it in the first place. Personally, I don't think Frank Mooney is our guy. Too many things have gone wrong. If it were him, he would have come in, hit his target—in this case, his wife—and gotten out again."

"Shonda said Ava wasn't there when the shooting started, though," I pointed out.

"So he would have waited until she came back." He shook his head. "I read the file on Megan's ex-husband while you were gone. Spoiled rich kid who fancied himself a world-class hunter. We know he got out of prison somehow—that to me is all we need. This sounds a lot more like someone like that than a professional like Frank."

"Knowing who it is doesn't really change the situation, though. Whether it's Justin or Frank, we're still stuck out here hoping we get to Megan, Violet, Ava, and Gabriella before the shooter does."

"True," Jack agreed. "To be honest, I think I'd rather go up against Frank when push comes to shove, though. If it's him, he has one objective: find his wife. Justin's completely erratic. He's just as likely to kill us as he is to kill Megan—we saw that with the warden he shot. He has nothing to lose."

With that grim thought to torment us, we fell silent and kept searching.

We continued on for another hour, Casper still vigilant

up ahead. My hands and feet were frozen despite the layers, but that just made me more determined. If this was bad for me, what must Megan be going through? And what about the other women out here? Ava Mooney: a woman with almost no English who had risen up against all odds to escape a man who, by all accounts, made his living as a hired killer. Then there was Gabriella Garcia, the subject of public scrutiny for all of her adult life and much of her childhood. She'd left her home much like Ava, only to find herself at the mercy of a monster the world viewed a hero.

And finally, there was Violet. Chase said she was working on her dissertation on domestic violence. Her mother's story made it clear that Violet had personal experience with the subject, but did that experience extend to her marriage? Was that what Sally Price had wanted to tell me, before the crash that nearly ended her life?

Casper stopped up ahead, so I forced myself out of my own head to tune into the dog. His gear was holding up well and his energy still seemed good, but this wasn't the kind of night when we could just search for hours with no thought of consequences. Casper was a young, healthy dog, but he wasn't invincible.

"What is it?" Jack asked, coming up beside me once more on the trail.

"I'm not sure," I said. I crouched beside Casper and scratched under his chin. "What have you got, boy? Need a break?"

He shifted his head away from me, clearly focused on something. Though his ears were cropped too close to his head for me to learn much, the tilt of his head told me he was listening for something.

Not so fast, baby girl, a voice whispered on the wind.

My stomach rolled, and I nearly lost my balance before I recovered. Heedless, the voice continued. *Don't worry. I've got bigger plans than that for you.*

I straightened with some effort, my vision blurred. Jack studied me, clearly unhappy.

"You're still hearing the voice?"

"Apparently so."

"What did he say?"

Go ahead—tell him, sweetheart, Brock growled. *Show him just what a basket case you are.*

I ignored Brock, or the voice in my head masquerading as him, and answered Jack's question. "I think he might have her."

When I tell you to do something, do it, the voice growled. The 'baby girl' voice—not Brock. The tension rose in the air around me, and something as real as a physical blow landed in the pit of my stomach. I gasped, staggering backward.

"Jamie?" Jack said. "What is it?"

I fought for my breath. I could feel her now—beyond the empty, hateful words Justin had been spewing in Brock's voice, I could feel Megan there.

"He has her," I repeated.

"Where?"

"I don't know." I shook my head, trying to clear it. "I don't see anything; I don't hear anything but his voice."

"Take it easy," Jack said. He touched my arm, but I flinched away. Jack took a step back, hands at his sides. "Sorry. Just try and breathe."

I nodded, and managed a deep breath through my nose while I considered what had just happened. He had hit her. I was unshakable on that fact. Were we too late?

Before we could discuss the issue any further, Casper's

head came up sharply. This time, I heard it too: barking, somewhere on the mountain.

"There's something happening out there," Jack said, nodding in that direction.

"Sounds like it," I said. "We should keep going. Hogan will let us know if we can stop."

"Right."

"Keep looking, Caz," I said to the dog. I pulled out the scent article in case he needed a refresher, but my guess was that the scent wasn't our problem. He couldn't track the missing women here if they never visited this spot, and it was looking more and more like that was the case. Regardless, Casper trudged on gamely, Jack and me sticking close behind now.

Minutes later, a crashing in the underbrush on the trail behind us had Casper barking furiously while I fought a near-fatal arrhythmia.

"I swear, you need the dang bell more than Phantom," I said as Hogan approached.

"They've got something?" Jack said to him. Hogan nodded.

"Gabriella Garcia—the model."

"Is she all right?" I asked.

"She is. They found her hiding in a gully not far from the camp—scared out of her mind, and near hypothermic. Otherwise, though, she'll be all right."

"Did she see the shooter?" I asked.

He shrugged, completely dispirited. "She doesn't speak much English, so we're having a hard time figuring that out. At the end of the day, though, what does it matter?"

Not much, I realized. And more and more, I was convinced Jack was right: Megan's ex-husband was the mysterious gunman roaming these woods. If we could find him, we could stop this thing. Assuming Megan was still alive.

"We keep gong?" I asked.

"We keep going," Hogan confirmed. "Gabriella had been there for a while—she was just too afraid to answer when people were out there searching. Which means Megan, Violet, and Ava could still be out there."

I hoped he was right, but the experience I'd just had made me think time could be running out for Megan.

•

By ten o'clock, snow had given way to a hard freezing rain that came down in a near-horizontal stream, the wind howling through the trees. Casper's head was down now, tail between his legs. Some humans may have the ability to continue with a job for years at a time even when they loath it; dogs do not. My goal as a SAR handler is to keep it fun and interesting for my dogs. As with people, there are dogs who'll continue to go through the motions even when the job is killing them, but even those dogs will never be as effective as an enthusiastic, fully engaged search and rescue dog.

Casper was definitely not enthusiastic at this point, and he wasn't even partially engaged. Beyond that, the weather conditions were such that even at his best, it was unlikely he'd be able to find much of anything out here.

"You know we can't stay out like this much longer," Jack said to me, reading my mind. We'd searched only about a quarter of the grid area we had been assigned. Farther on, I could hear the rushing of the Bear River, a fourteen-and-a-half-mile tributary of the Androscoggin River. When we first moved to Maine, this had been a favorite destination of Bear's.

"Are you sure that's really the name of this river?" he'd asked, more than once. I assured him that it was, but he hadn't believed me until I showed him on the map.

"I just talked to Steiner," Hogan said. "He wants us to check the river, then we're pulling the dogs out. Rain's supposed to let up in a couple of hours; we can get out again then."

"Sounds like a plan," I agreed.

We began our search of Bear River a few minutes later, heads down as we battled the elements. We hiked down in the dark, Casper up front while Jack and I trailed behind. Hogan, meanwhile, followed his own course—sometimes with us, sometimes not.

With the search team dwindling as the hours wore on, our search strategy remained clear cut: do everything possible to keep from surprising the shooter. We came in hard and bright, full force—a dozen searchers and their dogs in the dark at once, floodlights in tow.

"Our priority is finding these women," Steiner had reminded everyone before we set out. "And everybody coming back safe. Let the cops deal with the shooter. You guys just get in there and make sure he knows you're there, you're not alone, and you don't have any intention of being heroes."

Based on the noise of the group as we streamed toward the riverbanks, everyone was taking his orders seriously. The air was filled with the sound of searchers calling for the missing women. Dogs yowled, a wide range of vocalizations, from the deep, throaty barks of the German shepherds to Casper's high-pitched pit bull yap.

At the shore of the river, now partially frozen but far from stable, I followed the GPS to my assigned coordinates and gave Casper his command.

"Find them, Caz!" Casper's tail whipped back and forth, the dog newly energized now that we had a fresh, clear goal. He dove forward, but I kept him on a long line this time to maintain some control in case he was tempted to cross the river.

We'd been searching for well over an hour, the wet and the cold now soaked into my bones, when another search dog began barking in the search quadrant just a few meters down the line from Casper and me. Casper pulled up short, recognizing the distinct sound of a dog who's made a find.

"We've got something!" someone called just north of our position. Hogan, I realized after a minute. He'd gone on ahead of us. "Hold up."

All activity along the river stopped, with the exception of a single bobbing light to our left.

"I need assistance," Hogan called. "Stat. Jamie, get over here."

I realized with a start that I was closest, and brought Casper to heel as we charged into the fray.

Five minutes later, I saw Hogan wading into the icy, raging river as another search dog barked wildly from shore, his handler hanging tight to the dog's lead.

"What do you need?" Jack called to Hogan. I'd forgotten he was even beside me.

"There's someone in the water," Hogan called back toward us. "Careful coming in, though—it's freezing."

I shone the light toward him and saw what he had spotted immediately: something bulky and red caught on a rocky outcropping at the center of the river.

"Where the hell is your rope, Hogan?!" I called after him. There are protocols for nearly every situation in search and rescue. When going in to a rushing river, an anchor rope is required in order to ensure the searcher isn't swept away in the process of trying to rescue a victim.

"I'm fine," he called back. I shook my head in frustration.

"Stay," I ordered Casper. He sat reluctantly beside the other search dog, a black lab gone apoplectic at the action.

Jack already had his pack off and was digging out a safety line. He handed it to me, and I looped it around my waist and double checked to make sure it was secure. I handed Jack the other end.

"Okay?" I asked.

"I'll stay on my end if you stay on yours," he said. "Be careful, please."

"Always."

The shoreline was pure ice. I strode across on my cleats, aware of the searchlights and eyes on me from all around. Was this Megan in the water? Would I hear Justin's final words to her as I got closer?

I gasped as the icy water closed around my ankles… my shins…my knees. I nearly lost my footing between the temperature, the rocky bottom, and the rushing current, but I recovered quickly and forged ahead.

Hogan was waiting a few feet from the object, his expression grim. When I shone my flashlight toward it now, I understood why: still tucked into the parka, caught hopelessly in the current, a woman floated face up. She was blue, her hair waving in icy tendrils around her head.

Ava.

I couldn't imagine she could possibly be alive, but I wasn't there to make that call. Bodies submerged in freezing water stand a better chance of survival than those in warmer conditions. It was possible.

Based on Hogan's expressions and actions, he was praying for the same thing.

Carried in on the air like some insidious bacteria, I heard laughter. I ignored it, knowing I was the only one who could hear the sound.

"What do you need?" I asked Hogan.

"Go upstream," he shouted, his voice choked from the crippling cold. "I'm going to try and reach her, get her loose. If I can't hang on once she's free, you can catch her when she reaches you."

"At least tie yourself off," I said. "I've got an extra rope."

He shook his head. "No time. I'm fine, just go."

I nodded my understanding. I couldn't feel my feet, could barely navigate the rocky bottom or the rushing water as I stumbled farther upstream. Heart pounding, I watched Hogan as he struggled to close that final distance to the body.

He was within a couple of feet, just another step or two and he'd be able to grab hold. My breath caught when he stumbled, and went down hard. He flailed, caught in the current, cursing the whole while. Casper and the lab were both barking furiously now. I glanced back toward shore and watched as another of the searchers came forward to help keep the dogs at bay.

A second later, Hogan found his feet again. He swore roundly, water dripping down his face. Then, he started back, fighting the current once more to reach the body.

He produced a three-foot grappling hook from the bag he carried over his shoulder and slowly, carefully used it to bridge the distance between him and the body.

I didn't breathe. Didn't move. The water battered against me, moving me inches at a time even as I fought to hold my ground. All for what, though? Ava was certainly dead. We had failed.

After what seemed a lifetime, Hogan managed to maneuver the grappling hook under the red parka's material. He worked the fabric for several seconds, his entire body tensed with the effort to stay still. For a moment, the hook held.

The fabric shifted; the body rolled.

Face still up, dreadfully pale. Virtually inhuman. Sightless eyes stared up at the night sky. I heard others shouting along the shore, dogs barking, but I held my ground.

Braced myself.

The hook slipped, and the body remained caught on the rocks.

"Goddamn it," Hogan growled.

"Steady," I said. He looked up at me, grimacing. Icicles had formed in his hair, his lips blue in the pale wash of my flashlight beam.

"Easy for you to say," he said. He gathered himself for another attempt. "You ready?" he asked me.

"Hoo-yah," I returned, a nod to his past in the Marines. He grinned, and nodded.

"Damn right," he intoned, half under his breath.

With a mighty effort, he steadied the hook one more time. This time when he snagged the fabric, it held fast. Body rigid with the strain, he worked the implement back and forth three times. Four. And then, finally…

It came loose.

I barely had time to register the accomplishment before the body was rushing toward me. I braced myself, legs spread to better hold my ground, but the impact when it hit was nothing I could have prepared for. My legs buckled, and I felt myself being pulled under as the laughter swelled—that insidious echo that I couldn't shake.

An instant before I went down, strong arms caught me from behind.

"I've got you," Jack said. "Just hang on."

Together, we moved out of the worst of the current, dragging the body with us. I barely managed to stay on my feet once we reached the shore, but somehow we managed to get all three of us—Jack, me, and the lifeless body between us—to safety.

Paramedics pounced the second we were clear of the water, two of them going to work on the woman lying lifeless on the ground while others provided warming blankets for Jack, Hogan, and me.

"It's Ava, isn't it?" I asked Hogan through chattering teeth.

He nodded, though his attention was fixed on the paramedic working on the woman.

For three endless minutes, we stood riveted as the paramedic worked on Ava's lifeless body. Finally, just when I was sure all hope was lost, she coughed. A shout of triumph went up from the crowd. The EMT rolled Ava to her side, where she vomited half the river water onto its banks. I was shivering, soaked through myself, but felt a rush of relief regardless.

Through tears and near hysteria, Ava started talking in a steady stream of unintelligible Spanish. Unintelligible to most of us, anyway. After a few seconds when no one else responded, Jack stepped forward. He crouched beside the woman without touching her, careful to keep his distance, and spoke to her quietly in her native tongue.

I recognized "Miami" when Jack said it, and Ava reached out and took his hand. She clutched it to her, holding on with what little strength she had left. Jack asked her about Violet and Megan as the paramedics were preparing the sled to take her away, and she shook her head. I couldn't understand her answer.

"We need to get her out of here," one of the paramedics told Jack.

"What did she say about Megan?" Hogan asked, crowding in.

"You can ask her more questions after she's been treated," the paramedic insisted, pushing them both out of the way. "Not before."

24

FROM EVENING TO LONG PAST NIGHTFALL, they hiked under darkening skies. The last time Megan had seen a weather report, they'd been predicting snow or ice in the days ahead. The taste of moisture in the air made Megan think whatever that storm had become, they were about to experience the full weight of it.

The snow began shortly after dusk—heavy, wet flakes at first that quickly gave way to a sharp, relentless freezing rain. And wind. So much damned wind, Megan thought she would blow away with it.

"I can't keeping going in this," Justin complained as they trekked up another steep mountain pass.

"I'm happy to leave you here to die," Megan said. "Your choice."

Head down, mumbling curses under his breath, he kept going.

Before long, however, it became clear that Justin was right: they couldn't safely keep going in this weather. All three were already soaked through, and Megan would be damned if they died before she got a chance to use Justin's phone to save them all. The irony was just too good.

They stopped and used fallen trees, branches, and the tarp Justin carried with him to make a crude shelter, then hunkered down. The phone still had no reception here, but if they followed this trail another mile or so, Megan felt sure that would change. Just not right now, with ice slashing down at them and her body frozen through.

The shelter they came up with was barely six feet from end to end, the tarp providing only slight relief from the elements. Megan relegated Justin to one side of the structure and tied him tightly, ignoring his complaints. Then, she and Violet sat up together and waited—Violet with the rifle across her lap, Megan with the handgun she'd taken from Justin. Recluse, meanwhile, insisted on remaining outside despite the weather, curled into a tight ball and seemingly immune to the elements.

"You always thought you were so much better than me, didn't you?" Justin asked Violet at one point, after they'd been sitting in silence for at least an hour.

"The past twenty-four hours makes me think I was pretty on point about that," Violet said.

"Not to mention the decade before that," Megan chimed in.

"You and Chase, pristine in your ivory tower," Justin continued, undeterred. His speech was slurred, the words coming slowly. Megan hadn't looked at the wound from the dog bite, too afraid that Justin would try something if she got close. She wondered now if it was worse than she'd originally thought.

"What if I told you I know a secret about you and

Chase," Justin taunted. "I wonder what you'd give me if I told you that secret."

"Probably not more than we'd give you to shut up about it," Megan said.

Her curiosity was piqued, though—she hated that. Violet remained conspicuously quiet beside her. Megan glance at her in the darkness, wishing she could see the woman's face. Violet remained upright, silent, hanging onto the rifle for dear life.

"Why don't you take a break," Megan told her. "Close your eyes; get some sleep. We both don't need to stay awake through this. I'll handle this idiot for a while."

"You sure?" Violet asked wearily. "I'm okay if you need me."

"I'll be fine," Megan assured her. "Just lie down."

Violet managed to find a spot in the far corner and curled up, a sweatshirt from Justin's pack over her. Megan saw Justin watch the proceedings with interest, and prepared herself for his psychological warfare. It didn't take him long to begin.

"I bet you're wondering why Chase bought me all this gear. Boots, pack. Guns. He funded this whole operation, you know."

A few feet away, Megan saw Violet tense where she lay. So she wasn't asleep. Megan, on the other hand, forced herself to remain nonchalant.

"Not really, Justin. I wonder very little where you're concerned."

"Now that's a lie, baby girl. You know firsthand how thin that line between love and hate is."

"Not as thin as you think," she returned.

"Keep telling yourself that."

Megan didn't give him the satisfaction of responding. She was relieved when Violet, likewise, refused to engage. She had no doubt that he would continue regardless of whether either of them encouraged him. Justin had something he was dying to get off his chest, that much was clear.

Sure enough, he was the one to break the silence.

"You didn't happen to notice that Chase upped your insurance policy a few weeks ago, did you?" he asked, directing the question toward Violet's inert form. Megan watched her best friend's body go rigid. Justin chuckled.

"Yeah. Thought that would get your attention. You going on this trip was his idea, wasn't it? He was the one who thought it'd do your client so much good. But only if you were there, too."

"We both decided that," Violet said, the words breaking from her like she had no control over them. She sat up. "It was his idea, but we'd talked about it before."

"He pushed pretty hard to make it happen this time, though," he pressed.

"Shut up, Justin," Megan said.

"Why? You gonna sic your dog on me again? What have I got to lose? But maybe if you're willing to make a deal, I could tell you a little more."

"You make your deals with the lawyers," Megan said. "Not us. Now shut up, or I'll make you shut up."

He started up again regardless. Megan scooted across the short length of the shelter in a second and hit him squarely in the nose with the butt of the rifle. Justin screamed. Cursed. Bled.

He stopped talking, though.

25

AVA REMAINED HYSTERICAL and almost completely unintelligible as the paramedics carried her away from the river, where a snowmobile met them to take her to safety. She wouldn't let go of Jack's hand as they loaded her onto the sled that would take her to the hospital, sobbing when others tried to separate them.

"I'd like to go with her," Jack said to Hogan, now trying to pull the rescue together and get Ava out. "I promise, I won't get in the way. She needs someone who can communicate with her."

One of the police detectives intervened before Hogan could answer one way or the other. "We need to question her," the detective said. "Could you act as translator? We don't have anyone who speaks Spanish that well, and you've already established a rapport."

"Not until she's stable," Jack said. "But if she agrees, I'll ask her whatever you want."

"Go ahead then," Hogan said. "Whatever you can find out."

I stood by as they left, Casper standing solid beside me. Hogan turned to me when they were gone.

"You should get that dog back in. You're both going to get pneumonia if you don't get warmed up."

I knew he was right, but I couldn't stop thinking about Ava. Did finding her mean that we were close to Megan now? Or had those words I'd heard earlier mean that Justin still had her? Was she even still alive?

"I'll put Casper back in and let him get some rest. I'll get changed, but then I'd like to go to the hospital. We'll go out again once the rain's stopped."

To my surprise, Hogan was either too worried about Megan or too exhausted himself to argue.

I dropped Casper back at the house and found Bear and Ren on the couch watching a movie together, Minion, Whippet, and Phantom stretched out on the floor at their feet. I changed into clean clothes, then took a few minutes to check on Phantom, who was clearly still stiff when she got up to greet me. Bear and Ren hit me with a barrage of questions about how the search had gone, and I gave them whatever information I had before informing them that I was heading back out again.

"Do you know if Michelle's coming back tonight?" Bear asked.

I frowned. Ren was still curled up on the couch, looking tousled and cute and half asleep. "I'm not sure," I said. "I think we're pretty close on the trail of Megan and the other missing woman. She's probably planning on staying out as long as she can." I hesitated, then jerked my head toward the kitchen. "Can I talk to you for a minute?"

He stopped mid-eye roll at the look on my face, and nodded. "Yeah. Sure."

In the kitchen, I barely had time to open my mouth before Bear jumped in.

"You don't have to worry about us," he said immediately. "We're old enough to spend the night alone. It's not a big deal."

"I know you're old enough to spend the night alone," I said. As exhausted I was, I made a sincere effort to keep my tone even. "That's half the problem. I know the two of you are getting closer."

"Mom, you don't need to make a big deal about it, all right?"

"Actually, I do," I insisted. "I love you. I love Ren. I don't know where you are in your relationship, but it's up to me to talk to you about these things. You're alone in a romantic ski lodge. It's been an emotional couple of days. I know how this goes."

He frowned, but he didn't argue with me. I realized with a sinking heart that I'd very much wanted him to argue. Downplay the whole thing. Assure me that he and Ren were just friends. It had been a while since I'd heard that line, though.

"Regardless of how emotional it's been, though, I want you to be smart. You two can stay up until midnight, but we may need to get an early start tomorrow morning. Whether we do or we don't, I'll be back here in a couple of hours to get Casper again."

"You're really going out to search again tonight?"

"If possible," I said. "It feels like we're running out of time. I want to make sure I've done everything I can to find Megan and Violet before it's too late."

He nodded grimly. "I wish we could help."

"You're helping by watching the dogs," I assured him.

"That's huge—you know that. You and Ren should take them out one more time at twelve, then head to bed. In *separate beds,"* I added quickly.

His cheeks flushed, but he nodded. We'd had the sex talk innumerable times over the years—it's something you don't forget to cover when you've a been teen mom yourself. I didn't belabor the point now, knowing that he had the information he needed. I couldn't help but add,

"You know I trust you, right?"

"I know, Mom," he said. This time, his eye roll was impressive.

"Good. Be smart. That's all." I pulled him into a hug. "I love you."

"Love you too," he grumbled.

I poked my head around the corner and called, "I'm leaving, Ren. Give me a call if you need anything—I'll have my phone with me, and I'm not in the field for a couple of hours."

"Thanks, Jamie," she said, voice groggy.

I gave Phantom a final kiss on the top of her head, bid the rest of the pups goodnight, and—with too many reservations to list—left my two teenagers alone once more.

•

Stephens Memorial Hospital in Norway, Maine—the closest hospital to Bethel—was bustling when I got there that night, at just past midnight. Though there appeared to be only one patient, the combination of wardens, detectives, searchers, and reporters meant they were dealing with a packed house in the small rural hospital.

I walked the halls as I waited for Jack, pausing outside

Ava's hospital room door for only a moment before an armed detective shooed me away.

"Will you just let Mr. Juarez know I'll be in the waiting room when he's through?" I said, mildly annoyed at the treatment. The detective nodded, but somehow I doubted Jack would ever get the message. I hurriedly typed out a text and sent it along instead, then went in search of coffee.

At twelve-thirty, with crappy machine coffee in hand, I found a nook overlooking a wintry landscape and sat alone. Jack would let me know when he was done, I was sure. Right now, I just wanted a few minutes to myself to think about everything going on: Phantom's injury, the growing bond between Bear and Ren, the mounting danger I was sure Megan faced...

Unfortunately, the second I was on my own, Brock was right back in my head, whispering in my ear.

Have you missed me, James?

I ignored the question, and the voice. As a kid, how many times had I thought I was losing my mind when these voices first started? It was shortly after my sister Clara disappeared, or at least those are the first instances I can remember. I learned later that my grandmother had experienced the same thing, this ability to hear the voices of the dead. I suspect my mother may have as well, based on the violence of her reaction to my questions. If she did, she never admitted it.

Don't sit there and pretend you don't hear me, sweetheart, Brock said. I stood and stared out the window. I could ignore him—Bear was right, I didn't want to give him an opening into our lives. But was I already too late for that?

You look good, you know, Brock continued, undeterred. Death certainly hadn't changed him much. *A little old for my taste, but I wouldn't kick you out of bed.*

"Gee, thanks," I said aloud. I could almost feel his grin.

That's my girl. I knew you could hear me.

"I'm not your girl. I was *never your girl.*"

Beg to differ, sweetheart.

"Beg all you want. It doesn't change history."

"What doesn't change history?" a voice said behind me. I looked up, startled, to find Hogan's reflection beside mine in the window.

"Nothing," I said quickly. "Just thinking out loud."

I turned to face him. Brock was already gone; I could feel the change in the air, a lightness that hadn't been there before.

"Are you okay?" Hogan asked, clearly concerned.

"I'm fine. Do we know anything more about Ava or the shooter?"

"Jack is still in there talking to her, but she says it's definitely not her ex."

"Does she know who it was, then? Anything new about Megan or Violet?"

Hogan shook his head. "No. She says they got separated after the killer shot the warden—meaning Charlie Babcock, we're assuming. At least I hope to God that's who she means. She took off running in another direction from the others, and wound up by the river. Something spooked her, she tried to cross, and ended up falling in."

"What did she say about the shooter? Did she recognize him?"

"He said something to Megan right after he shot the guy. Ava was already running, but she was pretty sure it was Megan he was after when she heard that."

The look on Hogan's face said it all. He was terrified. "So it is her ex out there, then."

"Yeah. We just finally got word back from the Feds. They've had Frank Mooney under surveillance 24/7 for months now. They knew Ava left with the boys, so they've been watching him to make sure he doesn't make a move. He hasn't left Miami for the past month."

At this point, the revelation wasn't surprising. The thought of Justin out there still made my stomach turn, though. "Are you going back out?"

He frowned. "Steiner grounded me. Says I need to get my head together first, get some rest. He didn't care for the way I pulled Ava out of the river." He paused. "The way *we pulled her out.*"

"No, I don't expect he did. Still, we got the job done."

"Not without risking your neck," he said. "I should have done that by the book. You were right to follow protocol, even if I was too stupid to do so myself."

I didn't argue with him. "I know we haven't worked together in a few years, but things can't have changed that much. You're not working smart right now."

"Tell me about it. I'm sorry. The last thing I wanted to do when I called you in was put you in danger."

"You didn't call me in," I reminded him. "I mean, you made the phone call. Steiner's the one who requested me, though. And I'm glad he did. Anything I can do to help."

"Were you glad?" Hogan asked, sidelining any previous thought I might have had. "When you realized it was me, were you glad to hear from me again?"

I started to shrug off the question, but the pain in his eyes stopped me. Against my better judgment, I nodded. "Yes," I admitted. "I mean... I've wondered how you were since you left. I'm glad to know now."

"I never would have gone if you'd asked me to stay, you know."

"Hogan—" I began. I had no idea what I would say beyond that, though. He was exhausted, it was clear. Emotionally fried. This was so not the time to be having this conversation.

"It wasn't the right time," he said. "I know that. God, if there could have been a worse time for us, I'd love to hear what it might've been. It doesn't change the fact that it felt like the wrong thing to do." He paused. Frowned. "Leaving, I mean." He sighed. "Damn. I'm not making much sense here."

"You haven't been sleeping. Haven't been eating. You don't need to be coherent with me."

"Not much risk of that now." Silence fell between us, heavy with the conversation we'd started and, I knew, needed to finish.

"You leaving was the only thing to do," I finally said, pulling us back into the thick of it. "Bear needed me. And if you had stayed after the investigation was done and we'd ended up together, there would have been questions. It could have ended your career."

"It ended my career anyway," he reminded me.

"I didn't tell you to leave the force."

"No, you didn't. Ultimately, that was my choice and I stand by it. To be honest, it was one of the best decisions I ever made. It gave me a chance to get out of Maine, see a little of the world. Figure out what I wanted."

"And what is that?" I asked.

He shrugged. "A simple life, I guess," he said. "I've got a nice little house here. A job that keeps me outside instead of stuck behind a desk. A minimum of assholes to deal with every day."

"And Megan Hunter, just down the road," I said.

He lowered his eyes. Even blushed, a little. "And then there's that."

"So, are you going to do something about it when she gets back, or what?" I asked.

He ran a hand through his hair, tugging at the roots for a second before he let his arms fall back to his sides. "What about you?" he challenged. "I don't see you tearing up the dating scene where you are these days, either. Jack Juarez, for example—"

"Jack Juarez works for me," I said, fighting a blush of my own. "I don't date employees. It's as simple as that."

"But you *would* date him, otherwise."

I rolled my eyes and resisted the urge to go full-on adolescent and simply slug him in the arm. "This isn't about me."

"Uh huh. Sure."

Before we could continue, we were interrupted by Chase Carter as he rounded the corner.

"Oh—there you are," he said. "Sorry to interrupt."

"It's not a problem," Hogan said. "Is there something happening?"

"Sergeant Steiner wanted to talk to you," Chase said to Hogan. Hogan nodded quickly, but paused to look at me before he left. "Thanks for talking to me. This was good."

"It was," I agreed, then added, "We'll find her, Hogan. We'll find her, and we'll bring her home. It's up to you what happens after that."

"I hope it plays out that way." He walked away, leaving me with Chase—the last person I wanted to be alone with right now.

"Was there something you wanted?" I asked.

He smiled, an oily smile laced with innuendo. "I think your friend Jack's almost done."

"Great." I started to walk away but he stopped me, grabbing my arm hard enough to keep me in place momentarily. "He'll be another few minutes. What's your rush?"

"What do you want, Mr. Carter?"

"Call me Chase."

"No," I said. "What do you want?"

He studied me, hand still wrapped around my arm. "You don't like me very much. Why is that?"

"I don't trust you," I said simply.

"Some women are afraid of powerful men."

"I'm not one of them," I said. "And even if I were, I don't see what that has to do with you."

The smile widened, this time with the thread of arousal I had seen by the waterfall earlier. "Now, now. You should play nice with me."

"And why is that?"

He stepped closer, the grip on my arm tightening. "Because I can make your life better if you do."

"And if I don't?"

He said nothing out loud, but his eyes spoke volumes. Violence, through and through. I jerked my arm away. When he moved to grab me again, I swept his hand smoothly with my other arm and delivered a single snap kick to his shin. Light enough to do no real damage, but hard enough that he went down.

"Don't touch me again," I said. "Ever."

I walked away while he was still down on one knee swearing, the gentile Maine Guide all but forgotten.

•

It took three turns around the hospital before I'd calmed enough that I wasn't shaking with fury at my encounter with Chase. By then, Jack was done talking to Ava. The detective outside her door told me he'd gone to the lounge for coffee when I passed by. I walked the by-now-familiar corridor one more time, but paused just outside the lounge that held the vending machines. Hogan and Jack were inside talking. I would have gone in immediately, but something about Hogan's tone made me pause.

"You don't really know what she's been through," Hogan was saying. I tensed, praying that he was talking about Ava, even though I knew better. "She's tough, but I think you should know what her history was like with Brock."

"Jamie doesn't like to talk about that," Jack said.

"I don't blame her," Hogan replied. Instantly, my stomach was in a knot. All the things I hadn't shared with Jack, all the secrets Hogan knew... I imagined them spilling out like blood on that ugly green carpeting in there. Stains Jack could never ignore, once they were out.

"All the same, if you honestly care about her—and I think you do—it seems like you should know what she's dealt with."

"Jamie will tell me," Jack interrupted smoothly, before I could run in there and tell Hogan to shut his damned mouth. "If and when she wants me to know, she'll say something. If that never happens, so be it. But it's her decision. No one else's."

I couldn't hold still and wait to hear the response, and standing there lurking while they discussed my past was too much. I walked away, heart pounding faster than it had during the worst times in the search today.

Jack texted me two minutes later, while I was still in flight. *All set. Ready to go back?*

I texted back, *Meet you out front,* and left it at that. He'd had a chance to find out everything, all I hadn't been saying. And he had shut it down without getting even a taste of what Hogan had been hinting at. Why?

I waited outside the front entrance for him, just inside the portico as the freezing rain continued to fall. The world was frozen over, crystalline and deadly slick.

Are you going to tell him your secrets? Brock wheedled. *All those bloody little lies you keep buried?*

It was a dare, the way Brock said it. As though I would never dare speak those truths aloud. I hated the fact that he might be right about that.

I was still locked on that thought when Hogan emerged from the hospital, Jack on his heels.

"I'll give you a ride back to the lodge," Hogan said.

"You don't need to do that," I assured him. "I brought my van."

"The road's a nightmare," he said, dismissing me out of hand. "No way you should be out in that rig. I've got four-wheel drive."

I might have argued if the conditions had been even the least bit better, but I knew all too well what the results could be if I pushed for my own way and ended up in a wreck. No one had time for that right now.

It was one-thirty by the time I climbed into the passenger's seat of Hogan's four-by-four, while Jack climbed in the back in silence. The winds topped fifty miles an hour coming off the mountain, while sleet and freezing rain continued to pour down. Hogan drove us back to the lodge with his truck locked on four-wheel-drive the whole way. I noted the doused streetlights and darkened houses as we drove through Bethel.

"Power's been out for about an hour here," Hogan said. "There's ice on the cell towers, too. Radio signals are screwed up. Planes are still grounded."

"It's supposed to be better before dawn, though," Jack pointed out from behind me. "Tomorrow's supposed to be clear and cold. A good day for a search."

"I'm not waiting until tomorrow," Hogan said. "Remember what Ava said? Justin is out there, and he's got Megan in his sights. He won't stop until he has her. If he hasn't gotten hold of her already."

"I'll go back out with you," I said. "Casper's had time to dry off. So have I."

"There's a lot of 'I' in that sentence," Jack said. "Count me in too, please. I'm not interested in sitting out the final chapter."

I expected him to argue with us, but Hogan remained tense, silent, as he continued driving.

Bear and Ren were waiting for the latest news when we returned. Hogan came in and stood by the woodstove in silence as I gave them the highlights, while Jack went upstairs and changed into fresh clothes.

"You really think it's safe going back out there now?" Bear asked, when I had finished. "If this guy is as crazy he sounds, that plus the weather doesn't sound like the smartest combination."

"We have to try," I said. "He has to be tired himself by now. He'll be running. We're not trying to corner him; we just want to find Megan and Violet."

"Do you think Casper is up for the job?" Ren asked doubtfully.

Casper lifted his head at mention of his name. He was dry now, and remarkably bright eyed given the evening we'd had.

"He's fine," Bear said. "You guys were only out for a few hours. He's still got plenty of juice. I'm more worried about you and Jack," he said. "You're not as young as you used to be, you know."

Jack came down the stairs just in time to hear the words. "It's funny how kids age you," he said dryly. "But your mom and I should be fine. Thanks for the concern."

Hogan still hadn't moved from the stove, and I quickly got serious again.

"We'll be careful, but I'm not sure when we'll be back," I said to Bear. "You two are okay here on your own?"

They nodded, and I knew I had no choice but trust them. They were both responsible kids; I had to believe that good judgment would prevail right now.

Within ten minutes, we had everything sorted and Casper harnessed and ready to go.

"You ready?" I asked Hogan.

He turned. I was startled for a second by the darkness, the utter defeat, in his eyes. "Yeah," he agreed. "Let's go."

26

TWO SNOWMOBILES TOOK US through the woods and along the river until we reached the point where Charlie Babcock's body had been found. This was now the official Place Last Seen for Megan and Violet, according to what Ava said. As such, it was up to us to go through the area with our dogs one more time to see if we came up with anything.

Search teams were already spread through the area, the forest alive with floodlights and the shouts, barks, and yowls of the searchers and their dogs. Up ahead on the trail, I caught sight of another team. The warden among them, his features indistinguishable between his slicker and the driving sleet, waved at sight of us and hurried in our direction.

"Glad you could make it back out," the warden said. Up close now, I could see that he was a shorter man, wiry and lean. "We've got teams spread out across the southern quadrant here, but we need somebody to take the other side of the river. You up for it?"

"Sure," Hogan said briefly. "We can handle that. Any sightings at all?"

"Nothing yet," he said. "We found something over by the river, though. A rope, chewed through and tied to a tree.

There was a scrap of fabric with it, too."

"You think it belongs to Megan or Violet?" Hogan asked.

The warden reached into his coat and produced an evidence bag, a scrap of fabric about four inches square inside. Hogan took it. I looked over his shoulder as he examined it through the plastic, his flashlight trained on the item.

It was white fabric, or it had been at one time. Now, however, only a small corner remained the original color; the rest was stained a dull rust red. Blood. Hogan turned it over, and was silent for a full five seconds. I could just make out a faint line of black paw prints along the border of the fabric.

"This is Hunter's," he finally said. He sounded sick. Hollow. "She's got a long john shirt she wears on the trail, and it has this print on the sleeves. Though there was no blood the last time I saw it."

That's one, baby girl, a voice whispered on the air. Brock's voice. *Keep running, and we'll do this thing one bite at a time.*

"That doesn't have to be blood from a fresh wound, though," Jack pointed out, his own voice measured. "We know Megan was shot early in. She could have used her shirt as a bandage."

"That's most likely what it was," the other warden agreed, looking relieved. "So now we just need to find them before this nut gets there first."

"You said there was a rope, too?" I asked.

The warden produced a second baggie, this one with a length of heavy-duty blue climbing rope frayed at one end. I examined it through the bag, spotting specks of what looked like blood on the material.

"Looks like it was chewed through," I said. "Megan's dog is still missing. He was the only one they didn't find at the campsite. Maybe he's still with Megan."

"Where did you find the fabric?" Hogan asked.

"I've got the coordinates here, Lieutenant," he said.

"Good," Hogan said under his breath. "We'll start there."

The warden gave us the necessary coordinates, and left us to return to his own search.

We looked for a stable crossing point on the partially frozen river, and half-walked, half-slid across to the other shore. I started to take a scent article from my jacket when we reached our starting point, but Hogan stilled my hand.

"You got that from Chase?" he asked.

"I did. It's one of Violet's T-shirts."

"Hang on," he said. He took what looked like a bandanna from his pocket, already bagged and ready to go. "Use this instead."

At my questioning look, he said only, "Hunter left it at my place a couple of days before the trip. It should still have her scent."

I didn't ask any other questions, but called Casper to me. He was already prancing in place despite the weather, eager to get to the job. I opened the bag and put it down to him, where he eagerly snuffled the bandanna with his short bully nose.

"Ready, boy?" I said. He yapped his enthusiasm, tail whipping, body never stopping. "Find her, Casper!"

The second he got the command, Casper went into work mode. His head came up, nostrils flared. The night receded, as I watched Bear's dog sort through the scents on the air. For thirty seconds, he remained motionless.

Then, he began.

He stalked over the icy snow, paying no attention to the freezing rain that pelted us. Nostrils quivering. Head moving back and forth. Body never stopping.

We followed.

Within two hours, the freezing rain had turned to hail. Shouts in the distance were fainter now, coming less frequently and with a lot less enthusiasm. Casper's tail was tucked between his legs, his head down as he continued following the scent.

We'd traveled two miles from the river, moving uphill now. Despite my cleated boots, I'd fallen enough times that my knees and behind were bound to be a pretty shade of blue by morning. Jack had gone down even more than me, and continued to accept my helping hand with grace. This was definitely getting old, though.

Hogan alone kept his feet. He walked behind us, periodically calling Megan's name with growing urgency. It was just past three a.m., when I thought I couldn't stand the rain or the ice or the tense silence between we three searchers another minute, that Brock returned.

I'd just fallen hard on my behind, landing with a wallop that jolted my spine.

Out of nowhere, his voice was back.

Scream, and I kill you here.

Suddenly, I couldn't breathe—as though there was a hand locked around my throat. Jack offered his hand, but I shook my head, desperate to hang onto the words this time.

I closed my eyes and fought for breath, straining to hear. Why was I hearing this? How?

I want you to beg me for your life, the voice continued, the pressure tightening around my throat until I was gasping for air. *And then, when I'm done with you, I'll watch you beg me to put a bullet in your skull.*

The voice receded. I sat on the wet ground with hail pelting me, Hogan up ahead on the trail. Jack crouched beside me, forehead furrowed with concern.

"Breathe," he said quietly. "Just take a minute. Deep breath in."

I complied, because I didn't have it in me to fight him and I couldn't find my voice yet.

"Good. Now, slow exhale." He exhaled with me, and my heart began to return to a normal rhythm.

What's going on?" he asked. "That voice you heard before…"

"He has her," I said. "He was hurting her—"

"And you felt that?" The furrow in his forehead deepened. "You could feel what he was doing to her? How is that possible?"

"I don't know. It's never happened before. I think he was choking her."

Jack shifted his flashlight to my neck, gently pulling my scarf aside. The look in his eyes told me everything I needed to know about what he found.

"There's a mark?"

"Yeah." His voice was strained. "There's a mark."

This time, I accepted his hand when he offered to help me up. Casper was just ahead on the trail. I was about to call him back, but in the beam of my flashlight I saw him pause. An instant later, his body snapped into focus again.

The pit bull paused at something up ahead, though I couldn't tell what. Head down, he snuffled for a second with his tail going like mad, then bolted on ahead.

"He's got something," I said. Freezing rain continued to

pelt us along the way, wind occasionally strong enough to blow me right off the trail.

I paused at the spot where Casper had stopped, shining my flashlight over the snow and into the brush off to the side. It took three passes before I saw it:

A sodden piece of paper.

I crouched to get a closer look, and called back over my shoulder. "We've got something." I pulled a baggie from my pocket and gingerly picked the object up at the corner before dropping it into the bag. Then, I marked the spot on my GPS.

"What is it?" Hogan asked, coming up on me seconds before Jack did. I handed him the baggie.

"I'm not sure, but Casper was definitely interested."

He was silent, staring at the baggie.

"You know what it is?" Jack asked as he joined us.

"A birthday card," Hogan said, his voice hollow. There was grief there, pain, that I hadn't heard before. "I, uh—it was Hunter's birthday before she left on this trip. I gave it to her then."

He stuffed it into his pocket before I could ask anything more, a flash of realization crossing his face. "She was here. Your dog's got the trail."

I looked at my GPS, following the blinking red light that was Casper. "It looks that way. Come on."

We hurried on, Hogan at the front now, all of us heedless of the elements.

Fifteen minutes later, we'd scrambled up a steep hillside and just rounded a corner when I caught sight of Casper's orange vest as he continued on, head down. He, too, had no idea of anything going on around us. He'd found the scent.

Five minutes later, my breath coming hard and the world

slick underfoot, the dog stopped abruptly. I stared ahead of him, where the trees had opened up onto a clearing.

And, seemingly out of nowhere, a cabin appeared.

Gotcha, baby girl.

Casper's tail continued to wag as he started to approach the door, but I called him back. Hogan, however, didn't seem nearly as concerned about safety.

"Be careful," I said to him, whisper-calling the words.

"She's not there," Jack said, beside me. Casper, meanwhile, sat expectantly at my feet, grinning widely. Whatever else might be going on, he was clearly pleased with himself.

"What do you mean, she's not there?" I said. "She could be inside. They could be in there waiting for us."

Jack shook his head, then nodded toward the door as he shone his flashlight in that direction. "The door's sealed with ice—look at the snow buildup at the front there."

"Your dog backtracked," Hogan said, appearing in front of us. "He's been following a cold trail."

"He followed the trail that was there," I countered. The wind gusted through the trees, bringing with it a fresh onslaught of ice and hail. Casper barked at me, confused at my lack of response to his find. I shut out Hogan's pique to take care of my dog.

"Good boy, Caz," I praised the dog. He hadn't found them, I knew, but the pit bull had been working tirelessly for hours at this, and he had led us directly to the doorstep of a spot where Megan may have been not so long ago. I didn't give Casper the toy he got after a successful find, but still gave him a handful of treats and plenty of love.

Meanwhile, Hogan had gone back to stalking around the cabin alone, brooding.

"How much longer do you think he can keep this up?" Jack asked me.

"Casper or Hogan?" I asked.

"Both."

I shook my head. "I'm not sure."

We walked around the cabin, but I pulled Casper back at sight of a shattered window out front.

"Glass is on the inside," Hogan said from behind me. I turned to find him standing there soaked, staring disconsolately at the building. "He must have shot in from back here somewhere."

"But they obviously escaped that," I reminded him. "They were still alive at the river."

"Yeah. I know."

He looked up at the sky, cursing the ice and rain that fell. "Our radios are down," he said. "I just tried to reach base. We knew it was coming, but it still throws a monkey in the works. Another one."

"We only have another couple of hours before this passes, right?" Jack said. He nodded to the cabin. "We could hole up, at least get dry for a while."

"I was thinking the same thing," Hogan agreed. "Who knows how long it will be before communications are back, but it will still be easier searching once the storm's passed. We can see about patching the window. The dog could probably use a break."

I looked at Casper, soaked through and with head down. One look was all it took for me to agree. "That would be good. He's definitely more than earned it."

I kept Casper back while Jack and Hogan went inside to clean up the glass and patch the broken window with a tarp and some duct tape they found inside. Within ten minutes, they called us in.

It was hardly a place I'd want to spend a lot of time, but there was a roof and walls and a woodstove Jack was gradually coaxing to life. A double bed stood against one wall, a small table and two chairs the only other furniture. Hogan sat in one of the chairs, staring at the card I'd found on the ground. I toweled Casper off and lit a couple of oil lamps, grateful when the chill began to ease from the air.

"You guys carrying fresh clothes in your packs?" Hogan asked.

"Dry socks and long underwear," I said. "The outerwear is supposedly weather resistant. It should dry out fast."

He nodded approvingly.

"So, that card," Jack said, still seated on the floor in front of the woodstove. "It was for Megan's birthday?"

"Her fortieth," Hogan said. I was surprised he answered. "Heather threw a big party out at their place." He hesitated, and I could feel him weighing how much more to say. "I had a little too much to drink, so Hunter gave me a ride back to my place. Or… Well, I pretended to have a little too much to drink. I wanted to get a few minutes alone with her, though, so I could give her my present. That was the only way I could think to do it."

"What did you get her?" I asked.

"She'd been wanting…" He paused, and I was pleased when he actually laughed out loud. "She has this idea about making ice cream for the dogs. Like, going commercial with it. I don't know, Hunter's always got some crazy scheme she wants to try out. But they didn't want to get a goat and keep it at the WildFire base. Some of the dogs are a little nuts—if they got any kind of livestock, it wouldn't last long."

"So you got her a goat?" Jack asked.

"A couple of them," Hogan said. "I bought a house

here last year, and I have a little land. So I built a goat shelter and a nice pen, and got her a couple of milking goats. Told her she could keep them with me as long as she wanted."

Silence fell, for a couple of beats.

"Wow," I finally said. "You really do like her."

"Of course I like her," he said irritably. "She's strong willed and bull headed and stubborn as hell."

"Those things all basically mean the same thing," I pointed out. "But I get your point."

"She's a challenge," he said. "And she keeps things interesting around here. Keeps them real."

He stood abruptly, paced the room twice, and headed for the door. "I'm going back out. I want to keep looking for just a while longer, see if I can catch up with some of the other searchers out here, and find out what they've got."

Jack got up from the floor, somewhat painfully. "I'll go with you."

"You don't have to—" Hogan began.

"You shouldn't be out there alone, especially without a radio," Jack countered. "I'll come back here once you've met up with another team."

I looked at Casper, who had settled uncomfortably on the hard wooden floor beside the fire. "He really needs a break—"

"Don't worry about it," Jack assured me. "I'll be back as soon as I can."

"Be careful out there."

They promised they would be, and left me to fight the shadows of the abandoned cabin on my own.

•

I sat in front of the fire with Casper for a couple of minutes after the men had gone, too cold to contemplate peeling off my clothes yet, even if they were soaked. Lost in thought, I ran my fingers over the place on my throat where I had felt that hand close around my neck. Jack had been right: there was a mark. I could feel swelling, and I was sure I'd find bruises by morning. How was this happening? Why now?

Casper thumped his tail when I pet his head, rolling over onto his belly for a good scratch. I obliged, then got up and took a blanket from my pack and lay it on the floor for him. After the day he'd put in, he deserved a bed of his own more than any of us. As soon as the blanket was down, Casper got up and began pawing at it. He dug frantically for about ten seconds and then, exhausted but apparently satisfied, lay down on his newly made bed. Within a minute, his eyes were closed. Two minutes more, and he was snoring.

He really was a great dog. Still, I couldn't help but miss Phantom. Our working styles meshed so well: she was quiet and independent, but she'd come to trust me enough to take direction. I had to go through the same process with her before I, too, learned to trust that she knew what she was doing. The fall she'd had earlier followed by the attack, however, made me realize that, for her as much as me, I really needed to look for a dog to take her place in the field when the time for retirement came.

I put another log on the fire, watched until it had caught in the blaze, and stood once more. Dry clothes.

I glanced at the broken window Jack and Hogan had taped. It was a rough patch job at best, wind making the tarp balloon every few minutes or so. Still, it was better than leaving it open.

I took dry socks, long knit underwear, and a matching top from my backpack, and lay them on the bed. My jacket went on a hook not far from the fire, ski pants beside it. Socks went on the back of one of the chairs, pushed close to the woodstove. My shirt was added next, then pants, until I stood naked and shivering in front of the fire.

Suddenly, a gust of wind ripped through the room, tearing the canvas from the window. Casper woke with a start, jumped up, and began barking. At the same time, a low cat call pierced the air.

Never let it be said you didn't grow up fine, sweetheart, Brock said.

27

I RESISTED THE URGE to cover myself or cower at the sound of Brock's voice, and instead went to the window. With the cold stabbing through me, I got the tarp back in place and re-taped it as securely as possible.

Ignore me all you want. We've already established you can hear me.

I put my dry clothes on with my heart pounding, palms damp, and then settled myself on the bed. Casper was still on his feet, warily eyeing the window.

"It's okay, boy," I said. "Settle down. We're all right."

Reluctantly, the pit bull padded over and pawed once more at his blanket by the fire. I wished yet again that Phantom were here. Her calming presence had gotten me through many a long night before. An unexpected wave of grief washed over me at the thought of her mortality, the painful knowledge that our working relationship may be in the past.

As though sensing my darkening mood, Casper got up again and came over to the bed. Without waiting for an invitation, he hopped up beside me.

Now that's an ugly dog, Brock said. *What the hell are you doing to my business?*

"Fixing it," I said aloud. I got under the blankets on the bed, and Casper snuggled in against me.

I knew you heard me, Brock said, with a touch of smugness in his voice that I remembered well.

I lay in bed staring at the ceiling, letting Casper's warmth seep into me. I stretched my arm out and he lay his head on it immediately, with a happy little whimper. His body wriggled as his tail wagged, and I laughed out loud at the sloppy kiss that landed on my cheek.

"Sleep, sweet boy," I said. "I don't know how long we'll have here."

The pit bull closed his eyes with a sigh.

You can't go back to just ignoring me, Brock said. *Sorry. This genie's not going back in the bottle.*

In movies, the dogs always seem to sense whatever presence might be lurking in the ether, but that isn't generally the case for me. Phantom occasionally reacts to things I hear that no one else could, but I can never be sure whether she actually hears something, or is just reading me. Right now, Casper certainly didn't seem bothered by anything.

Makes you wonder if it's all in your head, doesn't it? Brock asked.

"Shut up."

A crash just outside the cabin cut our conversation short, and had both Casper and me out of bed and on our feet in an instant.

"It's just me," Jack called from just outside the door. I wrestled Casper away from the door while my heartbeat returned to a semi-normal rhythm. Brock made no comment, though I kept waiting to hear his voice once more.

After a minute of chaos, I eventually opened the door for Jack, who stood hunched and shivering just outside the door. A cold wind and still more rain burst through as soon as there was an opening, so I quickly stepped aside to let him in. Jack shed his boots upon crossing the threshold, but kept his jacket wrapped around him tight.

"You found other searchers for Hogan to join up with that soon?" I asked. They'd barely been gone half an hour.

"There was a team not far from here. I didn't want to leave you alone too long." He warmed his hands in front of the fire, hopping a little bit in place to speed the warming process.

"You could have stayed longer. We're fine." He glanced at me, about to defend himself, but I stopped him with a raised hand. "Not that I don't appreciate the thought."

His teeth were actually chattering, and I wondered whether he had a stitch of dry clothing left on his body.

"Why don't you get something dry from your pack? You'll feel better once you get dried off, get all that wet away from your skin."

"That would mean taking off clothes, though. I think at this point they may be fused to my skin." He paused. "Not to mention how cold naked sounds right now."

"Briefly naked," I said. "I promise, it's worth it."

I turned around to spare his modesty, and faced the wall. He hesitated another few seconds, and then I watched his shadow as he shimmied out of his wet clothes and stood for a moment in front of the fire, letting the flames warm him. Then, as though remembering himself and his situation, he pulled dry clothes from his pack and dressed.

"Okay," he said, after little more than a minute.

I turned to find him in long underwear and knit, long-sleeved T-shirt, still shivering.

"It gets better a lot faster from here," I assured him.

"Let's hope so."

I got back in the bed and under the blankets, feeling guilty at leaving him out in the cold. We hadn't really counted on spending the night somewhere, so neither of us had the gear for this. I'd brought the dog's blanket because I never went anywhere without it, but I'd neglected to bring a sleeping bag for myself. I doubted Jack had thought to bring one along if I hadn't.

"Did I hear you talking to someone in here when I got back?" Jack asked, while I was still wrestling with the logistics of who should sleep where.

"Just Casper," I said immediately.

I caught a glimpse of something unreadable on his face, but he nodded. "Ah."

"You don't believe me?"

He looked at me evenly. "You're not a very good liar."

I didn't know how to counter that. If I doubled down by saying I wasn't lying, I only dug myself in deeper. Which I really had no interest in doing.

"You know that voice I keep hearing?"

"The one that nearly strangled you back on the trail?" he said grimly. "I've got a vague recollection, yes."

"You asked before who it sounded like. If I recognized it?"

"And you said you didn't." He looked at me, eyes searching mine. "But that wasn't true, was it? Whose voice are you hearing, Jamie?"

I hesitated. The words got lodged in my throat for a second before I finally spit them out. "Brock Campbell." The name felt like poison on my tongue. Jack's reaction made it clear he felt the same way, though he didn't look as surprised as I would have expected.

"Do you have any idea why? This has never happened to you before?"

"No. Sometimes I hear the voices of the dead. Or maybe I'll catch a glimpse of the future—"

"Like the vision you had of you one day saving my life," Jack said.

"Right. Like that," I said. Back when Jack and I were fighting for our lives in Littlehope last winter, I'd made the mistake of telling him about a dream I'd had—one I felt sure would come true: One day, though I didn't know when or how, I would save his life. The dream had made a big impression on me. Apparently, it had made an even bigger one on Jack, who seemed unable to forget it.

He was still standing by the fire; still shivering. I sighed, and nodded toward the bed. "If you don't mind sharing with Casper and me, it's warmer here."

He hesitated only a moment before coming over to climb in beside me. There's not a lot of space in a double bed when it's shared between a full-grown man, woman, and dog. Somehow, we still managed to keep some space between Jack and me. I lay back with Casper beside me, Jack on his other side. Sleeping like this seemed implausible, if not downright impossible.

"What else do you see?" Jack asked, as we lay there. "Supernaturally speaking, I mean."

"Not that much. Bear's the one who sees things. Glastenbury was an exception I still don't really understand. If I see things, it's usually more an impression, you know?"

"Not really," Jack said. "An impression of what? Can you give an example?" He rolled over to face me, propped up on an elbow with his cheek resting on a fisted hand. Firelight played across his features, his eyes intent on mine. It took significant effort not to notice just how inviting he looked.

I considered his question. "Well... Take you, for example. There's this kind of light just over your left shoulder—sometimes bright, sometimes dim. But it's been there from the time I met you."

He sobered. "A light. What do you think it is?"

"Honestly?" I said, after a moment of hesitation. "I think it's your wife. Lucia."

I didn't say the name lightly, but regardless of the gravity I may have attached when it passed my lips, it was clear Jack wasn't ready for it. A shadow crossed his face. He lay back in bed, silent for one endless moment.

"Are you all right?" I asked.

"I am," he said. He sounded surprised. "Sorry. I guess I'm not used to talking about this kind of thing. I'm definitely not used to people saying they see my dead wife over my shoulder."

"No, I guess not. You did ask, though," I pointed out.

"I did," he agreed. "I want you to feel like you can talk about things with me. And I really would like to understand some of what you go through."

"Maybe we should just pace ourselves with that."

"Maybe so." A beat of silence passed between us, while the storm continued to rage outside. Casper, meanwhile, snored contentedly by my side. "We should try to get some sleep. I'd like to get back out there as soon as the storm slows down."

"Okay." Another beat passed, and I closed my eyes against the uncertainty and the storm and the knowledge of Jack Juarez lying just a dog's-width away. "Goodnight, Jamie."

"Goodnight, Jack."

28

I'M SURROUNDED BY SOIL. Mountains of it. It smells like clean earth, spring, and there's nothing I want more than to sink my hands in, elbow deep. Bear is beside me, but he's a little boy again—no more than three. Chubby, dirty cheeks and a mop of dark blond hair, his father's dark eyes always watching me from that intent little face. Phantom is beside him, seated patiently.

"We need to bury it," I say to my son.

I look down, and realize that we're standing on a box. A huge box—as big as a field, stretching as far as the eye can see. Despite the size, though, Bear doesn't hesitate. Doesn't argue. Instead, he nods seriously. He has on overalls that a friend of mine made for him in Washington, denim with grizzly bear patches at the knees. He refused to wear anything else when he was little, running naked whenever I had to wash them.

"Do you want me to use my hands?" he asks. I nod, because I don't have a shovel and I can't imagine where we'd find one.

Phantom lays down in the soil while we work, while a presence I can't shake bears down on us. He's getting closer. If we can't cover this up in time, he'll escape. And we'll never be safe again.

"I'm tired, Mom," Bear complains. "I don't want to do this anymore."

"Just keep covering it," I say. "Think of it like it's a game. Scoop up the dirt from here, and dump it down over here." I bend and scoop up a huge armful of soil, and I can feel the worms squirming against my skin as I hold it, pivot, and drop it on the box. It makes a hollow sound when it falls.

Bear imitates me, but I can tell he doesn't want to play this game. Neither do I.

And then suddenly, in the bizarre time jump of a dream, he is gone. Phantom is, too, and I am alone standing on a box the size of a football field, trying to cover it up using a pile of sand that wouldn't fill a litterbox.

Brock watches me.

He is whole now. Smiling. "You're really going to keep doing that?" he says.

I keep covering the box, desperate to find more dirt. "I'll do what I need to do."

Brock sits down a few feet away and watches me. His eyes are dark, his presence darker, and I don't know what he'll do or when he'll do it, but I know I'm not safe. Not as long as he's here.

"People need to know what you did," he says.

I don't look at him, continuing to pile more dirt on.

"You're acting like you're one thing, but we know you're something else," he continues. "I know better than anybody, exactly what you are. You think covering it up with a little bit of dirt can hide that?"

"Leave me alone. Just go back where you came from."

"Go back where you put me, you mean," he corrects me. I don't acknowledge him. I get down on my knees, more desperate than I can remember feeling in years, and try to scrounge for something more to cover the box. There's nothing there, though. There's no way I can hide this thing.

"Look at me when I'm talking to you, sweetheart," Brock says. I don't—I can't. I'm shaking. Furious and humiliated, out here in the dirt trying to bury this thing that won't stay buried.

"I said look at me," he says, the words a growl at my ear. And suddenly he is behind me. I can feel him, more real than anything else I know. His arm around my neck, his body pressed tight against me.

"Let me go."

"I'm never letting you go again," he says. "Beg all you want. You know how I love you on your knees."

I fight him, twisting to get away, my heart pounding hard enough to ache in my chest. I scream, when I feel him hold me tighter. "Get away from me!"

"Jamie," another voice says. A voice grounded in reality, not this nightmare dreamscape I can't get away from. Jack. "You're dreaming. Wake up."

•

"Are you sure you're okay?" Jack asked, for the third time in as many minutes. I was on my feet in the cold cabin, trying to get my heart settled back into a normal rhythm.

"It was just a dream," I said. "I'm fine."

He didn't challenge me on what was technically the truth, instead leaving me in peace as I went to the woodstove and put another log on the dying embers. We'd been asleep for almost three hours, a lot more than I had expected. An icy rain continued to fall outside, but it was winding down.

Casper lay by the fire now, having gotten up at the same time I had. He was already out again. I sincerely doubted that Jack or I would get any more sleep, though.

I sat on the floor and stared at the slowly growing blaze, trying to shut everything else out. The image of Bear flashed through my mind: a little boy in his favorite overalls, trying to hide that giant box. I felt a leering presence, a dark-throated behemoth that seemed to wrap around the entire cabin. There was no escaping Brock, it seemed.

"You've probably been wondering how I know Hogan," I said, when silence no longer felt like the safest option. I'd been thinking about what I should tell Jack—how much I should say. Now, the rehearsed speeches fell away. I swallowed past fear, guilt, rage. Grief.

Jack said nothing, though I had no doubt that he was listening.

"I met him when he worked as a detective with the Maine State Police," I began. "We worked a few searches together. I was still pretty green, just getting into search and rescue."

"And when was this?" Jack asked, when I paused.

I thought about it. "About ten years ago. I'd been living out west, in Washington, but Brock…" I stopped. Heard the voice in my head. Pictured Brock's face. "Brock wanted me to bring Bear to Maine, and help him out."

"I know he's mine, Jamie. I deserve to see my son."

"You have a son because I was fifteen, and didn't know what the hell I was doing—"

"That's not the way I remember it," Brock says, and I can picture him through the phone: blazing eyes and irreproachable certainty. "I've got the paperwork. You told me you were eighteen. And you were more

than happy to come to my bed. I'll show them your signature. Tell them what kind of woman you are. And they'll give me full custody of my son; you'll never see Bear again."

"So… I came back to Maine," I said, pushing past the memory suddenly overwhelming me. I had to force the words out.

"There's a rumor that Brock Campbell was Bear's father."

"Yeah," I said. I didn't have the energy to lie about it anymore. Outside, the wind howled and sleet pounded the windowpanes. I didn't look toward the window, half afraid that Brock would be there, his face pressed to the glass. Waiting for a way back in.

"We… Uh, yeah. I went to camp there when I was in high school. I already knew that I wanted to be a dog handler, and he was running a program."

"How old was he?" Jack asked. The tension in his voice was palpable, something I could feel from across the room.

"He was forty-two then."

"And how old were you?"

"I lied on my application," I said. "I'd gone there the year before for the kids' program, but I didn't feel like I'd learned anything there. He never actually attended the camp then, so I figured he would never find out if I faked it the following year so I could go to the adult camp. He thought—"

"How old were you?" Jack pressed.

"I was fifteen."

The words hung there. Rebounded off the walls. I waited for Brock's input. This time, he was silent.

"I'm sorry," Jack said, though his voice was still tight. "Keep going."

It took me a second to find my place—and my courage—again.

"Anyway… I went back years later, when Brock asked me to. And he was actually really good with Bear. I would have found a way to leave, to get Bear away from him, if it weren't for that."

"How was Brock with you?" Jack asked, when I went quiet.

How to even begin answering that question? I took a deep breath. "He didn't like women," I began. "Hated them, in fact, I think. I think he hated everything. Everything except Bear, I guess."

"Even the dogs? Wasn't that his thing?"

"He liked having power over the dogs. He was all about old-school training methods: prong collars, aversive training, flooding to get the desired result."

"Flooding?" Jack asked.

"He's afraid, Brock. Making him do it more won't help that."

Brock ignores me, focused on the shaking, cowering German shepherd in front of us. He holds a gun that he says is loaded with blanks.

I don't believe him.

Brock aims it at the blue sky overhead. "He needs to learn. You think a police dog will never hear shots fired?"

He fires again. The dog yelps, as though he's the one who's been shot. Brock and I both wear protective earmuffs, but the dog has none.

Brock fires again.

I watch as a puddle of urine forms beneath the dog. If he could run, he would, but Brock holds a leash attached to a prong collar that digs in deep enough to make the dog bleed.

I have never wanted so much to inflict pain on another human, as I do right now.

"What happened to the dog?" Jack asked, when the story was done.

Tell him what you did, bitch, Brock whispered. For the first time, I smiled at the voice.

"I stole him," I told Jack. "Sneaked into the kennels one night, got him, and drove him to a trainer who was experienced with fearful dogs. She ended up keeping him. He's ten now, a little older than Phantom. Lives a good life."

"What did Brock do when he found out?"

"He wasn't happy." I tried to make my voice light. I failed.

"Jamie," Jack said.

I hesitated. The fire was still flickering in front of me, and I watched the play of light and dark inside the woodstove.

These are our little secrets, sweetheart, Brock whispered to me, a caress so close to my ear that I felt his breath on my skin. *Shut that pretty mouth, and keep it shut.* This couldn't be real. How could he be here now?

Casper shifted beside me, his front paw twitching in dreams. It's been proven that dogs dream; that they process key parts of their day, reliving them in sleep. What did he dream about now?

"That scar on your side," Jack said, when I didn't elaborate on my answer. I stiffened. I had forgotten Jack had even seen that, back in the tunnel in Glastenbury. Clearly, he remembered. "Did he do that?"

I swallowed again, pushing back a sudden wave of nausea.

"He was waiting for me that night when I got back," I finally said. "It was about three a.m., and he knew what I'd done. Knew I'd taken the dog."

"You're too soft for this business, sweetheart," Brock says to me. He wears pajama pants and leather slippers, with a fitted T-shirt that accentuates his massive upper body, biceps bulging at the sleeves. Like everything he wears, I get the feeling the outfit was planned for this exact moment.

"The dog wouldn't have been any good at this—you saw him today. Better to get rid of him now. Save you the trouble."

It's an effort to keep my voice steady, keep myself from shaking, but I think of Birch—the dog I have just saved. I think of his terror, and my anger returns.

"You think you're justified in this," Brock says. He has an almost flawless ability to read people, and uses that ability to cut them down. But I won't let him. Not this time.

"You think you know dogs better than me, girl?" he asks. "A few years working with some hippies out west who wouldn't know a real dog if it bit them on the ass—"

"I know your methods are macho garbage," I say. The fury I've been feeling for this whole year suddenly overflows. "I know half the dogs you train are damaged beyond repair by the time they leave here, and if you ever looked into it you'd find out that was true."

"Careful, sweetheart," Brock says. He takes a step toward me, a vein standing out in his forehead. I know what's coming —or I think I do. I brace myself for the impact, tightening my gut. Brock never hits my face. Never leaves bruises. But he is a master at inflicting pain.

Instead of hitting, though, he reaches for me—fast as a snake, and his hand closes around my arm. Before I can get away, the other grips the back of my neck so hard that I go to my knees. I look up at him. He glares at me, eyes dark, the thrill of his power in this moment almost too much for him.

"You want me to show you how I first started teaching dogs who the master was?" he asks. His voice is low. He bends, still holding me *tight, and his breath caresses my ear. "You want me to show you how man gained dominion over dumb beasts all those years ago?"*

"Brock, please. I'm sorry. Just let me go. Let it go."

"Where did you take the dog?"

Tears sting my eyes. I am twenty-five, but he picks me up by the back of the neck like I weigh no more than a child. I force myself not to scream, not to cry for help. I don't want to wake Bear. Don't want him to see this.

Brock propels me forward, along the wood-paneled hallway and into his study. It smells like leather and books, cigar smoke and whiskey. An orgiastic experience for any Hemingway wannabe in the world. The fire is going in the woodstove. It's September, the air cool outside and in. There's a poker set inside the flames, already glowing orange, and I know what it's for. Know that Brock has been sitting here all night, waiting for this moment.

"Please, Brock," I say, and I hate that I'm begging him now, unable to be silent. He doesn't even acknowledge my plea, pushing me on. I fight him, trying desperately to be quiet. Bear can't see me this way.

I catch Brock in the knee with my boot and he stumbles. Roars. He's back on his feet before I can get away though, grabbing the back of my neck so hard I think he'll tear my head off before we're done.

"Please, Brock. No. Please let me go."

"Where's the dog?"

But I won't tell him, and he knows it. I keep trying to figure out what his next move will be. Is he going to force me to the ground? Brand me with the poker? Strangle me? Instead, he grabs the sweatshirt I wear. He forces it up. Pushes me forward, until the woodstove is directly in my path. He's tearing at my jeans.

"Don't do this, Brock. Please don't do this." I'm beyond reason, barely able to breathe through tears and snot and terror. But I know that when he asks me again, I won't tell him where the dog is. I will

never tell him.

I close my eyes as he pushes me that last step. I feel the heat before he bends me over the woodstove, but it doesn't prepare me for the hiss and burn when my flesh is laid bare on the cast iron.

"This is the way you teach someone who has the power. I should have done it with you years ago," Brock says. He leans down while I'm still braced there, and whispers in my ear. "Don't fuck with me, sweetheart."

And then, suddenly, I am not alone with him. Lights flash just outside the window. People shout. Dogs bark. I don't know how it happens, the sequence of events, but suddenly Hogan is there. Holding me. Bear is in the doorway crying. I watch, stunned and shaken, as Brock is led away in handcuffs.

But all I can feel is the burn.

I was sitting up, my body rigid, still staring into the flames when I finished the story. Jack wrapped a blanket around my shoulders, and sat down beside me on the floor. It was still grey outside, but dawn had broken. It looked like the storm had passed.

Aren't you going to tell him the rest? Brock asked.

"How did Hogan know?" Jack asked.

"Bear had his number. He called when he heard everything."

"And then what happened?"

I stared at the ground. Casper woke, stretched, and got up. He came to me and lay his head on my lap, and I was grateful for his warmth, solidity, under my hand.

"Jamie?" Jack prompted. "I looked through Brock's file. There was nothing about any of this. No record of an arrest."

"I had nothing," I finally said. My voice felt raw, like I'd been shouting. Or like I hadn't spoken a word in years.

"So?" Jack said. "What he did—"

"You don't understand," I said. My eyes were dry, and I was grateful. I'd cried enough tears in this lifetime over Brock Campbell. I turned, and faced Jack. He sat cross-legged on the floor beside me, his dark eyes mournful. Baffled.

"He was rich—and not just a little bit. He had prestige. Lawyers. The community behind him. I was this nothing girl from Georgia with a kid of my own to take care of."

"A kid he threatened to take if you pressed charges."

"And he would have," I said. "No doubt in my mind. He would have found a way." Jack didn't say anything. "You don't have to pity me. I know I was a coward."

"I don't pity you," he said, before I'd even gotten the sentence out. "I definitely don't think you're a coward." He studied me a moment, eyes piercing through me. "I think you're amazing."

I looked away, cheeks burning. I felt the cast iron again, that fire on my skin, as though it had just happened. Casper went back to the bed and lay back down, and I wished that I had Phantom with me. My silent protector.

"So… We've come this far," Jack finally said. "What happened after you didn't press charges?"

"Nothing," I said simply. I heard Brock roar, and felt a rush of power that took my breath away. I ignored him. And I kept talking. "I didn't press charges. He came back. That was in September." I looked at Jack. Held his eye. "By Halloween, he was dead."

Tell him everything, bitch, Brock screamed. *Tell him what you did.* The wind whipped furiously against the cabin walls. I thought for a second we would all be uprooted. Jack didn't look away. There was understanding in his eyes. I saw a faint hint of a smile, painful and knowing.

"Good," he said.

29

THE RAIN HAD STOPPED and dawn had broken, but it was still cold and damp when Megan topped the ascent she knew would have to be her last in this trek. She had nothing left; not an ounce of get-up-and-go left to be gotten.

She pulled out Justin's cell phone and turned it on, praying it would work. It did, with just twelve percent left on the battery. She checked the reception. With the ice storm last night, she didn't have a lot of hope. But there it was, as soon as the screen was illuminated:

Two beautiful bars.

Megan punched in the only number she could think of. The only number she could imagine calling right now.

"Hogan," a familiar voice barked in her ear. Megan's eyes welled.

"What's a girl got to do to get saved around here?" she croaked.

There was a long pause on the other end. Then:

"Hunter?"

"I haven't been gone that long, have I?" she asked.

"Jesus, Hunter, where are you? Are you okay? We've been looking everywhere—we've turned the mountain upside down."

She gave him Justin's phone number so the warden service could track the GPS. "Violet's with me," she said afterward. "And Justin—my ex. He'll need a paramedic."

"Okay," Hogan said. He took a second before he said anything more. "Just stay put, all right? Stay safe. I'll be there just as soon as I can."

"Good." She paused. She had no courage left to say more. Hogan, thankfully, had some to spare.

"I missed you, Hunter," he said suddenly. "You've got no idea, woman. No idea how much. Just…you should know that. I'll be there before you know it."

He hung up.

Megan held onto the phone and took a breath. She leaned back against the nearest tree, then slid to the cold ground. Recluse, matted and bloodied and weary, came over as soon as she was down and settled beside her. She looked at Violet, already seated with the rifle in her lap and a grim expression on her weary face.

Justin, meanwhile, appeared to be asleep, curled in the fetal position. From where she sat, she could see him shivering. Would he even survive this, when all was said and done?

"How are you holding up?" she asked Violet.

"You mean after learning my husband is a psychopath who wants me dead?"

"Among other things."

Violet considered the question for a few seconds. Finally, she shrugged. "I don't really know. I'm probably in shock. None of this has been easy to take in."

"Justin could be lying."

Violet shook her head, no trace of doubt on her face. "No. He's been up to his ears in debt for a while now. Then all of a sudden, he started talking about projects he wants to take on, stuff he wants to buy. A boat. A plane. He wants to finance your brother-in-law's movie, you know."

"Abe?" Megan asked in disbelief. "He's a nice guy, don't get me wrong. But why would anyone want to finance that thing? Does it even exist?"

"It's actually really good," Violet said. "He gave Chase a copy. We watched it, and Chase said he was going to write him a check just as soon as this thing he was working on panned out. Wanted to know if I thought it was good enough."

"So you're telling me he was getting your advice on whether to invest in a project he planned to finance with insurance money he got after having you killed."

Violet actually laughed out loud, though with no small amount of trauma in her eyes.

"Men suck," Megan said.

"Only some of them," Violet corrected her. It was the kind of thing she always said. Now, it seemed like it took more out of her to get the words out.

Megan thought of Hogan's voice on the other end of the line just now. The milking goats waiting for her at his house. Recluse lay his head in her lap with a sigh, one paw draped across her leg. "Yeah," she conceded. "Only some."

The words were barely out of her mouth before Recluse's head came up once more. He growled low in his throat, hackles raised, before the growl grew to a series of deep, menacing barks. Megan held him back, her hand wrapped tight around his collar.

"There you are," a man's voice said, as he emerged from the trees. "You have no idea how long I've been looking for you."

Chase Carter stood at the edge of the clearing, soaked through.

•

Justin's earlier words echoed in Megan's head, even as Violet turned her gun on Chase.

"Now is that any way to greet your loving husband, after he's braved all this to come save you?"

"How did you find us?" Megan asked. One hand still around Recluse's collar as the dog continued to bark at the newcomer, she used the other to reach for the pistol she'd taken from Justin. Before she got it, she found herself face to face with a shotgun leveled at her nose.

"Unh uh," Chase said. He had to raise his voice to be heard over Recluse. "Put it down. And, Vivvy, sweetheart, lay down that rifle please. And someone please, shut that dog up."

"Easy, Rec," Megan said quickly. "Hush."

The dog's full-throated barking fell to a whimper, and then died away as he looked at her. Megan caught Violet's pained gaze. "Do what he says," Megan said. She understood how to deal with Justin, but she didn't have a clue where to start with a man like Chase.

Obligingly, Violet put the rifle on the ground. Chase took the pistol from Megan, careful to avoid Recluse, then strode to Violet and kicked the rifle away from her. Then, he helped Justin to his feet none too gently and cut the zip tie that bound his hands.

"I'm hurt," Justin said. "The goddamn dog would've killed me if Megan didn't pull him off."

Chase looked at his arm distastefully, and cringed. "It doesn't look good. We'll find you a doctor just as soon as we're done here."

"Thanks, man. I knew you'd come through."

Chase returned his focus to Megan. "I'm sorry," he said. "You asked me a question. Justin, show the ladies how I found you."

Painfully, Justin bent and used his good arm to retrieve something from his boot. He held it up for both of them to see: a plastic button, about the size of a book of matches. "Look familiar?" he asked Megan.

"That's my transponder!"

Chase looked so pleased with himself that Megan wanted nothing more than to knock the smirk right off his face. "You remember that day I paid you ladies a surprise visit?" he asked. "I just couldn't go the whole week without seeing Vivvy... At least, I think that's the story I told."

"You stole it then," Megan said.

"I did. It wasn't hard from there to reconfigure it so it connected with my phone rather than the WildFire base. You environmental types are all about the re-purposing, right? I thought you'd be impressed with that."

Recluse remained rooted to the spot beside Megan, her hand loose on his collar now. Of course she was worried for herself, and she was worried for Violet. Mostly, though, she was worried about the dog. The second Justin made a move toward her, Recluse would go for him. This time, Justin wouldn't hesitate to kill the dog.

"What are you going to do with us?" Megan asked, trying to buy time. "I've already called for help. Nate Hogan's on his way with the police."

"Then we better get moving," Chase said. She saw a flicker of surprise at her words, but he didn't give away much beyond that.

"Where are we going?" Justin asked. It seemed shock and fatigue had combined to make him even dimmer than usual.

"You're going where we planned all along, just as soon as this thing is done. I'm staying exactly where I've been— more or less. A million bucks richer and newly single, but otherwise…"

Megan caught Violet's eye again. She looked ready to murder Chase where he stood. Chase followed her gaze, and smiled at his wife.

"I am sorry about this, Vivvy. It's not you, it's me."

"Oh, believe me, I know," Violet said bitterly.

"All right, ladies. On your feet," Chase said. "Let's get this over with."

With no alternative that she could see, Megan got to her feet. How far away was Hogan? It seemed impossible to her that they had come all this way, were this close to going home, only to have it end like this.

Justin led the way while Chase brought up the rear, with Megan, Violet, and Recluse in between. This time, however, their journey was a lot shorter than she'd expected. Barely half an hour had passed before Chase ordered them to stop.

"What happens now?" Megan asked. Justin was just a few feet away from her, but so far Chase had kept him at a distance. Now, however, he looked at his friend. She saw him nod, ever so slightly.

"I told you you'd get your chance," he said. "Whatever you need to do."

"It's about time," Justin said. Before he made a move, he

eyed Recluse. Chase had already given him his pistol back, since there was no way Justin could have handled the rifle with one good arm. Now, he lifted the gun. And aimed it at the dog.

"No!" Megan shouted. She tried to step in front of the gun, but Recluse had other plans. Before she could get in the way or call him off, the dog lunged.

Justin shrieked, but held the gun steady as the Malamute tackled him, hitting the man full force with seventy pounds of muscle and fury. Megan tried to pull him off, but she was too late.

A gunshot reverberated around her, beneath her, splitting the daylight in two.

30

OUTSIDE, IT LOOKED LIKE the sun was trying to make its way through the clouds. After I'd told my story, Jack had been quiet. Strangely, it wasn't awkward. I kept waiting to feel exposed, pitied, for the story I had told. Instead, I just felt lighter. There were still things I hadn't told him, but the fact that Jack knew some of the darkest parts of my history was surprisingly liberating. Nothing he might find out now could scare him away. More than that, though, I'd spoken the truth, and the world hadn't ended. I hadn't been struck by lightning for telling someone. Jack hadn't shaken his head or turned away; he didn't seem to view me as a weaker woman now that he knew what I'd been through with Brock.

"You sure you don't want to try and get a little more sleep?" Jack asked me eventually, interrupting my thoughts. He was still seated by the fire, just a couple of feet from me.

"No, I'm all right. I want to get in touch with Hogan and get back out there."

"Sounds good," he agreed. "I'm just going to go out and use the facilities. I'll be right back."

He stood somewhat stiffly, clearly feeling the effects of the past two days. As he passed by, his hand found the top of my head and rested there for a few seconds. It was an unexpected gesture, intimate and comforting, and I let myself relax into the feel of his touch for just a moment.

"Thanks for trusting me," he said. "I know it's not easy."

I said nothing, unsure how to respond. His hand lingered on my head for another second, stroking down the side with a touch so light, so gentle, that it felt almost ghostly.

"I'll be right back," he said.

"I'll be here."

He went out, leaving me alone in the cabin with Casper once more. The dog had been asleep on the bed, but got up when Jack headed out. I stood painfully, feeling the inevitable aches in muscles and joints in bones, and scratched under the pit bull's chin before going for my things.

"You think you're ready for another day's work?" I asked.

The dog's tail whipped back and forth, that happy grin back in place. Apparently, four hours was more than enough time to rejuvenate Casper. I wished I felt half so spry, but I reckoned I was in good enough shape to keep going for at least another few hours. Maybe, if luck was on our side, it wouldn't take that long before we were able to bring Megan and Violet home safely.

I was packing up my gear and thinking about how best to structure the day when I heard someone talking outside the cabin. I froze at around the same time Casper went ballistic. There was an instant of panic before I recognized the voices: Jack and Hogan. It sounded like there were others out there, as well. A few seconds later, there was a brief knock on the door before Jack opened up.

"Look who I found," he said, stepping aside to let Hogan cross the threshold first.

"It really is a small world," I said.

"Ain't it just," Hogan said dryly. Casper was going nuts trying to reach Hogan, but I pulled him back.

Outside were three other men, all of them rangers, while a cadre of policemen skirted the perimeter.

Hogan was in dry clothes, but it was the grin on his face that held my attention.

"You've got them," I said.

"We've got them," he agreed. "Or we will, anyway. Megan just called. They're safe. It's about an hour's hike from here, inaccessible by snowmobile or chopper. I'm going up, but I wanted to see if you'd like to come along. We don't have a pinpoint location. We could use Casper for that, if he's up for it."

"Of course," I assured him. "We were just about to come find you. How did she get to a phone?"

"Long story. Come on, let's go. I don't want to keep her waiting any longer. I'll brief you while we're moving."

Within minutes, we were on the trail with Hogan guiding us, GPS in hand. Despite the grin and the clean clothes, he really did look like hell. It was the lightness in his step and the determination emanating from him that made him look like a different man, though.

The forest seemed lighter now, thanks in part to the sunshine. The knowledge that Megan and Violet were safe and Justin apprehended made it less foreboding than it had seemed before. I wondered whether any of that had to do with the conversation I'd had with Jack a few hours ago, difficult as it may have been at the time.

Casper seemed to sense the change himself, and ran

eagerly ahead as we trekked up the mountain pass. Brock's voice was silent, though I was sure I'd hear more from him. Justin, on the other hand, seemed to be purged. I wondered silently what would have happened if he had successfully hurt, even killed, Megan. Would I have felt it? Was this simply a one-off, some bizarre occurrence like seeing the dead girl in Glastenbury? Or were my abilities changing somehow, in ways I wasn't sure I could handle?

"Penny for your thoughts," Jack asked, catching up to me on a stretch of slightly more even terrain. "Or are they worth more than that?"

"A penny will do," I said. "I'm just thinking about everything that's happened. Glastenbury. This."

"You mean the things you've seen and heard. And felt," he added grimly.

"Yeah," I admitted. "I'm not sure I'm ready for whatever comes next."

"Have you considered talking to someone?"

"Like a shrink for psychics? I can only imagine the nuts who line up to put that on their business card. No thank you."

"Give it some thought. If you're interested, I might know a guy."

I cast a sidelong glance to see if he was joking. It was clear he wasn't. "I'll let you know."

"Pick up the pace, you two," Hogan called back. "It should be just ahead."

The sky was purest blue, the air clear up here. It promised to be a gorgeous day. Hogan was practically running the last stretch. Caught up in his enthusiasm, Jack and I doubled our speed. But as we approached the clearing, I felt something ominous take shape just behind me. Some product of the elements that could take us all out at will.

"Casper, come!" I called to the pit bull, who was still moving further up ahead. Casper paused. His head came up as he looked back at me, questioning.

"Yes, you. Come."

Grudgingly, he returned to my side.

"You're sure this is where Megan called from?" I asked Hogan as we surveyed the snowy clearing.

"Look at the GPS," Hogan said, showing me his screen. "Not to mention the footprints."

He was right: upon closer inspection, I saw several scuffed boot prints. One quick pass was all it took to come up with a broken zip tie, blood coating the plastic on one side. They'd definitely been here. The next step would be to put Casper back on the trail, but we took a minute more to look around first.

"Hunter!" Hogan shouted. "What the hell? I'm too tired to play hide and seek."

"I don't think they're playing a game," Jack said. He knelt beside a downed spruce, eying something intently before he picked it up carefully in a gloved hand.

"Is this the phone you've been tracking?" he asked.

Hogan cursed under his breath, taking the object from Jack.

At the same time, that dark shadow I'd felt before flew directly overhead—blocking my sun, though things remained bright all around me. Though I heard no voices this time, felt nothing, there was no doubt in my mind that something had happened here.

"Where's your scent article for Megan?" I asked. "They can't have gone that far. You didn't talk to her that long ago, and she was fine."

I could hear the rest of the search team coming up the

trail behind us. What would Justin do if he was cornered? Or, the better question:

What wouldn't he do?

Hogan handed me Megan's handkerchief, and I gave it to Casper. The dog snuffled it eagerly, tail wagging. This time, there was almost no hesitation before his nose hit the ground and he began to move.

We had them now, I was sure. But would we be too late?

31

THE SEARCH TOOK just under half an hour, with Casper going all-out, nose to the ground. I waited for more horrible words, more angst or pain, but heard nothing. Felt nothing. Casper's pace typically increased the closer he was to whatever he was searching for; right now, there was no holding him back. My own dread gnawed at me at the thought of what we might find.

We lost sight of the dog on a twisting stretch of trail as he bolted, ignoring me when I called after him. Jack glanced at me. Hogan was a few steps ahead of us, his own body tight with the fear I knew he must be feeling right now. Up ahead, Casper barked twice. A deep bellow of a bark answered, apparently coming from the same spot. I broke into a run.

I turned the corner with Jack keeping pace beside me, neither of us mindful of the ice or the boulders or the craggy, snow-covered path that served as a trail here.

And suddenly, there they were.

"It's about time," Megan said wearily. She looked up from her spot just off the trail, perched on a felled tree. Her face was bloody and cut and beyond exhausted.

The woman I assumed was Violet Carter sat beside her,

looking equally ragged. I had been expecting Megan's ex, Justin, to be there, and he was: bound and sitting on the snowy ground, his face deathly pale and one coat sleeve soaked in blood. The surprise, however, was the man beside him.

Chase Carter.

Chase looked slightly more put together than Justin, though not by much. There was a welt on his cheek, but the bigger issue was the bloodstain just above the kneecap of his right leg. Like Justin, he sat on the ground with his hands bound behind him.

A woolly mammoth of a dog stood warily to greet Casper, who wisely kept his distance. After a quick butt sniff, Casper returned to my side and looked at me expectantly.

"Good find, buddy," I said. I didn't have to feign enthusiasm this time around. I took his tug toy from my jacket pocket and we played a rousing game as the remainder of the search team descended.

Hogan got Justin and Chase to their feet roughly, Chase's face growing paler with every passing second. Blood dripped from the wound in his leg, but Hogan made no attempt to go easy on either man. For which I was grateful.

"Good boy, Casper," I said to the dog as Jack looked on. Grinning widely, Casper took the tug that I offered. He went down on his front paws, tail wagging. This time, I made no effort to cut the game short.

EPILOGUE

BY THAT AFTERNOON, Megan and Violet were safely in the local hospital for observation. Chase and Justin were in the same hospital, where they would remain until they were taken into custody. Their wounds were more serious than the women's, both of whom were suffering from exposure and minor cuts and bruises. We didn't know yet what the prognosis was for the men, but their recovery would likely take a lot longer. The physical side of things, at least. The emotional side was a whole other story.

Meanwhile, inside our homey little lodge, Michelle was already gone, and we were on our way out. We'd cleaned up and packed our gear, though the dogs were still roaming free inside and Bear and Ren seemed to be having a particularly hard time saying goodbye to our oasis. While Casper and Minion raced each other up and down the stairs, Phantom stuck close beside me, every move stiff and awkward. The coyote had definitely gotten the better of her. Time alone would tell whether she would be able to join another search with me, but I was hoping this wouldn't mark the end of our partnership.

At just past four, Hogan showed up for a quick debrief. Bear and Ren joined us in the living room, both of them eager to hear the scoop behind the final twists and turns of the search.

"So Chase really hired Megan's ex to kill his wife?" Bear asked. He shook his head, frowning. "What a dirt bag."

"My thoughts exactly," Hogan agreed. "We don't have a lot of details beyond that, since Justin isn't talking. Seems he's the loyal one in the duo, since Chase is trying to lay it all at his friend's feet. We've got the transponder, Megan and Violet's testimony, and we're working on tracking the computer glitch that got Justin out… Dollars to donuts, that whole thing was thanks to Chase. Not to mention the fact that he apparently used his credit card to buy all of Justin's gear."

"Not exactly criminal masterminds, are they?" Jack asked.

"Not exactly," Hogan said. "It's a good thing, too. If either of them had been even remotely competent, armed with something a little more effective, things might have turned out differently."

"So what exactly happened up there?" I asked. "I still don't understand how you have two reasonably physically capable armed men, and they wind up being taken down by a dog and two hypothermic women. Badass women, don't get me wrong. But still…"

"There was apparently a struggle with the dog," Hogan said. "While Recluse was tackling Justin, Chase got distracted. Violet used the opportunity to steal an unattended rifle, and she got Chase in the knee. Justin was armed, but the gun jammed."

"So luck, a dog, and a woman quick on her feet," I said. "That's what saved the day."

"Sounds about right," Hogan agreed. "There's another

piece of good news, too—and one more nail in Chase's coffin, hopefully. Sally Price is conscious. She's got some short-term memory loss, but they expect her to make a full recovery. One thing she does remember, though: overhearing Chase on the phone with Justin just before she was in her accident. She was going to the WildFire base to tell Heather what was going on."

"That's a relief," Jack said. "I'm glad Violet didn't have to face losing her mother on top of everything she's going through with Chase."

"I think that'll make the difference for her," Hogan agreed. "She's tougher than she looks. She'll be all right."

"How's Megan handling everything?" I asked.

Hogan shook his head with a frown. "Time will tell, I guess. I'm not sure how to help, but I don't plan on going anywhere until I figure it out."

"Good," I said. "Just give her some time. But make sure she knows you're there. That's important."

"Count on it." He paused. "Thanks."

I shrugged. "Just make sure you invite me to the wedding."

I expected at least a faint blush. Instead, he cast a subtle sidelong glance toward Jack and grinned. "Only if you do the same."

I could have slugged him, though Jack seemed oblivious.

We chatted for a few minutes more before Hogan announced that he was headed back to the hospital to visit Megan. I walked him to the door. As we were saying goodbye, he pulled me into an impulsive hug.

"Take care of yourself, okay?" he said quietly, still holding me. "You should be proud of what you've done. Who you've become. Don't let anyone make you think you don't deserve every good thing that comes your way."

"Thank you. That means a lot, coming from you."

I imagined Brock's reaction to the words, but this time I heard nothing. Was he done? Had it really just taken me speaking those secrets out loud for him to lose his power? Or was he still lurking out there somewhere, waiting to pounce as soon as he found another opening?

I closed the door once more, and was plunged headfirst back into the world I knew best: Casper and Minion chasing each other over the furniture, under the table, up and down the stairs. Phantom lying peacefully on her bed by the fire. Jack, on the couch with long legs stretched out in front of him, a book in his lap.

"Why are we not ready to go?" I called up the stairs, where my teenagers seemed to have vanished once more.

"There's cable here," Bear called down from the top of the stairs. "Can we finish the show we were watching? It's just twenty more minutes."

I frowned, and looked at Jack. "Can you handle twenty more minutes?"

To my surprise, he actually looked nervous when he nodded. "Twenty minutes would be good, as a matter of fact. I had something I wanted to talk to you about."

"Of course," I agreed.

"You mind going for a walk with me?"

"Whatever you want. Sure."

I put on a jacket. Jack did the same. We left Casper and Minion behind, but I decided at the last minute to bring Phantom along.

The sun was shining, the air unseasonably warm, and the parking lot of Inn at the Rostay had already thinned out now that the missing had been found. Phantom hobbled along beside me, the wave of her tail enough to let me know she was happy to be out.

I nodded toward the dining hall just down the way. "We could grab a cup of coffee…"

"That would be good," he agreed.

Inside, the hall was now empty. A carafe of old, lukewarm coffee and a box of stale Dunkin Donuts were all that remained for any stragglers left behind. I snagged a cup for Jack and one for myself, and we took a table at the back. Phantom lay at my feet without being prompted and closed her eyes, immediately at ease.

Jack made a face at the first taste of coffee, and set it aside.

"Sorry," I said. "At it's best, that stuff wasn't great. It's not the kind of thing that gets better with age."

"True."

Awkward silence descended for only a few seconds before Jack finally cleared his throat, and began. "I wanted to let you know that I called my landlord this morning, and gave notice that I'd be moving out. I've had a month-to-month lease anyway, so he was fine with it. But it's seemed like I've just been spinning my wheels there."

"Really?" I said. I couldn't hide my surprise, but immediately started calculating. "We have a couple of rooms that are almost finished out on the island. I was assuming you'd be headed out there soon, so I've been pushing to get those done. There are—"

He held up his hand, his face coloring slightly. "I, uh… I wasn't planning on moving out to the island, actually. Not right now, at least. I'm thinking about setting up shop in Rockland."

My confusion must have shown, because he rushed to continue. "You've been incredibly patient with me over the past year, while I've been trying to figure out what my next step is. I'm not sure how I would have survived without that safety net. But, I think I've finally made a decision about what comes next."

"That being?"

"Last week, I passed the Maine Professional Investigators Exam. I'd applied a couple of months ago, but there've been a few hiccups with my background check. That's been resolved now, though."

"You're going to be a PI?" I said.

I tried to make it sound supportive, but I was still trying to figure out what this meant for my own business. If Carl was leaving and Jack wasn't actually working for me, that meant I really needed to get on the stick about hiring someone else. Bear would be leaving for school in a year, and I had no idea what the future held for Ren. What did any of that mean for Flint K-9?

"I am," Jack said. "But I know this puts you in an awkward spot, since I've been so unclear with you about what I wanted to do or what my role would be with Flint K-9. I'm happy to keep working with you as long as you need me."

"I appreciate that," I said. I took another sip of horrible coffee, and set the cup aside. Jack remained where he was, waiting for my reaction. I weighed my words carefully before I said anything. "I think this could actually be a really good thing for you. I can see you working for yourself and doing quite well, and God knows you have the experience necessary to make a go of this."

"But..."

"No buts," I said. "Really. I think this is good." I met his eye, studying him frankly for a few seconds as the air warmed between us. "*But*...why don't you want to work for me?"

"It's not that I don't want to," he said immediately. "At all. I just feel like this is a better fit for me, given my background. I'm hoping we'll still be able to work together sometimes, though. I could definitely use your services with the dogs on some of my cases, I'm sure."

"Sure," I agreed. "Just let me know."

I stood abruptly, nodding toward the window. Phantom got up more slowly than usual, and somewhere in the back of my mind I noted that she was favoring her left foreleg more than I'd realized.

"We should get going. Carl's got a lot on his plate, out on the island taking care of everything on his own."

"Wait a second," Jack said. "I wasn't done."

"It's a long drive back. I appreciate you letting me know where you are with things, though." I shrugged my coat back on and grabbed the still-half-full mug of coffee to take back to the counter.

Before I was halfway there, Jack caught me by the arm. I turned to face him, and was surprised at the intensity in his eyes when I did.

"You were right before," he said.

"Which time?"

"A minute ago, when you asked why I don't want to work for you." He scratched the back of his neck, dropping his other hand from my arm. "You're right about that, in a way."

I frowned. "If you have a problem working for a woman—"

"I don't. I've worked for lots of women before. Some of my best, most effective bosses have been women."

"Is it because of the whole vision thing? That dream I had about saving your life?"

"No." He hesitated. "Or maybe it is—a little. But that's not the real issue."

I sighed. We really did have a long drive back, and if I now needed to find replacements for both Jack and Carl, I had to get started. "Okay. Well, Jack, either spill it or let's just forget it. It's done now, anyway. You've got your next move figured out."

"Not completely," he said, half under his breath. Something in his voice made me stop. I stilled, waiting for him to continue. He wet his lips, and I was caught for a split second by the move. Jack had great lips.

"You don't date the men who work for you," he finally said. "That's a policy, isn't it?"

For a second, I had a hard time breathing. Jack studied me, bolder than I had expected. It took more time than it should have for me to find my voice. "It is. Dating my employees would make things too complicated. Ultimately, it isn't fair to them."

"Well, then…" Jack began. He paused. I was drawn to his eyes, darkened pools that I suddenly couldn't look away from. "It isn't that I don't want to work for Flint K-9. But if it means closing a door I'd rather keep open, I'll find another job."

"Oh," was the best I could manage, which made him smile. He took a step closer. The dining room was relatively dark. Completely deserted. Jack raised a hand to my face, and ran his knuckles along my cheekbone. There were other things I should be saying, a million reasons this wasn't the right choice for me. Or were there? I couldn't think straight. At the moment, all I could seem to focus on was the feel of his hand on my skin.

Phantom bumped up against my thigh, and I settled my hand on her head. Jack's smile widened as he continued reading my face. "We should go," he said, his hand still light on my cheek.

"Yeah," I agreed. "Bear and Ren are probably wondering where we are."

He dropped his hand, but he held my eye all the same. My cheeks were burning when he opened the door for me and I stepped outside once more, into clear skies and bright sun. Jack walked beside me on one side, Phantom on the other. I would need to make some phone calls, place a few ads, to round out my team on the island. Jack's hand brushed mine and, for a split second, our pinkies caught. And held.

I decided I could deal with one less employee.

Looking for more from Jen Blood?

Turn the page for a free excerpt from
the next novel in the critically acclaimed
Flint K-9 series,

THE REDEMPTION GAME.

1

IT WAS THE KIND of summer day that makes a body glad to be alive, and even more so to be alive in coastal Maine. Sun shining. Birds singing. All right with the world.

Except for, of course, the chorus of fifty or more dogs barking nearby and a stench to rival what you might find at a full-fledged, badly funded zoo. Which was, more or less, where we were headed.

I walked beside Jack Juarez, FBI Special Agent recently turned private investigator, along a deeply rutted dirt road off another deeply rutted dirt road off an infrequently traveled secondary road in Cushing. It was June, the sun reflecting off the deep blue of Muscongus Bay just across the way. On the other side, the barking of the aforementioned fifty or more dogs got impossibly louder the closer we got to our goal.

Bear, my eighteen-year-old son, walked on my other side, though he'd been quiet since we'd gotten out of the van. My own tension ratcheted higher as we approached our destination: a once-grand Victorian home that had long since gone to seed, set on ten acres of prime coastal real estate and flanked by two equally rundown old barns.

2 • JEN BLOOD

A surge of mangy-looking dogs of all shape and size rushed a rickety gate that barely looked sturdy enough to hold them back. I registered Jack's flinch beside me, though to his credit he didn't turn around and run.

"I'm going to check around out back," Bear said to me. "I want to get a look at the farm animals before Nancy comes out and runs us off the property."

"Be careful," I warned him. Nancy Davis was the owner of this ruin of a place, and was definitely not known around town for her hospitality. "If she comes out, tell her you're with us and don't engage. Just come find me."

He nodded without actually agreeing, but I had to hope he was smart enough by now to know when it was worth arguing with me and when it was better to just do as he was told.

Bear managed to skirt around the side of the building just as Nancy stepped out her front door and stood on the sagging stoop glaring at us. The dogs' snarls and yowls got worse as soon as Nancy set foot outside, as though they were drawing on their owner's ill will.

"Why are we here, exactly?" Jack asked me under his breath, his tone wary as he eyed the old woman now striding toward us.

"To evaluate the dogs. See if there are any we can take on at the island and rehabilitate there."

"My dogs don't need rehabilitating," Nancy shouted at us, still ten yards away. She had to be nearly seventy-five, but clearly her hearing wasn't suffering for it. Apart from that, though, Nancy wasn't wearing her years well. She wore a tattered house dress with a bathrobe over it, her white hair stringy and thinning across her scalp. Her right arm was in a cast, and she walked with a limp. The dogs in the yard—I counted twenty of them at first glance—vied for her attention, occasionally snapping at each other in the chaos.

"You know what's happening, Nancy," I said, my own tone softer than hers. There are times when I'm grateful for my Georgian accent, though I haven't lived in that part of the country for going on twenty years now. My drawl is gentler than the Maine accent, making me seem more compassionate than I necessarily am. This morning, I used that to full effect.

"You've got a choice," I continued. "Either find a place for the animals or the State will intervene and take them. Wouldn't you rather know where they're going?"

A dog who looked like a mix between a Sheltie and a rat came up to her and took a corner of her robe between his teeth, pulling at it with menacing little yips and growls.

"Knock it off, Oswald," she said, though there was tenderness underlying the words. "You wanna play, go find Albie. I ain't got the time."

Albie was Nancy's youngest son, a quiet, tense man with a number of cognitive challenges that had kept him reliant on his mother into his adult years. Discouraged, Oswald shifted his focus to us, still outside the fence. He nosed through the chicken wire, his attention fixed on Jack. The ex-agent took a step back. Jack Juarez had seen plenty in his day, I knew, but Oswald still seemed a little beyond him. I heard him curse under his breath, and he glanced at me as he bent to clean dog crap from his leather shoes.

"Have you thought about what we talked about the other day?" I pressed Nancy, ignoring Jack and Oswald for the moment. "If you can find a place for, say, three quarters of the dogs—"

"They're special needs," she said immediately, cutting me off.

Regardless of her animosity, she opened the gate and ushered us in, hollering and kicking at any dogs who dared try and escape. I glanced at Jack to see if he was still on board, but there was no time for a discussion. Game as always, he followed me through the gate and into territory I was sure was completely foreign to anything he'd ever seen before.

Two stunted pug mixes had taken up the charge with Oswald, successfully herding Jack back toward the gate before he'd managed more than a couple of steps into the yard.

"Nobody's gonna take them dogs," Nancy continued. "Half the ones in the house have health problems. And nobody's house trained in the lot. You tell me, who'll take that on but me? Besides, they've only ever known me."

Jack managed to extricate himself from the dogs, albeit momentarily, and stepped forward with the beguiling smile that was precisely the reason I'd asked him along in the first place.

"This is quite a setup you have here. If you don't mind me asking, how many dogs do you have, exactly?"

Nancy stared at him with dark, withering eyes for a full two seconds before she turned to me. "Who in hell is this?" So much for Jack Juarez's irresistible charm.

"Jack Juarez," I said. "He's helping me out today."

"Well, he doesn't need to be here." She stopped speaking altogether, arms folded over her bony chest while she waited.

"Why don't you go check in with Bear?" I said to Jack, nodding toward the back of the property. "I'll let you know when I need you two."

"You're not going to need them at all," Nancy said. Jack started to protest, but thought better of it when Oswald and his pack approached again.

"You know where to find me," he said. I waited until he was out of hearing range before I shifted my focus back to the old woman.

"What in Hades are you doing here, Nancy?" I said. I tried to infuse some compassion into the question, though that wasn't easy. "You need help here—you must see that. You've got dogs literally busting out the seams of that house, not to mention the state of the farm animals out in the field. Have you looked at those cows? I can count their ribs from here. The llamas' teeth need filing. The sheep need shearing…"

The more I went on, the tighter Nancy held herself. I watched the dogs circling around her, their attention shifting to me: the interloper. Someone their person clearly wasn't happy to see. A Newfoundland the size of a small pony, his coat patchy with mange, worked his way from behind a piece of cardboard and duct tape that patched a broken window in the house. At sight of Nancy, he loped our way with tail waving.

"Get back in there, Cody," she told the dog. "Go on, now."

The Newfie ignored her and headed for me. He would be magnificent if not for his circumstances, and a fresh surge of rage ran through me as he bumped his massive head into my stomach, nearly taking me down. "Do you know how many people are in line for rescued Newfoundlands?" I demanded. "Someone would take him in a heartbeat."

"I don't need anybody to take him. To hell with all of you," Nancy said. "You damned bureaucrats forget we're talking about living creatures here."

"Since when have I been a bureaucrat?" I returned. "And I think you're the one who's forgotten they're living creatures. You've saved their lives, and I thank you for that, I really do. But what kind of quality of life do they have now, if half of them are sick and all of them are starving?"

I stroked Cody's head, noting the ribs clearly defined through his ruin of a coat. A dog like this should be at least a hundred pounds, but I doubted Cody was more than sixty.

Nancy's lips tightened. She raised her good arm and pointed toward the gate. "Get out. You're no better than my son, trying to steal my animals and move me out of here just so he can have my land. He doesn't give a rat's ass what happens to these animals. None of them do."

"None of whom, Nancy?" I asked wearily. I'd known Nancy for a couple of years now, in some capacity or other. I was well acquainted with her conspiracy theories.

"Developers," she said. "Barbara and her fancy-fairy husband've got them sniffing at my land. She's been on me for months now to sell her this plot so she can expand her place. And it's not for my own good, I'll tell you that much."

I didn't know Nancy's neighbors—Barbara and her "fancy-fairy" husband—beyond maybe being able to recognize them in a police line-up, but I was sure this wasn't the whole story.

"So, don't sell," I said regardless, seizing the moment. "But don't try to do this alone. I thought Fred was helping you. Didn't he come back to try and sort this out?"

Fred was Nancy's oldest son, a strange, precise little man in his forties.

"He left," she said, with a trace of scorn. "Couldn't take it. Didn't even say goodbye. Just packed his things and left one night, just like his daddy did years before. Sent me a note from Cleveland, wishing me luck. Then next thing I know, I hear from his lawyer saying he wants to evict me and Albie. From my own damned house!"

"I'm sorry," I said, and meant it. Cody lay down in front of me, directly on my feet. "But maybe this is the only way he knows to help you. If not, there are plenty of other people around here more than willing to lend a hand. I've got space on the island to take some of your animals and work on training, and there's a whole network of others who'll pitch in. We'll clean this place up, set you up with a number you can actually handle."

She stepped forward silently and grabbed Cody by the collar, jerking the dog to his feet. Cody followed her willingly, then sat beside her and leaned against her hip. Nancy didn't say anything for a minute or more, still tense, before I noticed the sheen in her tired eyes.

"Please, Nancy."

She shook her head, more against the tears than my words. "If I weren't so damned old," she said. "I used to be able to handle it, you know. Could've run this place in my sleep."

This was actually true, I knew. Nancy had been doing animal rescue in the area for over twenty years, long before I came on the scene. She traveled around the country helping with cruelty cases; up until a couple of years ago, she'd run this place as smoothly as the proverbial Swiss watch. Her stellar track record was the major reason no one had shut her down sooner after it all got away from her.

"Does that mean you'll let me help?" I asked.

She took a deep breath, and looked around. Oswald and his buddies had returned, which made me wonder where Jack and Bear might be. They paced around us with a dozen other barking dogs, watching my every move. Cody ignored them completely.

"Is your friend gonna help?" Nancy asked.

"Jack?" I said. "I don't know. Maybe."

"Looks like he's being tracked by a grizzly bear every time Oswald looks at him sideways, you know."

I squelched a smile. "He does a little bit, yes."

"Nice to look at, though," she noted.

"Don't start."

She looked at me innocently, a trace of mischief in her eyes. "What? You don't think I notice something like that? I'm old and maybe half nuts, but I'm not dead. I can still appreciate a good-looking man when one comes around."

"You know I haven't forgotten the question," I said, getting us back on track. "Will you let us help?"

A few seconds of hesitation followed before she finally nodded. "Come back tomorrow—"

"We're here now. You know the police are set to come in tomorrow."

"Come back tomorrow," she repeated firmly. "Give me a few hours to pull myself together, talk this through with Albie and my other babies here."

Despite my reservations, I nodded. "We'll be back first thing," I said. "And we'll get this sorted out, all right? This can be a good thing."

"Sure it can," she said grimly.

Moments later, Nancy and Cody retreated back into her ruined house. I picked my way through rotting dog food, animal crap, and the carcasses of multiple rats—at least I hoped they were rats—toward the back of the property in search of Bear and Jack. I found them in a soggy pasture out behind the house, where Bear was giving an overgrown sheep a once-over while Albie—Nancy's younger son—looked on, arms crossed over his chest, face dark with anger. He wore a green sweatshirt with a pirate on the front, BUC PRIDE in large white letters across the bottom. It looked as old as the hills, and just as dirty.

Jack, meanwhile, crouched beside a grizzled black and white tomcat with one missing ear. The dogs that had been pursuing him, I noted, were now keeping a safe distance.

"I see you met Cash," I said.

"Is that his name?" Jack asked. The cat butted his over-large head against the palm of Jack's hand. "I'm not positive, but I think he saved my life."

"Cash keeps everyone in line here. They didn't mean you any harm, though," I said, nodding toward the pack of little dogs watching us from the fence line. "But you do give off a vibe. They can sense your fear."

"I'm not afraid of them," he said, a trifle indignant.

"Of course not."

"Now you're just patronizing me." He shifted his focus back to the cat. "What's his story?"

"Long-time neighborhood stray," I said. "He got into it with a coyote, though. You should have seen the coyote." Jack smiled faintly, focus still on Cash. "Nancy raised the money to cover the vet bills, and added him to the menagerie."

Jack nodded with apparent approval.

"So, what are we doing?" Bear interrupted us, returning from the field with one massive black and white sheep tottering along beside him. "Some of these guys are in bad shape. We need to get them out of here, but Albie's giving me a hard time about it."

Albie had followed Bear back toward us, his entire body coiled as tight as a rattlesnake about to strike.

"We're coming back tomorrow morning," I said. Bear started to protest, but I held up my hand. "Nancy needs a few hours to pull herself together. That's all she's asking. One more day won't kill these guys."

Bear looked at the ram beside him doubtfully. The wool was so thick I couldn't imagine what we would find underneath. Unlike wild sheep, which shed their wool naturally the same way a dog sheds its coat, domesticated sheep have been bred so that the wool will continue to grow until someone intercedes. If no one shears them, the coat can become so overgrown that flies lay eggs in the moist folds of their skin. Maggots hatch, and literally eat the animal from the outside in. Based on the smell coming from the poor thing, I was guessing we could well face a situation like that here.

"Do you think there's any way we could take him now?" Bear asked, nodding toward the sheep. "Therese should take a look at him. I don't think he should go another day."

Therese was the vet out on Windfall Island, our base of operations for Flint K-9 Search and Rescue and a growing animal rescue Bear had started. She was on standby today, with full knowledge of what we could be up against with Nancy's animals.

"I might be able to arrange something," I said. I surveyed the rest of the pasture, taking stock of the donkeys, llamas, cows, sheep, and goats in turn. "What about the rest of the place? Is there anyone else you think needs to come now?"

"There's a dog," he said. "They keep him chained out back. We should get him out of here as soon as we can."

"I'll check with Nancy. Anyone else?"

Bear took the place in critically, his gaze intent. "There are a couple of llamas that really need to get out of here sooner than later. Those, and that miniature donkey farther out." He nodded toward a thin, shaggy donkey at the back of the field. "You think you can talk her into letting them go now?"

"Mom says everybody stays," Albie ventured, joining in the conversation for the first time. He avoided my eye when he spoke, his gaze locked on the ground, arms still wrapped around his chest. "Nobody goes. This is the best place for everybody. Anybody who leaves here, they get killed."

"That's what we're trying to keep from happening," Bear said, with surprising gentleness. "You're a smart guy—you know some of these animals aren't doing too well right now. And your mom's having a hard time, too. We're just trying to help."

Albie took this in, glancing up to look at Bear for a split second before he looked back at the ground. "It's not safe," he said, half to himself. "Out there isn't safe. In here is the only safe place for us."

My heart clenched at the dangerous message Nancy had taught him over the years, and I struggled to find some way to reach the man. "I like your shirt," I finally said lamely, gesturing to his chest. "The pirate there…"

His face transformed in an instant. "Buccaneer," he said. There was reverence in the word. "It's a buccaneer, not a pirate. People always get that wrong. Coach gave it to me." He turned around, pointing awkwardly at the back. MVP was written at the top, with A. DAVIS and the number 7 beneath it. "You know what that means?" he asked.

"Most Valuable Player," a girl's voice said, behind us. I turned in surprise. A pretty blond girl likely a little younger than Bear strode toward us, taking Albie in with a casual nod. "Albie got MVP when he was in high school."

"Georges Valley," Albie added. "I went to Georges Valley High School. Class of 1990. Coach Pendleton. I played outfield on the baseball team."

"Hey, Bear," the girl said to my son, who nodded in her direction but otherwise remained mute. She cast a long look in Jack's direction, then shifted her attention to me. "I'm Julie Monroe," she said. "We live next door. My mom wanted me to come over and see if I could help."

"You're not supposed to be here," Albie said, in a whisper directed at Julie. "You know you're not—"

"I know, I know," Julie said, waving the comment away carelessly. "I'll go. I just figured if you need any help…" She let the statement trail off.

I watched with interest as she worked her way a little closer to Bear, who looked decidedly uncomfortable at her approach. Bear is a good-looking kid who hasn't quite figured that out yet, but it's bound to sink in eventually. Especially with the attention of girls like Julie Monroe.

I thought longingly of Ren Mensah—another member of the Flint K-9 team, and to date the only girl to steal Bear's heart. She'd left Windfall Island just over a month ago for California, where her father had just relocated. Ren was hard working and thoughtful and bright, and the least manipulative person I'd ever met. I could handle Ren dating my son.

I didn't have a clue what to do with girls like Julie Monroe.

Thankfully, based on the somewhat wild look in his eyes, Bear was even more clueless than me.

"I'll talk to Nancy about the llamas and the donkey," I said to Bear. "Go on over and check on this dog you want us to take, and I'll meet you there."

Bear nodded. Albie's momentary transformation at the memory of his glory days in high school was forgotten quickly at my words. He fixed me with a long, hard stare. "Nobody goes," the man said quietly. "Everybody has to stay."

"Everything will be okay, Albie," I said. "We'll take good care of anyone who leaves here. You don't have to worry about that."

He turned his back on me, visibly seething. A crawl of uneasiness ran through me, but I pushed it aside. Bear went to track down whatever dog he meant to save, while Julie tagged along beside him. I couldn't shake my anxiety when I saw Albie take off after them.

"You want me to go, too?" Jack asked. He stood with Cash still threading between his long legs, a throaty purr audible from a few feet away.

I nodded, relieved. "If you wouldn't mind, that would be great."

"No problem." He paused. I thought he was concerned about the dogs again, but when he shifted his gaze back to me it was clear that wasn't what was on his mind. "Be careful, all right? I don't have a good feeling about this."

"Yeah," I agreed with a sigh. "Same here. Watch your back."

For regular updates, free short stories, contests,
and giveaways between book releases,
visit http://jenblood.com/,
and like Jen on Facebook at
http://facebook.com/jenbloodauthor/.

More Mysteries from Jen Blood

In Between Days
Diggs & Solomon Shorts
1990 - 2000

Midnight Lullaby
Prequel to
The Erin Solomon Mysteries

The
Payson Pentalogy

Book I: All the Blue-Eyed Angels
Book II: Sins of the Father
Book III: Southern Cross
Book IV: Before the After
Book V: The Book of J

Flint K-9 Search and Rescue

The Darkest Thread
Inside the Echo
The Redemption Game

ACKNOWLEDGMENTS

This book has been a bear! Thanks to my family for providing the much-needed support to help me through the process. To Mom, for her multiple read-throughs and invaluable feedback; to Ben, for keeping me on level ground when I felt like I was going over the deep end; to everyone else for simply being there. You guys are amazing.

To Jan, for her incredible feedback, good humor, and great eye: you are the very best treasure on Treasure Island. Thank you, thank you, thank you.

A significant amount of research went into this novel, with some truly phenomenal professionals helping me along the way. Special thanks go out to Caroline Blair-Smith of Mornington Crescent Sled Dogs (www.sledpets.com) for her patience and expertise throughout this process; to Michelle Merrifield for answering a multitude of questions and, in particular, for giving me an invaluable day in the field with the K-9s and handlers of the Maine Warden Service; to Michele Fleury of Maine Search and Rescue Dogs, for even more field time and answered questions; and to Maine Warden Service veteran Roger Guay for walking me through the first incarnation of this plot, and helping me hone the details. This book would not be what it is without their help.

I always love to hear from readers! Email me at jen@jenblood.com or follow me on Facebook at www.facebook.com/jenbloodauthor or Twitter @jenblood, and don't forget to join the mailing list for all the latest news on projects and upcoming releases.

ABOUT THE AUTHOR

Jen Blood is a freelance journalist, certified dog trainer, and author of the bestselling Erin Solomon mystery series. She holds an MFA in Creative Writing/Popular Fiction, with influences ranging from Emily Bronte to Joss Whedon and the whole spectrum in between, and teaches workshops on writing, editing, and marketing for authors. Today, Jen lives in a big old farmhouse on the coast of Maine with a puppy named Marji, a Maine coon cat named Magnus, and a lovely bearded man named Ben.

Made in the USA
Monee, IL
06 July 2021

73037110R00204